THE
FABULIST

•

A NOVEL

•

STEPHEN
GLASS

SIMON & SCHUSTER
New York London Toronto Sydney Singapore

SIMON & SCHUSTER
Rockefeller Center
1230 Avenue of the Americas
New York, NY 10020

SIMON & SCHUSTER and colophon are registered
trademarks of Simon & Schuster, Inc.

For information about special discounts for bulk purchases,
please contact Simon & Schuster Special Sales:
1-800-456-6798 or business@simonandschuster.com

Designed by C. Linda Dingler

Manufactured in the United States of America

10 9 8 7 6 5 4 3 2 1

Library of Congress Cataloging-in-Publication Data is available.

ISBN: 0-7432-2712-3

AUTHOR'S NOTE

I was fired in 1998 from my job as a writer at *The New Republic,* and dismissed from several freelance assignments, for having fabricated dozens of magazine articles. I deeply regret my misconduct, and the pain it caused.

While this novel was inspired by certain events in my life, it does not recount the actual events of my life. Instead, it depicts an imaginary world of my own creation. This book is a work of fiction—a fabrication, and this time, an admitted one.

Of course, when I was fired and thereafter, I knew and interacted with many real-life people, including editors, colleagues, family members, and girlfriends. But the characters, events, and dialogue in this novel should not be understood as describing real people, real events, or actual conversations.

—Stephen Glass

To my mother, my father, Michael, and Julie

THE FABULIST

PART ONE
DOWNFALL

A SPECTACULAR crash, I've learned, is the quickest way to incredible accomplishment. In the summer of 1998, when I was twenty-five years old and sure of where I was going in the world, I suddenly became both Washington's most disgraced journalist and its fastest-rising star. It actually happened in that order: fall first, rise second. After I fell, my preceding achievements were greatly overstated so that my plunge, as deep and as fast as it was, would make sense.

Although I have been given many opportunities to explain myself, I have never previously discussed the events of that summer. My decision to step away now from years of self-imposed silence has more to do with physical distance than the passage of time. Removed from Washington, I am for the first time less ashamed—even less afraid.

Please don't misunderstand me: What I did was a terrible mistake—a serious, damaging wrong—and they are correct to say so. However, there are some individuals, journalists mainly, who think I should always be ashamed, and perhaps always afraid, too. Because they are liberals, and have faith in rehabilitation, they never speak of it that way, but I believe they feel it profoundly. They cannot understand how after violating all their rules, fair and important rules, I go on living among them. If I am not punished further, what good is the salutary order they have imposed?

Because I know of so many who feel this way, I am conscious that some of my colleagues and friends, present and former, will be suspicious of my motives in offering this account. They will see it as just one more lie; an eleventh-hour, last-gasp, back-from-the-dead effort to spin things my way again.

And, on one level, it is.

Nothing would make me so happy as your liking me once more. But I don't expect that. Not now, not after all that's happened. I can only tell my story and hope for the best.

• • •

Here are Allison and I, walking into our apartment, hand in hand. We're giggling, giddy, and pleased with the world. As usual, her pixie blond hair and gamine charm go straight to my heart: I can't believe how fortunate I am to be with her. Allison had me from our first kiss, maybe even from the first time I heard her slight Brazilian accent, and ever since, I've chosen to ignore the flaws in our relationship in favor of its virtues.

It is the middle of the afternoon, on the first day of our weeklong vacation, and we've just come back from the movies. Allison believed you were never as free as when you were sitting in a weekday matinee. Before that afternoon, though, we hadn't been to a movie in months, let alone a matinee. I had always been working, even on weekends. Although I was *The Washington Weekly*'s youngest staff writer, I was also one of its most prolific and, increasingly, one of its better known. And though I had expected and promised Allison that with some success would come a commensurate calm, my anxiety had only increased proportionately, and my efforts to allay it through long hours had only grown.

Allison checked our answering machine. "You have six new messages. First message: 10:49 A.M."

"Steve, it's Robert," the message began. Robert was the editorial director of the *Weekly*. "Give me a call when you get a second. I just got an email from a reporter at *Substance Monthly*. He says he wants to talk about one of your pieces. I don't know what it's about, so I thought I'd call you first. Sorry to bother you on your vacation."

"Next message: 11:21 A.M."

"Steve, it's Robert again. I just talked to the guy from *Substance,* and he was asking some questions about your story. It's the 'angry lottery winners' piece from a couple of weeks ago. Call me. I'm at the office."

"Next message: 1:45 P.M."

"Steve, it's Cliff Coolidge. Just want to make sure we're still on for dinner tonight. Give me a call and let me know."

Cliff was an acquaintance of Allison's and mine. He had gone to Stanford with Allison and now was a young writer at *District* magazine.

"I thought you canceled that," Allison said. "We have plans tonight with my brother. Remember?"

Allison had six brothers (she'd been the only girl in her family), and they all lived far away, on the West Coast or back in Brazil where they'd all gone to elementary school. So there was always a brother coming into town—but this brother I'd never met.

I knew I should apologize for forgetting his visit, but I couldn't. I stood there, frozen, and all I could pay attention to was Robert's voice. Allison's receded into the background like white noise.

"Next message: 2:07 P.M."

"Steve, it's Robert. This is my third message. Where are you? Call me. It's really important. Have them interrupt me if I'm on the phone."

"Next message: 2:41 P.M."

"Steve, cancel whatever you're doing and come over here, I mean it. Allison, if you hear this and know where Steve is, could you get him and tell him to call me? It's Robert."

"Next message: 3:48 P.M."

"Steve, Steve, Steve, Steve. Answer the goddamn phone. Where the fuck are you? I don't care if you're having some nice little romantic thing, call me. Do I have to come over to your apartment?"

"End of messages."

I stared at the machine, my stomach churning.

"You're going over there, aren't you?" Allison asked.

"Yes," I said.

"He always gets this way. Everything's an emergency. Can't you just not go?"

Allison was accustomed to Robert's persistence. Two weeks ago, he had called the apartment five times, and tried Allison at work, because he thought I'd forgotten to turn in a story. He had the wrong disk in the computer.

"If I don't go—"

"I know, I know. He'll just keep calling. At least promise me you'll be back in time for dinner?"

"Sure."

"Come back quick," she said.

I promised I would see her in about an hour. But, as it turned out, we wouldn't really see each other again, not in the same way at least. Here was where I would begin to lose Allison. I should have seen it even then, but I did not. By the time we saw each other next, the process of our unrecognition—by which we began to feel that we knew each other less and less, and in the end that we had never truly known each other at all—would have already begun.

The walk to the *Weekly*'s office from my apartment was brief, maybe twenty minutes. It was May, Washington's only agreeable month. The air was warm and thin, like a pleasant dream, and it was into a pleasant dream that I then began to make my escape.

My mind drifted to Allison and the picnic we'd had the night before, sushi and white wine on the Lincoln Memorial steps. I thought also of a klezmer concert I'd recently attended called Jews with Horns and how I'd popped a contact lens while dancing and had to drive home winking. I thought of my family too: my parents and Nathan, my brother.

Crossing through Dupont Circle, I watched the last few moves of a speed chess game and stopped at the CVS to buy a Mother's Day card. The card I selected had a picture of a mom telling a young boy to put the scissors away "where you found them," which is exactly what my mother used to say: "Make sure to put the scissors away, Stephen—where you found them."

Surely, you say, I must have known the trouble I was in—and to some extent I did. I must have been anxious and scheming, racking my brain for a way out, even then. I must have been buying time. That is what everyone who has never been caught thinks. But, in fact, I didn't plan; I didn't scheme; I didn't even envision what was to come—not yet. Instead, during the walk, I willed myself beyond recall. Had I concentrated on what I had done, I probably would have turned and run.

Here is the article Robert was referring to in his messages. It had appeared in the *Weekly* a little while before:

NOT-SO-LUCKY NUMBERS

by Stephen Aaron Glass

Every other Sunday, Gloria Pruitt, a graying, frail woman in her early seventies, stages an elaborate protest against the state lottery outside the Pennsylvania governor's mansion.

To make her demonstration more photogenic, Pruitt drapes herself over a seven-foot-high crucifix, which she has built out of white beach balls from Kmart, painted with black numerals. Above the cross she puts a placard that reads: "I won the lottery for your sins."

"It's my goal to have the lottery abolished before I die," Pruitt explained to me. "Having a mission with a good social purpose is what keeps me young."

Pruitt is part of a growing group of lottery winners who are planning to sue state governments that sponsor gambling. In the late 1980s, Pruitt won a $50 million jackpot. But like so many jackpot winners, the grandmother of six lost all of her money to sham investments and outlandish spending. She now folds shirts at an Eddie Bauer store outside Harrisburg; before her win, she was a successful middle manager.

"In January I had to sell off most of my winter clothes— sweaters, coats, Neiman Marcus furs, even a parka I'd had since high school," she said. "I'm in more debt now than ever before. The lottery ruined my life. I wish I had never won. Frankly, it's a crime that I won."

"Gloria didn't *win* the lottery," Stan Romaine, a lawyer who organized a Virginia conference for aggrieved winners, explained to me. "She was nearly destroyed by it."

It went on from there—with more on Gloria Pruitt and the Virginia conference, and more on other winners' tales of woe. I should have been thinking of the story as I walked—drifted, really—toward the *Weekly,* but I was not. Instead I thought of everything, anything, else that came to mind.

Soon I reached the magazine's office, and stopped to look at what had been my home since the day after I graduated from Cornell.

The *Weekly* occupies the eighth floor of a midsized commercial office building in Foggy Bottom, a neighborhood not far from the Lincoln Memorial. The structure's entryway is decked out in green-tinted glass and rose-colored marble, hand buffed to a perfect gleam every morning by a man named Jimmy, who also supervises the staff of nine that vacuums the hallways daily, polishes the hardware weekly, and washes the windows every third Monday when it's not raining. In all, 800 New Hampshire Avenue N.W. makes a perfect impression on one's mother.

Years ago, the magazine lived on Capitol Hill, in a weather-beaten storefront—the kind of building in which I had fantasized a magazine like the *Weekly* would be housed—with a clanking press in the basement, the flavor of printing chemicals in the air, and newsprint grime on every desk, door handle, and light switch. But the year before I was hired, the magazine's owner sold the storefront and moved us here.

The business staff invited advertisers to the shiny new space to watch the writers at work, but invariably they were disappointed. The magazine no longer looked anything like *All the President's Men,* with reporters crouched at desks flush against one another, grumbling about the day's news. Now the writers worked in their own offices at computers, alone. The editor no longer could yell, not even for show, "Stop the presses"—if he ever had, which I doubt—because the printing had been outsourced to a large corporation with a plant near the Chesapeake Bay. Every Monday afternoon, they delivered by courier the magazine's first press run, shrink-wrapped in plastic. As with a pack of Wrigley's gum, you had to pull one of those little red strings to open it up.

I loved arriving here every day. Working for my college newspaper, I had been a gadfly, detested by the campus authorities—the provost and the dean had come to hate me—but here, a gadfly was just what I was supposed to be. We were a nest of them. If an article didn't irritate someone, it had failed; if it didn't reveal embarrassing, even agitating information about its subject, it wasn't much of a story.

The *Weekly* had basically invented what became the dominant magazine journalism voice of the 1990s: the Ironic-Contrarian. *Weekly* pieces were attack pieces—but not angry, predictable polemics such as you might find in *The Nation* or *National Review*. They were sophisticated, low-key takedowns, all the more devastating because they used the source's own words to hang him: It was assisted suicide, not murder. The journalist's voice was cool, calm, even cold—at most, he or she might add the one-word sentence "Indeed," as if rolling up the noose for future use.

The key to a *Weekly* story was the capper: the most devastating remark by the source, in which he or she has been forced by the reporter's questions to take a position to a ridiculous extreme, a point where it is more laughable than logical. For instance, an Iowa congressman who was a leading defender of farm subsidies was pressed to say that if it was getting too expensive to pay farmers not to grow crops, then we should pay them a little less not to work at all.

Finally, the title of a *Weekly* piece had to be a tour de force. Whereas other magazines' titles were serviceable or vaguely clever, ours were little works of art: brief yet containing multiple meanings, pop culture references, and, again, veiled attacks that did not seem to come from the writer himself.

The headline for an article on Barbra Streisand's ill-informed attack on a conservative Israeli politician, for instance, was the manufactured word *Yental*. It would be a reference to both her movie *Yentl* and the Yiddish word *yenta,* meaning a gossip who gets into other people's business. (The echo of the grade-school insult *mental* would also be palpable.)

I'd adjusted quickly both to *Weekly* style, which was new to me but easy to learn, and *Weekly* culture, which was pretty similar to what I'd experienced at Cornell—no one dressed up, everyone procrastinated, everyone dated one another, and we all believed we were the center of the world. One of our favorite lunchtime games was, "If you had to cast *Washington Weekly: The Movie,* who would play whom?" I was invariably "a young Jeff Goldblum." My friend Brian was Matthew Broderick. And Lindsey, though she always hated it, was "Ally Sheedy in *The Breakfast Club.*"

Even though we had few subscribers compared to other magazines, and most of them were elderly men (an advertiser's least desirable audience), we convinced ourselves that it was the quality of the readers, not their number, that counted. When a reporter from another publication spotted a copy of the *Weekly* in the Oval Office and commented on it in print, the point was put beyond debate, as far as we were concerned. It wasn't important to be big, if you could be influential, and we were naïve enough to believe we were actually as important as we thought we were.

That belief was enhanced by the impression that we were special; we had been chosen. For a young writer, being hired by the *Weekly* opened doors; *Weekly* alumni would hire you to write later for the *Times,* the *Post,* or *The New Republic.* Our combined age was that of Helen Thomas; our combined journalism experience, before coming to the *Weekly,* that of George Stephanopoulos. Still, we were stars—precocious stars; Franny, Zooey, and Seymour on *It's a Wise Child*—and that was what mattered.

My own star was falling, though: I felt it falling even now.

Robert was standing at the door when I walked in. His black hair was just beginning to attain the distinguished salt-and-pepper hue that indicates a man who, while he may be eminent, is no longer quite young. The hair, however, was only a symbol of the transformation that had long been complete within. Robert had just turned forty-five, yet he was old hat at being old.

Apparently he had been pacing between his office and the desk of the receptionist, an elderly man and former preacher named Samuel.

"Where the fuck have you been, Steve?" Robert said the F-word a little louder than was appropriate around Samuel, who glared. As much as swearing and smoking and sinning were fundamental to the office's culture—hell, even encouraged by the editors—none of it was ever permitted in front of Samuel.

It was then that I began to focus ever so slightly on how wrong things were. Normally when things go wrong, even small things, I become panicky, but now I was more absorbed and intrigued than anxious, as if things were going wrong for someone else, someone from whom I was removed and to whom I was otherwise indifferent.

"I'm sorry," I said. "I was on vacation with Allie. It's our first real vacation in a long time and it's important to her."

"Okay, Steve, that's fine. But come with me."

Robert's office was immaculate; everything was in its place. Framed copies of his cover stories lined the walls, as did his awards, and there were dozens of them.

After Robert sat down, he buzzed Ian, the magazine's vice editorial director and Robert's second in command, and asked him to join us.

I was sitting—actually, sinking—into Robert's low-slung sofa, while he positioned himself several feet above me in his swivel chair. We were separated by his new, oversized desk, a desk too big for the room, but which he had ordered specially. Robert had organized his computer, telephone, and all of his stuff in the corner of the desk's L. It resembled a cockpit.

"Is some—something wrong, Robert?" I asked. The stutter surprised me. I was beginning to sweat, too. The anxiety I'd always felt at the *Weekly* was beginning to bubble up, as if from depths, to threaten the serenity I'd willed myself into as I walked over.

"Hopefully it's something you can clear up quickly. Let's just let Ian get in here, and then do it all at once." His voice was firm, with a hint of annoyance or maybe anger, I couldn't tell.

Robert took out an extra-large Filofax, the kind that is so big it has a belt buckle to keep it closed, and a felt-tip pen. He was looking at me and writing—scribbling actually, and moving his hand so fast you would have thought he was sketching my portrait.

"Can I ask what you're writing?" I ventured cautiously. I wondered what he was thinking, and what he knew.

"Let's just wait until Ian gets here, okay?"

"I'm sorry," I said.

Thirty seconds passed, and Robert continued to write. I shifted in my seat, trying to straighten up, to rise a bit out of the couch cushions. I tried not to think about how many of the writers had had sex on this couch after hours. I knew of several; there had to be more.

Robert coughed once or twice. I thought about how weird it is that people seem to cough more often, and at greater volume, just when they are supposed to be quiet. For instance, it's very rare for someone to cough when you're at a party, chatting. It's worrisome if they cough powerfully. But in, say, the theater, just after the house lights go dark, it might as well be a high school infirmary ten minutes before a big test, with all the hacking and wheezing going on.

Despite myself, I coughed.

"Don't get me sick, Steve."

"I'm sorry."

About a minute later, Ian, who looks a bit like the cartoon moose Bullwinkle, arrived. I was immediately reassured. Nothing too terrible had ever happened when Ian was around. Nothing too good either, but right now Ian was just what I needed.

Another good sign: Bullwinkle sat next to me on the couch. He grinned at both of us.

"Okay, let's begin," Robert said. "Steve, we'll start from square one: I got a phone call today from a reporter at *Substance Monthly*. He said he was trying to re-report your story about the lottery winners, and he was having a hard time doing it. He says he can't find Gloria Pruitt, the protester. He's saying he thinks the woman might be made up—fabricated."

Robert didn't say anything more right away; he just considered me, studying my eyes, my hands, my mouth. But he saw nothing. In the years since, much has been made of my steady composure. Mostly it has been deemed a sure sign of cold-bloodedness. But I didn't lack for emotion in that moment; I only buried it deep within me, knowing that if I didn't, I would never make it through. Dissociation, and the anxiety and even the despair it masks, are often mistaken for arrogance.

Robert: "Was Gloria Pruitt made up, Steve?"

"No. No. Of course not." I said it because I knew it was what I was supposed to say. As I listened to my own response, my nervousness and fear only worsened.

Bullwinkle, though, was visibly and audibly relieved. He exhaled loudly. "Well then," he said. "This won't be hard to straighten out. I should get back to my editing."

Bullwinkle stood up and was about to walk out, when Robert motioned for him to remain seated.

"I looked online for Gloria Pruitt's number and I couldn't find it," Robert announced. "And Ian looked online too. Ian, did you find a number for Ms. Pruitt?"

"No, I didn't. But I looked quickly, not all that thoroughly. Couldn't really say if there was one." Bullwinkle's speech was rushed.

"What about it, Steve?"

"I don't know, Robert. She's a senior citizen, if I remember correctly. Lots of elderly people don't have their own phones, right? They live with their grown children, or in nursing homes. Or she could be listed only under her husband's name. Some senior citizens are very traditional. You know, my grandfather had his number unlisted after he got a series of prank calls."

"That makes sense to me," Bullwinkle said approvingly.

Robert nodded, relaxing a bit. My explanation made sense to him as well. It sounded reasonable. For a moment I relaxed too, and allowed myself to hope that everything might be okay.

Bullwinkle laughed uneasily. "All right, then. I think it's all making sense now. Just a little confusion there, huh? I still haven't finished editing the cover story, so I better go do that." He began to get up again.

"Ian, sit down, and don't get up until this is done," Robert said. He did not speak again until Bullwinkle was firmly planted, once again, on the couch next to me.

"Even if she's not listed, you must have had her number to call her, right?" Robert pressed.

"Yes, of course, but I'm pretty sure the interview mainly occurred at a conference—not on the phone."

"You're *pretty* sure?"

"I mean, I'm sure, Robert. I'm sorry I'm not watching my every word. I should be, I guess. Most of the reporting occurred at a conference."

"The story said that," he replied slowly. "But do you think we can get this number somehow? If not from you, maybe from someone else at the conference?"

"I don't really know. I'd need to check my notes. . . . Can I get them?"

After some silence, I repeated my request, this time in the form of a statement: "I'll just go down the hall to my office and get my notes." I pointed out the door, but Robert's eyes didn't follow my finger; they remained focused on me.

Bullwinkle, though, turned his head and looked where I was pointing. He spoke uncertainly. "Makes sense to me, right? Should make this all go a little faster, at least I think—I mean, it should, no?"

"Come back, though," Robert instructed me.

"I will."

"I want to see you when I talk to you."

"Okay."

"Not over the phone."

"Okay."

I stood up from the couch and walked out of Robert's office. My gait was deliberate but unhurried, the step of someone who is sure. If I had followed my emotions, though, I would have curled up in a fetal ball on the carpet.

During the walk down the hallway, I became, for the first time, truly terrified. I was apprehensive as to what I would find in my files, though surely at some level I knew perfectly well what was, and was not, there.

• • •

My tiny office was furnished with only a desk, a filing cabinet, and a sofa inherited from the previous occupant. Despite the hundreds of hours I spent there every month, the white walls were bare, as if I had never felt entitled to move in. The only decoration was a Rock 'em Sock 'em Robots game, which sat, midpunch, on my desk. It belonged to Brian Lipton, my closest friend at the magazine; he liked to come over during the day and challenge me to oppose his tiny pugilist, yelling, "Knock his block off!" the way the advertisements had years ago, when we were children.

I took a deep breath and walked to the filing cabinet in the rear corner of the office. Inside were dozens of meticulously arranged manila files, containing my notes for every story I had ever written for the *Weekly*. If the notes weren't here, they didn't exist. If there were no Gloria Pruitt notes in these files, I would know for certain I had never actually spoken to her.

My thumb was poised to press the handle's little release button, but I couldn't actually bring myself to open the drawer. I sat down on the couch, placed my head between my legs, and pulled the trash can next to me. But after some time, the nausea passed, and a calmness again descended upon me. Fear turned to a strange inquisitiveness; anxiety again fell below the surface, somewhere where I could feel it circling, patrolling, waiting to rise.

I stood up and yanked open the drawer. I pulled the file for April 1998 and brought it to my desk. I sat down and opened it cautiously, like an important letter. There were four documents inside. Two were receipts: one for the US Airways Shuttle to New York, and one for lunch with a source at the China Grill. Two were sets of notes. One was about a congresswoman who slept in her office, supposedly to save the taxpayers money. I had demonstrated that after the additional cleaning costs and security expenses, the congresswoman was actually costing the taxpayer more than if she had rented a Georgetown apartment.

The second set of notes was about a man who had invented a "Tip-O-Meter," a small digital screen that displayed what the diner was inclined to tip the waiter, as the anticipated tip fluctuated over the course of the meal. The inventor told me that the conventional system, by which diners revealed their tip only at the very end of a meal, failed to create the right incentives for waiters to improve. "If the appetizer comes late, the diner can reduce the anticipated tip and then the waiter might bring the entrée faster to try and rally," the inventor explained. "For hundreds of years diners have needed a way to express real-time information about the quality of their customer-service experience. Now they will have it."

There were no notes about Gloria Pruitt. I checked and double-checked, but there were none. There were no notes about the lottery conference at all. There were no fucking notes.

My neck, my chest, my legs, every part of my body throbbed with fear. And with every moment, the pain amplified. My fingers prickled and the sensation moved up my hands, as if I were putting on gloves of nails.

Lindsey Ditmar, another writer at the magazine, chatted with someone across the hall, at a normal volume, but her voice hammered into my head. She was on what we had nicknamed the "re-obit" beat—writing contrarian assessments of the newly deceased, to contrast with *The New York Times*'s whitewashes. Currently she was writing about Fred Astaire: He hadn't been that good of a dancer, she was claiming; in fact, Ginger Rogers led *him*.

Meanwhile, as Lindsey cross-examined one of Astaire's former choreographers, the ringing of Brian's phone, four rooms away, shot through my ears, into my brain, and down my spine, until it pulsed in my lower back.

I could not concentrate. I could not focus. I could not think. But I needed to think. I urgently needed to think, more now than ever before in my life. I closed the door, closed the file folder, sat down at my desk, and closed my eyes. I tried to will the Gloria Pruitt notes to appear in the folder. I prayed to God, which I only did when something was really wrong, for the notes to turn up. I thought if I just wished hard enough, if I just wanted it badly enough, the notes would materialize. Before this, much of life had yielded easily to my desires—enough that I'd become, over the years, an intractable optimist. Now I thought: This is what I want, this is what I need. I need those notes to be in the file. I need them to appear.

After a few minutes of this, I closed the April folder and put it back in the filing cabinet. I walked out of my office and into the hall, took a deep breath, turned around, and reentered.

Once inside, I opened the top drawer, removed the folder again, and placed it on my desk unopened. I promised God that if the notes were inside, I would never do anything bad, ever again. I would study Torah and observe the Shabbat and keep kosher and I would be a good Jew, the best Jew ever. I would be like Moses.

I opened the folder carefully. As before, on top was the US Airways receipt. No big deal, I told myself, there are still three documents to go. Beneath it was the receipt for China Grill. Okay, I was nervous, but hopeful—still two more papers to go. Next were the notes about the Tip-O-Meter. Yes! A good sign. Last time, those notes were the fourth document. Now they were third. So there was one more document beneath them. Maybe God had rearranged the papers and placed the notes I needed at the end. Maybe it would all be okay. Maybe, maybe. Please, please, please. I held my breath as I turned over the only remaining document. It was the notes about the congresswoman who slept in her office.

No, no, no. I raced through the notes twice more. US Airways, China Grill, Tip-O-Meter, congresswoman. *No Gloria Pruitt.* US Airways, China Grill, Tip-O-Meter, congresswoman. *No Gloria Pruitt. No fucking Gloria Pruitt. Where the fuck was Gloria Pruitt?*

My entire body was slick with sweat. My shirt stuck to my chest and my chinos to my crotch; my glasses slid down the length of my greasy nose. I wanted to scream, but I couldn't; I couldn't let people know I was in trouble. I should have cried, but I couldn't let myself know I needed to, or else I would have fallen apart utterly.

What I needed, I told myself, was to think. I needed to figure out what I was going to do. But I couldn't think here. I couldn't do anything here. So I needed to leave, I needed to go home.

I buzzed Robert. He instantly picked up. "Um. Robert?"

"Steve, I told you to come to my office, *not* to buzz me."

"Hi, Steve. How are you?" That was Bullwinkle. I knew he'd still be sitting there.

"I need to run out," I said. "I think my notes are at home."

"They're not in your office? You should really be more organized."

"You're right, I should be. I'm sorry."

There was a long silence, as static burbled through the speakerphone. Robert said nothing. I said nothing. Bullwinkle knew better than to say anything.

"Steve, I think you should come down here," Robert finally intoned.

"No, Robert. I need to get these notes. So I'm going home. I'm going home now." It was the first and only time I ever contested Robert openly. "I'll call you when I get home," I blurted. And with that, I hung up the phone and exited out the back door.

Once I hit the street, I began to run toward my apartment. Buildings, cars, tourists, businessmen, everything whizzed by me. I wished for my legs to slow, but they refused. It was like trying to tell your kidneys to shut down. I didn't want to get home; I feared what I would find there.

When I passed Dupont Circle, I realized I was halfway to my apartment and only ten minutes had passed. Ten minutes more, and I was at my front door. I stood outside the apartment—my sweaty belly adhering to my shirt so tightly, the outline of my navel was visible through the cotton. I tried to clear my mind, but I couldn't.

Reluctantly, I went inside. There I found Allison in a long evening dress, fully made up.

"We're running late," she said. "Are you going like that, Steve? You're . . . not going to . . . dress up a bit? At least a fresh shirt?"

Her speech was broken up because she was applying lipstick. I still remember the color: M.A.C Grid. The cosmetics company classifies it in the lilac family, but I've always thought of it as more of a steel blue. Allison wore it on our first date and I couldn't take my eyes off her pouty blue lips. I wanted to taste her mouth. I know it sounds strange, but I hoped she would have the flavor of metal. I told her that, just after I kissed her for the first time. I probably shouldn't have.

"My brother is in town. Remember? We're supposed to have dinner with him?"

"I'm so sorry, Allie," I said. "I just don't think I can do it tonight. Something really bad has happened at work."

Just as I was catching my breath from the run, I began to breathe very quickly again, panicking as I remembered I was supposed to be getting my notes for Robert. I steadied myself a bit against the couch's arm.

"What do you mean? You *have* to come. You've never met him, and he's only here tonight. Don't tell me it's work stuff. You're on vacation, and you promised."

My field of vision began to turn clockwise; slowly things blurred. Leaning on the couch was no longer enough. I sat on the floor.

"Are you okay?" she asked.

I said nothing. Her voice distorted somewhere between my ears and brain. It sounded something like: "Ow-re yooo oohhhhh kay?"

She spoke again: "Steeee-veeen, ow-re yooo oohhhhh kay?"

I didn't look up. I was feeling sick, a special kind of sick that I had never felt before, but that I have since come to know well. The walls of my stomach sting as it squeezes into a fist. Sour acid molecules chew on the lining of my innards as if they had teeth. The light-headedness becomes more severe as blood rushes from everywhere to my center. If I'm not already lying down, I must, and so that day I lay down on the floor.

I have felt the sickness hundreds of times since then. I felt it when I saw my name on the front page of the newspaper. I felt it months later when I saw Bullwinkle at a movie theater, sitting a few rows in front of me. I felt it when the receptionist at my eye doctor's office asked if I was "the famous Stephen Glass." I feel it even now, five years and 225 miles removed, as I tell you what happened that summer. The sickness has become a physical memory, summoned to consciousness by so many triggers that I doubt I'll ever be totally free of it.

Allison handed me a glass of water and I sat up, sipped it, and cooled down a bit. After a minute, the sick feeling began to clear. I drank the water carefully, as if I were swallowing something sharp. I breathed a few more times and then, without looking up, I asked Allison to sit beside me. Now we were both on the floor with our backs against the sofa, she in her evening dress bunched at the knees.

"Look, I'm really sorry about your brother," I said. "You know I'd be there if I could. But Robert is really upset with me. There's some questions about a story I wrote, and I have to get my stuff together or he's going to be really mad at me."

"Steve, Robert is always pissed at someone. If it's not you, it's Brian or Lindsey. You just can't keep letting him invade your life like this. You need to set boundaries."

"I promise you, this one's different. I might be in serious trouble if I don't take care of it."

Couldn't she see how important this was to me? Usually I would have just acceded; Allison was headstrong, and since I tended to be indecisive, I generally acquiesced in whatever she wanted, figuring her preferences were stronger than mine. I hoped she could see that I wouldn't do this rare thing—I wouldn't outright refuse—except out of pure and total desperation. The truth was, I'd never stood up to her before or even thought about it; I'd only tried to placate her, to make her happy. But she seemed oblivious to my new tone of voice, to its barely controlled panic, to my unusual insistence on my own way.

Her eyes, usually so gentle, scrutinized me in the same measuring way Robert's had. Then she looked at her watch. "Fuck you, Steve. I should have known this would happen. You never put me before the magazine."

She stood up, took her purse, and walked out the door. She did it all without looking at me, and my heart sank. I had loved Allison for a long time, and I knew the tension between us now was my fault, not hers. Despite our problems, I wanted, more instinctively than rationally, to stay with her.

As soon as the door closed, I ran to the window and yelled down, "Allie, I love you." But she didn't turn to look. She was hard where I was soft; if it were me, I couldn't have helped but turn, but she kept her back to me, and did not even pause. I watched, and kept watching even after she rounded the corner and I could no longer see her.

And then I got to work.

Our apartment was a spacious, one-bedroom duplex that overflowed with light. We were on the fourth and fifth floors, and even though there were only two reedy spruces outside, if you opened the windows after a good rain, it smelled like a forest.

When we moved in, we'd converted the upstairs walk-in closet into an office for me, and it was the only place in the apartment I felt was totally mine. I spent almost every night in there, reading and writing. Even after Allison went to sleep, when I could have used the whole downstairs to work, I preferred the room's cooped-up feeling. Friends who visited said the room smelled like me. I never knew what to think of that.

I took the stairs two at a time. As I reached the landing, the phone rang. I didn't want to answer it—whoever it was, it couldn't be good. One more ring, and then the machine picked up. The outgoing message played. My voice, recorded months earlier, when Allison and I first moved in together, was buoyant. And then a beep.

There was just breathing. Noisy, shallow breaths. It was angry breathing, masculine angry breathing. And then a hang up. No message.

Robert.

I walked into the office, dropped into my chair, and turned on my laptop. While it was booting up, I looked at my desk, stainless steel and spotless. On the left of the computer was a neat stack of lined paper; on the right was a long row of ceramic coffee mugs from the Sunday morning talk shows on which I had appeared, each filled with different-colored pens. I didn't need to rummage around; I knew there were no misplaced notes here. Things were too clean, too organized.

I knew I needed to get something together—anything, really— before Robert called again.

I pulled up the *Weekly*'s website and printed a copy of my lottery story. I skimmed it, to see what I would have to prove. The most important person in the story was Gloria Pruitt, the activist who had built the crucifix out of lottery balls. I had quoted her four times.

I looked at the printed-out article and then I looked at the blank screen of my computer. I looked back and forth one more time, and then I typed Gloria's quotes into my word processor.

You must want to know: Did I think about the implications of what I was doing? No, not then, anyway. The truth is, I thought only about what would happen to me if I didn't come up with the notes. I couldn't think of anything else. There have been so many times since when I've wished that I had thought more broadly, but the fact is, I didn't.

I read over the typed quotes on my screen. They looked too perfect. The notes were supposed to have been taken during a phone interview; there was no way I could have gotten everything down so precisely. These notes were obviously faked.

So I futzed with them. First, I transposed letters. *Weird* became "wierd" and *the* became "teh," and so on. I changed some of the words to homemade abbreviations: *Because* became "bc"; *Gloria* became "G"; *lottery* was "lt." But the notes were still too exact. No one, at least no one at the *Weekly,* could phone-type that well. I went back to the beginning and used the space bar like a shotgun—adding spaces before words, after words, even in the middle of words, sometimes three or four at a time. I put in so many extra spaces that the page looked holey. After that, I went back over the text with the delete key in the same way.

When I was finished, I read the notes aloud with satisfaction, even speaking the typos and pausing for the extra spaces. I remember thinking that the notes had been *distressed,* which at the time was the hip interior-design word for making new things look old. For the first time that afternoon, I was feeling better.

Then it occurred to me that I had to add text around the quotes. Journalists take far more notes than they use in their articles, but my quotes were entirely bare. I began inventing additional sentences, but it was difficult. At moments I felt like I was in the flow, but most of the time I was struggling to compose. I couldn't write just anything: Gloria was a character, and the surrounding text had to feel like part of an interview she would give.

I tried to make myself be Gloria, to imagine what she would say. To do this, I spoke questions aloud in my normal voice and then, with a picture of her in my mind, I answered in the high-pitched, scratchy tone of a woman triple my age. My hands were poised over the keyboard, ready to transcribe what she said.

But it didn't come. I was too self-conscious, too keenly aware of being Stephen Glass pretending to be Gloria Pruitt. I needed to become Gloria Pruitt.

Props! That's what I needed! Costumes!

I ran to the bathroom.

Rouge! I was sure Gloria would wear a lot of rouge. I dumped Allison's makeup bag on the counter. She didn't have rouge, but she did have a Bobbi Brown Cream Blush Stick. Okay, I thought, it's got to be close to the same thing—rouge for young people.

Unfortunately, Allison didn't have the severe colors I was looking for. Her shades were far too light. They blended into her skin. Elderly women like Gloria wouldn't use makeup that blended in. "Why buy it if you can't see it?" Gloria would say. Gloria would wear strong— almost alcoholic—red. But I didn't have time to shop for the real thing, so I took Allison's Sand Pink and used a lot of it.

Once, months ago, Allison had taken me with her to Nordstrom to have her colors done. The senior colorist—I loved her title—said Allison was an "Autumn" with a few hints of "Winter."

"Like, early November?" I said, trying to be helpful.

"It's not coordinated to the months," the colorist told me.

"Forgive him," Allison said to the woman. "He's a Spring."

"Of course," the colorist agreed. "Springs know nothing. It's part of their whimsy."

Fortunately for me, Gloria's season was easy—it was whenever the seventy-year-old drunk prostitutes came out to play.

Unsure of how to operate Allison's blush stick, I held it like a piece of chalk and drew large circles on both my cheeks. I used so much, probably half the tube, that the blush spots were raised off my skin a millimeter or two.

I looked at myself in the mirror. I needed lipstick. Allison had probably twenty different types of lipstick, but again none of them were as garish as Gloria's tastes. There were browns and roses and lavenders, but nothing that would make it look like Gloria had just finished a cherry Tootsie Pop. I knew that was the color she would wear.

My only hope was to combine Allison's colors. First, I put on a layer of her darkest brown lipstick and on top of that, a layer of her deepest red. I didn't realize how hard it is to do your lips. My hand jiggled all over the place. I lipsticked my cheeks and my chin, even the underside of my nose.

I looked in the mirror.

"Hello, Ms. Pruitt," I said. "You look gorgeous."

I ran back to my desk, leaving Allison's makeup scattered throughout the bathroom, and sat down at my computer, ready to perform Gloria's interview. Now my fingers would merely transcribe.

Gloria provided further commentary on the lottery, such as: "It's the number-one public policy problem today." She sought reassurance from me, making comments like: "You'll be sure to quote me correctly, dear?" When I got too personal, she would cut me off, saying, "I really don't think I want to talk about that." And often—probably because, despite the rouge and lipstick and high-pitched voice, I didn't have a firm enough handle on her character—she rambled, making little sense at all. Still, a half hour later, I had pages of notes on our conversation.

To make the notes believable, I knew I needed to include Gloria's phone number. Every journalist at the *Weekly* puts the interview subject's number in the header of his or her notes. I knew that, and Robert knew that; it was probably why he hadn't stopped me from leaving the office. Even if I'd spoken to her at a conference, I was supposed to have a number on file for her. If I did have a number, it would solve all our problems; if not, it would be the conclusive evidence against me that I think Robert was already searching for, even then.

I began dialing random numbers in the Harrisburg area code. If I could just find one that was disconnected, I would use it. Gloria must have moved, I would tell Robert.

But a person or answering machine picked up at each of the numbers I dialed. No good. This wasn't going to work. It seemed every one of the billion numbers in Harrisburg was being used.

Then it occurred to me to create a voicemail box for Gloria. I found dozens listed in the online Yellow Pages, but only one company promised "instant activation" for every area code in the country. I called it.

"Voice-O-Rama—where you get the *very special Voice-O-Rama treatment.* This is Holly."

"Hi, Holly. I need a voicemail box in the 717 area code— Harrisburg, Pennsylvania—and I need it set up immediately."

"Just a moment . . . Unfortunately, sir, we have nothing available in that area code right now. Would you like one in the Fort Lauderdale suburban area code, 954? We're having a *very special* special on those."

"I need 717. She's supposed to live in Harrisburg."

"Well, how about 649? We're having a *very special* special on those too."

"Where's that?"

"The Turks and Caicos Islands."

"Where?"

"They're near the Bahamas. The islands were part of the United Kingdom's Jamaican colony until 1962. When Jamaica won its independence, they were made a separate crown colony."

"No. No. No. You don't understand. I need 717, Harrisburg, *Pennsylvania.* Can't you help me?"

"Not with a 717 number. I'm sorry, sir."

"This isn't really the *very special Voice-O-Rama treatment* now, is it, Holly?"

"Sir, I can only do what I can do. Is there something else I can help you with?"

"This is really bad."

"Okay, sir. I'm going to disconnect from this call now. . . ."

"No. No. I'll take the Fort Lauderdale number. I'll take it. And, here's my other question: How private is it? I don't want anyone to know I opened this voicemail box."

"If you don't tell them, they won't know, sir. Do you want a secret password?"

"Yes."

Holly gave me one, and asked if I would like to buy two more voicemail boxes. Apparently Voice-O-Rama was having yet another *very special* special, three boxes for ten dollars a month.

"I'll take it," I said.

She assigned me three numbers: the Florida number, and two in Alabama. I had no idea how I was going to explain the Alabama area codes to Robert. The state doesn't even have a lottery.

She also gave me a toll-free number to use to record the outgoing messages. I hadn't thought of that. What was I going to say? How was I going to pretend to be three different people?

I decided to record Gloria's message first, since that was the number Robert had been asking about, and by now I was accustomed to impersonating her. I typed out a brief message and read it into the phone, in the same high-pitched voice I had used before. It was no good. The message sounded like me pretending to be an old woman. I redid it, trying to make my voice breathy, but now it sounded like me pretending to be an old woman with a cold. I tried to talk fast, like the guy from the old FedEx commercials, so you couldn't make out my gender or age. No go: a freak on helium. I tried to talk overly slowly. I spoke with gum in my mouth. I pretended I was retarded. I pretended I was British. The recordings all sounded like me having fun with my voice.

Ultimately, I covered the phone with a sock and recorded the following message, in as deep a voice as I could muster: "This is Fred. Me and Gloria aren't here. Leave a message and we'll get back to you. It may take a while, because we're spending much of the summer in the R.V. "

I liked the last detail, which I made up on the fly. I thought it would help explain why Gloria wouldn't be returning Robert's messages anytime soon.

I handled the other two voicemail boxes more quickly. For one, I recorded just dead air. For the other, I recorded my AOL software saying "You've Got Mail!" I figured that couldn't be traced to me.

Then I rolled back in my chair and surveyed what I had done. It was something, at least—maybe it was even enough, I dared to hope. This was the first moment when I felt I could pause—I'd done all I could do for now to protect myself, to try to ensure that everything would return to normal again. But when I did pause, I had to face my growing belief that it wouldn't be that way; it was going to be different for me this time, different and terrible.

A few moments later, the phone rang. It was Robert.

"Did you find your notes?" he demanded. "Why aren't you back here?"

"Yes, I found them."

I expected that he would be excited or express some sound of relief, but Robert just hmm-ed twice, maybe three times.

"I have the phone number," I added.

"Are you sure, Steve? How is it possible you got her number when I couldn't? Give it to me."

I gave him the voicemail box number I had just established.

"Have you called it?" he asked me.

"No."

"Good. Don't. I don't want you calling anyone until I've called them."

"That might make it hard to track things down. Don't you think?"

He didn't respond. Neither of us spoke for a few seconds.

"I have more, Robert. I have more to give you." I told him the two other voicemail numbers, which I ascribed to two other lottery winners mentioned in the story. As I spoke, I wrote down which number corresponded to which person on an index card, so I wouldn't later forget.

"I have notes too," I added. "But I don't have a fax machine at my apartment. Can I give them to you tomorrow?"

Robert didn't answer the question. Instead, he said he had spoken with the editor of *Substance,* and we were all supposed to talk at 10:30 A.M.

"Okay, Robert. I'll have all my stuff ready for them."

And then, without any forewarning, Robert disconnected. I wouldn't say Robert "hung up on me." Rather, he turned me off, like a TV program he could no longer bear. It was only when the phone company's triple tone sounded, and the recording came on instructing me to replace the receiver, that I knew he was gone.

Soon after he hung up, I drove my car to the *Weekly,* parked in the underground garage, and rode the elevator up to the eighth floor. Allison was coming home soon, and I did not want to have the fight I knew would happen if I was there when she returned to the apartment.

Here, I could work by myself. It was late enough that all the writers had gone home. Only the cleaning guy, whose nickname was Throw, remained. He had just started his evening rounds, and was vacuuming inside. He heard me insert my key into the *Weekly*'s front door, and he opened it before I could finish with the lock.

"I knew it was going to be you," he said.

"Thanks," I replied faintly. I walked past him, heading toward my office.

Throw was a lonely immigrant from Paraguay, and because I was frequently the last person to leave the office, he would come by my desk many nights and tell me about his wife and two daughters. They remained in South America, and he hadn't been back in more than two years. He told me he missed them terribly and had no friends in Washington.

One night, when I had stayed very late, I asked Throw if he wanted a ride home. He had once mentioned that he rented an apartment not far from the magazine. But he declined. "This is my home," he said.

I asked him again, thinking he had misheard me. Throw's English was generally excellent, but occasionally he just completely misunderstood a word.

"Esteban, esta es mi casa," he repeated.

Throw told me that after everyone had left, he would walk around the office and pretend he lived there. He confided that he liked to pretend all the writers were his children. He imagined we were all just out for the night. "I sometimes think everyone's at a big celebration. I couldn't go to it because I had to work late," he explained. "But they'll be back soon from the party and I'll be here waiting for them."

Throw would sometimes stay at the office until 2 or 3 A.M., long after all the other cleaners had gone home. His enthusiasm for the job creeped out most of the magazine's staff. When they were working late, he would come to their offices and try to start up a conversation. He wouldn't know where to begin, so he'd ask if things could be thrown out: "Throw? Throw?" That's how he earned his nickname.

When I asked Throw about his apartment, he said he spent almost no time there. He used it to sleep, but as soon as he woke up, he would go out. In the summer, he spent the afternoons in the city's parks. In the winter, he preferred Washington's museums. His favorite was the Air and Space Museum, which he said he had been to more than one hundred times over the past two years. When I told him I didn't believe anyone could have gone there so frequently, he climbed on top of my desk and recited Neil Armstrong's moon-landing speech, using his duster as a microphone. When he came to "one giant leap for mankind," he jumped off the lunar lander.

Convinced, I asked why he always went back to that museum.

"They have astronaut ice cream," he said. He told me he sent some of the candy back to Paraguay for Christmas.

The previous February, I had held a small birthday party for Throw. Brian, Lindsey, and Allison came and we waited in my office until he passed by on his rounds. When he showed up, I had a cake with candles ready. Brian took a couple of Polaroids of Throw with me. On the one Throw sent to his wife, he wrote in the white area under the image: "Mi amigo mejor." My best friend.

"Are you surprised I knew it was you?" Throw asked me now. "Everyone turns their key in the lock a different way. You're very gentle, Esteban."

I said thank you, and turned toward him for the first time.

"I was right. You're back from the party," he said when he saw me. "Are the others coming?"

"What?" I asked him. I was annoyed; I wanted to be alone. More people meant more complications, which would be more than I could bear.

"Your cheeks are rosy and your lips are made up. A costume party?"

Of course. I still was wearing all the Gloria makeup. I'd have to remove it.

"No, no one's coming," I assured him, and myself.

I turned and started toward the bathroom.

"Esteban?" he said. His voice was tender.

"Yes?" I replied. I stopped, but just barely; I didn't even turn to look at him this time.

Throw didn't say anything right away; he was waiting for me to face him, but I didn't. I heard the metal clank of a garbage can being lifted from under a desk. "Throw, Esteban? Throw?"

"Yes," I said, even though I had no idea what he was pointing to. "Go ahead. Throw it away. Throw it all away."

After I returned from the bathroom, where I'd scrubbed off the makeup, I saw that the voicemail light on my office phone was blinking. There were three messages. The first was from Cliff. He said he was waiting at the restaurant and I was thirty minutes late. He said he would give me another fifteen. That had been more than an hour ago. He must be long gone by now, I realized. He was going to be annoyed, but I didn't have time to call and explain.

The second message was from Brian: "Glass, call me at home.

I'm worried about you. Lindsey said Robert's on the warpath. This has got to suck for you. Call me if you need anything. Call me even if you don't. Just call me."

Brian and I had grown up at the magazine together. We had gone to college together, where we'd worked together on the *Cornell Daily Sun*. We were hired together, started on the same day, and had planned to stay at the *Weekly* forever, or at least until we were shriveled, crotchety ninety-year-old men who could no longer type. Then, we'd said, we would simply be avid *Weekly* readers; we'd finally fit the demographic. We would also be the perfect age to begin an active Letter to the Editor writing career. This was our dream. We had discussed it many times over drinks. Even our girlfriends had talked about it.

The third message was from Robert. He said he had left a message for Gloria but she hadn't called him back yet, and he didn't understand why. His phone call was important. "Doesn't she understand that?" he asked.

I ignored the message, took out the lottery story, and read it again. This time I highlighted everything that required supporting evidence. To be complete, I would need to come up with contact information for several more interview subjects and corroborate a lottery winners' newsletter from which I had quoted. That was much more than I could accomplish in one night, but I hoped that if I just established a critical mass of stuff, Robert would believe me.

Stanley Romaine was first; he was the lawyer I'd quoted in the article—the one who I'd said had organized the conference. I created a new email account, LawyerStan@aol.com, and clicked on the section of America Online that allows you to make your own homepage. I composed the simplest one possible. It was mostly text, but I knew I needed at least one photo to make it more credible. I typed "pictures of professional men" into a search engine, and it spit out a gay porno site that featured men in suits. I swiped the pic of "Graying Gary" and pasted it onto Lawyer Stan's homepage. Graying Gary held a thick book in one hand and wore wire-rimmed glasses. He looked just the way Mr. Romaine should. Plus, even if Robert knew who the guy really was, and the movies he had starred in, he would never say so.

One more thing: Lawyer Stan needed a phone number. I couldn't give him an address—Robert would try to visit his office, or he would call the Recorder of Deeds or something—but he had to at least have a phone number, and the Voice-O-Rama sales office was closed for the night.

I called Nathan, my brother, a junior at Dartmouth.

"Hi, Steve."

"Nat, I love you, but I don't have time to talk."

"Um. Okay."

"I need your help."

"Okay," he said again. "Shoot."

"I need you to change the voicemail message on your cell phone. I need it to say this: 'You've reached the law offices of Stanley Romaine. No one can help you at this time. Please leave your name and number and we'll get back to you just as soon as we can.' Do you have that? No, wait, make it 'Stanley Romaine *and Associates,*' it sounds more established."

"Uh-huh," he said, perplexed. "But can I ask you one question?"

"Yes. I'm sorry I'm so hurried. I should have said thank you."

"That's all right. My question is, isn't Stanley Romaine the lawyer from your story last week?"

"Yes."

"I read that story. I liked it a lot."

"Thanks."

There was a pause. I suddenly felt overwhelmingly, crushingly sad. My brother admired me; he read all my stories. He was proud of me. He believed I really was a good journalist. And now he, like Robert, would slowly begin to change his mind.

"So," Nathan said, when it became clear that I didn't want to clarify. "Can I ask why you're doing this?"

"I can't get in touch with the guy, and I need to, because Robert is on me about it. You don't have to do anything big, just change the voicemail message and don't answer your phone for a while. I really can't talk about it right now."

I swallowed. I had never lied to my brother before—at least, not like this. I had never asked him to do anything like this, either. But I was desperate; I had no one else to ask and I couldn't bear not to ask—I couldn't bear just to let the world collapse around me.

Even though my request must have sounded extremely fishy, loyalty was foremost between Nathan and me. We both knew he wouldn't press me further.

"So will you do it?" I asked.

He didn't even need a second to think about it. "Of course."

"Thank you, Nat, I love you."

"I love you too."

From the way he said it, I knew he probably knew. And then we hung up.

The night went on. I created a fake newsletter called *The Lottery Update,* which I had described in my article as having editorialized against the rebellious winners. One of the *Update*'s stories profiled a lottery winner who had picked his numbers with the help of his goldfish. I created another article, "Wendy Windfall's Good Luck Recipes," to look like a regular feature. I lifted the recipes from an online cookbook, but changed the measurements a bit—more sugar in everything.

I wrote pages and pages of fake notes. I created notes for lottery winners and lottery losers and lottery martyrs—lottery activists of every possible persuasion. I created fake notes for almost everyone who appeared in the article, and a couple of people who didn't appear, so I could tell Robert, "See, there are even more people, too; people I didn't even quote."

Sometime in the middle of all this, I called Allison, but she didn't answer the phone. Then I called Lindsey. I wanted to call Brian, but I was too ashamed. I thought Lindsey might be understanding.

"Sorry to get you so late, Lin."

"Not a problem. Robert called me. Are you all right?"

I should have expected as much. No matter what decision had to be made at the magazine, whether it was about a cover line or where to eat lunch, Robert felt the need to drum up support.

"I'm pretty pissed. I think I'm going to quit," I said. "Robert's the editor; he should be supporting his staff. It's like he's prosecuting me instead of defending me. I can't work for someone who doesn't stand behind me."

She listened carefully, and said supportive things, and I calmed down a bit. She retold the story of the time Robert accidentally locked himself in the supply closet and, unable to find fault in himself, demanded at a staff meeting that "the one who did this dastardly thing" come forward "and be a man of honor." At the meeting, Lindsey had attempted to defuse the situation, but made it so much worse: "And what if the perpetrator was a woman, Robert? What then? Should *she* too be a *man* of honor?"

"So has he called you *dastardly* yet?" Lindsey asked me now. "Are you a *man of honor*?"

She had me laughing. I was looking for one ally at the magazine, just one.

"Lin, why didn't you and I ever go out?" I ventured.

But she didn't go there. "I'll see you tomorrow, Steve."

"See you tomorrow."

And for one precious minute after I hung up, I really thought everything might be okay.

Robert found me at 8:30 the next morning, slumped over my desk, asleep. He cleared his throat at me loudly.

"What TV show are you going on?" I asked him, as I wiped the sleep and a gritty trace of mascara out of my eyes. He was dressed in a suit; the only time anyone ever wore a suit to the *Weekly* was when they were planning to appear on television.

He didn't answer. "Steve, I was up most of the night working on this," was all he said.

"So was I. I never went home."

"Steve, it's different. You're really angering me. You're not organized. You take forever to get me stuff. Being here is keeping me from seeing my daughter, who is home from college for the week. How can you do that to me? How can you do that to my daughter?" He was waving his hands around, somewhat wildly.

"I'm sorry, Robert. I'm working on it. I stayed here all night." I paused for a bit. "Robert, I'm hurt that you're not defending me. I'm your writer. That's what Ted would have done. He would have defended any of his writers. And you know that."

Ted Davidson was the editor who had preceded Robert. There had been a virtual cult of personality around Ted, and his secret nickname had been Co-author, or just Co. When editing, Ted always added text— sometimes thousands of words—and in adding, he always improved articles dramatically, buttressing the reporter's weaker prose. And yet he never took any credit for what he had done, referring to it as "tinkering," "noodling," or simply "typing." Unfortunately for us, though, Ted's very skill soon meant that the vultures descended: Other publications wanted him, and the *Weekly* couldn't afford to keep him. He went off to L.A., where we'd heard he had married a stunning short-story writer. (Shortly after their wedding, and to no one's surprise, she reworked one of her stories into an acclaimed six-hundred-page novel.)

Ted was known not only for his prolixity on others' behalf, but also for his loyalty. He would praise your virtues to anyone who'd listen, and it was because of Ted's large and beneficent mouth that under his editorship, the *Weekly*'s circulation increased for the first time in more than a decade. It was also because of him that many of us at the *Weekly* had succeeded despite our youth. Ted believed in us.

After the adulation Ted had received from us all, no wonder Robert felt embattled. He could never have measured up, no matter what he'd done. He was LBJ after JFK. His response had been to become testy and controlling. Other people might have responded differently, but there was no real solution; Robert had been doomed from the start, and it hadn't been fair. Ted in memory was even worse competition than Ted in person. To be fair, Robert had many virtues—he was an outstanding domestic policy writer, especially on health-care reform and economics; he was a keen editor of copy, an excellent mentor to the younger reporters, and a fair manager who never played favorites among the writers—but since they weren't Ted's virtues, it was hard for us to appreciate him as much as we had Ted.

But I had to stop thinking about Ted. He was not going to save me now. Ted was gone: He was probably sitting with his brilliant wife next to a huge kidney-shaped pool, in a tastefully landscaped grotto, somewhere where the weather was perfect.

Robert sat down on the couch across from my desk.

"Stephen, I am *trying* to defend you, but you're making it impossible for me to help you. Look, Gloria didn't call me back last night, and I've gone through all the other names in your story. I can't find any of them in any phone directory anywhere on the Web, and they're businesspeople, lottery winners, lawyers. How can that be? These are public people. And there's something else. Do you know how one can set up a voicemail box?"

"What do you mean?"

"All three numbers you gave me go to voicemail, and not only that, they all go to the same *kind* of voicemail. If you hit the Pound key, the same computer voice comes on and says the same thing. So I'm asking, do you know how anyone could set up a voicemail box?"

The way Robert had raised his volume at the end of his sentences betrayed how much anger he was feeling. He was onto me; he'd suspected, but now he felt he knew, and I saw how furious it made him, and I was afraid.

I responded cautiously: "Most people get voicemail at work, Robert? Or through the phone company?"

"Is there any other way, Steve? Think about it."

Even though I paused at this point, it was just to catch my breath. I didn't think about what I was going to say next. I just spoke: "Well,

I've seen in the phone book that you can set up a voicemail box for a fee. There's tons of ads for voicemail services in the Yellow Pages."

"I know, Steve, I looked in the phone book, too," Robert said in a heh-heh voice.

I have often wondered why, after working so hard to hold it all back, I gave up this bit of truth so easily. It was damning in the most absurd Perry Mason way: "Aha! Members of the jury, I ask you, how could Stephen have known of the phone book voicemail services if he had not used one himself? Coincidence? I think not."

In the months that followed, Robert would point to this moment with a detectivelike pride. He would say he had outsmarted me; he had carefully coaxed a near confession out of me when I let down my guard. But I'm pretty sure Robert actually had nothing to do with my slip. The words just rose up from deep inside me. It was a momentary eruption from the war being waged within my subconscious, and it was the first evidence of which side was going to win.

"Is there anything else you want to tell me?" Robert pressed. "Something important, before we go any further?"

"No."

"Nothing you want to get off your chest?"

"Not really."

"You sure?" Robert asked once more. "There's nothing you'd feel better about letting me know about now? Because I am going to fig-ure this all out in the end. You can bet I will."

He said it in the way journalists sometimes pressure their sub-jects, and police officers their suspects—warning them that talking will give them more control than silence.

There was a long quiet.

"Well, I guess there is," I said softly. He waited expectantly. "I'd like to show you some of my notes from interviews. I think that might be helpful." I handed him the stack of pages I had manufactured the night before.

"Oh," he said. Robert looked at me. He seemed astonished by the stack's volume. I could see he didn't know what to think. One moment ago, he had believed our tête-à-tête was nearly over, with only my tearful confession and appeal for mercy remaining. But now Robert, the esteemed editor of the *Weekly,* who had worked his way up for more than twenty years to this top post at the pinnacle of the Washington media establishment, thought he might have to apologize to me, a twenty-five-year-old writer.

Robert thumbed through the evidence. There was so much of it, and it was beautifully organized. He didn't really read the notes. It was more like he was weighing them.

"Okay, I see your notes, Steve, but answer me this: How come I couldn't find anyone on the web? Don't you find that strange?"

"I don't know. I only found one of them, Gloria's lawyer."

"Where? I'll take that link right now. None of this running back to your apartment to get it."

"Um. Okay," I said, as I looked through my papers. "Here it is. Here's the link."

"Pull it up on the screen right there."

I typed in the URL, and up came the picture of Graying Gary in his featured performance as Lawyer Stan. Never before and never again has a porno star looked so good to me.

Robert sat down, astounded. He scrolled through the page twice and then he walked out of my office wordlessly. His silence, though, was brief. When he got to his office, he buzzed me. "Don't go anywhere, Steve. I need to think."

"I'll be right here. I have nowhere to go, except maybe the bathroom. That's okay, right?"

"Don't be a smartass. We're not out of the woods on this yet."

"I didn't mean to be, Robert. I'm tired. I'm sorry."

Robert said nothing more to me, but before he disconnected the intercom, I heard him yell to Ian, "I told you to stay here. I told you not to leave my office. . . ."

I closed my office door, turned off the lights, and stretched out on the couch. I urgently needed to get some sleep; I was beginning to feel dizzy.

I was just beginning to fall away when my cell phone rang. I let it go to voicemail, but then it immediately rang again. In my family, the double call is the signal that it's really important. It's not to be used lightly. I picked up the phone.

"Hello?"

"Steve?"

"Hi, Nat. I'm sorry I didn't pick up the first time. This has been the worst day."

"Robert just called my cell. He left a voicemail, a long one saying it's urgent that I call him back—well, not me, but the lawyer, Mr. Romaine—and he's sorry to disturb me, or him, or whoever, but that I need to call him ASAP."

"Well, don't call him."

"Are you sure, Steve? . . . Wait, Steve, that's call waiting . . . hold on . . . my caller ID says it's him. What should I do?"

"Don't pick up. Let him go to voicemail again."

"Is he going to keep calling all day?"

"He might."

"I really don't want my phone ringing all day. How long is this going to go on?"

"I don't know just yet. Can you leave the ringer off?"

"No, there are some calls I have to take."

"Nat, I've been thinking I may have to buy you a new phone."

"What?"

"I may have to use this number for some time."

"Steve, it's call waiting *again*. And it's Robert *again*. He's persistent, isn't he?"

"Well, maybe you should call him back, actually. He just wants confirmation that Mr. Romaine exists. Can you say you're him, and confirm that I interviewed you last week?"

"But what if he asks me questions?"

"Well, you might have to improvise."

"That's kind of dangerous. I might screw it up."

"Nat, you're supposed to be a lawyer, so why don't you say your client doesn't want you talking to the press? He'll try to keep you on the phone, but don't let him. Just say you have to go. Don't be afraid to hang up on him. Can you do that?"

"You won't believe it. He just called again."

"Well, let's put this into action. You cool?"

"Um."

"Okay, we'll rehearse it once or twice. Pretend I'm Robert."

We went through it three times, actually. I asked all kinds of questions. By the second time, Nathan had it nailed. By the third, he was doing it with such gusto that Robert would be embarrassed he had ever called Stanley Romaine and Associates.

"And don't be calling people so many times. It's just not nice," Nathan roared before hanging up in the final dummy run.

But afterward, Nat said he was nervous. "I feel like I'm flying blind here."

"You can do it, Nat. I know you can."

"This is really serious for you, isn't it?"

"Yes, it is. I need this like I've never needed anything else. I hate asking you, but I need you."

Pause.

"All right, Steve, I'll do it. I'll call you back when it's over. . . . Hopefully you'll still have your job."

Eight minutes and forty-two seconds passed before Nathan called me back.

"So how'd it go? Did it work?"

"I don't know. I think he's somewhat suspicious. He asked me if I talked to you and all, and that part went okay. He also asked me about specific people in the story, a Gloria, I think. I told him I don't talk about my clients. He kept asking me more and more questions and I kept just saying 'I don't talk about my clients.'"

"And?"

"Well, he would never get off the phone, and I knew I would just have to keep saying, 'I don't talk about my clients,' so I yelled at him and hung up on him."

"Perfect."

"It didn't end there, though. He called back and left another voicemail. He said he's sorry he pushed me so hard. It's weird, he was actually apologetic-sounding. He said it was really important, and he needed to know, and he's sorry if my clients don't like it, but please explain to them that it's very, very important his questions get answered."

"Did he sound like he believed you were Mr. Romaine?"

"Yeah, I think so."

"Nat, you sound too quiet on this. Is something wrong? Something you're not telling me?"

"Don't worry about it," he said.

After Nat and I hung up, I lay down on the couch again and closed my eyes. I felt awful about what I'd gotten Nat to do, and I wanted to sleep to escape it—to escape everything. I couldn't sleep, but I couldn't stay awake either. I went on in this state until Robert buzzed me again. He asked me to come to his office so we could have our conference call with *Substance*.

I found Robert alone in his office. The hairy-chested smell of a man rising to the occasion had taken over the room. Bullwinkle had either been sent away or, more likely, he had escaped.

"Steve, as soon as we're done with this call—and we're going to make it quick—you and I are going to go to wherever this conference took place and we're going to ask people about it," Robert instructed me. "Someone there will put us straight. Don't say you're not, because that's what we're going to do. You got that?"

I said I understood.

"Good. Let's get going."

The call was brief. I gave the *Substance* reporter and editor the same evidence I'd given Robert, including the information for Lawyer Stan's website. They seemed surprised. They asked a few more questions about the story, and I tried to answer them as best as I could. My tone was helpful, but perturbed.

At one point, a question worried me, and I appealed for help: "Robert, could you put the phone on mute so I could talk to you for a second? I want to ask you something."

"No, Steve. Answer them. I want to know the answer as well."

It was then that I knew things had changed forever for me. In that single remark, Robert had communicated to *Substance* that he wasn't on my side; he too was disturbed by my story, he too wanted answers. It was his way of telling them, "If you're going to hang Steve out to dry, okay, but know I had nothing to do with it, and I don't believe him either."

I fumbled some answer to that question, and to the next few. Then Robert said we had some work to do, and ended the call.

"It's time for us to leave," he said, putting on his jacket.

"I'll get my car keys," I replied. "They're in my desk. I'll be back in a minute." I had thought that together my notes, the web page, and Nat's conversation with Robert would settle things, but they had only made things worse; now Robert and I were heading out to Virginia. How long could I go on like this?

I hated continuing, and yet I also hated the thought of reversing course. The hope that life could somehow go back to the way it had been, any day before today, persisted even as it became more and more irrational. My hope didn't die, no matter how much evidence mounted up against it. I wondered what, in the end, would kill it.

I bumped into Lindsey on my way to my office.

"I've been thinking about it all night," she said, touching my shoulder. "It's really terrible what he's done to you. You're right, I think you should quit when this is over. We probably all should do something, to protest it. It could have been any one of us they accused."

"Thanks, Lin, but I have to be going now."

"No, wait. Robert shouldn't really even dignify their questions with an answer. He should just tell them to fuck off, and they can write whatever they want. If they want to write a Letter to the Editor, so be it. We're always printing letters that say our stories are wrong.

That's what Letters to the Editor are for. But they should leave it at that."

Lindsey looked at me with woeful eyes. I didn't say anything.

"Do you want me to say something to him? It might be helpful," she offered. I should have told her no, but I said nothing. I longed for Lin's passionate, even if erroneous, defense.

She started to say more, but I excused myself, walked on, and got my keys. Later, I knew, she would think I had betrayed her—she, my last ally. And she would be right: Like a drowning man, I'd grabbed at others near me—Lin, and my brother—without a thought as to whether I might pull them down too.

Reluctantly, I returned to Robert's office, and with a sigh, he stood up and walked with me down the hall and into the elevator, where we each stewed separately.

I exited the elevator first, and Robert followed me to my white Saturn. Since I had arrived last night, beating everyone to the office, my car was parked in the space closest to the elevator.

"Nice spot," Robert said. He made it sound as if I had done something wrong to get it.

I walked to the passenger side of the car, unlocked the door, opened it, waited for Robert to get all the way inside, told him to watch his hands, and then closed the door. I walked slowly around the front of the car to the driver's side, studying Robert through the windshield. Come on, Robert, reach over and unlock my door, I said to myself. Pull up the little button. Do it. Do it.

Robert's arms remained fixed across his chest, his fingers wedged under his arms.

I let myself into the car, started it up, and backed out, little by little, using my turn signal even though there was no one else to see it. I slowly drove up the ramp and waited for the automatic door to open fully, not the usual just-enough-to-clear-the-car. Then I pulled out onto New Hampshire Avenue.

"This is not a driver's test, Steve. You've got to go faster."

"I'm a safe driver, a very safe driver. I won't change now."

"I wasn't asking you to be unsafe, but. . . . Never mind. So, where to?" Robert asked.

"To where the conference took place," I said.

"And where would that be?"

"Jeffersonville."

"You said that, Steve, but where in Jeffersonville? I want to know specifically."

"I don't know the Virginia suburbs all that well, but I can take us there. It was on a major road. I can show it to you."

"That's what you're going to do. You're going to walk us through everything that happened."

It had started raining, and the only sound inside the car was the rush of the wipers. *Blub-blub.* Every two seconds they pushed another wave of water off the side of the windshield. *Blub-blub.* Like a metronome, the wipers parceled out time. *Blub-blub.* I couldn't help but think they were counting down.

I drove on and soon passed the White House. I thought of President Clinton inside. He was in worse trouble even than me.

"We're going too slow, Stephen."

I had fallen below fifteen miles per hour. I had planned to use this time to think, to put together what I was going to say when we reached the conference site, but I was having trouble coming up with a story. I decided to go to the only place in Jeffersonville I knew I could find in my car, a small building complex called Olde Jeffersonville Square. Olde Jeff was a risky choice because I had been there only once before, years ago, and I couldn't really remember what it looked like. But I figured my ability to persuade Robert would have less to do with the location, and much more to do with my storytelling skills.

We crossed the Fourteenth Street bridge and passed National Airport. Traffic was heavy and with the rain, we moved at a funereal pace.

"This has got to be the worst way to Jeffersonville, Steve. Take the Parkway. It will be faster."

"I'm sorry. This is the only way I know. I won't be able to figure out how to get there if we take a different road."

Twenty minutes later, we arrived. On the approach, I saw that Olde Jeff consisted of four office buildings and a hotel. In the center was a cement park, dominated by a large Civil War memorial. A few people were standing outside, smoking under the awnings and trying to stay dry. Otherwise the area looked as if it had been evacuated. Was that good or bad? I couldn't decide. No one would be there to help me, but no one would be there to rebut me either, and that might be the best I could hope for.

I pulled the car up to the first office building. "We're here," I said.

"This is it?"

"Well, this is basically the area," I said weakly.

"I don't want to see 'basically the area,' Steve, I want to see *it*— where everything happened. So park the car and show me."

I turned off the ignition. We were parked in the office building's driveway.

"You can't park here. Park somewhere legal. I don't want you complaining while we're looking around that you have to get back to your car because you're going to get a ticket."

"It's pouring out."

"You won't melt. Park it legally."

I restarted the car and began driving around the block, looking for a parking lot.

"Where'd you park when you were here for the conference? We'll park there."

"I took the Metro."

"Really? I don't think there is a Metro around here." He began writing in his Filofax again.

"Or maybe Allison drove me."

Just ahead I saw a sign for a public lot. I pulled into it. "You know what, Robert, this is looking very familiar," I said as I took the ticket from the machine. "Now that we're here, I think *I* parked in this lot. That's right. Allison didn't drive me, now that I think about it."

Robert said nothing. I felt sick inside.

We got out of the car and walked to the hotel, which was in the middle building of the complex. I didn't have an umbrella, and Robert, who was shorter, held his too low for us to share.

"I want you to stay one step ahead of me," he directed. "You're leading me. Not the other way around."

I nodded.

The Democratic Hotel was a graceless fifteen-story pile of chrome and glass. Flags for different countries, dozens of them, with plaques identifying their nationalities, adorned the entryway. A bellman opened the door for us, and Robert unholstered his notebook again.

"So this is where we started," I told Robert, once we were in the lobby.

"Are you sure?"

"I remember the flags. See that one there? It's the flag for the Turks and Caicos Islands." I pointed to a blue flag, the third from the right. "Mr. Romaine, the lawyer, he told me about the flag," I explained. "The islands were part of the U.K.'s Jamaican colony until 1962, when Jamaica won its independence and they were made a separate crown colony. That's when they got their own flag. Mr. Romaine's family descended from the colonists, so he knew a lot about it."

Truth be told, as a child I had memorized the flags section of the *Encyclopedia Britannica* my grandmother had given my brother and me, because they were the only pictures that were in color. I had Holly at Voice-O-Rama to thank for the history lesson.

"Where were you sitting, Steve, when you had this fascinating discussion?"

I walked to the center of the lobby, near the glass elevator. I spun 180 degrees and pointed to a pair of dilapidated couches. "We sat there. Yes, there."

"Okay. Do you remember if any of the people behind the check-in desk over there were also here when you were here?"

"I don't recall."

"Or maybe the porter who opened the door? Was he here when you were here?"

"I don't remember."

"You remember an awful lot about the flags, but nothing about the people," Robert said, his volume rising. "The flags can't talk, Steve."

"Robert, the flags I remember because they might have been interesting to add as color to my story. The bellman, the concierge, et cetera, I didn't give a shit about."

I had raised my voice, too, and the bellman and the concierge, who had heard their titles spoken, looked at us, puzzled.

"I'm sorry," I said softly in their direction. "I didn't mean you."

"Okay. What happened next?"

I took Robert on a tour of the hotel lobby. He counted our paces and wrote down the figures. He took notes on everything. I explained that Mr. Romaine and I had sat on the couch for some time, talking. I asked Robert to sit on the couch with me so he could "feel what it was like." Full reenactment allowed me to improvise more fluently.

"When we'd been talking for about fifteen minutes, Gloria emerged from the elevator over here."

I then noticed there was a smoking section on the other side of the elevator.

"She wanted a cigarette, so we all had to get up and walk over here, to these other couches, so she could smoke." I pointed to the smoking area.

"These couches?"

"Yes. I remember this couch because it was so uncomfortable. The fabric is all pilled."

"Stop it. I don't care about the upholstery. I don't care about the goddamn flags. Here's what I care about: I care about you telling me what the fuck happened that day. Enough already, Stephen."

Robert was yelling at this point. The bellman, check-in staff, and maintenance crew looked at us gravely. One counterwoman picked up a telephone and whispered something. I continued with my tour, but in a hushed voice.

As we walked to the back of the lobby, I saw there was a small restaurant in the rear. "We considered getting a bite to eat here at the Congressional Café, because Mr. Romaine was hungry," I continued. "Did I tell you he was incredibly obese? That picture on his website must have been taken years ago; he's gained like a hundred pounds since then. But we were tight for time since we had to get to the conference, so he said he could wait until the banquet. We could hear his stomach growling, though."

"Steve . . ."

"Sorry, sorry."

"So where was the conference? Here at the hotel, right?"

I looked around. I didn't see any conference rooms, and even if the hotel had them, there would surely be a register of who had rented them, and I would be caught.

"No, not here," I said hesitantly.

At that point, an older man in a suit interrupted Robert and me. He said he was the hotel manager and asked if he could help us. Apparently some of the hotel's staff had told him we looked "confused."

Robert thanked him for coming by, and said we were trying to check into a news article that had been published about the hotel. "Could you please tell me if two people, a Gloria Pruitt and a Stanley Romaine, were guests of the hotel in the last month or so?" he asked.

"Yes," I said. "Could you? It would be very, very helpful. We don't want to invade anyone's privacy, but it would save us a lot of trouble and put a great deal of confusion to rest."

I said the bit about privacy very slowly, looking directly into the manager's eyes. At this point, I felt as if I were trying to extend my life by minutes, even seconds. I felt as if I were fighting for one more moment of the life I'd loved, the life I'd always wanted, the life I'd probably forfeited but couldn't quite let go of yet.

"No, I'm sorry. I can't do that," the manager said. "We *do* protect our guests' privacy. We don't discuss their arrangements with us. So is there anything more you need from us then?"

"It's very important," Robert said again, more sharply this time.

"Well, I'm sorry, but I don't think I can do anything for you."

The manager had led us to the door without our even noticing it. "Can we hail you gentlemen a cab?" he asked. He raised a single finger to get the bellman's attention.

"It's okay," I said. "We drove here, but thank you for your help."

Robert and I were once more standing alone outside the hotel, beneath the large flags.

"Never, never again speak like that," Robert said, yelling at me so loudly that the hotel employees turned to watch us through the windows.

"I'm sorry," I said.

"I was getting him to give us the information and then you brought up all the privacy stuff. I am running the show here, not you."

"I don't think you could have gotten him to give it to us anyway. You can't get that kind of information."

"You don't know what I can get. You don't know, Stephen. I—not you—am the editor of the *Weekly*. Don't ever forget that."

We stood there in silence for a few seconds more.

"Robert, can I ask you a serious question?"

"What?"

"Do you want me to resign? Would that be better? Because I'll do it. I really don't want to put you and the magazine through all this. I can just leave and work somewhere else, if you think that would be best."

Robert spoke very slowly in response. "It might come to that. But first you're going to show me where the conference was. Where was it?"

I spotted a diner called the Worthwhile Waffle next door. "Well, before that, we're going to pass the restaurant where we ate afterward, so let's go there."

I pointed to the Worthwhile Waffle and started walking.

"This is it, Steve? You went to the *Worthwhile Waffle*?"

"Yes."

"Steve, you said in the article it was a *banquet*—the guests at the meeting attended a banquet afterward. You're telling me they had a *banquet* at the Worthwhile Waffle?"

"Yes. It was convenient, I guess. And Mr. Romaine was hungry."

"You said a 'banquet'—that was your word. . . ."

"Well, a banquet means a group of people and a lot of food, right? Well, there was a group of people and a lot of food. But you're right, maybe I should have chosen another word. . . ."

"This is crazy. Okay, okay. Fine. I don't want to get into semantics with you, Stephen. You're saying there was a banquet here, a *waffle banquet*. Let's just go ask."

We walked into the Worthwhile Waffle and were greeted by the hostess. Robert asked to speak with the manager.

A young, pimply man in his early twenties, wearing a hair net, came over. He introduced himself as John, and shook our hands. His palm was sticky, probably from all the syrup.

"Well, John, we're trying to figure out whether there was a banquet here about a month ago," Robert said to him.

"A banquet, huh? I'm sure there probably was. There are a lot of them here. We're open all night," he explained enthusiastically.

"Could we see the list of people who rented out the restaurant last month, then?"

"It's not possible to rent the whole restaurant. Frankly, we're thankful if they call and make a reservation. That doesn't happen too much around here. But if they do, we're happy to give them adjoining booths."

"A banquet," Robert insisted. "Was there a banquet? That's all I want to know."

"Look, maybe we don't mean the same thing by 'banquet,'" the manager replied. "To me it just means people getting together and eating a ton of food. That's all. We have birthday parties here all the time; they don't rent out the restaurant, and I think those count as banquets."

Robert's face flushed. "Fine. Do you recognize this guy? He says he was at the banquet. Steve, come closer. Stand in the light and turn around so John can get a good look at you."

I rotated slowly, hands extended, like a pint-sized ballerina on display for all the parents at her junior high recital.

John looked at me carefully. "Who's asking, anyway?" he inquired.

"Excuse me?" Robert asked.

"Sorry. I thought that was what I was supposed to say. That's what people always say in the movies, when you come in and ask if they've seen someone. Say, we're not on *America's Funniest Home Videos,* are we?"

He waved out the window, where he thought there might be a hidden camera, and mouthed, "Hi, Mom."

"No, John. We're just trying to prove a news article that discussed a banquet at this place."

"We were in the news? I didn't see an article about us—not that we're not deserving, of course. This is the most profitable Worthwhile Waffle in the Mid-Atlantic region. Was the article in the *Post*?"

"Don't worry about it. It didn't mention the Worthwhile Waffle by name. So, did you see him last month, or not? He probably would have been holding a reporter's notebook or a tape recorder, and there would have been about a dozen people together."

John paused, and a mystified look came across his face. "So we're not going to do the part where I say I haven't seen anything until you give me the twenty-dollar bill, are we?"

"No, we're not."

"Because that's the part I was looking forward to."

"Come on, we're busy. Did you see him or not?"

"Might have. Can't tell for sure. He doesn't look so unfamiliar."

"That's the best you can do?" Robert snapped.

"That's the best I can do."

I said thank you, Robert said nothing, and we both walked out.

"That doesn't prove anything, Steve."

"I didn't say it did."

"But you were thinking it, I could tell."

"How can you tell what I was thinking?"

"Goddammit, Steve. Take me to the place where you had the conference. That's what I want to see. None of this other horseshit."

We walked toward the first building beyond the Worthwhile Waffle. It was an ordinary 1970s-era office building, a few floors shorter than the Democratic Hotel. It didn't look much like a conference center. Instead, it had the feel of a state government building—maybe a DMV.

For a moment, I considered doubling back. The buildings behind us seemed more promising. One had a little dome on top. Surely there had to be an auditorium under there. But because I had told Robert the restaurant was on the way to the conference, I felt committed to proceeding in this direction.

"This is the place?" Robert asked.

"This is it."

We entered the lobby: black linoleum floors and cement walls, vacant except for a security guard, the drone of forced air circulating, all else silent. Robert walked to the elevator and pressed the Up button.

"What floor?"

"No floor. We're here. The conference took place here."

"In the lobby?"

"That's right. There were tables all along the walls."

"No way."

"Yes, way. That's how it happened."

"You're telling me a lawyer held a meeting with clients in the lobby?"

"That's right."

"No lawyer would have that kind of meeting. Especially not *this* lawyer. I talked to him, Steve. He was all about privacy. He wouldn't even tell me his clients' names."

"Well, I suppose they probably met somewhere else afterward to do the private stuff, but I wasn't invited to that part, except the banquet. Obviously, they wouldn't have done the private stuff in front of me."

"Steve, if it happened here in the lobby, it wasn't a conference. At a conference, you *check in* in the lobby, you get your name tag there, you don't *meet* there."

"You're probably right. I should have called it something else. Maybe a 'fair' is more like it? Or a 'meeting in the lobby'?"

Robert looked at the floor for a full ten seconds, boiling, restraining himself. Then he looked at me. His face was flushed again. His speech was dead calm. "I don't believe you, Steve. Now I'm going to go look at that directory and see if there are any lawyers in this building, and if indeed there are, we're going to ask each and every one of them if there was a conference here or if they've ever heard of this guy Stanley Romaine, and I think each and every one of them is going to say no."

Robert walked over to the illuminated directory on the wall near the entrance. I stood next to him. He moved from panel to panel, running his finger over the entire board, carefully going over the names. When he was done, his voice remained eerily even. No word was emphasized over another. It was as if he were dictating something very important, something that had to be taken down exactly.

"There's no Stanley Romaine," he said. "There are no lawyers at all."

My anxiety was becoming overwhelming. Even my palms had begun to sweat. I started thinking of any other place but here—a warm bed, an office as friendly as the *Weekly* used to be for me, a booth and a Belgian Breakfast at the Worthwhile Waffle. Even then, I think I knew the world was about to turn hard and cold to me and so I started remembering its softnesses and warmnesses, as if I could save them up.

Then, in my reverie, something occurred to me. "I didn't say he worked here," I reminded Robert. "I never said that. I think his website even listed a 603 number, which is in New Hampshire."

"I noticed that too." He paused. "I'm glad you reminded me. Steve, where does your brother live?"

"What are you saying?"

"Just answer my question. Where does your brother live?"

"He goes to Dartmouth."

"Which is where?"

"Hanover."

"Hanover's in New Hampshire, right?"

"Yes, it is."

"Now I'm going to ask you this, Steve. Who was it I talked to on the phone? Who was it who said he was Stan Romaine?"

"I don't know, I didn't speak to him. I suppose it was Mr. Romaine."

"Are you sure it wasn't your brother?"

"Yes, I'm sure."

I felt a drop of sweat fall from my right armpit against the side of my belly. It wouldn't be long now. I looked out the lobby windows and watched the rain, which wouldn't let up.

"Okay then. There are no lawyers in this building. That's that. Case closed."

"There are too lawyers in this building." I pointed to a VERNER & JONES, LLP on the directory. "Maybe they're accountants, but they sound like lawyers to me."

"We'll see, won't we? We're going to go up there."

We took the elevator up. Just down the hallway was the firm's name stenciled in black on the glass door. Underneath were the words ATTORNEYS AT LAW.

Okay, I told myself, there's still hope. If I'm lucky they'll give a non-answer. They'll save me like the waffle man did.

Inside the office was a plump receptionist. "Can I help you, gentlemen?" she asked politely.

Robert pressed his hand firmly on my shoulder to silence me.

In his palm I felt the weight of his building fury. He seemed to hang on me.

"Yes, ma'am, I'd like to know if a Stan Romaine works here."

"No, we have no one by that name here. Anything else I can help you with?"

"I'd like to know, was there a conference in the lobby a month or so ago? There were supposedly lawyers there. Or at least *a* lawyer was supposedly there."

"I'm sorry. I have no idea. I just started work here."

"Who would know?"

"I guess Mr. Verner, he's the managing partner."

"May I speak to him please?"

"He's not in today, and anyway you'd have to schedule an appointment with his secretary. What's this about?"

"Can you tell me if there are *ever* conferences in the lobby?"

"Look, I really can't help you. You're going to have to leave."

We took the elevator back to the lobby. In it, Robert silently fumed and I silently whimpered. Finally, we reached the lobby and the elevator doors eased open.

"Steve, now I'm going to find out for sure whether there was a conference here," Robert informed me. "Follow me."

Robert walked to the security guard's desk near the entrance. I remained a few paces behind. My stomach tightened. Why was I making him go through this? Where did this crazy hope, the hope that I could somehow be saved, come from? My stomach wrenched with the excruciating, gradual loss of this irrational hope.

The guard was eating a sandwich and watching a soap opera on a portable TV. He didn't notice us until we were standing above him.

"Excuse us." Robert said it like a command.

"Oh, hey. Hi there, guys. I'm on lunch, so I'm not really on duty, but can I help you?"

"Yes, I think you can," Robert said. "I want to know if you have security cameras that record the lobby."

"Are you crazy? That's none of your business. I can't help you with that." The guard pushed his books and papers over the black-and-white monitors to hide what they were displaying.

"If you can't help us, then give me the phone number of your supervisor," Robert demanded. "I'm sure he will."

"Are you going to get me in trouble or something? I'm just trying to do my job. There's no way I can tell you this stuff. And, I'm on lunch. I don't even have to talk to you guys."

"Give me your supervisor's number. I will speak with him directly."

"Is this guy serious?" the guard asked me, pointing to Robert.

I nodded. The guard gave Robert the phone number.

"Now, Steve, you and I are going to the car," Robert instructed me.

We left the building with the guard loping after us. "What's this all about? Come on. You gotta tell me," he shouted. But neither of us answered him. Robert was too busy pushing ahead, and I was too busy thinking about how to turn back time.

Robert and I walked to the parking garage. I drove the car out of the lot, and onto a street named after Robert E. Lee. It was raining heavily now and my wipers were unable to move the water fast enough. Everything seemed colorless, except for the occasional red flicker of taillights bouncing off the street. The car in front of us accelerated, leaving us in its rooster tail, and then Robert and I were totally alone.

"Steve, hear me clearly: This morning I faxed a note to the Pennsylvania Lottery and by tomorrow I will have a list of every single lottery winner, and we'll see if Gloria Pruitt's name is on it. And soon I am going to call that man's supervisor and get those security tapes, too. That's right, I will. And I am going to watch them, every last hour of them if I have to, and I will find out once and for all whether there even *was* a conference."

I didn't say anything.

"When I do that, what am I going to find?"

Silence.

"What am I going to find, Steve? Tell me, Steve, what the fuck am I going to find?"

Neither of us spoke for thirty more horrendous seconds, and the silence strengthened; the longer it went on, the harder it was to break. At sixty seconds, the silence was stronger than I was.

A red warning light appeared on my dashboard, indicating that Robert had unbuckled his safety belt. I felt him shift in his seat. Twisting his torso, Robert raised himself up and leaned in to face me, positioning his head less than an inch from mine. I could feel his exhalation, hot and damp against my right temple. I continued to face forward, too scared to look at him, my hands on the wheel.

"God fucking dammit, Steve. *What am I going to find?*"

"I'm sorry, Robert. I'm really very sorry."

"What the fuck are you sorry for?"

"Please, please believe me that I'm sorry."

That was when I started to cry. My tears were noiseless at first. But weeping gave way to blubbering, which itself broke down into all-out bawling. It was the uncontrollable sound of unmanageable fear, a staccato mix of squeals and yelps and shrieks.

"I'm sorry. I'm sorry for everything," I said.

"I've heard that. Now tell me what happened."

Tears were flowing full-throttle down my face. The cuff of my shirt was soon so soaked from wiping my eyes that it no longer provided absorption. I steadily moved up my sleeve to find relief, until I was somewhere between the elbow and the shoulder.

"I'm sorry. I didn't—I didn't—I didn't really go to the conference."

"Oh fuck you. You didn't go to the conference?"

"I'm sorry. I am. I didn't mean to hurt you or anyone else. . . . Someone told me about it and I just wrote it like I was there. That was wrong."

"I don't believe that. And neither do you."

"I'm so sorry, Robert. I shouldn't have lied to you." But I was still lying, of course. For me lying had become more than a vice, or a comfort, or a habit, or the easiest thing to do: It had begun to seem vital.

I could no longer work my hands. They began to shake, slipping far from their driving-school-perfect ten o'clock and two o'clock positions. The car drifted onto the shoulder, pebbles clattered under the tires, and Robert screamed, "Holy shit. You're off the road. What the fuck are you doing?"

I tried too hard to correct, and we jerked to the left. Robert, whose seat belt was still unbuckled, was thrown against the dash. The car came off of the shoulder, passed over our lane, and approached the center yellow lines, verging toward oncoming traffic.

"You're going to kill us, Steve. You're in the wrong fucking lane."

A car's horn bleated, but because of the rain and tears I couldn't see where it was coming from. In front of us. It's in front of us. Oh shit. Headlights. They're getting closer. I merged hard to the right and back into my lane. *Whoosh.* The oncoming car passed, spraying us with a torrent of water.

"We could have died," Robert yelled at me. He was panting, out of breath.

I am dead, I thought silently. I slowed down the car and the tears returned, as soundless as the thought.

Robert pulled a handkerchief out of his suit jacket's inside pocket. It was monogrammed and because his surname's initial, *U* for Underwood, was placed in the middle, it spelled *RUT*. He blotted his forehead. "Let me tell you, Steve, this is really bad. I mean really bad. I don't know how you're ever going to survive this."

"Can . . . can I borrow . . . your handkerchief?" Despite my sharp inhalations, I could no longer prevent mucus from running down my nose. I was snuffling between my words.

"Don't you have your own?"

"No. . . . I use . . . tissues and I'm out. . . . Please?"

"Well, you'll just have to hold it in, then."

I wiped my nose on my shoulder.

"Do you think you can drive safely now?" he asked.

I tried to focus on the street sign just ahead, but everything was fuzzy. "No, you better take over."

I pulled the car onto the shoulder and got out, leaving the keys in the ignition. I walked around the back of the car. The rain was still coming down in sheets. Robert climbed over the emergency brake and slid into the driver's seat. I knocked on the window for him to unlock the passenger-side door. He waited a moment, then let me in. I was drenched. When I sat down, I made a squishing noise.

No one spoke for a few minutes and then Robert began, in a cold and clinical tone. "You're in a bad situation. You've jeopardized everyone at the *Weekly,* everyone who trusted you. And then you lied to me."

He paused for a few seconds.

"The magazine might be savable and I'm going to do my best to save it from what you've done. But you, Steve, you've done something very, very terrible. Things like this don't end well. I guess I can't really know what will happen to you. I don't know that anyone can. Liars always end badly, though."

During the rest of the trip to the office, we drove in silence. Robert parked the car in the same spot we had taken it from, and we waited for the elevator.

After an agonizing minute of quiet, the elevator arrived. We got in, and Robert pushed the 8 button. We stood side by side, looking up, studying the digits above the double doors as if we had never seen the number line before. The accomplishment of each floor climbed was celebrated with the chime of a bell.

One. *Bing.*

"How could you do this to me, Steve? You might have ruined me. What did I ever do to hurt you?"

I said nothing.

Two. *Bing.*

"How? How? I have a family that depends—" Robert's voice cracked as he was saying it. It was extinguished before he finished.

Three. *Bing.*

Silently I begged Robert to hit me.

Four. *Bing.*

Please punch me, Robert.

Five. *Bing.*

I pushed my chin farther out to make an easier target. Take out your anger on my body, I thought. Do what men do, Robert. Yes, you have a family that depends on you. Hit me. I deserve it. Break my nose. Scar me.

Six. *Bing.*

Hit me, Robert. I know you want to.

If you hit me, people will see how horrible you are. No matter what I've done, it will be excused when compared to your violence, compared to what *you've* done. I won't respond with violence. No, for sure not. I will politely exit the elevator and use the receptionist's phone to call the police. Tomorrow, the headline will read: EDITOR ASSAULTS WRITER CAUGHT FABRICATING. Maybe, if I'm really lucky, the last part will even be reduced to a subhead.

Seven. *Bing.*

I imagined the trial. It would air on Court TV. They would convict Robert, of course, and the tabloids would call him the Journabeater. Dressed in an orange prison jumpsuit, Robert—now the Jack Ruby of journalism—would stand before the judge and say he was sorry, very sorry, truly and sincerely sorry for what he had done. He would say he was essentially a good person—one who had made a mistake, a serious mistake but a mistake nonetheless, and if allowed to go free he would never, ever do it again, he promised. He would point to all the other good things he had done in his life—his kindness to friends and family, his years of journalism for the public good. Unmoved, the judge would sentence Robert to ten to twenty-five.

Seconds later, on the courthouse steps, reporters with microphones would tell their live TV audiences what had happened. Talk shows would offer experts opining about the sorry state of modern journalism, and audience members would call the stations to express outrage. And all the callers would say, all of them, that no matter what Stephen Glass did wrong, it wasn't as bad as this.

Please hurt me, Robert. Please. We both deserve it.

Eight. *Bing.*

The doors opened and we were back at the *Weekly.*

Robert exited the elevator first, and I followed him.

"Steve, I want you in my office. Don't go anywhere but my office. Don't talk to anyone. Don't use the phone. And do not test me now."

Robert walked into Ian's office and closed the door behind him. Just before the door was completely closed, I heard him say, "You're not going to believe this." I walked to Robert's office as I'd been instructed to do, stepped in, and closed the door behind me.

After some time, Ian came in. Bullwinkle looked solemn.

"Hey, Steve."

"Hey."

"Robert told me what happened."

"Uh-huh."

"I need to talk to you about something. Robert thought you might be more willing to talk with me than with him. Things went pretty badly between you two, and we've been friends, right?"

"Yes, we have."

"Good. I'm glad. I like our friendship."

"Me too."

"Okay. So, it's a question about another story," he said. "The one about the underground sports games between white supremacists in Connecticut. They played capture the flag and drank Hi-C and stuff. Do you remember that article?"

"I remember it."

"The leader of one of the militias was named Clay Ortman. Remember?"

"Yes."

There was a pause. Ian swallowed before he spoke again. "We can't find him on the Internet anywhere. You see, Robert started picking out random details from other stories you wrote, to check them. I suggested it, actually. He wanted to fire you, and I said you'd done so much other good work, we should do something less—a suspension maybe. So Robert punched a few of the names from your other stories into the Internet and some were there, but some were not. Now, I'm not saying they don't exist. Not everything that exists is on the Internet. But it's really hard for me to make my case unless I know it's true."

"I see."

"So does Clay Ortman exist?"

"Huh? Yes. No. I don't know, Ian, I'm so confused right now. I think I'm going to throw up. Can you give me a little space, a little air?"

I lay down on the couch, just trying to breathe steadily. Ian sat in Robert's chair and waited patiently. "Are you feeling better?" he asked after a while.

"Not really."

"Steve, I need to ask you only this one question."

"Can I talk to you as a friend, Ian? Off the record? Between you and me only?"

"Of course. That's why I'm here, as a friend."

"What if I knew Clay Ortman existed, say, but I also knew I could never prove it, and no one would ever believe me?"

"Well, if he existed, I know we could prove it. I'd help you. We'd go out there and find him if we had to."

He smiled. I think he was ready, right then, to leave and drive with me to find Ortman—as ready as Robert had been to go to Jeffersonville, but for a different reason: Ian wanted to see me through this, he truly did. But I knew by then that he couldn't.

"No, Ian," I said softly. "Take my hypothetical just as it is."

"Okay, then. I guess what I would do is, I would ask for mercy from the court. That's what you do in situations like this. You throw yourself on the court and beg for mercy."

"The court?"

"Well, Robert would be the court in this situation."

Ian forced himself to smile again even though he knew as well as I did that Robert's mercy wouldn't be forthcoming anytime soon. I could see he was in pain. He hated having to do this. As much as I sometimes mocked Ian's genial mushiness, I also saw how kind he was—how much he was trying to help me.

"I'm sorry," he told me.

"Me too, Ian."

There were a few moments of quiet. Then Ian reluctantly spoke: "So, Robert said I can't leave until I get an answer to my question. So, um, can you please answer it?"

"I guess I have to." I sat up on the couch and raised my back straight. My mom had always told me to have perfect posture during the really important things in life. "Clay Ortman exists, but I'll never be able to prove it."

I choked back tears as I said it. I was describing the world, I knew even then, as I wished it to be, not as it was. I had visualized Clay Ortman so clearly—his tattoos, the way he chugged his orange Hi-C—that I almost believed in him.

"Okay then." Bullwinkle, sad and gentle, began to walk to the door.

"Wait, Ian. Can I ask you a favor?"

"Sure. Anything you want."

"When people ask about this conversation later, people here, would you please tell them I said I was sorry, and I didn't mean to hurt anyone?"

"Absolutely."

"I mean if things get really bad, will you tell them that?"

"I will. And I'll tell them I believe you, too."

Ian forced a last smile, and closed the door behind him. I thought I saw a tear in one of his eyes as he walked out, but it might have been just the light bouncing off the tears in my own.

I waited in Robert's office for a while longer, since I didn't know where else at the magazine to hide, and Robert had told me to stay there. At least here I was safe. No one had ever visited Robert's office unnecessarily.

I stood at the window. It was late afternoon and the rain had finally subsided. Some people were leaving work early, pleasantly surprised not to need their umbrellas. Others were running out for a lunch break they probably had delayed because they didn't want to get wet. I saw one guy on the street, about my age, reading a newspaper while he walked. What was his life like? I wanted to switch with him, without an inkling.

"Steve, please sit down."

It was Robert. I hadn't heard him come in. I sat down and he continued: "I've been thinking long and hard about all this, and I've let you have your chance to convince me otherwise. I think I've been fair. I went with you to Jeffersonville. I chased down all your notes. I called your phone numbers. And they all lead me to a single conclusion: the lottery conference never happened. It's not that you didn't bother to go. It's that it didn't exist. I'm convinced of that. I don't want to debate it anymore.

"The question then is, what do I do with you? You've lied in this magazine at least once, and now, when I press a little bit, it looks like you may have lied more. That cannot stand. Lies left unchecked will destroy not only this magazine, but the whole of journalism, and it has fallen to me to make a judgment here on what is the right course for all of us."

Robert paused to collect himself.

"Journalism is a beautiful thing, Stephen. It's the practice of reporters figuring out what actually happened and writing it just that way. I should be able to take any story in our magazine and go out and re-report it and get the exact same results. It's like science or math that way. Every morning the press pool writes what color tie the President is wearing, red or blue, and if I were to go back a month later and call the White House's valet and ask what color the President's tie was on any day, he would tell me the very same color the pool reporter reported. This is because the reporter wrote the article just the way he saw it. He didn't write it the way he thought it should be, or the way he was told it was, or the way he hoped it was, or the way he felt it was, and he certainly didn't write it the way that made for the best story. He wrote that the tie was the color it was because he observed it to be that color. And that is the most elegant thing a journalist can do. That's what I've been doing for two decades.

"What you have done, Steve, has caused me to think about the deeper purposes here. There's a reason journalists have these strict rules about truth. Journalism is fragile. Our only asset is the credibility readers place in us. If our readers no longer believe what we print, if they think we are reporting anything less than what is literally true, if they can't bank on what we say happened, we don't have a magazine anymore.

"That means your lies take away credibility not just from you, but from me too. And it gets worse. That credibility is a shared pool. Every lie you told hurts not just this magazine and our writers, but the industry as a whole. You've poured poison into the stream. Readers, who are already increasingly cynical, will lump magazines together. Because of Stephen Glass's lies, they'll say, you can't believe journalists as a class. I'm not making that up. That's the way they talk about politicians, and lawyers. Journalists can't afford that. The readers' trust is our currency. Credibility, Steve, is the only thing that holds journalism together. We're not novelists or poets or moviemakers, we're reporters, and as much as all those other groups say they understand truth, we're the only ones who tell it just as it happened. Eyewitnesses to history. That's what journalism has over all the rest. And if any of us stops doing that, he betrays journalism.

"And there's something else, Steve. You lied to me. Even if I could make all this go away and keep the readers' trust and rescue the magazine and help journalism . . . You can see you've given me a task that would test the strength of Atlas. Even if I could do all that, I could never trust you again. I cannot have someone on staff who was disloyal to me. That is something which I will never allow.

"For all of those reasons, I have to fire you. Effective today, you're terminated.

"I also want to tell you something else, and it's important: You're a fucked-up kid. You need serious psychological help so you can get back to a place where you can separate truth from fiction."

Robert sat down. I looked at him. He was waiting for me to respond, but there was nothing to say.

"Thank you," I said idiotically. I might have been the first person in the world ever to thank their boss for firing them. "I understand why you feel you have to do this," I added. And to try to make their boss feel better about it.

And with that, I stood up and extended my right hand. Robert looked surprised. I think he had expected some plea for forgiveness, compassion, and a second chance. He certainly didn't seem to want to shake my hand. My arm remained outstretched for an awkwardly long time. Robert just looked at it as if it were infectious.

"Don't leave me hanging," I said.

He nodded, shook my hand briefly and reluctantly, and withdrew his.

"Good-bye," I told him.

"I want you to have your stuff packed up and cleaned out before you leave."

"Okay," I said—I would have done anything to get out of his office—but I knew I couldn't pack up my office right then. I needed to leave before the reporters, inevitably, arrived.

Robert said something else, but I couldn't make it out. I had already closed the door behind me.

I walked toward my office. On the way, I passed Clovis, the literary editor; he was in his office with the door open, talking with a poet. I knocked on the open door, and without waiting for an answer, I stepped in.

"I just wanted to say thank you for all your help over these years," I told him; the words came out in a rush. "You were great, and a source for inspiration, and if I were in better spirits right now I would say something more eloquent and appropriate, but just know I think a lot of you."

"I heard about it all. What'd he say?" Clovis asked.

"He told me I was fired."

"Fucker. I wasn't expecting that. Did you ask him how he's going to talk about it to the media? That's really important."

This was Clovis's way of expressing affection; he wanted to protect me, I knew, but there was no way. No one could protect me now.

"I don't think it will matter, in this case. Robert's going to come down on me as hard as he can," I said.

"Fucker."

"Anyway, thanks. I meant everything I said and much more."

"Be good, Steve."

I walked the rest of the way to my office, somehow managing to avoid running into anyone else. When I got there, I heard a female voice inside. I figured it was Lindsey, who sometimes borrowed my space in order to get away from her own constantly ringing phone. Ugh. I didn't want to see her now, but I wanted to get my laptop before I went home. I knocked on the door and heard the click of the phone being hung up. Then I opened the door nervously.

It was Allison.

I took her into my arms and held her. In my mind, I took back all my doubts: she'd come through for me when it mattered.

"Brian called me," she said. "He said I should come over, that you would want me nearby."

"So, will you help me get out of here?" I asked.

"Of course. Hold my hand tight. There's going to be a lot of people out there."

Allison and I walked the long way around, so I could go out the front door. I told her I didn't want to leave out the back. Five or six writers were hanging out by the front entrance, waiting for me. Lindsey wasn't among them, and I realized she had probably gone home to avoid Robert's inquisition. I felt horribly guilty; I'd let her back me up, and now she might be in trouble too.

One by one, the writers embraced me, and made me promise to keep in touch. I said good-bye to Brian last. "You know this doesn't mean anything between us, Steve," he told me. "You're still going to dance at my wedding someday, our kids are still going to play together, and we're still going to grow old together."

"Please don't be mad at me, Brian. Please, please don't hate me."

"Why would I hate you?" he asked. I didn't answer. I knew he still didn't really understand what was happening; no one but Robert and Ian did, yet.

I heard the high-pitched beep made by the intercom system to signal an office-wide page. It was Robert: "There will be a meeting in my office in five minutes if you want to hear *my* side of what happened."

"I better go. I don't think I'm invited to that," I said, and then I gripped Allison's hand even more tightly, and walked out the front door of the office.

Allison and I took the elevator to the garage. On our way down, the doors opened on the ground floor, revealing Throw, who must have arrived at work early, as usual. He shouted for me to hold it open, which I did.

Throw didn't get in, but only ran up and spoke to me breathlessly. "I'm so glad I caught you. A camera crew from CNN is looking for you, Esteban. They just took the other elevator up. I think they want to interview you."

"No thanks. See you tomorrow," I said, forgetting momentarily that I might never see him again. Daunted, he withdrew the hand that had been holding the doors open, and gave me a puzzled look.

The elevator doors closed with a thud and it occurred to me that I now understood why Robert had worn a suit to the office.

When we got to the garage, Allison assumed the wheel, even though she had never driven my car before. I was thankful when she did, even though I was a little concerned that no one allowed me to drive anymore.

The drive back to our apartment was mercifully quiet. Halfway home, Allison placed her fingers on my neck. I lowered my head and raised my shoulder to enclose her petite hand. Allison had paper-thin skin and I could feel her pulse whenever our bodies made contact. She wasn't as calm as she appeared.

Soon we neared the apartment, and Allison broke the silence. "Magic spot!" she cheered, as if she had just scored a touchdown.

Magic spots were the few spaces outside our apartment that, because the street signs had been stolen, didn't require the car to be moved every two hours. If you got one, it meant free parking for days—weeks, even, if you could make do without your car. If we saw one open up, we would stop whatever we were doing—dinner, work, we probably even would have interrupted sex, if our windows had faced that way—and race, sometimes against fierce competition from our neighbors, to seize it.

Magic spots had become a currency within our relationship, the way flowers work for some couples. When I had to cancel on a date, or when I'd said something insensitive, I'd quietly switch Allison's car into my magic spot. I often held one, because I could walk to work and never move my car. I knew my never leaving the magic spot defeated the purpose of having one a bit, but I loved possessing the space, even so. It meant I had something I could always give Allison, something she would always want.

"See, everything's going to be all right," Allison said as she pulled in. "Things are already looking up. We landed a magic spot."

I didn't say anything.

"Just kidding," she added. Allison "just kiddinged" whenever something she said didn't go over well. It was a habit I hated. I once told her I thought it was a way for her to avoid ownership of her misstatements. She shrugged it off and told me I just didn't under-stand her sense of humor. More avoidance of responsibility, I insisted. More humorlessness, she maintained. It all seemed so petty now.

"It was just a joke, Steve," Allison remarked, as if she'd read my mind.

"Don't worry about it," I said. "I know you were just trying to be nice."

Allison and I walked silently up the stairs and into the apartment, which was immaculate. Merry Maids had come, as scheduled, earlier that day. The gleaming hardwood floor smelled of lemon cleaner, and the couch cushions swelled from being fluffed. Even the remote controls—and we had six of them, one of which was a "universal remote" that was supposed to replace all the others but in actual fact, only augmented our remote load—were once again sensibly moored to the coffee table. Like an evening guest, I wasn't even sure where to put my bag down.

The answering machine blinked in beats of five, but I decided to ignore it.

"So what should we do?" Allison said, and then she added, almost inaudibly, "I'm still upset with you, but it can wait."

"I should probably call my parents."

"That's a good idea," she said, meaning that it wasn't. I could tell she wanted me to talk with her, and I knew that was a reasonable request, but I urgently wanted to talk with my parents now, and so I remained quiet. She walked upstairs to the bedroom to give me privacy.

As soon as she was gone, I dialed my parents' home in Lakeside, a suburb of Chicago. My mom answered. She was cheerful, and said she had just been thinking about calling me.

"Mom, something really bad has happened."

"What are you talking about?" Her voice was hurried and scared. "What's going on?"

"Are you sitting down?"

"Just tell me."

"This is really big and difficult."

"Stephen, tell me."

"Okay. I was fired today."

"Oh. Thank God. I thought you were going to tell me something really terrible, like you were sick or something."

"Well, it's pretty bad. I'm really upset about it."

"Don't scare me like that. Things are so bad that I need to sit down? Who do you think I am, Natalie Wood? I've heard a lot of bad news in the past and I can handle it. You made it sound like you've got a horrendous disease or who knows what."

"I'm sorry."

"Don't ever do that again, scaring me half to death like that."

"I won't," I said, and then we both paused for a bit before I spoke again. "I'm so sorry. . . . I'm so sorry to disappoint you."

"Tell me what happened."

There was quiet and then I began to sob.

"Oh, Stevie, it's going to be okay, I promise you."

"I think I'd like to come home."

"Sure. If you want to, we'd always love to have you."

"I'll get tickets and tell you when I'm coming. Probably tomorrow morning," I said.

"Did you tell Dad yet?"

"No, I'm going to call him now."

"He'll be fine with it. This is not a huge deal. I love you. When you get here, you'll see it will be fine."

"I love you too. I'm so sorry, Mom."

I hung up and called my dad at his office.

"Dad, I have some bad news."

"Are you all right?"

"Not really. I was fired today. I'm really sorry, Dad. I'm sorry I let you down."

"You didn't let me down. You've never let me down. What happened?"

"Robert and I had a disagreement."

"That asshole."

"No, it's my fault, not his. Really it is. I'm sorry, Dad. I really am. . . . I think I'm going to come home tomorrow."

"Great. Come home. By then, things will have calmed down and you can put this in perspective. You know, I was fired once. I was working for a friend of Grandpa's selling candy door to door. I couldn't sell the candy, which was awful off-brand stuff like green licorice, and so they fired me. I was embarrassed, but when I told Grandpa, he just told me to get another job. 'You have to get back in the saddle,' he said. And that was it. It's part of growing up. Now you have your green licorice story. You have to get back in the saddle, that's all."

"I don't think it's going to be that easy."

"It will be."

"I don't think you understand."

"I think I do," my dad said. "Things will be okay. I promise you that. And have I ever made you a promise I didn't keep?"

"No. You haven't," I said. I knew that, as with my mom, I'd have to wait until I saw him to convince him that things were much, much worse than he thought.

"I love you," I told my father. "I'll see you tomorrow morning, probably around nine o'clock."

"Mom and I will both be at work by then, Stevie, so you're going to have to take a cab to the house."

"Okay."

"And do you have cash on you?"

"I'll get some before I leave."

"Make sure you do. Don't travel without any money on you."

That was one of my father's life rules. He said it whenever Nathan or I went anywhere. "Okay. I love you," I said.

And we hung up.

Allison came downstairs as soon as my call was finished. I suspected she had been eavesdropping, but I didn't care.

"So what happened?" she asked suspiciously.

"I'm going back to Lakeside for a few days. I want to see my parents, regroup a bit."

"What about our trip?"

"Oh, shit. I'm sorry, Allison. I wasn't thinking."

"No, you weren't."

"I'm just really upset right now. We can go another time, right? I just think it's probably best for me to go home right now."

"Can't you stay here?" she asked.

"I can't. The reporters will start arriving tomorrow." But that wasn't the real reason I had to go home. I needed to go because I knew my parents, more than anyone else in the world, loved me without recompense or reward and always would; Allison's love, I had to earn, and now all I could do was spend it until there was none left.

"Okay," she said slowly. "You should call Coastal Airlines. I got an email about a special—Dulles to O'Hare for cheap. And when you're on the phone booking the tickets, you can cancel our vacation tickets too."

"Will you come to Lakeside with me?" I suggested.

"That, Stephen, is asking too much. If we're not going to have a real vacation, I'm going back to work so I can take one later, with or without you."

And so I booked the tickets to see my parents. It was immature, it was cowardly, I know that, but I also knew Allison, and I knew she would be too angry to help me make it through. I hoped my parents would be different.

I missed Allison's and my old relationship—the one we'd had before I'd worked so many hours, and disappointed her so many times, that I'd begun to feel a kind of keen and constant resentment beneath every word we exchanged. As I canceled our vacation tickets, I remembered how it used to be, and how the point of the Savannah vacation had been to bring it back.

Allison and I had been going to Savannah for long weekends ever since our first trip over Valentine's Day weekend in 1995. I had wanted to take her somewhere for the holiday that was warm, inexpensive, less than two hours away since she hated to fly, and most of all, completely private.

"Maybe we'll love it," I said to Allison that first year before we left, trying to create enthusiasm. "Who knows? Maybe we'll move there."

"There are no Jews in Savannah," she said.

But she was wrong. There were. Not too many, but they were there. In fact, there was even a majestic synagogue in the town center, one of America's oldest, and it was headed by a brilliant rabbi from

New Jersey. We never attended synagogue in Washington, but we always went when we were in Savannah.

That's not all we found there. It was warm year-round. There was a sandy beach and great food, and most of all, it was devoid of everything Washington. Back home there was always a journalist or one of Allison's colleagues—she worked for the Smithsonian—to be bumped into during a Friday night dinner date, or a party to go to on Saturday night that was more about journalism or museum politics than about our having fun.

In Savannah there were just lazy days and private nights. We always stayed in the same inn overlooking the river and lounged in bed until noon. Lunch was the same both days: fried chicken, sweet tea, and red velvet cake. We'd spend the afternoons sitting in one of the town's little squares, or playing in the ocean at Tybee Island, or, if they were at home, watching the minor-league Savannah Sand Gnats lose another game. At night, we would read and laugh and get drunk and play Boggle while half-submerged in the bed and breakfast's Jacuzzi.

The first time we went, on our last full day in Savannah we spent a few hours wandering among the headstones in Bonaventure Cemetery until just before closing, after the charter buses filled with *Midnight in the Garden of Good and Evil* fans had left. Then, at twilight, under the Spanish moss–draped trees, we sat near Johnny Mercer's grave and made out. At some point, I sang the only verse I knew from the only song I knew that he wrote, "Something's Gotta Give." At the end, I crescendoed,

> *You can bet as sure as you live*
> *Something's gotta give, something's gotta give, something's gotta*
> *give.*

Something gave. After I was done, Allison looked at me lovingly, ran her hand through my hair, and asked me to promise never, ever to sing to her again.

. . .

"What do you want to do now?" Allison asked, once my flight to Chicago was set. She handed me a mug of vanilla tea, my favorite. I heard that familiar grate, that undercurrent beneath her words, and despite myself I stiffened against it.

"I think I'd like to go to sleep," I told her. "I'm very tired. I really didn't get any rest last night and I have to get up at six for my plane."

"I think we should talk a bit first, don't you?" she said calmly.

"The flight's out of Dulles," I added.

Allison sat down on the couch, sinking deep into the plumped-up pillows. She held her tea cautiously and blew directly down on it, creating a depression in the liquid. "How's the tea?" she asked.

"Good, thank you," I said, sloshing it around in the mug. The sugar wasn't fully dissolved and I didn't have a spoon, and didn't want to go to the kitchen to get one.

"Do you want to talk to me about it?" she asked.

"Honestly?"

"Yes, of course," she said. "Why would I want you to say something that wasn't honest?"

"I didn't mean it that way. I was using it as an expression."

"An expression?"

"You know, I wanted to cushion it—to say, This is going to be hard, I have something to say that you're not going to like."

"Being honest means I won't like it?" She was shrill; I could see it was painful for her, and I knew I wasn't helping.

"Come on, Allie, you know what I mean," I offered weakly.

"No, I don't think I do. I want you to tell me what happened. You're going to tell me, aren't you?"

"I don't think I'm ready to talk about it," I finally said.

She leaned back. "That's really hard on me," she said.

"I know."

"Tell me at least what you told Robert. I shouldn't know less than he does."

"Okay," I said.

I told Allison a very condensed version of what had happened, but I didn't tell her the truth. I knew, even as I said it, that I shouldn't be lying, but I also knew that if I didn't lie, she'd leave me. She might leave me anyway, but this way, I thought, at least I had a chance.

At first, I told Allison what I had initially told Robert—that the basic thrust of the lottery story had been told to me by the lawyer, Stan Romaine, but under deadline pressure, I had written it as if I'd actually seen it all myself. Then I backed down a little, and said that even beyond that, the story wasn't entirely true, it was partly made up. I told her there'd been problems with other stories too—details that turned out not to be true. But I couldn't bring myself to tell her the whole truth, the true story of all the lies and how they were all my fault, none of them mistakes and all of them fabrications.

Allison listened carefully. She nodded at the appropriate moments, and once even touched me reassuringly on the knee. When I was done, she sighed loudly.

"Do you want to go to sleep?" she asked.

"Yes," I said. She surprised me. That's it? No questions? No pressing me on the details? She must be saving up her comments for later, I figured.

"Go to bed," she told me.

Then suddenly I wanted—no, I needed—to talk with her about it. Allison must hate me, I thought. She must know I'm still lying. She must be so angry with me, she's unable to formulate her words. I can't go to bed this way. I'll never get her back; things will never really return to the way they used to be, before we started having problems. I'll go to Lakeside and that'll be it. For a moment, I wondered again if I should stay here, but I still felt I had to go. If I stayed, I feared I would just lie and lie and lose her more and more each day.

"Look, I know you want to talk about it, Allie," I said. "We can talk about it. I'm tired, but let's try."

"Well, do you want to add anything?" she asked.

Quiet.

"No, not really," I said. "Do you want to ask me a question?"

"Yeah. Why the fuck didn't you tell me this was going on?"

"I'm not sure," I said. "I'm still working this out for myself."

"What do you mean, you're not sure?"

"I wasn't even really telling myself I was doing it as I went along."

"So were you out of your mind? Is that what you're telling me?"

"No, not really."

"Then what were you thinking?" she asked.

Quiet.

Now I really wanted to go to sleep. Why didn't I take her up on the earlier offer to release me? She gave me the way out and I refused it. I am an idiot. The only way this relationship will survive is if I can somehow get out of here without discussing this, if I can come back in a better state of mind, and tell her the truth. I can't bear to tell her the truth now, and I can't lie anymore either, and so as much as I might want to, I can't stay here.

"Stephen, why?" she burst out. "How can I explain this to myself, if you won't explain it to me? How did you write these stories? How did you do it for so long? How did they not catch you? And how did I not know anything about it? *How did this all happen?*"

"I don't know, Allison. I don't know. I'm sorry. I'm really very sorry. I just can't talk about this now."

I had trapped myself: I didn't want to confess my earlier halfway lies, I didn't want to tell her more lies, and I didn't really want to tell her the truth either. I was ashamed and I felt my life giving way in yet another respect. I had tried not to lie to Allison before. For a long time, I had kept my working life very separate—in retrospect, secret, I suppose—from her. At some level I did it to protect her from complicity in all that I had done, and at some level, I did it to protect myself from her—to avoid, I think, this very confrontation. I had both wanted to avoid her judgments and to keep her pristine, untainted by my mistakes. Now I saw that I had only guaranteed that the confrontation, when it came, would be all the more hurtful to her. You can't deceive people and protect them at the same time, but it took me a long time to learn that was true.

I stood up and leaned over to kiss Allison on the lips. She

accepted the kiss, but gave nothing in return. I walked over to the staircase slowly, staring at her the whole time, trying to figure out what she was thinking. When I crossed behind her, I ran my hand through her blond hair. She didn't lean back, but she also didn't withdraw.

On the third stair, I said, "I love you," but it was somewhere between a statement and a question.

She said nothing.

By the sixth stair, I couldn't bear it any longer. I had to ask her directly: "Do you still love me, Allie?" I stopped, held the banister, and waited for her answer.

"Yes," she said.

I ran up the remainder of the stairs at full clip, shed my clothes, and slid into bed without brushing my teeth. Within a minute, I was asleep, too tired to fear the nightmares readying themselves to rush in.

My dreams that night were filled with wild colors and violence and loud noises. I remember being in pain and crying for help and finding no one to rescue me. I dreamed that it was time for me to wake up, but still I did not awaken.

I woke before the alarm went off. I turned it off before it began to buzz, and slipped out of bed silently, lest Allison stir in her sleep, and awaken. If I woke Allison, I knew she would resume last night's questions. "Now do you know how you did it?" she would ask. "And more important, do you know *why* you did it?"

I didn't want to get mired in that discussion, especially not when I was running late for the airport. Frankly, if it were possible to avoid it, I didn't want to have that discussion ever.

I skipped the shower, which made a thunderous moaning sound whenever the hot-water dial came within twenty degrees of a tolerable temperature. And I carefully peed against the part of the bowl just above the waterline, where urination is its most quiet. I did not flush.

Even opening the creaky dresser would have made too much noise, so I gathered yesterday's clothes off the floor and tiptoed down the stairs. While I was dressing in the kitchen, it occurred to me that I had worn the same outfit for forty-eight straight hours. I had sweated in these clothes, I had been rained on in them, and I had been fired in them, and while I might be able to wear the shirt and pants for another few hours, I absolutely could not bear the underwear and socks for another minute.

I ruled out going commando; the zipper on the pants was slightly broken, and it would have scratched me. I couldn't risk going back into the bedroom for clean underwear either.

I tiptoed back upstairs and peeked in the dryer, which was in the bathroom. There were only a few items inside, all Allison's: a pair of tiny, white cotton socks, two T-shirts, and a pair of beige underwear. I decided to give the beige underwear a chance. They were her least sexy pair, more like bloomers than panties, and the elastic looked overextended. Maybe, just maybe, they'd fit.

Back downstairs in the kitchen, I thrashed about, trying to pull the underwear on, but I couldn't get them over my knees. It occurred to me to attempt it one leg at a time. Sitting on the kitchen counter, I got my left leg through the left leg hole and pulled the underwear up to my thigh. Next, I bent my right leg until my knee was hoisted up as high as my neck. I was trying to thread my right foot in through the unoccupied underwear hole, but I just wasn't high enough above it. I leaned back, way back, extending my spine as far as possible, which pulled my bent leg up a few more inches. Just a little more and I'd have my foot over the hole.

I lay lengthwise on the edge of the kitchen counter, with my left leg tethered in dumpy women's bloomers, my right leg pulled up past my ear, and my right big toe fishing for the ever-changing position of the underwear aperture. Come on. My heart beat a little faster. Come on, Toe. You can do it. I know you can. You're a big toe! A thumb toe! Just a little farther back.

And then . . . *Boom!*

Just as I passed the right toe into the opening, my weight shifted slightly and I toppled over the counter's edge, landing hard on the floor; I couldn't even break my fall with my hands. There would be bruises all along my side, tomorrow, but I couldn't worry about that now. The noise of my fall, which was pretty loud itself, had been amplified by the screech of the cotton ripping under the force of my right leg shooting through: a pyrrhic victory.

"What was that noise?" Allison yelled from upstairs.

"Don't worry about it, honey. I love you. Please go back to sleep," I yelled back while removing the shreds of her underwear from around my waist. My whole body ached.

"I'm coming down," she said.

I heard her stumbling around upstairs.

"No. No. It's very early, Allie. Go back to sleep."

"I'm awake. I'm going to come down."

I heard her at the top of the stairs and shoved the underwear scraps into the nearest cabinet. "Really, it's nothing," I shouted. "Go back to sleep."

She yawned and headed back to bed.

Bottomless again, I began searching the kitchen for a creative solution. The only thing I could find was a box of plastic garbage bags. With a paring knife, I cut two holes in a bag and donned the Glad.

Fortunately, it was one of those fancy garbage bags with the red plastic handles, which I tied around my waist. To be honest, it felt pretty good. Like leather pants, but loose. The only problem I noticed was that I made a slight rustling noise when I walked.

For socks, I used two Ziploc storage bags. They were less comfortable, but kept my feet dry in shoes that were still waterlogged from traipsing in the rain with Robert.

Finally, I sat down on the couch and wrote Allison a brief note. It was simple, formal, and probably inadvertently cold, as all of my most personal notes are, although I tried to make it much warmer. I reminded her of my parents' phone number and asked her to call when she had a few free moments. I said I would call later that evening. I also told her that I would miss her, and that I loved her very much. I told her, though I knew it wasn't true, that everything would soon be okay, and I prayed it to myself too: Please let it all be okay again.

PART TWO
DEBACLE

THE TRIP to Dulles was unusually effortless. I quickly found a taxi and made it there with plenty of time to spare. I was actually feeling pretty good about the new underwear—plastic lingerie could catch on, I thought. I wondered if I should call one of those toll-free invention lines to talk to a lawyer about applying for a patent. See, there were things other than journalism I could do: I could become a plastic undergarments mogul.

After getting my boarding pass, I bought a *Washington Herald* at the newsstand and skimmed the headlines while I waited in line to go through security. There was nothing significant on the front page, and, as was my habit, I next opened the paper to the features section. There, just below the fold, was the following headline: WASHINGTON WEEKLY STORY FABRICATED, WRITER FIRED.

The story was written by Gil Garvey, the dean of American media writing. In the early 1980s, Garvey had single-handedly invented the journalism beat. Before Garvey, journalism's stories were thought to have as little news value as insider reports of any other industry's office politics. Then Garvey was assigned to write about a union dispute between reporters and editors at a Seattle newspaper. An editor had been injured when a reporter burned stacks of newspapers to protest management's use of scabs. The story ran big, in part because the paper had excellent photos of the burned editor. And afterward, dozens of journalists, who obviously read and thought a great deal about newspapers, wrote to the *Herald* about it. Based on the volume of mail, the *Herald*'s editors figured readers wanted more journalism coverage, so they assigned Garvey to work on it. And the more Garvey wrote about journalists, the more journalists talked about Garvey's stories. Within two years, every major newspaper had assigned a reporter to cover journalism—thinking that because they were all talking about journalism, their readers must be as well.

I started sweating profusely and became cold inside. I didn't want to read Garvey's article. And even if I had, I'm not sure I would have been able to force my eyes to do it. My pupils focused on the headline, refusing to budge, until the words dissolved into individual meaningless letters and after that, into mere dots of ink.

"Sir, please step through," the airport security guard said to me. "Can you hear me? Please step through."

But my eyes wouldn't progress beyond the headline. I mumbled it to myself: "Washington Weekly Story Fabricated, Writer Fired."

"What did you say?" the guard asked. People behind me were murmuring. I didn't care.

"Did you say something, sir? This is the last time I'm going to ask you. Please step through security." The guard was yelling at me now. I didn't respond; I only stared at the newspaper in my hands, as passengers walked around me and passed through the magnetometer.

A tall man in a blue blazer put his hand on my arm and guided me away from the metal detector. He said his name was Guillermo and he was a security supervisor. I could see he had a pistol under his jacket. He wanded me carefully and I came out clean.

"I've heard you've been having trouble passing through the security checkpoint," he said. "What's going on? Can you hear me?"

I still said nothing. Realizing that if Guillermo saw the Ziploc baggies budding up from my shoes, he would doubtless think I was a drug courier, I started to tremble. Suddenly, answering his questions seemed perilous. When he found out I had just been fired for lying, and was wearing a Glad bag for underwear, who knew how long the interrogation could go on?

Guillermo removed the plane ticket from my shirt's breast pocket. "So, Mr. Glass," he said, reading my name off the boarding pass. "It looks like you're going to Chicago."

Again I said nothing. I shifted my legs nervously, and the garbage bag made a crinkling sound. Guillermo looked around, to try to identify the source of the noise.

"You can't hear me, can you?" he asked.

What was I going to do? Suddenly hear him? How would I explain that, too? I rubbed my face to show I was animate, even if I wasn't speaking.

"Hey, Roger," Guillermo yelled to the security guard. "This man's deaf."

"Really? I don't think so," Roger yelled back. "I heard him mumble something."

"Just because he can talk, doesn't mean he can hear. He might have lost his hearing sometime after he learned to speak. Get me a wheelchair, will you?"

"But he can walk—"

"Just get me the chair. He can't be told where he has to go. Someone's going to have to push him there. Unless you know sign language."

Roger pushed a wheelchair over to us. When it arrived, I sat down in it.

"I'll roll him over to the gate," Guillermo said to Roger. "Somehow he got an exit row. The ticket-counter people are idiots. How's he going to help in the event of an emergency?"

"This is a terrible, terrible mistake," Guillermo told the agent when we got to the gate.

The agent, similarly horrified, asked me how I got the exit row. I started to answer her, when I remembered I was supposed to be unable to hear. I turned the first sound of the word *from* into an awkward noise, something like *fraaawww.*

Careful, I told myself. Trying to explain my fake deafness would, especially in light of everything else, be disastrous. Technically, it might be a federal crime. And the newspapers. Oh, the newspapers. Surely Garvey would run a follow-up item on my fictitious impairment. Best to stay silent—while I knew it was a kind of lying, too, I believed I had let it go on too long to stop now. It would take a long time for me to learn to tell the truth when I knew that only anger and recriminations would result.

The agent told Guillermo she would switch my seat. Guillermo made clear that he didn't want me getting a worse seat just because I was deaf. "It's not his fault," Guillermo repeated over and over.

"The aircraft is very full. This passenger will have to be accommodated in a middle seat," the gate agent explained.

"You're punishing him because of your airline's mistake," Guillermo insisted. "And you're doing it because he can't hear. I won't stand for that. And, stop talking about him in the third person! Just because Mr. Glass can't hear you, doesn't mean he's not present."

"There's nowhere else to put *him*. I mean *you*. I mean . . . whatever. There's no room."

"Well, put Mr. Glass in first class then," Guillermo ordered.

"I can't do that."

"You absolutely can and I absolutely will make a stink if you don't."

Grudgingly she printed out a ticket assigning me seat 3C—in first class and on the aisle.

Then Guillermo waited with me at the gate, keeping me in the wheelchair. Soon I heard someone call my name. The voice seemed familiar, and I almost turned to see who it was.

Stay still, Stephen. I caught myself. Deaf people don't hear such summonses.

"Steve?" the voice from behind said again. Guillermo looked over his shoulder, but I remained facing forward.

"Steve Glass?" The voice was closer. Guillermo was shifting more. He started to turn my chair.

I was racking my brain trying to place the voice. Distant relation? No. Someone from the *Weekly*? No. But a journalist? Yes.

"Steve, is that you?" the voice said. I was halfway turned around at this point, but I didn't turn my head toward the voice. I tried to look out the corner of my eye, but I saw nothing.

I went back to searching my memory. It was definitely a journalist. One I hadn't seen in some time. Who was it? Who was it? Cliff Coolidge. I knew it. Shit. I don't want to see him now. He's probably seen the piece in the *Herald,* I thought; he knows I don't need a wheelchair, and based on our many conversations, he's probably fairly confident in his assessment that I'm not deaf. And, fuck, I blew him off for dinner the other night. What to do? I was now three-fourths of the way turned toward him. I couldn't go anywhere. I couldn't talk. How would I escape?

I closed my eyes and began lightly snoring. Immediately, Guillermo stopped moving the wheelchair.

"Hey, Steve, are you okay?" Cliff asked. He was right up next to us now. "A wheelchair, huh? Now I know why you never showed up for dinner. What the hell happened? Were you in an accident?"

"Can't you see Mr. Glass is asleep?" Guillermo said to him. "Go away."

"What are you talking about? He's a friend of mine."

"Your friends don't sleep?" Guillermo responded louder now. "Move on, sir."

I snored a little louder.

"See you on the plane," Cliff called out.

"Friend! Ha!" Guillermo said to no one in particular. "If he really was a friend, he'd have known this man is deaf."

I continued to fake sleep until the flight attendant called my row. Guillermo boarded with me, showed me to my seat, and exited the plane only after I was buckled in. He told the gate agent he wanted to make sure no one took the first-class seat away from me after he left. Remembering to stay quiet, I didn't say anything, but tried at least to invent a hand signal for thank you, which he then returned.

Pretending to be deaf was much easier on the plane. (I had to keep it up. Guillermo told the flight attendants and the first-class passengers to keep an eye on me, in case "something needed to be heard.") The flight attendant wrote down questions for me such as, "What would you like to drink?" and I wrote my answers.

I also wrote her a note saying that a man seated in coach, Cliff Coolidge, would likely try to visit me during the flight and I'd like it if she kept him away.

"Don't worry, he won't bother you," she wrote back, and for the entire flight she prevented any and all passengers from crossing between coach and first class.

The plane was hot and I was anxious and, not surprisingly, I began to sweat. It was such a sudden output on my forehead, it looked as if I'd swallowed a habanero pepper. But the real problem was hidden from view; an underground spring of perspiration had developed beneath my pants.

With no cool air circulating in the garbage-bag delta between my belt and my knees, the subterranean temperature had surged. Heat was rising off my thighs, and when the hot vapor made contact with the plastic, it condensed into a lukewarm liquid. It felt as if a complex industrial process was going on down there. The more I tried to focus my brain on cooling down my body, the more anxious I became, and the more perspiration my thighs pumped out. I had a steam bath in my pants.

Soon the plane lifted off the tarmac, and I realized I was trapped. If I stood up, the growing reservoir of sweat—and it sure felt like a lot; my penis was treading water—would spill out of the creases of the garbage bag and wet me all over. I just had to wait it out and hope that the next time the flight attendant came around I could signal her—without speaking, of course—to bring me . . . what? An in-flight pillow? A huge dinner napkin? A lap bib?

With nothing to do but wait, I planned how I was going to explain the lying, the cover-up, and the firing to my parents.

The last time I had disappointed my parents so brutally was six years ago, as a college sophomore, when I'd failed organic chemistry, effectively ending their hopes that I would be admitted to medical school and someday become a doctor, like my father.

I had attended only two lectures all semester and instead spent all my time at the newspaper, which was what I really loved. As soon as I opened the exam, I realized I was fated to fail. The test packet consisted of dozens of blank pages that I was supposed to fill with diagrams of chemical reactions; we were allowed to bring models to help us do it. While the other students busily constructed long, twist-ing contraptions of multicolored balls and sticks, I anxiously fitted the pieces together for the first time. While they rotated their con-trivances in midair, drawing diagrams of the molecules in motion, I tried to jam molecules together by banging the pieces against my desk.

Accidentally, I connected a carbon ball to an oxygen ball and made carbon monoxide. I held the model high above my head and looked at it from below. I added another oxygen ball and got carbon dioxide. Now I was on a roll. But that was where it ended. I wrote "carbon monoxide + oxygen = carbon dioxide" under every question, hoping that somewhere, I might earn a point.

I frantically searched the textbook for answers, but none of it made sense; it seemed I just didn't speak the language of organic chemistry. I cursed myself for buying a new textbook. If I had bought a used one, I might have been able to work from whatever the last stu-dent had highlighted. At least someone would have read my book.

And so, with nothing else to do for the rest of the exam period, I wrote the professor an essay in the broad expanse of white space around the chemistry questions, the way one writes a message in a Hallmark card around the preprinted "Happy Birthday!" But there wasn't enough room. When I asked the proctor for additional pages, the students sitting near me looked up, panicked. The proctor handed me more paper and whispered, "You must be a genius. You're not even using the models."

"Just trying to be thorough," I demurred.

In the essay, I explained why my becoming a doctor was impor-tant to me, my parents, and, frankly, the whole of society. I empha-sized how a passing grade in this class was essential, despite how lit-tle (if ever) physicians actually used organic in their daily practice. I also discussed the importance of academic freedom and professors having the inalienable right to give a student whatever grade they see fit—noting that during the Vietnam War, for example, professors rou-tinely passed failing students so they could maintain their military deferments. Passing me, I concluded, would be a small victory for compassionate medicine and a tremendous defeat for rigidity. I ended with this sentence: "Please, Professor, look kindly on my exam; look kindly on my life."

Afterward, I knew I was almost certain to fail despite my plea, and I was terrified of what my parents' reaction would be. I had never failed anything before.

A few days later, I flew back to Lakeside to start a summer job as a research assistant at a Chicago medical school. When I got there, I told my parents that the exam was "tough—the toughest I've ever taken."

My dad, probably thinking back to the organic exam *he* took at Cornell—which he no doubt pulled all-nighters studying for, in a tie no less, because he had read somewhere that students who study with a tie retain more of what they read—nodded at me knowingly. "A real gut-check, huh?" he said.

"Yeah. Some people even walked out before it was over." Which was true, but it was probably because they had finished early.

"We only care that you tried your hardest," my dad added.

"Which you did, right?" my mom asked.

"Yes, but I'm not sure it was enough," I answered quietly.

"Trying your hardest will always be enough," my dad said.

My mom looked at me suspiciously. She knew I was up to something.

Meanwhile, the medical school assigned me to a nephrology professor who was studying fetal rats. My job for the summer was to produce a steady supply of baby rats. At first, I thought this would be easy—just put the boy rats and the girl rats together, dim the lights, drop Tom Jones into the CD player, and voilà! Baby rats. But you couldn't just mix the males in with the females. The guys would freeze up and sit in the corner all night, as if they were at a junior high school dance.

I knew I needed to succeed at this job like none of the research assistants before me, if I was ever going to escape the organic chemistry humiliation. I needed to learn how to rush rat love. I began to use positive reinforcement, rewarding the stud who sired the most rats with more and younger virgins. The key to getting the most pregnancies, I learned, was to make sure the eligible females were in heat. To do this, I Pap smeared the females daily. At first, I'll admit, I was squeamish. None of my prior jobs or education had prepared me for their minuscule cervices. Rat sex was only slightly less mysterious than snake sex, which still confounds me.

But within days, I found I was a natural. I could Pap smear a rat with astonishing speed and, apparently, no pain. Grab her, flip her, in and out, and onto the slide. I may have been projecting, but I think the rats even enjoyed my work. Given more time I would have located the rat G-spot.

A month into the job, the head of the program called my father. "I'll be happy to let the admissions committee know that Stephen is a true talent," he said. My father immediately called my mother, who bought me a cake from my favorite bakery to celebrate. She had them write "#1 Mouse Mater" on the top, and draw little white rats in icing where there would normally have been flowers. For a brief moment, I was the perfect medical school–bound son.

The next day, I received a notice from Cornell that my grades were available on the school's automated voicemail system. I called and when prompted, entered my student ID number. Then I held my breath.

"In . . . Organic Chemistry . . . you received . . . an F," the computer said in a mechanized voice. It sounded out the "ch" in *chemistry* the way it's pronounced in *change* and *China.*

Feeling woozy, I pressed the star key to have the computer repeat the grade. Maybe there had been a mix-up.

"In . . . Organic Chemistry . . . you received . . . an F."

"What the fuck do you know?" I yelled into the phone. "You can't even pronounce 'chemistry.'"

"In . . . Organic Chemistry . . . you received . . . an F," it replied.

I hung up and slunk downstairs to the kitchen, where my parents were having some of the leftover cake for dessert. I thought about delaying further, but figured I had to tell them while they still felt the warm glow from my doing well at the summer job.

So I told them my other grades, which were good, and then I said

I had some bad news: "I didn't do well in chemistry. I told you it was very hard and I didn't really understand it."

"What did you get?" my mom asked. "A C?"

I said nothing.

"Worse?" she said.

I nodded. Then I hesitated. "I got an F," I finally admitted.

"What?" my mom asked. "Did you say you failed?"

"Yes."

"How do you know?" my dad asked. "Did you get a report card?"

"No. Cornell has an automated voicemail system."

"Are you absolutely sure you heard right?" my dad asked.

"Unfortunately, I think so."

"Let us hear it then," he said. "Maybe there's been a mistake."

I dialed the number, queued up the grade for them, and handed them the phone.

"It pronounces *chemistry* wrong," my dad said. "You'll have to call the professor."

"Why?" I asked. I didn't think the professor would care that the computer mispronounced *chemistry*.

"You have to call and ask him if there's anything you can do."

"What could I possibly could do at this point?" I asked.

"Steve, you can't get a worse grade," my dad said. "So call him and see what he says. I don't really see what you have to lose."

"Right now?"

"Right now," my mom said.

"It's very late," I said. "I doubt he's there."

"Then you'll leave him a message to call you back," my mom replied.

I left a message for the professor, and he called back during dinner the next evening. I explained to him that I had failed his class and wanted to see if there was anything I could do to improve the grade.

"No, I don't think so. It's really a little late for extra credit," he said. "Why? Was there something you were thinking of doing?"

"I was hoping you might show some kindness," I said. "It's really important for me to pass the course."

"I gathered that from your essay. It was very fluent. But you should have studied instead."

"I'm sorry."

"Don't be. It was a nice essay. I showed it to my wife. In a different world, you'd pass. But not in this one. Maybe you should consider working on the newspaper, being an editorialist or something."

"Thank you," I said just before I hung up; at least he'd managed to soften the blow a bit.

"What'd he say?" my dad asked.

"He suggested I join the paper."

"I was going to suggest you quit the paper to get better grades," my dad said.

"It's going to be okay," my mom said. "You're doing very well at your summer job. Knock on wood. And you're just going to have to retake the class next semester and do well. It's bad, but that's how it goes."

Wow. I never expected to get off so easily. And so I learned then that bad news, in my family, could be diluted with good news. For all their pressure and demands for perfection, my parents also saw things in proportion to their importance.

The problem this time—now that I was flying back to Lakeside, having been dismissed from the *Weekly*—was that I didn't have any good news to counter the bad. I had been fired, I was on the verge of becoming infamous, and I was wearing a garbage bag for underwear. Worse, any credit I had banked with my successful journalism was about to become tainted by the revelation of my fabrication. This time I was going to disappoint my parents not just partially, but profoundly.

The flight arrived at O'Hare a few minutes after nine o'clock Central Time. Immediately after touchdown, the pilot came on the public address system. Instinctively, my head jerked up to listen, but I quickly remembered my hearing impairment and, just in case the flight attendant was watching, I rubbed my neck as if it were sore.

When the plane finally came to a full stop, I stood up, along with most of the first class cabin, and made my move for the exit. I didn't mind the river running through my pants. All I cared about was getting off the plane before Cliff, who was somewhere in the back, caught up with me. But the flight attendant waved at me to sit down, and reluctantly I did.

Soon all of my first-class companions had exited the plane, while I sat patiently in my seat. I crooked my neck so I could look down the long aisle toward the back of the plane. Cliff was about thirty people behind me and getting closer.

I stood up again, determined to make my break this time. The flight attendant began waving at me furiously, but I refused to make eye contact. "Mr. Glass is getting up," she announced. "He needs to remain in his seat until everyone else has deplaned." Her tone was the same one used by flight attendants universally to warn passengers of impending turbulence.

Naturally, because I was supposed to be deaf, I didn't pay any attention to what she was saying, no matter how grave she made it sound. Instead, I stepped into the aisle and began shuffling toward the front exit, while still facing the rear of the plane to avoid her eye.

Everyone else on this airplane, and probably everyone else in the history of air travel, at least since they stopped wearing long scarves and aviator goggles, has walked off aircraft facing forward. Let me tell you, there's a reason for this. If you're facing backward, the carry-on bags stampede you like the Running of the Bulls.

"Mr. Glass is moving in the aisle," the flight attendant said. "Alert the captain!" she shouted to a colleague close to the cockpit.

Now I definitely could not turn around, so I began waving frantically toward the back of the plane as if I knew someone, an old friend maybe, who had been seated in coach. (Of course I did know someone, Cliff, but since I didn't want to talk to him, I waved as if I knew someone else too, someone who was much closer to me in line.)

The passengers, struggling to bridle their charging luggage, didn't know what to make of my frenzy. Finally, a large middle-aged woman who was dressed completely in purple—sweatpants, socks, barrettes, and a sweatshirt with I LOVE PURPLE printed across the front in violet glitter—pointed to herself. "Do we know each other?" she asked. Desperation relieved me of my deafness, at least momentarily: I nodded yes, yes we absolutely did. I allowed someone to pass us, and then I embraced her.

Ms. Purple did not look like a woman who was accustomed to young men heroically fighting their way through crowded aisles to hug her. Excited, she took me fully in her arms and kissed me on the cheek. I continued to shuffle backward—heading toward the front door of the plane, while facing the rear. Clinging to her, as she walked forward, I stared at my purple guardian angel. Until that very moment, I had not known that purple came in so many shades. She said something about how it had been so long, and she hadn't recognized me at first, and I nodded in total agreement.

By the time we got to the front of the aircraft, where the flight crew thanks the passengers, Ms. Purple and I looked like old friends. But when we took the left turn and were about to deplane, the captain's heavy hand clasped my shoulder, and guided me firmly into a first-row seat.

"What are you doing?" Ms. Purple demanded to know.

The captain explained that he had been instructed not to allow me off the plane unless I was in a wheelchair.

"This is an outrage," Ms. Purple said. I held her hand tightly in support. "This must be a violation of the law," she added in a louder voice, when no one responded. "I'll call my son; he's a lawyer."

I couldn't imagine what Ms. Purple's son would argue on my behalf, let alone what he would be wearing.

The captain, noticing that the other passengers couldn't deplane, thrust Ms. Purple into the seat next to me.

"At least this will give us time to write down witnesses' names," Ms. Purple said. She took a lavender pen out of her purse.

The captain watched us very carefully.

"Don't be nervous," she said to me. "He's just a big stuffed shirt. Everything's going to be all right."

With that, the captain leaned over and said to Ms. Purple, "Excuse me. You know your friend is deaf, right?"

Ms. Purple's face flushed. "Of course I know that, sir—" she began weakly. And then it came to her: "But, he reads lips."

Suddenly, Cliff was upon us. As he came up from behind, he punched me on the shoulder. It was supposed to be friendly, but it hurt. "I'm so glad to see you," he said. "I've been so worried about you."

Cliff wasn't worried at all. He was excited to see me. Now he could report back to all our journalist friends, informing them I obviously wasn't doing well—I was being detained by the captain with some large woman dressed like a character out of Clue. I knew how he felt because I too would have been giddy, had our positions been reversed. It was such a juicy story, I probably would even have called someone from the airport—no, from the plane, on the airphone.

The captain told Cliff to deplane. He was in the other passengers' way.

"I'll just step to the side here. He's a friend of mine," Cliff said, pointing to me.

For the captain, that was the finishing touch. "I'm sick and tired of his friends. No more friends. He's got one friend already, Purple over here. Now get off the plane."

"I'll call you in Lakeside," Cliff shouted as he exited. It couldn't have turned out better for him. Now Cliff would not just be reporting what he saw happening to me, he'd be part of the story, too. Garvey was sure to print his name in a follow-up article.

I shrugged toward the captain, as if I were very confused.

"If you weren't deaf, I'd yell at you too for being so unbelievably disruptive," he said, and I smiled, pretending not to hear.

Ms. Purple wrote down the captain's name under the lavender words: "Mean To Airline Patrons."

After everyone deplaned, a wheelchair was brought aboard. The captain pointed for me to sit in it, which I did. A porter arrived to push me, and started to do so, at a slow but even pace.

"You'll regret ever meeting us," Ms. Purple yelled back at the captain. She began jogging alongside the porter and me.

Seeing that there were no airline staff nearby, I turned to the porter and spoke. "Look, I'm really sorry to tell you how to do your job, but there's a man out there looking for me. You have to do whatever you can to avoid him."

"You're supposed to be deaf," the porter remarked.

"If I've told you airline people once, I've told you a million times. *He reads lips,"* Ms. Purple said.

"Ma'am, I don't care what he reads, Double-Oh-Seven here is talking, not watching my lips."

"'Deaf' doesn't mean he can't talk," she replied.

"What in God's name is going on?" the porter asked me.

"Look, you're supposed to wheel me and I'm supposed to be deaf," I told him. "Let's just leave it at that. Everything will go much faster if we can just avoid this guy." I described what Cliff was wearing.

"I just want to get you safely to your destination so I can be finished with this job, and let me tell you, I want to be done with this job," the porter said.

"I'm putting you on my list for being sarcastic and hostile," Ms. Purple said. She wrote his name under the captain's.

"Who the fuck is she?" the porter asked me.

"An old friend," I said.

"Well, you better tell her to get off my ass because if I want to, I can wheel you real slow so you'll be seen by everyone in this whole goddamn airport."

"Swears, too," Ms. Purple said. She was still writing.

I turned to Ms. Purple and hugged her magenta hips. "It was so great to run into you after so many years," I told her earnestly. "My mom will be so excited to hear that I saw you. But I really have to go now. Will it be okay if I just get in touch with you again soon?"

She held me forcefully and kissed me on the head. "Of course, my sweetie. Of course."

And we were off. The porter pushed me through the terminal at Wheelchair Olympics speed. We jumped the line at the taxi stand and within a minute, I was on my way to Lakeside.

When the taxi dropped me off, no one came out to greet me. The driveway was empty and lonely, and I remembered my dad had said he and my mom would be at work when I arrived. I paid the driver and watched him back out onto the street and head back toward the highway. And then I was completely alone.

Don't tell anyone, but the key to my parents' house is in the hollow of a fake rock in the garden near the front door. When my dad bought the plastic rock at a Sharper Image store, it resembled our front garden's real stones. But fifteen Illinois winters have intervened, weathering all the rocks except this one. Now the artificial rock is bigger, shinier, and prettier than its peers. A flawless specimen, the fake rock demands to be noticed and to be held. It practically screams, "I am an artificial rock with a key to the house inside. Open me up and rob this home."

But no one in my family worried too much about the fake rock. Buying a new fake rock to match the weathered ones would have been too much of a hassle. Buying new real rocks to camouflage the fake one seemed excessive. And, in Lakeside, trusting your neighbors with a key puts you more at risk that they'll come over to snoop, or to size up your new TV and see if it's bigger than theirs, than you ever were at risk of being burgled.

That day, I found the fake rock with ease, took the key out, and let myself in. Once inside the house, I went upstairs to the corridor that led to Nathan's and my rooms.

If a house says anything about a family's values, ours proves that my brother's and my welfare was of paramount importance to our parents. Our old bedrooms are perfect for studying. In each, there's a spacious desk and even now, when we no longer live here, plenty of writing paper and sharp pencils in the drawer. Both rooms face west to allow in plenty of after-school light, and each has a thick door to provide us with the luxury of silence.

I went into my childhood bedroom and lay down and tried to sleep. My plan was to nap for a few hours before my parents came home from work, but I couldn't. My mind was racing and my whole body felt jittery. After a few minutes, I stood up and began looking around the room, trying to distract myself with memories, to calm myself with the familiarities of my years growing up in this house, so that I might somehow find some rest.

My old bedroom is dominated by a massive wraparound wall unit that houses bookshelves, a chest of drawers, a bed, and a desk. The wall unit, and the half-dozen others like it throughout the house, were the brainchild of a futuristic interior decorator who believed all of a home's furniture should be connected. While the idea once had Jetsons-like appeal, it turned out to be a design blunder. Because of it, no piece of furniture has ever moved rooms.

On one of the shelves in the huge unit are the little clay pots I made in third grade. That day, I held one of them for a few minutes and realized they're terribly ugly, even by a child's standards. Then I opened a shoebox in a cabinet near my bed and found a collection of baseball cards, which I had organized better than any of my friends', to hide the fact that I didn't care about sports at all. Finally, from the large corkboard above my desk I removed a pink construction-paper-and-doily valentine my brother had made for me when he was in second grade. He'd spelled out words with each of the letters in my first name: S = Super, T = Terrific, E = Eats a lot, P = Perfict, H = Hungary always, E = _____, N = Nice. The space next to the second *E* was blank because he'd run out of time and Mrs. Nance, his teacher, said he had to put it away. I sat at my desk and held the valentine and was tempted to fill in the blank space next to the *E* now. What should I write? Egocentric? Emetic? Evil? Expatriate? Exposed? Embarrassment? Extinct?

Everything I'd looked at just made me think of all the potential I had now squandered. Feeling even worse than before I'd made my little survey, I began to haunt the rest of the second floor. I went into my brother's room. It's similar to mine except that unlike me, he was always being given the kind of photo collages high school girls make for their boyfriends. There must have been ten of them, all on white poster board, displaying panoramic photos of friends with their arms draped over each other's shoulders, and words clipped out of women's magazines: SEXY, WHAT HE REALLY WANTS, and HOW TO KNOW IF HE LOVES YOU. Bubble letters spelled out things like "B.F.F."—Best Friends Forever. Despite Nathan's popularity, I'd never felt very jealous of him—I'd always thought he had his strengths and I had mine. But now I didn't know what my strengths were anymore, and for a moment I longed for my brother's happier life.

Finally, at the end of the hall, I reached the playroom, an enormous space over the garage. When Nathan and I were small, it had been the ultimate landscape for building sofa-cushion forts. Later it became a computer game sanctuary where we'd spent years pretending to be Olympic athletes and dragon slayers on our Commodore 64. And, when I was in high school, it was the room where I would have held boy-girl parties, and played Twister until everyone was so tired they couldn't hold themselves up on one arm and one leg anymore. That's what it became for Nathan, but back then, I never knew any girls well enough to invite.

In the playroom there was a small rocking chair, no more than three feet high, with my name stitched into the cushion. Lying next to it were my brother's dumbbells—the ones that for a week, during my sophomore year in high school, I'd used secretly, when everyone was asleep, because I was too embarrassed to tell anyone I wanted to get into shape. Under the bathroom sink was a tiny orange stepstool, with Geoffrey the Toys "Я" Us giraffe painted on the base; I'd used it to reach the toilet when I first escaped diapers. I looked at it, bowed my head, and wondered, When did it start? When did I begin to be this person?

The house was so silent, and the past—our family's past—was still there in it, intact. I couldn't understand how everything could be so quiet, so unsullied, when my life was falling apart. I flipped on my father's clock radio and turned the volume all the way up. It was a talk station—the wrong sound. I needed the clash of cymbals or the mixed-up noise of an orchestra tuning its instruments. Then, from outside somewhere, I heard the growl of a lawnmower. I opened the windows to allow the motor's noise in. But just like that it petered out, as if the machine had tried to start, but couldn't; and I was caught again in this heavy, empty silence. I turned off the radio and sat on the edge of my parents' bed. There was nothing to do but wait.

Very soon—much sooner than I had anticipated—I heard the rumbling of the garage door opening. For years, that noise had served as an early warning system for my brother and me. From the moment the rumble began, we knew we had exactly forty-five seconds to get into our bedrooms, slip under the covers, turn out the lights, and slow our breathing enough to have plausibly been asleep when our parents came in to kiss us good night.

On this day, however, no matter how much time I had had, I would never have been prepared for their arrival.

"Stephen! Are you home?" my mom yelled, within a few seconds of the rumble's beginning. "Where are you? Where are you? I need to see you." I heard footsteps. She hadn't parked her car all the way in the garage, or even turned off the ignition. She had jumped out as soon as she was close enough to run into the house.

"Yes, Mom," I yelled back from the top of the stairs. "I'm coming down."

I could hear the pounding of her feet as she raced toward my voice. Suddenly she came into view in the downstairs hallway, below the staircase. Tears streamed down her cheeks as she rushed up toward me.

"Are you okay?" She was still yelling, even though we were now both on the staircase, five steps apart.

"Yes, Mom. I'll be okay."

"Thank God." She held me tight and cried on my chest, gripping my shirt with her fists. Still two steps above her, I rested my chin against the top of her head. We stood like that on the staircase for a long while.

"Come downstairs," she finally said. "Dad's on his way home, and I made you a blueberry buckle."

Blueberry buckle is a kind of crumb cake my mom has made every time I've returned home since I was six years old and visited my grandparents for a long weekend. My family has no inherited recipes; blueberry buckle, which a neighbor gave us, is as close as we come.

I went to the driveway, pulled her car into the garage, and turned off the ignition, while she cut a slice of buckle for each of us. When I came back, I sat at the kitchen counter and she stood near the sink, obviously too worked up to sit down.

"Allison called here sometime after you left this morning," she said. "I was already at work, but I checked my messages on the machine and called her back. She said it was very important that I call her, so I did. When I got Allison on the phone, she was crying. She said she thought you were going to kill yourself. Someone from the *Weekly* called your apartment to talk to you and mentioned they thought you were leaving out of National, not Dulles. Allison thought you were lying to her about Dulles so no one would follow you, and you could run your car off the road. She said you left a note and said you were going to miss her. Did you do that?"

"Yes," I explained. "But I *was* going to miss her, because I was coming here for a while. I *do* miss her."

My mom shook her head in exasperation. "Well, Allison read the note and became anxious. She called the airline, and at first they wouldn't tell her anything—not if you were on the plane, not if you were even scheduled to fly. But when she told them you were possibly going to hurt yourself, they went crazy. They transferred her to some airline health specialist, who told her they weren't going to leave you alone at any time."

I realized that the flight attendant, the pilot, and the porter must have thought I was both deaf *and* suicidal.

At that point, the other garage door rumbled and my father rushed in, still wearing his white doctor's coat over his shirt and tie. His stethoscope was slung around his neck, barely hanging on. "Thank God you're okay," he yelled, as if it were some kind of triumph.

The dishwasher clicked off and for a moment, the room was completely silent. Then my mom—who hadn't had the chance to tell my dad anything, except that he had to come home because Allison had said I might be dead—explained everything again.

From the way they looked at each other, I understood that my parents now thought Allison had wildly overreacted. I also saw that in the twenty minutes it had taken each of them to drive home, they had already begun to mourn me. My dad had been trying to figure out how he would keep the family together if I had died; my mom had been trying to figure out how she would withstand it. Now, while we talked, they both held some part of me—my mom held my right elbow; my dad, my left shoulder—as if to reassure themselves I was still there.

"Allison was scared," I explained in her defense. "Think about it from her position. She really believed I might kill myself. If that were true, you'd have wanted her to call, right?"

Neither of them responded.

"Well, it looks like everything is going to be okay," my dad said. "I have to get back to the office. There's probably a patient wondering where I am."

"Go back," my mother said. "We'll talk about this when you get home."

My dad kissed both of us good-bye and left through the door to the garage. Before he was fully out, though, he poked his head back into the house and shouted, "Anyway, Stevie, I'm glad you're still alive."

"Me too, Dad, me too."

After he left, I started to explain to my mom about the firing, but she insisted that I go to my room and get some sleep. She led me up the stairs and back into my childhood bedroom. As soon as I lay down, I knew, in the way the body physically remembers some things more powerfully than the mind, that I desperately needed to sleep.

Eight hours later, my dad woke me up. "How're you doing?" he asked, sitting on the edge of my bed. He placed his hand on my sweaty forehead and held it there for a few seconds.

"All right, I guess. I didn't realize how tired I was."

"You were talking in your sleep. You made a lot of noise. We were worried about you."

As long as I've been able to talk and walk, I've done both in my sleep. Every so often, I convince myself I've grown out of my nocturnal activities—I'm told most people do, during adolescence—but then I sleep beside someone new, or share a hotel room with a friend, and over breakfast they let me know, as gently as they can while keeping a safe distance, that I was yelling about aliens coming in through the window. Or something like that.

"What'd I say this time?" I asked my dad. We had a long history of his filling me in on my sleeptalking.

"Hard to tell exactly. You were talking about the Turks and Caicos Islands, and flags, and a banquet, and a 'worthwhile waffle' . . ."

My dream came rushing back to me: I had relived the firing, moment by moment.

"You walked some too," my dad said. "We heard you stomping around. I came up a couple of times and helped you back into bed, but within a few minutes you were back up again, storming around the room."

My dad handed me my glasses. The chair was on top of the desk. The closets were open and clothes were scattered on the floor. I had twirled in a circle for the Worthwhile Waffle manager. I had run between Robert's and my offices, and driven to Olde Jeff and partway back. And I had done it all in the four-foot perimeter around my bed.

"I'm sorry about that. I'll clean it up after I shower."

"Don't worry about it. You can get to it when you have a chance. Why don't you put something on and have dinner with Mom and me?"

Next to the bed was a neat pile of clothes. My mom had washed and folded the shirt and pants I had worn on the plane, the same clothes I had been fired in. I hadn't brought anything else with me, and all my high school stuff had long ago been donated, so, as much as I hated that outfit by now, I had to wear it again.

"Sure. Thanks. I'm going to take a shower first, though. I'll see you downstairs in a bit."

When I returned from the bathroom, I saw that inserted between the shirt and the pants was a new, neatly folded garbage bag.

Nobody said much while we ate. When we did talk, it was about safe topics: my parents' work, our friends and neighbors, local politics.

I remained quiet, pretending to listen. In truth, I couldn't think of anything but my firing, and it was too painful to think about that, so mostly I thought of nothing. I thought about nothing aggressively. I told my mind to think of nothing and when it resisted, I thought about how one convinces one's mind to think of nothing. I thought about whether it was even possible to think of nothing.

When that didn't work, I wished I were drunk. I pretended that the bottled water I was drinking with my deep dish pizza was scotch. I poured two fingers of Evian into my glass and threw it back. I told myself it burned. A few bites of pizza later, I downed another shot. But I felt nothing.

"Are you all right?" my mom asked. I had been so busy doing water shots that I had forgotten my parents were even present.

"Yeah. I think so."

"You're not going to feel well if you keep doing that," my dad said.

I looked up at him. Could I really be hurting myself in this tiny attempt to drown out my pain? Fuck it. It was just water.

I knocked back another one.

"You'll get indigestion," he said. "Nothing serious, but it won't make you happy."

I nodded. He was probably right. I already felt waterlogged. I stood up, cleared the dishes, and took out the garbage.

When I got back, I sat down at the counter and looked at my parents. We all knew we needed to talk. They were just waiting for the most comfortable moment, the moment when it would be easiest for me, and I loved them for that. But as much as I wanted to delay it, everyone knew now was the right time.

"This came while you were sleeping," my mom said. She pushed a fax across the counter toward me. My parents' antiquated fax machine printed on thermal paper, which curled into a tight scroll. The warped paper bounced on the countertop and I had to press down on its edges so it would stay still while I read it. It was a brief, hand-written note from Gil Garvey. It said he was working on a follow-up article, and he wanted to get my side of the story. It asked me to call him at the paper.

"He also called here asking for you," my mom said. "I didn't say anything. How do you think he knows you're here?"

"I'm sure Robert told him," I said.

"Doesn't Robert understand you came here to be alone for a little bit? Why does he have to give out this number?"

"I could be wrong. Anyone at the *Weekly* might have told Gil I went back home, and after that he might have just looked us up in the phone book."

"No way. This guy doesn't seem too smart," my dad said. "I picked up the phone once when he called, and he said he also wanted to ask you specifically about your being detained by a captain on an airplane. I told him he was nuts and hung up on him."

"He called a second time?" I asked.

"Actually, he called three times," my mom said.

"Three times?"

"Well, there were a couple of hang-ups, too. They could have been him."

"Could be phone solicitors, though," my dad said. "They call a lot."

"Could be," my mom said. But I knew neither of them believed it really was.

"How many of those were there?" I asked.

"Six," she said.

"The phone's not ringing now, though."

"Eventually we turned the ringer off, so you could sleep."

"Who else called?" I asked.

"A few people from Washington . . ." Her voice dropped off.

"You don't want to tell me who?"

"No, that's not it," my mom said.

"What is it then?"

"Stevie, we can go through the list later. I promise you. But at some point, and I think that point is now, we have to talk about what happened."

I could see my mom was very worried. The letter from Gil Garvey had suddenly made everything horrible seem very tangible. His fax might as well have been my suicide note.

"Okay," I said. "I need to ask you a favor before we talk about this. Do you promise not to be mad at me?"

They said nothing.

"I know that's really an impossible promise to extract from someone, especially when you haven't even told them what you've done wrong. But I need it. I feel like there's no one in the world who will be nice to me anymore, no one in the world who will love me anymore, no one who's not mad at me. Robert hates me, and Allison barely tolerates me, and Brian and Lindsey are going to hate me soon, if they don't already. I'm not really in a position to be asking favors of you right now, I know that. But I need you to promise not to be mad at me. Is there any way you can do that?"

My parents looked at each other. In some ways they were such different people. And so while they almost always agreed, especially on how to raise Nathan and me, their reasoning was often very different. And this difference in reasoning often resulted in disagreements—disagreements that, while a lawyer would have said they were moot, were very much alive in my house. It was important to my parents that they come to an agreement not just on the result, but on the way of thinking too. But this time there was no argument; they agreed for exactly the same reason.

"We promise, Steve," my dad said calmly. "We love you. You're our son. But you have to tell us what's happened. We can't help you if you don't tell us."

My mom, too nervous to speak at this point, got ice cream out of the freezer and scooped the entire container into three mugs, one for each of us. No one could ever be angry over ice cream, my mom always said. She learned that technique from Nancy Reagan; she'd once seen a photo in the newspaper of the First Lady serving ice cream during a particularly difficult press conference. My mom didn't like Fancy Nancy, too conservative and goyish, but she was impressed with the trick.

I was nervous too. I knew what I said now would be critical. It would define me to my parents forever, and in a way it would define me to *myself* forever. If I kept on lying even to those who loved me most, who loved me unconditionally, and who I believed would never desert me, no matter what I did, then who would I ever tell the truth to again? If I didn't tell the truth here, I was a liar and would always be a liar, but if I did, maybe someday I could become a person who once had lied, who used to lie but didn't anymore.

And so over chocolate chip mint, I explained to my parents, truthfully, what had happened. I told them I had fabricated details in some articles, and that other articles were wholly made up. I told them I had lied to Robert and tried to cover up the entire thing, to save my job and to save any respect I might still have had. Finally, I told them I had employed Nathan in the cover-up. I was most worried to tell that last detail, that I had dragged my brother into this mess.

"What are you thinking?" I asked my mom, after I finished explaining it all. She was leaning on the kitchen counter with her head in her hands. All our ice creams had melted in their cups, unfinished.

"I'm thinking a lot of things."

"Do you want to tell me what they are?" I asked.

"I'm thinking you have a problem telling the truth. And you've had this problem for some time. And now that problem has really, for lack of a better phrase, come to roost.

"I remember when you were six and I took you to Dr. Goldberg. During the first appointment, you asked him if he knew your previous dentist, Dr. Fein. And he said yes, they were friends. And you told Dr. Goldberg, the next time he sees Dr. Fein, to tell him to go to hell. Do you remember that? Well, Dr. Goldberg asked you why you thought so poorly of Dr. Fein. He said it so kindheartedly, like he heard these things all the time out of little kids, which I'm sure he didn't. And you said it's because Dr. Fein made you throw up by shoving so many instruments down your throat, and then—and this is the kicker—you said he made you clean it up. You said *you* had to scrub off the ziti you vomited all over the dental chair. Well, it's true that you did throw up, but no one made *you* clean up the office. I was there, I would never have let them do that to you. You were sick and I took you home and got you into bed. So I had to explain to Dr. Goldberg that it didn't really happen that way, so he wouldn't think worse of Dr. Fein. Although he probably would've known not to believe you anyway."

"Mom—"

"There were other times too, Stevie. Don't interrupt me. Remember when you were thirteen years old, and it was Rosh Hashanah, and you and Nathan walked home from temple? When I got home, I saw a bit of icing on both your faces and I asked you if you had eaten anything. You said 'no' and he said 'yes.' Then he said 'no' and you said 'yes.' Finally I got you to confess that you'd each eaten a yellow smiley-face cookie. On Rosh Hashanah no less! You don't eat *schmutz* like that on Rosh Hashanah."

"One of the holiest days of the year," my dad added, disappointed still.

"I agree that was bad, but—"

"Or what about the time in high school when you said the principal had had a fling with a student on the women's basketball team?" my mom continued.

"Come on, Mom, that's not fair. That was an epic poem I wrote for the literary club. I was trying to communicate how the principal didn't care about the students who weren't athletes, and I presented it in a classical form using his seduction of the students as a metaphor. So it's not as if—"

"Stephen, you read it over the P.A. system with the morning announcements. They were saying things like 'chess club meets after school today,' and 'tomorrow there's rehearsal for the student musical.' And then you get on and talk about how the principal has slept with a freshman girl."

"Everyone knew it was a poem. It was in verse."

"That's not what the principal thought when he called us to his office."

"Come on, Mom, he was an idiot, and he looked like a game show host, and you know he only cared about the athletes."

"There were other times, too." My mom spoke softly now. "I'm remembering them now. There was that time last year, at Thanksgiving dinner when you told everyone that Allison's mom had once appeared on the *Sally Jessy Raphaël* show about women who were over forty, but looked younger. It turned out Allison's mother was *in the audience,* not on stage with Sally."

"Mom, I'm sorry. I really am. And I know I'm not really in a position to defend myself here, but what you're saying is not totally fair. Sally let Allison's mom ask a question, and after she asked it, Sally asked her how old she was, and when she said her age, Sally said she looked so good, she should have been on stage too, and so I thought—"

"Stephen, enough with the excuses. I could list a thousand things like this. I could list them from day 'til night. And I'm sure there's a reason you could come up with for each one. But you know what? Most people don't have these things to excuse. They don't need to explain them away, because they don't do them."

A long and horrible quiet descended upon us. I knew talking would only anger my mother more, so I waited it out. My dad knew not to speak either. We both saw that my mom wasn't finished. She gripped her short hair with both of her fists and shook them, and then spoke again.

"There's one good thing," my mom said, but her voice was completely clinical. There wasn't a hint of optimism in her tone.

"Really?" I said. I wasn't expecting her to say that.

"The good thing is that this, this thing, is something that happened far away. It happened in Washington. No matter what happens there, you can always move back to Chicago and have a new career here."

"Yes," my dad said, latching on to this idea. "She's right."

"You'll move out here," my mom said matter-of-factly. "You'll live downtown and you'll have a good life here. It'll work out."

"You should think about it, Steve," my dad added. "No one's going to care about this out here. No one's going to even know about it."

"I'm not so sure about that," I said softly, deferentially. I didn't want to oppose them—especially not on this, the lone sliver of hope they had found—but I also wanted to prepare them for what I believed was coming.

"Not sure about what?" my mom asked.

"I think people out here are going to know," I said. "Robert's talking to the *Herald*. He's probably already talked to the *Post* and the *Times* and it's bound to be picked up here too."

"No way," my dad said. "People out here, they don't care about these things. I know in Washington this can seem so huge, but here they care about local news, what's going on in Chicago. People here don't read *The New York Times,* they read the *Tribune.*"

"*We* get *The New York Times,* Dad—delivered."

"We're different. Your mother and I grew up in Brooklyn. I drive out every morning very early to work, and I see what papers people get. The *Trib* is wrapped in blue, and the *Times* and *The Wall Street Journal,* they're wrapped in yellow. We're the only house around with a yellow paper."

"And few even get the *Trib,*" my mom said. "*The Lakeside Letter* is what people read here. I know you think it's provincial out here, but this is an advantage. People in Lakeside won't even know what's occurred."

"I don't want to be the naysayer," I said cautiously, "and I certainly don't want to make this bigger than it is. I've made enough of a mess already, I know that. But I need to be realistic with you, and I'm sure everyone in Lakeside is going to know."

My parents were shaking their heads in disagreement.

"Look, what's the one thing everyone reads in *The Lakeside Letter*?" I continued. "The police log. Everyone wants to see their neighbors, or better yet their neighbor's kids, get arrested for DUI or speeding or a few ounces of pot or whatever. Right? Well this story, the story about me, is basically one big item for the police log. 'Local Boy, Thought to Have Done Good, Actually Did Bad.'"

"Stephen, how are they even going to find out about it?" my mom asked. "We're certainly not going to tell them, and you're not going to tell them."

"Robert is going to tell them. Robert is going to tell everyone who will possibly listen."

"That's it, then. I'm going to call Robert," my dad said.

"What? No you're not!"

"Does he have children, Steve?"

"He has a daughter. Why? What are you going to say?"

"Well, I'm going to call him and talk to him, father to father. I'm going to tell him to keep a lid on this. I'm going to tell him I wouldn't hurt his daughter, and he shouldn't hurt my son."

"Dad, that sounds a little threatening. You can't do that."

"Well maybe someone around here needs to sound a little threatening. The way you're painting it, everyone is going to know, because he's going to tell everyone, and then you're going to be ruined. I think that's a little threatening. Don't you?"

"Dad, you can't call him."

"Why?"

"It won't help, Dad. Robert will become reenergized. He'll lash out more."

"I don't think so, Steve. I'm a bit older than you."

"Dad, Clovis nicknamed Robert 'Khrushchev' for a reason. Trust me. It won't go well."

"We have to trust Steve on this one," my mom said. "You and I don't know Robert. We've never met him, and he does seem angry, if he's talking to the *Herald*."

"All right, we won't call Robert," my dad said. "I don't think there's anything he can say that anyone out here is going to care about anyway. In the end, this will all be okay."

I too was sure that "in the end" it would all work out okay, but I think my dad and I had different feelings about when "in the end" would come. I was hoping it would be sometime before I died.

"Dad, this may go away, but I don't think it will be soon. The problem is, it's about journalism, and so journalists are going to keep it alive." I didn't want them to someday think I had misled them into believing this would just blow over.

"There are going to be other stories, Stephen—more important stories. The President might be impeached!" my father pointed out.

"Yes, but to journalists, right now this is the most important story in the world. Most people, people who are not journalists, care about their jobs, their families, and that's what they should care about. But journalists see me as their job *and* their family—I was one of them. Now I'm their black sheep. And they're going to write about me, and write about me viciously, and everyone will read about it. Finally, at some point, regular people who've never even heard of the *Weekly* may think *they* should care about it too. The journalists will convince them this isn't just one twenty-five-year-old fuck-up who got fired, it's a symbol of national moral decline. God forbid there's another case of this, and they'll claim I'm a trend. It's like a virus. It's not going to go away anytime soon. Look at Janet Cooke. It still haunts her."

"Don't use all these names," my mom interjected. "We don't know who this Janet Cooke is."

"She worked for *The Washington Post* in the 1980s and was caught fabricating a story, which she won the Pulitzer Prize for, and then she was fired. She eventually moved to Paris."

"Well, that's not going to happen to you," my mom said.

"How do we know that? I made up more than one story—lots of stories, Mom. It's worse."

"But you didn't win the Pulitzer Prize," my mom said. "Which is a good thing, given the current situation. I don't know this Janet Cooke, but *you're* not going to leave the country over this, I can tell you that. You're being a little hysterical, Stephen. You're making this sound like you have to run from the Vietnam War or something."

My dad jumped back in. "That woman didn't have to move out of the country, she chose to," he said. "Mom and I have no idea who this Janet Cooke is. We've never heard of her, and we hear a lot about people in the media, because for the past few years you've called us every other day and told us obscure gossip about the media business. So if we don't know her, people outside of Washington don't know her. Trust me, she could move to Lakeside and no one would be the wiser. She would just slip into town, set up a life for herself, and nobody would know a thing about her past."

My mom nodded.

"I think you're wrong on this one," I said to both of them. "We all know everyone else's business in Lakeside, why wouldn't we figure out hers too?"

"And how would we go about that?" my dad asked.

"The Internet. It doesn't matter if I move to North Korea, where the *Herald*, the *Post*, and the *Times* are probably illegal. Anyone with a computer can do a search and have the story in a second."

"I hate the Internet," my dad lamented. My mom nodded, and so did I. That was the one thing we all could agree on right now.

And then my father's beeper went off. "It's the answering service," he said. "It's probably the ER. I'm sorry, Stevie, I have to call them."

"It's okay. In the meantime, I'll go upstairs and call Allie. I told her I would."

My mom nodded. She was silent, her head resting on her fingertips. I could tell she didn't know what to think anymore.

Allison was screening calls. I pleaded with her to pick up, but after three minutes of begging, the machine beeped at me and disconnected. I tried a second time, and a third: "Come on, Allie. I know you're there. Please, please, please get the phone."

Finally she picked up. "I've been trying to call you over and over again in Lakeside, but no one picks up," she said without saying hello. "I wanted you to know what it feels like to not be able to get through."

"My parents turned off the ringer."

"You could have turned it back on! I was worried you'd killed yourself, and you didn't even bother to call me to tell me you were okay. Didn't your mom even tell you I called?"

"Yes, she did."

"Why didn't you call back? You're pissed at me for calling your mom. That's it, right?"

"No, not really."

"So *she's* pissed at me?"

"I didn't say that."

"Then why are you sounding that way, Stephen?"

"It's been a hard day. We've been getting a ton of calls."

"You think *you've* been getting a ton of calls. Right now I have the phone buried inside the dish cabinet. I only left it plugged in because I wanted you to be able to get through—which, by the way, means we better say everything we've got to talk about now, because when this conversation is over, I'm unplugging it, and I don't know when it's going back into the wall. Oh yeah, and what the fuck is my underwear—shredded—doing in with the dishes? What were you doing down here this morning?"

"I'm sorry, honey. I'll get you another pair."

"I don't want another pair! I want to know what happened to *that* pair."

"It's a long story. So who called?"

"No. No. No. This time you're going to have to tell me what happened. What happened to the underpants, Stephen?"

"Okay, okay." I explained to her, step by step, how the underwear ended up in the cabinet and the garbage bag on my ass. I told her every detail of everything that happened, from when I woke up to when I left the apartment.

"See, doesn't that feel better, now that you've told me the truth?"

"Um. I guess so." In fact, it didn't feel that much better, and I wondered why. It had felt a little better to tell my parents the truth— it had been a relief, at least. But it didn't feel better to tell Allison the truth (or at least some of it), it only felt worse somehow. Maybe, I thought, it was because I knew she would use it as a reason to leave me.

It struck me that this was exactly why I had lied: to avoid this type of consequence. But I had to start steeling myself to this: I was going to have to start telling the hard truths, the ones people would dislike me for, maybe even hate me for. Even the truths that would drive them away. As I had destroyed myself with lying, I was going to have to destroy myself further with truth telling. It was the only way.

"Allison," I said hesitantly, "actually it didn't make me feel better to say that, because I feel like you're judging me for it."

"That's because I *am* judging you, Stephen. Telling the truth is not a Get Out of Jail Free card. I want to know the truth because I *deserve* to know it. I'm being harassed here. Reporters are probably outside right now, Stephen—they're always there, waiting for me to leave."

"Look, I'm really sorry about that," I told her. "I know that's got to be hard on you."

"The people outside are only the half of it. The phone rings every five seconds. Literally, I put it on the hook and it rings again. It's journalists, but you know, it's also your friends, people who saw the story in the *Herald* and want to see if you're all right. They all know you went to your parents instead of me, and it's humiliating. I don't even know what to say to them. All I can tell them is, you're in Lakeside, and you're recovering, and you'll be okay. It's one thing to blow off the journalists, but I can't tell your friends to go away. And you don't even bother to tell me if you're alive or dead—to tell me anything I can tell *them*. They're worried about you, Stephen. It's not decent—some of them were my friends too. Like Brian, and Lindsey, and Cliff."

She sounded somewhat calmer, as if she were advising me, rather than arguing with me, but I could sense she was trying to control the anger beneath her words.

"I'm sorry about that, too, Allie. Can you just tell them I'm not ready to talk about it yet?"

She said nothing.

"Anything else going on?" I blurted.

"Steve, how the fuck can anything else be going on? This is the biggest fucking thing that has ever happened in our relationship. You're *in* the *Herald* today. Not writing *for* a newspaper—*in* the newspaper. Just because I'm being nice doesn't mean . . . We don't have to go over that now. I know you're under a lot of stress, so I'm trying to be calm for you. I'm just glad you're alive."

"I love you."

She said nothing.

"I said 'I love you,' Allison. You're not going to say you love me back?"

"My mom says I should."

"What?"

"I told my mom about what happened. I had to talk with some-one."

"She didn't tell you to break up with me, did she?"

"No. The opposite, actually. She likes you, and she said I had to help you through this, and it's not such a big deal. She said you would feel like no one loved you, and I had to be extra careful to make sure you knew I did."

"That's great. That's the best thing I've heard all day."

"I'm sure it is. Maybe you should date my mom."

"So are you going to tell me you love me?"

"Okay. I do."

"Come on, Allie. I want to hear it."

"All right. I love you. There you go. Okay? I'm trying my best over here. It's really hard. . . . You've put me through a lot, Stephen, and I don't just mean that you got fired, it's much more than that. It's how you acted after, how you're acting now. I think I want to go to sleep. I'm really tired. I was scared about you and then totally confused by you. My whole life seemed shaken up a bit today. I think tomorrow will be better. It has to be better. I just want to go to sleep now."

"Then I guess we should get off the phone. I promise to call you earlier tomorrow. I'm sorry about all this. I love you, Allison."

She hung up.

I ran down the stairs and back into the kitchen. I knew my relation-ship with Allison was precarious, but at least there was one glimmer of hope: I couldn't wait to tell my parents that Allison's mom thought my being fired was a trifling event. Maybe my parents were right. Maybe the rest of the world outside Washington would think everything I had done was inconsequential. Maybe they would think Robert was overreacting. Maybe, maybe. Please, please, please.

"Mom! Dad! I have good news."

"What's that?" my mom asked. She was sitting at the counter, looking beleaguered.

"First, did everything work out okay with the hospital, Dad? Do you have to go in?"

"It wasn't the hospital." He looked worn down. "It was a reporter. When no one picked up the phone here at the house, he called my office and the answering service picked up. He told them it was an emergency, so they paged me."

"Is this ever going to end?" my mom asked.

"Well, maybe sooner than I thought. I spoke to Allison, and she said she told her mom what happened, and her mom thought it was fine, no big deal. I guess you're right—people outside D.C. don't care about this kind of stuff."

My mom and dad looked even wearier after I told them. My dad sat down and shook his head back and forth. "Why'd she do that?" he asked.

"Well, Allison said when she saw it in the *Herald* this morning, she wanted to talk with someone about it, and she couldn't reach me so she called her mom. Is that a problem?"

"It absolutely is a problem," my mom shouted. "Allison's mom is a huge yenta. If her mom knows, everyone in all of South Orange is going to know." Allison had gone to high school in South Orange, New Jersey, where her mom and dad still lived and owned a South American restaurant.

My mom was now standing up and pacing.

"Make that the past tense," my dad added. "She's probably already told everyone in South Orange. She's moving on to Livingston by now."

"And that means everyone in Lakeside is soon going to know too, Stephen," my mom added.

"Mom, how do you know she's such a big yenta?"

"Trust me, Stephen, she's a huge yenta. Do you know what the

Zweigs said about her? They went on an Alaskan cruise with Allison's parents last year. They said she knew everyone's business on the cruise boat before they even left Juneau. They said she would have known which polar bears were cheating on their bear wives with the seals if she had been allowed off the boat and onto the glaciers to talk with the animals."

"She's a very big yenta, Steve," my dad said, rolling his eyes. "A huge yenta."

His arms were outstretched to show how big of a yenta she was.

"Okay, so even if she's a big yenta, she lives in New Jersey. We live in Illinois."

"Don't be so naïve, Stephen. All these suburbs are interconnected, and you know that. Dad's got it right. Here we come, Livingston. All aboard!"

She was right, of course. All of the Jewish suburbs splattered across the country—Lakeside, South Orange, Highland Park, Shaker Heights, Whitefish Bay, Scottsdale, West Bloomfield, Scarsdale, Potomac, just to name a few—are impossibly interconnected, as if by underground tunnels. As children, we went to overnight camp with kids from the other suburbs. We saw them again in college, and after we graduated, we ended up marrying them. And then, when our kids came, we were supposed to move out of the cities we lived in, and into still another one of these suburbs. Life would become a series of holiday commutes: Rosh Hashanah in Lakeside, Passover in Potomac, Thanksgiving in Shaker Heights. Winter vacations, when possible, were to be spent seeing grandparents in Fort Lauderdale, which seemed to be the final stop on the tunnels' route.

"Well, maybe it's not too late," I said to my parents. "I'll call Allison and tell her not to tell anyone else."

"I think Dad should call her," my mom said. "You're too eager to get approval. I don't think you're going to tell Allison forcefully enough."

"I'm not comfortable with that," I said.

"You're not comfortable with me calling anyone, it seems," my dad said. "I think this is a good idea. I agreed not to call Robert because we don't know him. But Mom and I do know Allison. We've met her and talked with her and she's been here, to our house, and you say she likes us. So I think I can call her."

"I'm really nervous about this, Dad. What are you going to say?"

"I'm going to tell her it's really important she doesn't talk to anyone else about this, and her mom shouldn't either."

"If it comes from Dad, she'll take it more seriously," my mom said. "You're not going to impress the importance of this on her clearly enough, Stevie. We know you. You're probably really worried she's angry with you. Right? How are you going to tell her this important stuff when you're worried about whether she loves you?"

I looked down; she had me to an almost psychic extent.

"Once everyone knows about this, your life is going to become much, much more difficult," my dad added. "We have to put a stop to it now."

"And Allison is the leak we have to plug," my mom said.

"It's futile. All the *Weekly* writers come from these suburbs too," I said. "What are we going to do? Call all of them?"

"We'll cross that bridge when we come to it," my mom said.

"I'm going to call Allison now," my dad said. "You'll see, it's all going to be fine."

He picked up the phone in the kitchen and dialed my apartment in Washington. I hoped Allison had made good on her threat to disconnect the phone. "It's ringing," he said. About thirty seconds passed. With each passing second I grew more hopeful that she had ripped the phone out of the wall. Please, let it ring into time without end.

"The answering machine picked up," he said. "Hello. Allison, it's David Glass, Stephen's father. How're you doing? Please pick up the phone if you're there. Allison, are you there?

"Steve, I don't know if she's there or not. Isn't she normally there? No one's picking up. I wonder why. I'm just talking into the answering machine. I don't want to tell her on the answering machine, I want to tell her in person."

Come on, Allison, sleep through this call. I tried to transmit my plea to her telepathically.

"I wonder where she could be," my dad said, while still on the line and still being recorded. "Oh wait, wait. Allison, is that you?

"Allison, I'm sorry to wake you up. I know it's late and I know you have to work tomorrow. . . . No, no. He's okay. . . . Yes, we're all okay. Thank you for asking, and thank you for calling before, too. Stephen mentioned you spoke to your mom about what happened to him. His firing and all. The problem is, we don't want anyone talking about this at all. . . . Can you tell your mom, too? . . . I understand why you might feel that way, but . . . Well, I know it was in the paper, but it's very destructive to Stephen if people talk about it. We're trying to protect him here and I think we're all on the same team. . . . Great. I'm glad you agree, Allison. Okay, then. . . . Yes. I look forward to seeing you too, next time we're in D.C. Good night. I'm sorry to have woken you. Good night."

He hung up the phone and I exhaled for the first time in more than a minute.

"What'd she say?" I asked.

"She said she understood," my dad said. "She's on board. She's smart. She understands how this can hurt you, and she said she wouldn't say anything to anyone anymore, and neither would her mom."

"That's all we can ask of her. Thank God you called, David," my mom said. "That worked out well, didn't it, Steve?"

"I guess so. I'm not sure, though."

"Why not?" my dad asked.

"I won't know, I guess, until I talk to her," I said.

"And that's why you were the wrong person to make the call," my mom said. "I think we should all go to bed. It's getting late and we've had a crazy day."

"Yes, absolutely," I said while faking a yawn. "We all need to go to bed."

I wanted to have some privacy, so I could call Allison and see if there was a way to repair whatever damage had been done.

"Good night," I said. "I'll see you in the morning."

• • •

I raced up the stairs and into the playroom. I started to dial, but then I heard the door open behind me. I hung up.

It was my mom and dad.

"Stephen, let her go to sleep," my mom said. "You can talk to her about it in the morning. Don't you think you've had enough for one day?"

"Go to bed," my dad agreed.

"I told her I would say good night to her," I lied.

"Didn't you already do that?" my mom asked.

"No, *Dad* said good night to her. I want to call her. I'll be quick."

"All right," my mom said, too tired to argue anymore. "Good night."

They headed off to bed. When they were down the hall, I dialed again and it started ringing. After ten rings, Allison still hadn't picked up. I figured she must be on the phone and didn't want to pick up call waiting. Maybe she was talking to her mom about what my dad had said. That's probably it. Come on, Allison, pick up call waiting. It's me, Stephen. Come on.

The phone rang another five times. Of course; I'm an idiot. Allison wouldn't pick up call waiting, especially after what my dad had said to her. It could be a reporter and then she would be stuck.

I waited a few minutes and tried again. Again it rang ten times, and no one picked up. Fuck.

I called the operator.

"Operator. How can I help you?"

"I'm trying to call my apartment to talk to my girlfriend, but there's no answer. I think she's on the phone and not picking up call waiting. I'd like to do an emergency breakthrough."

"Is it really an emergency?"

"Absolutely," I said. And that was the truth: I had never felt so panicked in my life.

"Well, there's a five-dollar fee for breaking through. Are you willing to pay the fee?"

"Yes. Best five dollars I'll have ever spent."

She asked for our phone number in D.C. and I gave it to her.

"I'll try the line. Hold on one minute," she told me.

More than a minute passed. I was beginning to get lightheaded. I lay down on the floor. My fingers were turning white, and I was beginning to lose feeling in my right hand from gripping the phone too hard.

"Where the fuck are you, Operator?" I muttered.

"I'm right here, Mr. Glass."

"I'm sorry, I didn't realize you could hear me."

I stood up again.

"I just clicked back over," she said.

"So the line's free, then?" I asked eagerly.

"No, I'm sorry, it's not. There's no talking on the line. That's what took me so long. I was checking to see if it was just a long pause in the conversation. That sometimes happens if someone has to check the oven or something, and just leaves the phone on the table. But I didn't hear anything for a long time. And there's no fast busy like it was left off the hook. It seems someone has disconnected the phone from the wall."

"Is there any way you can get through?"

"I'm sorry, no. It's not like I can just yell into the line and the noise will pop out of the wall."

"You're saying there's nothing you can do? Nothing?"

"Mr. Glass, the only thing I can do is transfer you to 911, and they'll dispatch someone to the apartment if she's in trouble. Would you like me to do that?"

"No," I said. "Fuck. Fuck. Fuck. Fuck you."

And then I slammed the phone down.

As soon as I hung up, I realized I shouldn't have yelled at the operator. She was just doing her job. I dialed 0 again. I got a different operator this time.

"Operator. Can I help you?"

"Hi, I just hung up on an operator and told her to fuck off. I feel bad that I did that. Is there a way I can pass on an apology?"

"Sir, I don't know with whom you spoke."

"Well, can you look in my record, please?"

"I'm sorry, sir, we don't keep records like that."

"Well, can I make a general apology to all of the operators or something, then?"

"I don't see why not."

"Please tell all the operators I know they work hard, and they work hours when no one else is working, and they're always there for me. And they're better than the 411 people. And I'm sorry. I can't have any more people hate me," I said.

"Excuse me, sir?"

"I said, 'I can't have any more people hate me.'"

"Sir, are you okay? Do you want me to connect you with 911, or maybe a hotline?"

"No," I said. "Good-bye. Please tell all the operators what I said and if you see an operator who says I told her to fuck off, please tell her I'm sorry. I am truly sorry. I'm sorry for so much. I'm sorry for everything, I really am."

I replaced the receiver and cried myself to sleep.

The next morning, my mom woke me early.

"There's a person at the door for you," she said. "His name is Cliff Coolidge, and he says you told him to come over. He said he's a friend of yours from Washington. Did you ask him to come?"

"He's not really a friend. He writes for *District* magazine. And, no, I didn't tell anyone to come over."

"That's what I thought," she said. "I'll tell him to go away."

"Just tell him I'm not talking to anyone right now."

My mom left the room, but she left the door open and I heard what happened. There was angry shouting, and my mom's quiet voice. My dad yelled something, and I heard the door close abruptly and lock. The bell rang again and again, as if someone was leaning on it, but no one answered it and eventually it stopped.

A few minutes later, I put on some of my dad's clothes and went downstairs to the kitchen. A place had been set for me. There was cereal and raspberries and hot tea waiting.

I asked my parents for the newspaper to read with breakfast.

"I put the papers away," my mom said. "I don't think you should read them right now."

"It's everywhere," my dad said. "You're everywhere."

"David, why don't you tell him how we woke up," my mom said.

My dad said a reporter and cameraman from Channel 6 had shown up at 4:45 A.M. They said they were sorry to come so early, but they needed the spot for their morning show, and they assumed I probably couldn't sleep anyway.

My mom chimed in. She told me that overhearing this from the upstairs bedroom, she came down in her nightgown. "The camera was on and Dad was standing in the doorway. And I see he's becoming more and more angry. I told him to close the door. They're filming him in his tomatoes." My dad's favorite pair of pajamas was all red except for some green trim around the collar. Everyone in my family called them his "tomatoes."

"So I said 'no comment' and closed the door," my dad added. "But I have to say, I did it reluctantly. I just think there's another side to this story, and someone has got to tell it."

They looked at me.

"I don't have a side," I said. "I'm wrong. I did wrong."

"What you did was not huge national news, like a natural disaster—FEMA is not here. That's a side," my dad said. "Other journalists have done stuff like this before. Another side. You're only a few years out of school—another side. These are all sides that need to be put out there, and they're just the ones I came up with this second. Let me tell you, I've read the stories. You're coming off like Jack the Ripper. So give me one good reason why we're not out there telling the other side, any other side?"

"I don't have another side that journalists will find sympathetic," I said.

"And they're the ones who control the story," my mom pointed out.

My father sat down at the counter. Six and a half feet and two hundred pounds of Jewish father balanced on the small wooden stool.

"I am your father," he said. "When you were born, I committed myself to protecting you. Not just when you were a little child, but for the whole of your life. I cannot accept that there is nothing I can do for you. I won't accept that—not now, not ever. There is always something that can be done. Tell me what it is."

I explained to my dad that the best thing was not to comment at all. "It's just not endlessly interesting to hear Robert and all the journalists of the world beat up on me forever. At least, I hope it isn't. But if I talk, it becomes more interesting. Then they have conflict. If we're quiet, they'll go away someday."

"I guess I did the right thing then," he said. "Although it sure didn't feel like it."

"Well, not exactly," I said. "You said 'no comment.' That's different than not commenting. The press treats 'no comment' as if it were a comment. It looks like a defensive denial. Like taking the Fifth."

"They shouldn't be able to do that," my dad said. "The point of no comment is that you don't want to comment."

"Well, they do. So, for future reference, the best way not to comment is actually not to comment."

"Don't be snide, Stephen. Anyway, that's what we started to do, after the first time," my mom said. "We just hung up on them, or closed the door."

She explained that shortly after Channel 6 left, other TV crews had begun to show up. Then, at around 7 A.M., newspaper reporters and magazine writers appeared.

"There were also people who were very sketchy about what news group they worked for," she added. "One journalist just said he was a reporter from L.A. I asked him which paper, but he just kept repeating himself. 'I'm from L.A.' 'I'm from L.A.' Big deal. It's easy to be from L.A. All you need is plane fare."

I knew what they all wanted: the first interview. The exclusive. I remembered what it had been like when I had wanted those things too, but now, in retrospect, I saw myself as a predator, an animal waiting at the door.

I had been predatory, and now I was powerless: My fate would be decided in articles written by others, appearing in publications for which I would never again write. Now others would tell my story, and there would be nothing I could do. That is the power of the press; there is nothing that one can do about them. Even if what they wrote was false or wrongheaded or merely mis-spun, I would have no recourse, for who would believe me now? And while I knew that it was fitting, it was fair—it was my comeuppance—it was also so frightening: I knew all about the media, I knew what they would do. If there were a special hell designed personally for me, it would probably have been this very hell. And my parents were going to share it, I soon learned.

My mom explained that when she and my father refused to comment, the media began visiting their neighbors. Most of them also refused to talk, and some even called the police to try to get rid of the reporters. "But not the Wordens," my mom said. "We'll get to them in a minute." The Wordens lived down the street from us.

Around 7:30 A.M., the police had come to our house, my mom recounted. They ordered the reporters off everyone's lawns and put yellow police tape in front of our driveway to keep them away.

"I didn't like that they used 'Crime Scene—Do Not Enter' tape," my father said. "Mom and I thought it would look bad on TV, but it was the only tape they had."

"So what did the Wordens say?" I asked.

"This is the stupidest thing ever," my mom said. "They announced they were having a press conference at 9:15 A.M."

That was right now.

The three of us walked to the den, where my mom turned on the TV. The press conference—carried live on one of the local morning shows—was just beginning. Dr. and Mrs. Worden were standing in front of our driveway, looking somber. He is a very short man, under five feet, and she is a very tall woman, over six feet, which made for an odd pairing behind the dozen microphones that had been taped together to make a little post for them to talk from.

"We have a statement we would like to make, before we take any questions," Mrs. Worden said. "Stephen Glass and his family have been our neighbors for many years. Our granddaughter went to the same school as Stephen. He often ate at our home and played with our grandkids. Accordingly, we were saddened this morning to read about what he had done.

"This comes at a time, as you all know, when journalism and the other major institutions of our great country are in crisis. We have seen it particularly in medicine. My husband, Harold, is an obstetrician and every day he has to deal with people who no longer trust their physician. He is a man who makes babies come into the world. There is no greater thing than that, and yet people don't trust him anymore. At least, not as they used to. We therefore believe that Stephen's actions are part of a terrible movement in the direction of a national mistrust."

"What the heck is she talking about?" my dad shouted at the TV.

"But we also believe that people are not guilty before they are proven to be guilty. That is the American way. Therefore, we are forming a neighborhood committee to investigate these claims against Stephen, and determine what should be done. When we have determined what occurred, we will announce our findings and what we believe to be the proper punishment, if any. We will take your questions now."

In the corner of the screen, you could see a small old woman with gray hair and way too much eye makeup walking up our front driveway holding a plate of brownies.

"Who's that woman?" one of the reporters asked.

"That's Zuza, the Glasses' housekeeper," Mrs. Worden said. "Next question."

But the TV crews sprinted away from Mrs. Worden and ran over to Zuza, shouting questions at her. From our family room, we could hear muffled noises outside. A split second later, they were clear, distinct questions on TV.

"What do you think of what's happened?" one reporter yelled.

"Will you still work for the Glass family?" yelled another.

"Are you *the* Zuza?"

"How do you spell 'Zuza'?"

Zuza then stopped and turned to the cameras. She was wearing a royal-blue apron with 29 AND HOLDING on the front. Zuza was almost sixty years old.

"Yes, I am *the* Zuza," she said. "And these are Stephen's favorite brownies. He is the best boy I have ever met. Now go away."

My mom sprinted out of the den and opened the front door for Zuza, and my father turned off the TV.

The next five days passed in much the same way. I kept trying to call Allison and failing to get through. TV reporters showed up every morning and took footage of the house. Because none of us ever spoke to the press, there was very little to film, and they mostly sat in lawn chairs, eating pizza and talking on their cell phones, waiting to see if we would emerge. In the mornings, they filmed my father and mother driving to work, and once even followed them to their offices, but the police soon put up yellow crime scene tape there as well.

It was around this time that I began to be introduced not only to nightmares, but also to night terrors. Not only did I relive the firing, but I began to believe I was awake as I did so. Previously, underlying my dreams, there had always been some secret, comforting feeling that I would eventually awaken; that no matter how real it felt, it was still a dream. But now that feeling was gone: I was *inside* the dreams, I lived in them. There seemed to be no difference between my waking state and my dreaming, and sometimes when I was awake, I actually wondered if I might be dreaming.

I relived the firing again and again, not only in my mind but with my body. It was not just that I pirouetted or walked, it was that I sweated and shook. More than this, it was that I felt, deep inside myself, that it was—that it had to be—real.

I recount my night terrors in part because journalists would later accuse me of not truly regretting what I had done, and not having suffered nearly enough for it. After all, they pointed out, I'd never tried to kill myself—an attempt many seemed to expect I would inevitably make. One journalist remarked that these stories "always end in death," but mine hadn't—not yet, anyway. And so the journalists, all of them, seemed to me always to be hanging on and waiting for my death—or at the very least, my breakdown and subsequent institutionalization—to come.

It never did. Indeed, I never even took medication, and no psychiatrist ever suggested I should. (I saw several therapists, but not until much later, in a different city.) I confess this hesitantly—for many will take this as corroboration of their version of me: the version in which I am a sane but evil trickster, mocking the world and undermining its rules at the same time, maliciously and without regret or remorse.

In truth, I think those who have suffered both anxiety and depression likely have no favorite as between the two—no clear lesser evil. And anxiety, at least, I suffered intensely. My thoughts raced until they were a mental blur; I stared, night after night, up into the darkness and even when I slept, I never rested. My brain played out darker and darker worst-case scenarios of my future and replayed ever more grotesque versions of my past. Sometimes I could not even sort out my worries, regrets, and fears to choose one to focus on. I was more anxious than depressed, but still I cried—in shame and frustration and despair. I cried because I had so much to worry about, and nothing I felt capable of doing to allay the worry, and because things were happening in my mind, and to my mind, that I couldn't stop. I cried because for so long I had tried so hard to control my life, and now it was so far beyond me.

Nathan called nightly to reassure me. He never said that it would all blow over or that it would soon go away. He didn't suggest things for me to do next in my life. And he didn't want me to apologize to him. "We're brothers," he said. "We're beyond that." Nathan just listened. He listened when I talked about Allison, and he listened when I talked about how sorry I was, and he listened when I explained how I had never intended to cause this much pain, and he even listened when I said nothing. It is a gift to have someone to listen to you even when you have nothing to say.

• • •

During this time, newspaper and magazine writers, and radio and TV reporters, called ceaselessly and, when they could not get through, wrote letters asking for interviews. Here are a few:

Mr. Glass,

I am writing an article about you for *The New York Times,* and seek to interview you for said article.

On three occasions I have called and left a message at your apartment, setting a time for us to talk on the phone. You have not, however, called at any of these times.

I am writing this letter because it occurs to me that it is possible you are not getting your messages.

In the unlikely event that you are indeed getting the messages and merely ignoring them, I would expect at least a callback telling me you do not intend to comment. As a former journalist, you have a duty to journalism. As the nation's paper of record, *The New York Times* has a duty to make sure this event is recorded for history in its fullest. I hope that you'll help the *Times* effectuate our important role.

Sincerely,

Laurence Cooper

Dear Stephen Glass:

I am a hand at Norway National Television, Washington Bureau. I produce the newsprogram *All Morning Long,* which is watched by 82% of the Norwegians all morning long. This is a very big deal in Norway. More people watch us there than the Katie Couric.

Norwegians are greatly compelled by the problems in this country with "fact verifiers," "magazine-workers' trustworthiness," and "honesty."

Norway knows this has been problematical. You have caused great commotion in Norway. We want to talk to you about it. You must clarify this.

I am told that you are smart and diligent worker. Therefore I believe that you had good reasons to write stories which do not exist. Maybe you did not have good reasons. I hope not. But even if you had no good reasons, it is very gripping to Norway.

I am also told that you stay up very late because you work very hard. This is good for me. To be on my show live, you have to be up very late. Norway is six hours ahead of us. When it is 7 A.M. in Norway, it is 1 A.M. here. I am a night owl.

No way is this the first letter you have gotten on this subject. I am told that it is not even the first letter you have received from Norway. I hope it is the first letter that you have received from *All Morning Long* or someone is trying to take my job. (Hee-Hee.)

Okay here is the part that gives me goose-bumps: I am killing myself to interview you. All of Norway is killing themselves to hear from you.

Why should you talk to all of Norway? Because Norway is far away. Or another reason.

Please hear from me.

I hope your life is perfect!

Yours,

Jens Erik Thon
Norway National Television, Washington Bureau

Steve,

I don't know what to say. When I read about what happened, I was shocked. I didn't believe the story was true. I thought it might be an April Fool's joke. How can it be? I was hoping you had done it on purpose, to write a book about it or something— the ultimate investigative journalism about journalism, a historic exposé. And you got caught too early. That's it, right? Please let it be so.

Also, I'm sorry to say, but I have a tiny bit of business to
bring up too. We're planning a story about you and I would love to
interview you.

It doesn't surprise me that you haven't returned any of my
calls, I know you haven't given an interview to anyone. But what I
do want to know is, are you planning to talk to Cliff Coolidge? He
told *Now* that you were (see enclosed article), and I want to try to
convince you that talking to us is better. I don't want to pitch you
or snow you—just take a look at our last few issues. We do try to
be fair here, unlike some.

If you're weighing between the two, call me—and don't forget
what Cliff wrote in *District* about Monica Lewinsky. They've got
the sharp knives out for you over there.

Josh Miller
Capital Reporter magazine

Enclosed was the following printout from the online magazine *Now*,
with a circle around the sentence that said Cliff had landed an interview
with me. I wondered exactly why Josh had sent it—and then I realized
he must have sensed that Cliff's claim probably wasn't correct. (As
someone who knew me, he knew I wasn't especially close to Cliff.

Once I read the printed-out piece, I also thought Josh had probably wanted to try to send me an example of an article about me that
wasn't merely an attack piece. It seemed to me to be an implicit
promise that Josh wouldn't write an attack piece either—or at least
that, if he did, it would be a thoughtful one.

GLASS-GAZING

By Royden Blake

This is the true story of how I, a man who has made his living
as a Washington cynic, blew the media scoop of the year.

Last January, this magazine sent me to Atlantic City to interview Claire Rollins, the author of *There's No Such Thing as Magic,* a bestselling children's book revealing magicians' tricks. The book had been in the news because it had infuriated many small-town illusionists, who were suddenly confronted with booing Boy Scouts and jeering birthday girls.

Before I went, I read a previous piece about Rollins—authored by none other than the nefarious, and now notorious, Stephen Glass, the young reporter recently fired by *The Washington Weekly* for having made up dozens of articles. Glass claimed, among other things, that an angry Indiana magician, who insisted he really did perform magic, had cast a spell on Rollins to render her unable to write again. The magician was identified only by his stage name, Open Sesame.

Glass reported that when he told Open Sesame that Rollins's publisher was planning a sequel, the magician laughed, and commented, "I didn't say she wouldn't *try* to write again. I just said she would be *unable* to write again." And, sure enough, Glass reported, Rollins was experiencing writer's block on her second book.

I spent much of a day interviewing Rollins, and over dinner, I asked her if she was surprised that a magician had cursed her.

"I assumed it would happen eventually," she told me. She said many magicians, after performing their tricks so many times, begin to think that they actually do possess magical abilities. "It's not as crazy as it sounds," she explained. "I'm sure by the end, Yul Brynner thought he was the King, too."

So last week, when the *Weekly* dismissed Glass, I immediately tried to find Open Sesame. After examining Indiana telephone directories and calling national magician's associations, I couldn't locate anyone by that stage name.

In the days that have followed his firing, many in the media have stroked their chins about why Glass fabricated. They've speculated about the pressures in his life, the expectations his parents imposed upon him, and the content of his soul. I say "speculated" because thus far, Glass has never spoken publicly about what happened. (That won't stand for long. As has been widely reported, Glass has agreed to an interview with *District* magazine writer

Cliff Coolidge. Coolidge got him to commit to half an hour. Hopefully he'll get him to say at least one sentence that is not a lie. I wish Coolidge luck.)

I, however, was able, at least, to land an interview with myself. In the course of it, I tried to figure out why it was that I didn't catch Glass in his ridiculous "Open Sesame" charade. In retrospect, the story seems obviously absurd. At the time, though, it didn't even give me pause; I blithely accepted it.

The easier explanation is that Glass was exceedingly capable at mixing fact and fiction. Looking at his stories now, I can't help but notice that Glass's fictions are generally preceded by a series of easily accepted facts. You're with him for Point A, Point B, and Point C. So why would you drop him at the fictional Point D? This is true of Glass's wholly fabricated stories too. They build gradually. The early fabrications are so easily digestible that the last whopper goes down smoothly too.

The harder, and more worrisome, explanation is that I accepted Glass's lies because I wanted to believe they were true. Glass's writings cheered on his readers' biases. Take the famous lottery-winners story for which Glass was nailed. As a liberal who is wary of gambling, I wanted to think that I was, in fact, right to believe poor people are hurt by the lottery—a regressive tax if there ever was one. I loved that there were even lottery *winners* who agreed with me.

So far, so good. But why, you ask, would I also want to believe in Open Sesame? Perhaps because, on some level, as a Washington journalist, I need to believe that you people out there, far outside the Beltway, in the middle of the country where I can't see you, carry out and believe all kinds of crazy shit. It makes life more exciting and varied, and it spices up our job.

One side note and a prediction: What distinguishes a true Washington scandal from a mere Washington disgrace is the speed at which the principals stop distancing themselves from the event, and instead start connecting themselves to it all the more closely. Ironically, Glass's firing will do more for Robert Underwood than his topnotch reporting, writing, and editing ever did. He will become famous for being the editor who fired the fabulist. This isn't a bad thing. Underwood deserves more credit than he's ever gotten. He's a damn good journalist. What's ironic is that firing Glass was probably the most straightforward task of his career. Anyone would have fired Glass—even *Glass* would have fired Glass. But Underwood is now a participant in an event that other people are intensely curious about—and this, like proximity to the President, gives him cachet within the Beltway. My bet: He'll soon have a big gig of his own. Maybe a talk show. I'd call it *Underwood Uncovers*.

And how about Rollins, the victim of the alleged curse? Why didn't she catch Glass either?

"For me, it was sort of a fear-fulfillment," she said, when I inquired. "I was prepared—I'm still prepared—to think that people curse me."

Wish-fulfillment or fear-fulfillment, Glass honed in on our wishes, prejudices, and fears—mine and Rollins's certainly, and probably yours too. No wonder we believed him.

I didn't mind receiving the copy of the article, but I was still too nervous to call Josh—especially since I didn't want to give him, or anyone else, an interview—and so I did not. I did, however, appreciate his kindness in the letter, which I believed had both sincerely wished me well and been candid about its motives, unlike so many of the others.

The closest anyone got to interviewing me came on the third day. It was Tuesday, trash day in Lakeside, and I went outside to move the garbage can from the garage to the curb. My mom offered to do it, so I could stay out of the reporters' sight, but I felt it was unfair for her and my dad to have to do everything.

I walked the length of the driveway, carrying the plastic bin at chest level and focusing on a tree straight ahead. When I reached the curb, I let go of the can abruptly, turned around sharply, and walked straight back into the house, looking forward the whole time. I pretended not to hear any of the questions being shouted at me.

Later that night, Channel 6 showed the footage, midway through the ten-o'clock news. It looked like I was marching with the trash at a parade.

The correspondent reported that they were "live from Lakeside" where "embattled local journalism whiz kid" Stephen Glass was having a "normal day" at his parents' suburban home.

"Mostly embattled by *you*," my dad said to the TV.

"But in related news, back in Washington, Robert Underwood, the editor of the *Washington Weekly,* the prestigious magazine where Glass was employed, announced today that he would be conducting a full investigation into Glass's fabrications."

The newscast switched to footage of Robert working at his computer. He was dressed in the same suit he'd been wearing the day I was fired, his best. Next, they showed a shot of the conference room. Everyone at the *Weekly* was dressed in a suit—even Lindsey, who generally dressed up by adding a shiny barrette to her T-shirt-and-cargo-pants ensemble. I worried that Robert had come down hard on her for defending me and felt bad again for my part in encouraging her defense.

Above the conference room table was a sign that said PROJECT SHARDS OF GLASS. "This is where the investigation will take place," Robert said. "We promise our readers they'll know everything that went wrong. We are committed to our readers and to quality journalism. The fact checkers will go over all of Glass's stories with a fine-tooth comb."

The reporter came back on the screen: "Underwood promised the results would be announced soon."

The video then cut to my dad in his tomatoes, filmed three days earlier, saying "no comment." At the bottom of the screen it said DAVID GLASS, FATHER OF FABRICATOR.

"Sounds like things are pretty heated," the TV anchor said to the reporter.

"They are," the reporter continued. "Glass was taking the trash out to show he's still alive and well. He's trying to get back in the swing of things and put this behind him. Glass was a wunderkind, but it's not clear whether he'll ever get past this. Not until there's a full accounting, at any rate."

"Thank you," the anchor said to the reporter. Turning back to the camera, he said, "Channel 6 will keep you up-to-date on this important story."

"At least they think you were a big *macher*, a 'wunderkind,'" my dad commented after I turned off the TV.

I told him not to believe the hype. "They should call it *blunderkind*—journalists only use the word after the *kind* has fallen. You didn't see them talking about me on TV before this happened, did you?"

"We saw you on C-SPAN . . ." my dad said. I think he was trying to make me feel a little better.

"Everyone at the *Weekly* was on C-SPAN. They're desperate for commentators—no one else wants to talk about whether the General Accounting Office's budget should be increased. And, Dad, it wasn't even C-SPAN. It was C-SPAN 2."

My dad said nothing more. I think he realized it was bad either way: if I'd taken a great fall, or if I had never succeeded so spectacularly in the first place (which was actually the case).

A day later, I received a letter from Evelyn Worden, our neighbor. She said her committee had met "to talk about the situation." In fact, my mom had heard that while many neighbors had showed up at the meeting, it was mostly because they wanted to coordinate their approach to keeping the TV trucks from blocking their driveways.

Mrs. Worden, however, claimed in her letter that the meeting had focused on "the subject of your journalism conduct." "The ad hoc committee understands it might not have all the facts and would like you to come to our next meeting to explain what happened," she wrote. "We wish you well in these hard times, but also remind you that accountability is the essence of democracy."

"No way you're going to that," my mom said. I agreed. Mrs. Worden scared the hell out of me.

• • •

As the days passed, the calls continued. Reporters, old friends, and even random people I didn't know, with no connection to the media, phoned. I got hate calls, threat calls, and a few surprising, weird, admiring calls.

Usually they got the answering machine. In the few seconds they had to leave a message, the reporters always tried to connect with me on a personal level. Some said how sorry they were this had happened; they had loved my stories in the *Weekly.* Others said they had grown up near Lakeside, and had childhood friends who knew me. Still others said they understood the emotional pressures I had been under, and had felt the same pressures themselves. (No one confessed to fabricating, though; the closest anyone came was one reporter who said he knew "how lonely it can be.")

I didn't return any of their calls, and I never picked up the phone. But sometimes one of my parents would answer it, thinking it might be a friend or neighbor, or maybe Nathan checking in. Reporters who got them often would say that it was "important" or "critical" or "vital" that I speak with them—that they had information I would like to know, no, that I absolutely *needed* to know. If my parents asked what this information was, they would say they could tell only me—it was also very private information, so private they needed my comment before they ran it in their newspaper, to make sure it wasn't, by chance, erroneous—and then my mother or father would hang up.

Still others sent gifts. A Cleveland drive-time DJ who went by the moniker Todd Turtle sent me a large stuffed tortoise, with a note asking me to call his producer so we could "make this happen." A Seattle morning-show producer sent me coffee beans—"a taste of the Pacific Northwest," she wrote, in the hope that "you'll give me a taste of your thoughts." A Dallas Internet journalist sent me three digital cameras and asked me to set them up throughout my parents' home, so he could broadcast my "life in exile." I sent them back C.O.D.

And then there were the old friends I had lost touch with years ago. They wrote kind letters, some so gentle they didn't even mention what had brought them to think of me again. A few wrote to say they still lived in Chicago, and had heard that I was back in Lakeside, and would love to see me if I had the time.

From their perspective, we had become close again. Through the news, they had reconnected with me, reading about my success and my scandal. They had seen my high school yearbook photo in the *Chicago Tribune* and there I was again, the skinny Stephen Glass they remembered walking the halls of Lakeside High. Seeing me in trouble, they had reached out to tell me they remembered that Stephen Glass, the old, the original one, and they believed I was still him.

But as much as I appreciated their kind letters, and often read them several times over, I never responded. I simply did not know what to say. The idea of seeing old friends was too painful. If we had gotten together, I would have been thinking the entire time that the only reason we were there, they and I, was because I had lost everything and was now forced to go back into the past and begin anew.

Brian called when I had been in Lakeside about a week, and I picked up as soon as I heard his voice on the machine. The first thing he said was, "I don't know what to say."

"I don't know either, except that I'm sorry," I said. "I'm genuinely, honestly, sincerely sorry."

He didn't want to hear it. "Robert says you made up a ton of stories. People here are pretty upset."

"They're right to be."

"I mean *really* upset," he said. "They've been saying crazy things. Lindsey says you were never really her friend. In fact, she's told everyone that she's taken back the friendship retroactively—whatever that means. She says you can't be friends with someone who lies about their life as much as you did. She thinks your friendship itself was a lie. Did you ever really care about me, or any of us?"

"Of course," I said. "I cared and still care about you very much, and everyone else there too. . . . You don't believe me, do you?"

"No, I don't think I do," he said. "I think deep down you're a need junkie. You have an uncanny ability to tap in to people's deep psychological needs and satisfy them. You did it in your stories, and I think you did it in your friendships too. And I don't think the friendships are any more true. They're all just ways to satiate your craving for other people's approval. I don't think you have any idea of the difference between what you want, and what other people want from you.

"This morning, I was thinking about the time you drove to Pennsylvania to pick me up. Do you remember that?"

I said I did. Two years ago, Brian's car had broken down near York, Pennsylvania, around midnight, the night before his article was due. Brian's AAA membership had expired, there were no all-night mechanics nearby, and there were no trains back to Washington until the next afternoon. He was stuck. Brian called to ask me for advice on how to handle Robert, but I didn't have any advice to give. Because of the tight deadline, I knew that if Brian's article was late, it wouldn't make it into that week's issue; in fact, since it was an of-the-moment piece, it might never run at all. And so even though he didn't ask me to, I drove up to York that night, arriving after 3 A.M., and brought Brian home. He finished the piece, and it ran in the magazine after all.

"At the time I thought, Holy shit, what an amazing friend," Brian explained. "I wouldn't have driven that far, that late, for *anyone*. But after you did that for me, I absolutely would have done the same for you. Hell, I would have driven to Alaska for you. It was like some kind of logic game. You took the first step, and proved to me you would be my great friend, and after that I would have been happy to repay you tenfold.

"But, Steve, you never called in the debt. I never really thought about that, or maybe I thought you had your life so together, you never really needed to ask me for a favor in return. But that's not right, is it? I've talked to other people. Lindsey realizes it now too. You never asked any of us for favors. Which is really strange, since you were always doing them for us.

"Steve, you do favors people don't even ask for. You noticed what we liked to eat, what we liked to read—then you'd always get it for us. Those parties you had, where you chose every possible kind of cookie, every kind of beer, then you alphabetized them—it was so pathetic, but in a way it was so charming too. Oatmeal raisin before peanut butter, Amstel before Budweiser. You catered to our every need, didn't you? And if we thought it made you a loser, it was all the better—it masked how manipulative it was. I saw it when you were with Allison too: the movies were the ones she wanted to see, the restaurants were the ones she picked. You didn't have a say in it because you didn't want one. You wanted it to be all her.

"I now realize why you do all these favors. It's because you're asking for a favor every day—your own kind of favor. You ask for our trust and approval and kindness and love. That's what you want. You want the things we give away for free. But that's not friendship, that's buying us."

I said nothing. I was silenced by shame but also, for the first time, by anger. I hadn't felt entitled to feel anger since I'd been fired—after all, I was the one who'd done wrong, the one everyone should be angry *at;* I was the perp, the culprit, not the victim—but now, as I listened to Brian, anger crept in anyway, like a mouse into a wall. Didn't *anything* I had done stand? I wondered. Didn't it count at all? I had still gone to York. I had still driven there, exhausted, and made myself sick on caffeine to stay awake, and messed up my own deadlines. And now in Brian's eyes, it was worse than if I had sat at home with the remote, slept soundly through the night, and left him to his fate. Was it so terrible, after all, that I had done all this to get Brian's approval? So, too, do children seek their parents' nod. I might have been immature, manipulative, and destructive—yet I had been there, at 3 A.M., to take Brian home. Still I said nothing.

"Anyway, I could have lived with all of that. Really, I could," Brian continued, apparently unaware of either my sadness or the fury that was seeping in beneath it. "But you went one step further, Steve. You tried to take me down too. Now they're questioning my writing because we edited each other's pieces. One innocent mistake and I'll be lumped together with you. And it's not just me. It's cast suspicion on the entire magazine. Everyone knows this isn't the first time a young *Weekly* writer has come under fire.

"Do you realize your fuck-ups could kill the magazine? The place you said you loved, and I actually do love. I love it a lot. It's like killing my family, Steve, or making me homeless when I used to live in this mansion. It was a mansion for me, anyway. And that's why I don't think I can ever forgive you."

I just listed to his carefully planned speech, which had burst out of him in one crazy blast. He was right, and it wasn't my place to ask him to be more sympathetic. He didn't want my apology either; he had already rejected it.

"So I guess that's it," he said. "I'm going to go try to write my next piece—you know, make my little contribution to trying to keep this magazine afloat. It was the only place I ever wanted to work, and you knew that, and you tried to destroy it. Good-bye, Stephen. Good-bye." And he hung up on me.

Looking back, I think I should have tried to apologize to Brian anyway—even though, in a way, it was impossible. Nothing I could say would have excused me in his eyes. The truth was, I had no defense for what I had done. And worse, I couldn't even really explain to him how I had come to do it. I had crossed a line that some journalists—and I suspected Brian was one of them—would never cross even in fantasy. And even those who might have crossed it in fantasy still could not understand. For them, I had gone somewhere only fantasy could go. It would be like trying to explain to someone how to suspend disbelief: either you could, or you couldn't. If you had to ask how I possibly could have fabricated, how I could have erred and how I could have dared, you'd never know—and you'd be fortunate not to. Brian had asked, but he hadn't wanted to hear an answer; he too must have known that no answer I could give would placate, nothing I could say would satisfy. I had crossed a line and he stood on the other side of it, looking at me, and as we watched each other, the line rose up and grew to an impossible wall between us.

I never took another call about my firing again. Journalists seemed to perceive my silence as arrogant, crafty, obfuscating—just another trick. In truth, I was simply, paralyzingly sad and afraid. And Brian's call had shown me, as well, that it would do no good to apologize.

Lindsey did call, days later, but now that Brian had told me she didn't even consider herself my friend anymore, I was too wary to take her call. It sounds weak or petty, I know, but I worried that for her, as for so many people, I might only be a story now. She was dating a *New York Times* reporter, and both her parents were journalists too—they would all speak to her, I thought, and speak against me, and soon they'd be suggesting that at least, after all I'd done to her, she could get an article out of it. It would be cathartic, they'd say. It would help her put this behind her.

Meanwhile, over the same week, I called Allison every day, several times a day, leaving messages. But she never called back, and on the rare occasions when she picked up the phone, she immediately hung up on me.

In each of my calls, I tried to apologize. I said I was sorry for having lied to her, even after I was fired. I apologized for running back to my parents in Lakeside, rather than working through my problems with her; I admitted it had been cowardly. I promised to come back immediately, answer all of her questions, and make things right in every way, if she would only talk to me. But she wouldn't. And I was scared to go back to see her without an invitation because I felt certain by now that she didn't want me there.

On the eighth day, I sent gerber daises, Allison's favorite flower, with what I hoped was a moving (and honest) note about how the only pleasant part of my dreams these days was when I imagined being with her. Immediately after the florist confirmed delivery, I called Allison. She let it go to the machine.

On the ninth day—the day on which I had promised myself that if I didn't finally get through, I would return to Washington and plead with Allison for forgiveness in person—I had a virtual grand mal of messaging. I called her four times, begging her to take me back.

After I finished the fourth call, I realized I had concluded my message with a slow restatement of my telephone number. I called back immediately and apologized—saying I realized her reason for not calling had nothing to do with her not having my number, and everything to do with my behavior. Unfortunately, at the very end of that message, I left my number once more.

Or at least I thought I might have. After I hung up the phone, I couldn't remember exactly. After about ten minutes of trying to remember, I called Allison one more time, and explained that I had been concentrating so fully on my apology for leaving my phone number, I might have somehow inadvertently done it again. I said I hoped she understood if I had left my number another time, and that she would excuse this final message if I hadn't. She still didn't call.

On the tenth and final day of my messages, I attempted a new strategy. I knew I needed to prove my love. I was finished with all the promises of contrition; they weren't getting me anywhere. I was sure Allison wanted something tangible. I needed to make it clear to her how much I loved her, and I needed to do it with unadulterated masculinity. So I concocted a plan.

In high school, I had once seen a guy win back his girlfriend with great success. During my junior year, Tommy Graham, the center of our varsity basketball team, announced during a pep rally that he was going to win the next game for Stephanie James. Stephanie had been his girlfriend for two years, but she had dumped him when she caught him hooking up with Katie Heywood. Sure enough, with less than a minute left to play, Tommy sunk the winning free throw, and Stephanie took him back.

But the story doesn't end there. When Katie lost Tommy, she told everyone that *she* was going to win *him* back by coming in first at *her* next competition. Katie was the captain of the Dolphins, Lakeside High School's synchronized swimming team. She practiced her routine for months and mastered an impossible underwater double split-swivel maneuver.

I had always had a crush on Katie and often went to her tournaments so I could watch her dance around in a bathing suit. I worried that going to her games would make my crush too obvious, so I claimed to be a huge synchronized swimming fan. This rightfully struck many people as strange. It wasn't like basketball or football. Few people who weren't either close friends or parents of a swimmer went to synchronized swimming matches. (I don't believe the principal ever made it to a game.) Certainly I was the only student who regularly traveled to their away tournaments. To make my "I'm just a fan" story plausible, I went all out. I subscribed to *Strokes,* the sport's top magazine, and on game days I would write "Go Dolphins!" on classroom chalkboards.

In the stands, I would watch Katie and dream that, someday, her love for Tommy would shift to me. I fantasized that I would be the only guy to show up to a match and while Katie was underwater, flipping and turning, she would have an epiphany. She would come to realize she absolutely had to be with me forever.

Initially, the night Katie tried to win back Tommy proceeded according to my fantasy. I was, in fact, the only boy from our school to show up. Katie's parents thanked me for coming (again) and invited me to sit with them, which I did enthusiastically. During high school, I operated under the mistaken notion that parental approval was a way in with their daughters. So when Katie's dad told me he was a lawyer, I asked him about a recent Supreme Court case I had read about in the paper. He was impressed, and told me I should come by their house sometime.

"I can't get Katie to talk about these things," he said. "And I absolutely couldn't get Tommy interested in anything at all."

Woo hoo! Things were going well! Getting into Katie's house, I believed, was the first step to getting into her pants.

"By the way, where is Tommy?" I asked Mr. Heywood.

"He's not coming tonight," the father said. "He said Stephanie wouldn't let him."

"I'm sorry to hear that," I said. "I know Katie was hoping he would be here."

Bring it on! Katie and I are going home together tonight!

Shortly before her performance, Katie looked up in the stands and saw me sitting with her mom and dad, and I swear she smiled.

That evening, the swimmers were made up to look like mimes, and their routine, daringly, was silent. Katie and her team won the competition by a unanimous vote of the judges. When they handed her the first-place trophy, I tried to organize some of the spectators to rush the pool. Only her father followed me. The two of us stood there next to Katie for a few pictures, and then I tried to hoist her onto her dad's shoulders. She didn't like that, however, so I got onto his shoulders and we did a victory lap around the diving boards.

After the event, her parents offered me a ride home, but I declined, claiming I had "things to do." Katie's dad winked at me, and I went to wait outside the girls' locker room, with a bouquet of flowers I had hidden under my windbreaker.

The mimes' waterproof white face paint must have taken forever to remove. While I waited for Katie, I threw out a few of the flowers. They had gotten crumpled while pressed up against my chest. But then the bouquet looked lopsided. I threw out a few good flowers from the other side, to even things out, but I overcompensated and had to thin out the first half even more. When I was done, I had winnowed the bunch to only a third of its original size. The remaining stems didn't look so hot either. Only the cheap greenery and that prom staple, baby's breath, seemed to keep their shape.

More than forty-five minutes passed, and Katie still hadn't left the locker room. I dreamed she was getting herself ready to start dating me with gusto. I imagined that I wouldn't have to say anything at all; she would just kiss me when she saw the flowers. I had decided we would count this night as our first night together, even though it had not been planned (at least, not by her). It was the first of the month and I liked the symmetry of it, how easy it would be to count our month anniversaries.

I heard Katie behind the door and hid the flowers behind my back, like they do in the movies. I thought it would go over better if I popped them on her. When she appeared, she seemed surprised to see me. She was a mime no longer, I noticed.

"Whatcha got behind your back, Glass? A gun?"

Yes, Katie, a *love gun,* is what I wanted to say, but I said nothing. I revealed the destroyed flower arrangement.

She laughed a little. It was a tiny little laugh, more like a hiccup, and she said, "I hope they're not for me."

My face flushed, although I doubt she saw it because of the gray-and-white Dolphins face paint I was still wearing. I stammered and said no, they weren't for her. I told her they were a gift *to* me, but I had nowhere to put them down.

"From who?" she said. "They look like they were run over by a car."

I couldn't think of anyone to say, so I said I had received them from my mother. I congratulated her on winning, and walked off.

A decade later, as I was designing my plan to win back Allison, I figured I needed to be more like Tommy, and less like myself. I had been a spectator; Tommy had been a doer. "Be Aggressive. Be, Be Aggressive," our high school cheerleaders had shouted, and Tommy had acted. I would act too.

This was a problem, seeing as I've never been particularly sporty, and certainly didn't have the time to practice before my next call to Allison. Also, Allison was far away, so even if I could train for some competition, she wouldn't see me win. Working within these constraints, the only thing I could think of was to set the world record for nonstop pleading of one's love.

I didn't know what the present record was. The *Guinness Book of World Records* lists only the longest kiss. So I decided my goal would be to fill Allison's and my answering machine—two full hours—with *amore*. The machine was programmed to disconnect a caller if there were just five consecutive seconds of silence, so there was no way I could cheat (not that I would have—I intended to play by the rules for rest of my life). Plus, the tape would be the proof I could send to *Guinness*.

As I saw it, Allison would have to forgive someone who was listed in the *Guinness Book of World Records* for pleading their love to her. She would have no choice. Our sponsors would require her to pretend. It would be like the movie *Can't Buy Me Love:* Allison would make believe she loved me, and over the course of a month, she would genuinely learn to love me again.

I prepared myself for the task by downing a bottle of Gatorade and dissecting a PowerBar into tiny energy morsels. I figured I'd snack (swallowing whole, no time to chew) between words.

And I was off!

"Hi, Allison, it's me Steve. Funny, I don't know why I'm starting that way, introducing myself and all. You've got to know my voice by now. We've been dating for years. . . . That's why I'm calling. After all this time, I want to tell you how much I love you. Most of all, I want to apologize for everything. I know we can work this out, if you'll only talk to me. . . ."

I was a natural. I was Tommy Graham, sinking the last-minute free throw to win the game. No, I was better than Tommy. I was a love jock. I could go pro. I was better than Limbaugh, better than Stern.

Suddenly, remembering my plan, I froze: Why wasn't Allison picking up? I got worried, and it was then that I almost messed everything up. Looking at the clock, I realized I had paused for three seconds. Two more seconds, and the machine would cut me off.

"Hallelujah!" I screamed. It was the first word that came to mind, and I couldn't risk getting disconnected.

Then, unexpectedly, Allison picked up the phone. "Stephen?"

"Oh, Allie, it's you!"

"Stephen, stop this craziness."

"But, Allie, how can you say that after—"

Allison interrupted me and said she had called the landlord to inform him we were moving out. We had to vacate by the day after tomorrow.

"I've been thinking a lot about this and I think it's better for us to separate," she said. "And not just for me—I think it'll be better for both of us. You have a lot of things to sort through. You're probably better off doing that on your own."

I started to say something more, anything to keep her on the phone, but Allison said she had to go, reminded me that we had to be completely moved out in two days, and hung up.

I called an airline—not Coastal—and booked a ticket back to D.C. Then I went downstairs to tell my parents what Allison had said, and to let them know that I had to return to Washington the next morning.

"I'm glad she's doing this," my dad said.

My mom nodded in agreement.

"But I thought you liked Allison," I said. "Just last night you were saying I was lucky to be with her."

"She's got style," my dad told me one night, after I worried aloud that she might never talk to me again.

"She's resourceful," my mom said the next night, after I only half jokingly speculated that journalists had kidnapped her to get her to talk about me.

Previously my parents had had mixed feelings about Allison, so I suspected their recent outpouring of unqualified approval, at a time when she would not return my calls, came from their appreciation that she hadn't spoken to the media about me. Now they'd reversed position, seemingly instantaneously.

"Our feelings have changed," my mom explained.

"When?"

"When you told us she was breaking up with you."

"But that was only a few seconds ago. How could your feelings change so dramatically? It's only been a few seconds."

"Things change," my dad said. "Sometimes they change fast."

"She said she no longer wanted to be with you," my mom added. "You think we want *our son* to be with someone who doesn't want to be with him?"

"No way, José," my dad interjected.

"The problem is," my mom continued, "you don't have the confidence right now to end it with someone, even when you know they don't want to be with you. Imagine if you were dating someone with as little confidence as you. Then she wouldn't be able to break it off either. Both of you would be dating people you don't want to date."

"We call that the worst possible situation," my dad said. "The good news is that Allison *is* strong enough to break it off with you."

"That's something to admire in her," my mom said. Now it sounded like they were back to liking her again.

"Well, Allison didn't really say she's breaking it off," I backpedaled hesitantly. "She said we were moving out. . . . It's not the same thing."

They looked at me incredulously.

"No, really, it's very different," I said. "Maybe she wants us to have a place farther from the city, so we won't be disturbed by all the reporters."

"And not live together anymore?" my mom asked.

"Who knows? Maybe she thinks if we were apart, it would be easier for me to have my privacy from the media, but we'll still see each other all the time."

"Kooky talk," my dad jumped in. "She's breaking up with you. She said the landlord would throw out your things or sell them."

I bowed my head and looked at the kitchen counter. I realized he was right—I was escaping into fantasy again.

They told me they wouldn't allow me to go back to Washington if my goal was to salvage my relationship with Allison. "I'm putting my foot down," my dad said. He stamped his foot to show he meant it.

"You want what's best for me, right?" I said. "So if I want this relationship back, shouldn't you then want it too?"

"You're mixed up," my dad said. "Listen to me. Right now, I don't think you're in any position to know what's best for you. You need to concentrate on putting your life back together, which is absolutely doable if you put in the work."

"I don't think I'm that mixed up."

"You are. People who are as mixed up as you, sometimes don't even realize how mixed up they are. Do you get what I'm saying?"

Part of me knew he was probably right, but all of me knew I should just agree.

"Yes," I said.

"Don't just yes us," my mom said. "You always yes us and then do what you want to do. You've done that since you were a little child."

My dad nodded. "I remember when Mom and I allowed you to leave synagogue early on Rosh Hashanah one year. You said you had a lot of homework. We asked if you would walk directly home. No stops. You said, 'Yes, Dad.' And then what happened? You stopped at the White Hen Pantry and got a smiley-face cookie."

"On one of the holiest days of the year," my mom added.

"We went through this already. I was thirteen years old. And Nathan did it too—it wasn't just me. That's not going to happen—"

"Do you know how much it hurt us?" my dad said. "You can bear to hear it a second time."

The incident with the cookie, and the degree to which it angered my parents, have remained with me for years. I remember standing in my bedroom beside Nathan, facing the massive weight of my parents' disappointment, and thinking that I had to either accept that I was the boy who had disappointed them so greatly, or to learn to better wipe the icing off my face.

I wondered if Nathan had thought about it differently—thought about more than just getting caught—and if that was why he'd turned out differently. Better, I admitted to myself—he'd turned out better, more honorable, and much more honest. Nathan didn't care so much what other people thought, and he didn't lie to them either. So why did I?

"I've known you your whole life, Stevie," my mom said. "Whatever you're telling us now, you're going to go back to D.C. and try to get back together with Allison."

There was silence.

"I think I need to go with you," my mom said.

"What?"

"You heard me. What do you think, David?"

"You're going to come to Washington with me?" I said, before my dad could answer.

"That's right," my mom said.

"But—"

"I don't know," my dad said. He was wavering.

"Someone needs to help Stephen pack up and find a new apartment and move," my mom argued to my dad. Neither of them even looked in my direction. They were two Security Council nations deciding the fate of a rogue state.

"I'm right here," I said.

"Who's going to help you if Mom doesn't go?" my dad asked.

"I don't know," I said. "No one."

"You're going to need the help," she said.

My mom was right. There was too much for me to do alone in two days, and I doubted I had any friends left to help me.

"Are you going to be mean to Allison?" I asked. "Because whatever happens between her and me, I want to be on good terms with her. So you have to be nice to her, Mom. Can you do that?"

"Definitely," she said. "I'll prove it. Let's practice. Dad will be Allison. You and I will be ourselves."

My father brushed his hand over his ear as if he were pushing back one of Allison's blond locks. His tight Jewfro didn't move.

My mom knocked on the kitchen wall.

"Who is it?" my dad said in a high-pitched voice.

My mom looked at me. "It's your line," she said. "I don't think I should say hello first. It'd be too in-your-face to her."

"I thought I heard the door. Is anyone there?" my dad asked again.

"Uh, hi, Allison, it's me, Steve."

"Steve who?" my dad said, a soprano again.

"She knows who he is, David," my mom said.

"Trust me, she's going to be resistant every step of the way," my dad explained.

"It's Steve Glass," I said.

"I'm sorry. I still can't hear you," my dad yelled. "I'm behind a lot of boxes because I'm packing up to leave my boyfriend at the very moment when he most needs my support and love."

"Fine, I'll just use my key," I said. I pretended to walk in the door.

My mom then followed me into the imaginary apartment, which was in actuality the breakfast nook of our kitchen. She ran up to my dad and embraced him.

"Allison, it's so good to see you," she said. "How's your mom?"

Even my dad was caught off guard. "Fine," he said in Allison's voice. "I'm really busy packing."

He looked me in the eye and moved his eyebrows up and down. "Pretend I'm giving you dagger eyes," he said.

My mom then asked Allison/my dad what she could do to be helpful. They talked about moving boxes and packing up clothes.

They laughed and Allison/my dad said several times how happy she was that my mom had come. They pantomimed working together in harmony.

I tried to breed anger. "Isn't my mom's being here awkward for you, Allison?"

"Not at all," my dad said. "It's kind of nice. Gives the place a bit of a *feminine feeling.*"

Finally, I gave up. "Okay, Mom," I said. "You can come. You just have to promise you'll keep an open mind about Allison while you're there."

"My name is open mind," my mom said.

PART THREE
DISAPPEARANCE

THE NEXT morning, my mom and I took the first flight to Washington. On the plane, we decided I would begin packing while she went to look for a new place for me to live, somewhere far from reporters, in the Maryland or Virginia suburbs.

While she napped on the flight, I looked over at her and thought about how other parents would have reacted, and how my parents hadn't reacted that way. I thought about what my dad had said about what it meant to him to be a parent, and I knew it applied to my mom, too. When she woke up, I thanked her.

"Don't thank me at all. It'll be fun," she said. "We'll rent the new place, move you in, go out to eat, maybe even see a movie."

When we got to D.C., my mom dropped me off at the apartment I'd shared with Allison, and said she would come back at the end of the day or when she'd found a new apartment for me, whichever came first. I was amazed not to find a single journalist staking out our apartment—they still plagued us in Lakeside. Maybe the story was dying? Or they'd given up? Maybe we could still live here, and Allison would stay with me, and it would all go away. Could it have gone away already? I dared to hope.

I waved at my mom as she drove off, held my breath, and unlocked the door. When I opened it, I saw Allison, standing over a cardboard box, wrapping a dish in newspaper.

I stood there before her for about a minute, waiting to be acknowledged, but she pretended not to notice me. I considered making a fake "ahem" cough to call attention to my presence, but I knew she knew I was there.

"Hi, Allie. It's me," I finally said. "I'm sorry I left."

"I'm sure you are."

"No, I mean it. I'm really sorry. I'm sorry for what I did wrong, and I'm sorry I fled when it all came down on you."

"A producer from one of those talk shows showed up on our doorstep last night," she informed me. "She said she was doing a show on women who love men who lie. I slammed the door on her. Two hours later, another producer is here: she's doing a show on women who *stay* with men who lie. Well, I'm not among them." She paused to let it sink in. "This is the shit I have to put up with every single day. The only reason no one is here now, is Cliff."

"Cliff?"

"He called last night, supposedly to see how I was doing. I told him I was going out of town for a few weeks. Suddenly, this morning, all the reporters packed up and left. But I'm sure they'll be back the minute they hear you're in town. They're going to film us moving, Stephen—film our breakup if they can. Sounds like fun! Do you see now why I'm leaving you? Do you get it yet?"

"Allison, I honestly didn't mean to hurt you."

"I'm sure you didn't," she said. "But so what? I don't want to be with someone who just doesn't mean to hurt me. I want to be with someone who *actually* doesn't hurt me."

"Allie, please—I'll be completely honest from here on out. You will never hear me tell a lie again. I want to be with you. When this all went bad, I began thinking about how much I wanted to have children with you. I'm coming to think about my life differently, and I'm willing to make changes and become a better person. Please, Allie, at least think about staying. I'm willing to do whatever it takes to keep you."

"I'm sure you are. I'm the only thing you have now. You've lost your job. You've got a fucked-up family. Oh, I didn't even begin to tell you how pissed I am about your father. Who are you, that you think you can have your dad call me and speak to me like that?"

"He was just trying to help me, but, yes, I'm sorry for that."

"And the operator. You cook up the craziest schemes. A woman claiming to be a telephone operator—who the hell knows who she really is—calls me at six A.M. She says she'd just gotten off work and was at home, but she'd spoken to you and knew you really wanted to talk with me. She asked if I would call you. Did you tell her to do that?"

"I tried to break in on your call, but her calling you directly was her idea."

"I don't think I even want to know what happened there. Where was I? Oh, yeah. You've lost your job. Your family is crazy. And you're known nationwide—probably *world*wide—as a liar. That's not what I signed up for. Do you know what I hate the most?"

"My family was trying to be as good as they can for me. I love them for that." Again I felt a little anger, as I had with Brian. Didn't she see that even if her life was bad, mine was in tatters? I knew I wasn't supposed to feel this way, and I tried to suppress it and collect myself. "I'm sorry," I added. "Please go ahead. What do you hate the most?"

"I hate that everyone knows my business. When I go to work, everyone looks at me and thinks, There's the poor girl whose boyfriend is a famous liar. When I go out and see our friends, they whisper. That's why I left New Jersey, so everyone wouldn't always know everything about me."

"Allison, please, I just want the opportunity to win back your love. Don't you think we might be able to find that love again? You know, like that song 'Where Is the Love?' "

"Listen to me carefully. I am only going to say this one time. I am not your mother. I have no obligation to love you unconditionally, because *you are not my child.* I love you conditionally, and you violated the conditions. End of story."

I looked at the ground. Then I asked her quietly if there was anything that could possibly save our relationship.

"Anything?"

"Anything. If we had endless time and endless resources, would there be something that could save us?"

"Endless couples therapy might do it," she said. "But we don't have endless time, and you're taxing my resources. So I need to get back to packing."

"Hold on one second. Is it possible that something less than infinite therapy might save our relationship? Say, a whole lifetime of therapy?"

"Yes, it is conceivable—although unlikely—that would work. But we're not going to—"

"So if it's possible that something less than infinite therapy might save us, then might it also be true that something less than that would at least give you enough information to know our relationship could be saved? Say, maybe ten years of therapy would convince you that with a lifetime of therapy, our relationship would be okay?"

"Yes, but—"

"So can't you imagine that just a month or two of therapy might show you what ten years might hold, and from there a lifetime?"

"I'm not going to a month or two of therapy with you, Stephen."

"Okay, what about one day? Just one session. After three years together, won't you give me one session to prove what might be done?"

"No."

"Why not? After three years, I'm only asking for one hour. They don't even give you the full hour, just forty-five minutes."

"I said no."

"Why?"

"First of all, I'm busy."

"You can't always be busy."

"After all the days I took off work to escape reporters, I'm going to be busy for a long time."

"You're not at work today."

"Fine, Stephen. If you can find a therapist who will take us today, I'll go for one session."

"You've got a deal."

I knew I didn't have time for a referral, so I just opened the Yellow Pages and began calling therapists, one after the other. I called dozens of psychiatrists, psychologists, and clinical social workers, but I reached only their answering machines or secretaries. Finally, after an hour of desperation, Dr. Irv Kantor called me back. He said he'd had a cancellation, and could see us at noon.

• • •

Allison and I arrived at Dr. Kantor's office in Cleveland Park a half hour early. We sat in chairs beside each other, separated by a pile of magazines. Allison drew a volume off the top and offered it to me, but I declined it.

"It's *National Geographic*," she pointed out. "I'm positive you're not going to bump into a story about yourself—unless you lied about a chimp."

"I said I was fine."

"You've got to read something, Stephen."

"Why?"

"Because I don't want to talk, and when you're not reading, you're talking."

"I'll be quiet. I just need to spend some time thinking about what I'm going to say in there."

Allison put down her magazine. "You're not supposed to plan out what you're going to say," she said. "When you think about what you're going to say, you don't end up saying what you're really thinking. Instead you say what you planned to say. There's a difference."

"So you're saying it's not therapeutic to think about the therapy?"

"Exactly."

I took a *National Geographic* off the pile and began to read. I just wanted to do this right, the way she wanted me to. It was my last chance.

Twenty minutes later, Dr. Kantor invited us into his office. He was a fat, bald man with a bushy brown beard and plaintive brown eyes. He was wearing a tie covered with leprechauns, rainbows, and treasure chests.

"Sit wherever you're most comfortable," Dr. Kantor instructed us.

Allison and I sat in chairs near the door. Across from us, there was a long, brown leather couch. It was old, and badly damaged, and I wondered if it was an antique placed in the office for appearance, rather than actual use.

"Does anyone lie on that?" I asked.

Dr. Kantor just looked at me.

"I was wondering if anyone actually used the couch, or if it was more like a prop."

"It's interesting that you use the word *prop,*" he said.

Shit. I had already said something wrong. I shouldn't have listened to Allison. I should have spent my time planning what I was going to say. At least I could have plotted out the opening few lines, which would have held me until I got comfortable.

"It's a theater term," Dr. Kantor went on. "It's like you're saying therapy is all some big performance."

"The word *prop* isn't that narrow," I said. "It can be used as a synonym for *accoutrement.* Anyway—"

"No, let's stick with this for a second," he said. "Allison, outside of the theater, have you ever heard the word *prop* used?"

"Absolutely not," she said. "When Stephen said *prop,* I too was thinking 'big show.'"

"And what do you make of that?" Dr. Kantor asked her.

"It's evidence that he's lost in the make-believe," she said.

"Very insightful," he replied.

I didn't protest any further. I wanted to stay focused on my goal: saving my relationship with Allison.

Allison explained briefly why we had come to therapy. She told Dr. Kantor about the stories I had invented, and my firing. He nodded and said he had read about it in the paper. Uh-oh. That was bad.

Allison spoke some more, but I didn't listen; I knew what she was going to say—she had said it all in the apartment, and I knew she was mostly right. The key, I thought, was what I could say in response, to convince her, and Dr. Kantor, that this relationship could work again.

But as I was trying to think about that, my attention was distracted by the sight of Dr. Kantor's navel. It had been revealed in a gap in his shirt where a button had come undone. Whenever Dr. Kantor shifted in his chair, which he did a lot, the leprechaun tie would swing slightly and, for a second, the navel would be exposed and it was the most intriguing belly button I had ever come across.

Dr. Kantor had an outie. I had never before seen an outie on an adult, excluding pregnant women. In fact, before this witnessing, I think I had believed outies were like baby teeth; I had assumed they fell out during adolescence, leaving only an innie behind.

"What do you think?" Dr. Kantor asked me after some time had passed—lost in my thoughts, I had no idea how much.

"I'm sorry. I wasn't paying attention."

"What were you thinking about?" he asked.

"I don't think I want to say."

"You have to say," he said. "That's the rule of therapy. You have to tell us what comes to mind. That's how we come to understand what you're really thinking."

He shifted in his chair another time, and the leprechaun tie swung once more, and I said the first thing that came to mind. Actually, I sang it: *"Frosted Lucky Charms. They're magically delicious!"*

"On the other hand, Stephen, I think we may have to move on to the second rule of therapy with you. And that rule is this: You need to listen to Allison when she is speaking. When she's speaking, she's the most important person in the room. Not cereal."

"Yes, sir," I said, for some reason.

Allison looked at me suspiciously, to check that I was paying attention now. Then she said she did not think she could continue in the relationship, and she wanted to end it. I had persuaded her to give one session of therapy a shot, but since I wasn't even listening to her, she should probably just forget about it. Dr. Kantor smiled at her kindly and nodded. Then he turned to me, and asked me why I wanted to stay in the relationship.

"I know I've made mistakes, but I will change," I said.

"That's *how* you'll stay in the relationship," he said. "My question is *why*. Allison thinks you only want to hold on to her because you've lost everything else. Why do you think *you* want to?"

"Can I think about it?"

"You can do whatever you want," he said. "But you only have

a limited time here—especially because you're only doing one session—so use it wisely."

"I think it's wise for me to think for a moment," I said.

No one said anything for a minute. Allison looked at Dr. Kantor, and Dr. Kantor looked at me. I thought about it carefully and realized, to my surprise, that succeeding in keeping Allison might not make me happier or better off. I had loved Allison in the beginning, but because I'd kept her so distant from the realities of my life—my fabrication and all the anxiety it both brought and vanquished—we hadn't been close for a long time. It might have changed if I'd stayed here in D.C. after I'd been fired, but our relationship had been so strained that I'd wanted to go home instead, and for once, I'd done what I wanted to do. It was all my fault, but the fact remained: We were no longer close, and now she was being cold and mean to me. Even if I'd caused it, it still affected me.

Still, even if I wasn't sure I wanted to stay with Allison, at least I knew I wanted to try to see if we could make it. And at last, I knew what I wanted to say—and it was the truth.

"I know there are problems in our relationship," I began, "but I think we used to have—we have—something wonderful, beneath it all. I still love Allison, and if Allison were to stick it out with me, I would know she'd love me no matter what, and I think, in time, we could get back what we had."

There was quiet.

"Well, we're getting toward the end of our time," Dr. Kantor said. "Normally with my patients I lean back more—I let them come to their own understandings over a period of time. But since you say you're only coming in for one session, I think I should just give you my opinions now, without any reservations. Is that okay with you?"

Allison and I both said yes.

"I think you should break up. Allison, I think you feel incredibly violated that everyone, as you say, 'knows your business.' I don't think you'll get over that anytime soon. You would probably get over it faster if you could work on it on your own, without the burden Stephen has placed on you. Stephen has lied to you and done some serious damage to your self-esteem and your sense of security and privacy. You are a victim, and it will be empowering for you to move out and get your own life started without him.

"Stephen, you need some serious help. You don't seem to recognize the seriousness of what you did. You seem to think, somewhere deep down, that Allison should be more forgiving of you. I can see you saying to yourself, 'Give me a break. This wasn't murder.' I think in fact what you did was very much *like* murder, and you need to come to terms with that. You hurt Allison deeply, in a way you don't yet seem to acknowledge. You killed the reputation of a magazine and dealt a serious blow to journalism as a whole."

I couldn't believe what he was saying. I had unwittingly chosen a psychiatrist who agreed with my worst critics. He would probably nod along with an article Nathan had mentioned that said I'd committed journalism genocide, and was the "Milosevic of magazines." Worse, Dr. Kantor had backed me into a corner: Protesting the murder comparison would seem to be an effort to disown what I had done, or at least to minimize it.

"My advice is this," Dr. Kantor concluded. "Move away from each other. Go to therapy separately. And, each of you should build a life for yourself apart from the other."

Allison accepted his card. I stood there mute.

I was stunned. I don't remember how I got myself from the chair out the door. All my blood pooled in my feet. My body felt like it weighed five hundred pounds. I doubted I could make it from the office to the car, a distance of maybe fifty yards. I had thought nothing bad could come of this: At worst, the therapist would side with Allison, but suggest more therapy; at best, Allison would agree to give the relationship another chance. Instead, the therapist had simply finalized our breakup—effectuated it, like a lawyer inking a deal.

Allison and I left the building in silence, walking side by side. Someday, I knew, I'd probably have to find another therapist—one who didn't judge me so harshly, and one I'd see alone—but the experience had hardly encouraged me to seek one out. I had learned something about myself in the session, but I thought it was despite Dr.

Kantor, not because of him. At least I'd told the truth; I wondered if Allison had sensed it, if she'd appreciated it.

Halfway to the car, Allison stepped ahead of me and turned, gripped me by the shoulders, and kissed me on the mouth.

"Let's go home and have breakup sex," she said.

"What?"

"You heard me."

In the car, Allison told me she had been moved by what I had said about our once having had something wonderful. While she probably didn't want to continue to date me, she said, she at least wanted to have one last fling. We could see what happened from there, but I shouldn't be too hopeful.

My heart was fluttering. I thought she must still care about me if she wanted to have sex with me one last time. Even if she claimed it was for "closure," I believed it was a sign that I still had a chance. I had to be good in bed, very good. And then, I had to be even better when the event was over. Perhaps I could win her back after all, if everything went perfectly. I still wasn't completely sure things between us would ever work, but at least I wanted the chance to try. And I definitely didn't want it to be Dr. Kantor who closed this door; if it had to be closed, if I had to lose this too, Allison and I should end it together.

As soon as we'd entered the apartment, Allison began taking off my shirt. In the foyer she had my belt off. In the living room, she pulled down my pants.

"We have to slow it down," I pleaded. "I'm going to go too fast."

"Well, let's go to the bedroom then," she said flirtatiously.

Allison ran up the steps, nimbly shucking her clothes as she went. She disappeared into the bedroom just as I, handicapped by the pants around my knees, made it to the stairway. There, I slipped off my pants and boxers and scurried upwards.

Suddenly there was a loud noise, and something fell and shattered, and Allison screamed, "Oh my fucking God." She ran out of the bedroom with a sheet pulled over her, screaming. I halted at the bedroom door and saw a terrifying sight.

There, standing in the bedroom, was my mother, packing my clothes.

Totally naked, I also screamed. With no bedsheet left to grab, I ran into the bathroom.

"Could someone please send in a towel?" I yelled. The bathroom was completely bare.

"They're all packed," my mom yelled back. "I have a T-shirt I was using as a rag."

"Fine, anything." I reached out and grasped for the shirt. It smelled of Lysol. I put it on anyway, caught my breath, and walked back out.

"I'm sorry. The super let me in," my mom said. "I found a new apartment for you already, so I came over here to get some of the packing done. I didn't know . . ."

Allison was holding the sheet around herself toga style. "It's over, Stephen," she said.

"But I thought . . ."

"I can't deal with this shit anymore."

"It's not my mother's fault that she's here. You said we had to be out in two days. She was just trying to help."

"I know it's not her fault. It's your fault, Stephen. I blame *you*. I just can't deal with you. Do you hear me? It's over."

"What about 'the something wonderful'?" I asked.

"Something wonderful? If it ever was wonderful, it is long gone. Now what we have is this," she said, and gestured to the sheet around her and then to my mom in the bedroom.

I told Allison that my mother and I would stay in a hotel for the night, and we would be back in the morning to pack and move out.

I didn't see Allison the next morning. And although I called and called, in the days that followed, sneaking the calls in when I knew my mom wouldn't overhear, I never saw Allison again. It was then

that I made the decision, having lost everything I had loved and val-
ued in this profession and in this city, to disappear from it and from
here.

It is only after one loses everything, and nothing more can be
taken away, that one can truly disappear. Disappearing and its companion, silence, are the ultimate in passive-aggression: the only
remaining powers the subject has against the journalist; the only powers the former journalist, who can no longer ask questions, but is
instead forced to face them, retains.

And so I disappeared.

The next day, I moved into the new apartment my mom had found. As
we'd discussed, it was outside the District—a studio on the eighth
floor of a high-rise named The Harvey, which was in Jeffersonville,
Virginia. Unfortunately, it was less than one mile from the Olde Jeff
office complex that had been the site of my undoing—the place where
I'd lost everything, where Robert had had his final face-off with the
security guard and then with me. I might not have chosen to live in
Jeffersonville, if I'd been looking for a place myself, but I hadn't told
my mom to avoid it, and anyway, at least the Olde Jeff complex
wasn't visible from my new home, so I didn't mind being here so
much. At least it wasn't D.C.—or anywhere like it.

Technically, The Harvey was twelve and one-tenth miles, by the
car's odometer, from Dupont Circle. But each of those miles might
have been a hundred. Jeffersonville is a leafy, inside-the-Beltway Virginia suburb where the retired elderly and the well-off young live. Its
tree-lined streets are littered with children's bikes and toys. Fathers
(and sometimes mothers) take the Brown Line to work, and always
come home in time for dinner. It is a bit like Lakeside that way, and
that may have been why it appealed to my mother.

The Harvey, however, did not partake of this general bucolic
pleasantness. It was a halfway house for people in transit, or at least
in transition—students, recent immigrants, and contract workers on
temporary assignments whose families had stayed back at home. No

one wanted to stay at The Harvey for more than a few years; everyone was waiting for a graduation, a better offer, a green card. But some stayed anyway, despite their best intentions.

The Harvey, in accordance with its limbo-like nature, was defined by urgent uniformity. The apartments, each precisely the same size and painted Liquid Paper white, were plugged into the building like fuses. I imagined that somewhere in the Nevada desert, near Yucca Mountain, there existed a plat filled with identical, prefabricated empty apartments stacked one on top of the other, waiting to be substituted into the building when ours wore out.

The Harvey, I thought, was the perfect place for my exile— which had been both real, I believed, and self-imposed. If I'd tried to stay in Dupont Circle, I think the same journalists who had hounded Allison would have tried to drive me out—making it literally impossible for me to stay there; banishing me, in effect, from the jurisdiction. But I could have moved anywhere, and I had chosen—or let my mother choose—this place just outside D.C., perhaps to make my exile palpable, to remind myself that I had not left but been cast out.

Over the next few days, my mom helped me move in. She unpacked my boxes, ran my errands, and organized my single closet, which, when she was finished, housed a double rainbow of clothing. On the left were my shirts, ordered one by one from dark blue to light blue to white; on the right were my pants, sorted in descending gradations of brown and gray.

Under her direction, every nook of the apartment was brought into order. Toiletries were arranged by height in the medicine cabinet, so that every bottle of Advil, roll of dental floss, and nail clipper could be removed without disturbing any other article. In my top dresser drawer, socks were organized, pair by pair, in a little death row, according to the life they had left. "Make sure you use the oldest socks first," my mom said. "That way you always have a brand-new, perfect pair in case you need them."

Most of the time, I sat on the couch, broke down the boxes my mother had so carefully unpacked, and plotted ways to send her home. "When do you think you'll be going back to Lakeside?" I asked.

"I hope that doesn't sound like I'm forcing you out," I added, before she could respond. "I'm just wondering."

"I don't really know," she replied, and returned to her work dusting my videotapes.

"That's cool," I said.

One of the reasons for my feeling of exigency was that when I slept, my mom lay near me on the sofa bed, which, when unfolded, was separated from my own bed by a mere six inches. She was quiet, but her presence there couldn't help but remind me how much I'd disappointed her, and so I found it hard to sleep. When I tried, I'd haul out old, nearly forgotten dreams—the pre-firing dreams, the happy ones—and attempt to return into them. But after a minute or two, the picture would go dead and my mother would appear, like a house manager bringing up the lights, and announce that due to circumstances beyond her control, the night's dreams were canceled.

Not only was she in my house, now she was also occupying my mind.

When my dad called the following day, I tried a slightly more aggressive approach. "It really sounds like he misses you," I said. "Maybe you'd like to head home tomorrow? I'm sure I could take care of the rest here."

"He's fifty-five years old. He can handle himself."

But I persisted. "Mom, I don't mean to be pushy, but I think you can probably go home tomorrow," I said. "You've done virtually everything."

"I'm not going back until you're settled in here."

"But I am settled," I said. "Everything's put away."

"You're moved in, but you're not settled. There's a difference."

"How will we know when I'm settled?"

"I'll know when you're settled."

"But how?"

"I'm your mother. A mother knows when her son is settled."

I gave up for the moment, but as the day passed, it wore on me. At 9:30 P.M., already exhausted, I washed my face, brushed my teeth, and got into bed.

"You're going to sleep so early?" my mom asked.

"I'm very tired from all the unpacking," I explained.

My mother changed into a sweatsuit and climbed into the sofa bed, and both of us began to read quietly. About an hour later, when I came to the end of a chapter, I clicked off the only light in the apartment that was still on.

"Hey, I'm here too," my mom said in the dark. "You could ask me before you turn out the light. I'm in the middle of a sentence."

"Sorry," I said, and turned it back on. "Can we go to sleep now?"

She didn't have time to reply before I shouted, "Good!" and switched the light off again.

In the dark, I could tell my mother was fuming.

"What do you want from me?" she burst out. "I'm trying to be a good mother. Don't you see that? It's not my idea of a fun time, coming here and helping you move, schlepping your boxes, unpacking you. Hip, hip, hooray—let's move Stephen! You think this is the way I want to spend my time?"

I said nothing, but I turned on the light again. My mother was sitting up straight in the bed, and she was angry. "Answer me," she demanded. "Do you?"

"No," I said.

"You're right, it isn't. I'm doing this for you. If I weren't here, you'd be in a mess of boxes and you wouldn't be unpacked and . . . Stevie, your life is falling apart. You don't have a job, and you're not looking. I see you staring off into space all the time. You only have an apartment because I found you one. You need help."

My mom stood up and faced me, looking small and weary in her sweatsuit. "You need me," she said. "Even if you don't realize it. You needed someone to help you, and I did that. You didn't have anyone else. You need to get something straight: I'm not asking for you to be thankful. Honestly. I'm not even asking for you to understand everything I've done to help you. I recognize that you can't see things clearly right now. I'm just asking you not to be mean to me. You turn off the light on me and pretend I don't exist?"

"I'm sorry, Mom. I didn't mean to do that. I just want to be on my own a bit. Can't you see it's hard on me?"

"Hard on you? Do you know how much harder it would be if I weren't here? Do you know what most parents would have done? Do you know what Jamie Roth's mom did, when Jamie's husband divorced her? Did she help her move into a new apartment? No. Jamie had an eighteen-month-old and was moving heavy boxes by herself, with the baby at her feet. How would you like that?"

"I wouldn't, but . . ."

"No, you wouldn't. So before you get all angry with me for being here, think about why I'm doing this. I'm trying to help you get on with your life again. Now let's go to sleep."

She turned out the light again and climbed back into the sofa bed. I should have stayed quiet and gone to sleep. In the morning, everything would have been fine. But I couldn't.

"Mom, I don't think you're doing this just for me," I said in the dark. "I think you're doing this for *you* too. I think you can't stand the idea of being in Lakeside while this is happening to me. Your friends are all talking about it. It embarrasses you. It's easier for you to be here than there. I know you want to make it better, but making it better is not the same as doing it *for* me. I need to do it by myself."

"Are you saying you want to flail about, for God knows how long, until you figure out what you're going to do?" she asked. "That's just stupid, Stephen. What makes sense is for you to take help from me when you need it. And I can't think of a time when you've needed it more."

"Maybe that's the reason I fucked up, Mom. I've been thinking about it a lot. I never really grew up. I'm not my own person. I'm your son, or Dad's son, or Allison's boyfriend, or Brian's best friend, or the *Weekly*'s star writer, trying to make everyone happy. I was always trying to please everyone and then I just couldn't do it anymore."

"Hold on. You're blaming me for *your* making up stories?"

"No."

"It sure sounds like it."

"I'm not. Not at all, Mom. All I'm saying is that maybe, just maybe, me doing this on my own will get me onto a better track."

"What are you talking about?"

"Mom, I want you to go home. I want you to go back to Lakeside."

"So let it be written, so let it be done," she replied and then she got up, turned on the light once again, and began loudly packing her single bag, noisily zipping and unzipping it a dozen times.

"What are you doing?" I asked. "It's almost midnight."

"I'm going to the airport."

"There are no flights for hours. Let's go to sleep and talk about it in the morning."

"No, Stephen. You've been really clear. You want me to stop trying to fix your life. Well, I'm stopping right now. I'll wait at the airport and get on the first plane out. It will let you get started sooner at putting your life back together on your own, all by yourself. I'm sure it will be better that way."

And with that, she walked out.

I opened the door and called out to her, "Mom, please, come back. Please!" But she said nothing in return, and I heard the elevator doors close behind her.

I scrambled back into my apartment, threw on pants and a shirt, rushed back into the hall, and pressed the Down button.

The Harvey had four elevators, but only one ever seemed to be working. I could see my mother's elevator slowly moving down to the first floor, while the other three remained asleep. As it began its excruciating return, as I yelled at it to move faster.

"Come on, you fucking elevator. Do your job."

Yes, it's at three! We're making progress. But moments go by and we're not at four. What the fuck is it doing? Who, at this hour, is picking up the elevator at three and wants to go up? No one. It's nighttime. People are either leaving the building or coming in. No one is going from floor three to, say, six. It can't be a person. The elevator must be stopping to talk to its fellow nonfunctional elevators—an elevator sympathy call.

Finally, when hope seemed lost, the elevator smugly exposed itself to me, as if it had hauled itself up from the Earth's core. It was empty. Warily, I got in.

Two floors below, the elevator stopped, and a brunette woman in her thirties entered. She had a small Lhasa apso on a plaid leash. Her hair was back in a ponytail, and even in my rush, I noticed that she was beautiful. She put her hand in the door, to keep it open for a friend who was nowhere to be seen.

"I'm sorry, but is anyone coming?" I said after about ten seconds. "I'm in a hurry."

"My friend just went back to get her makeup," the woman explained.

Ten more seconds passed.

"Do you think you could maybe step out and just get the next one?"

"There is no next one," she said. "It's the only one working, and it takes forever to come. You should know that, you live here, don't you? She'll only be a second. Plus, Milton Rosenbaum really has to pee."

I looked around for an old Jewish man.

"That's my dog's name," she said.

Many more seconds passed. All valuable time for my mother to get away.

"What's your rush, anyway?" she asked.

"My mom is mad at me," I told her lamely. "She fled."

"Oh, I see," she said, and kept holding the elevator door.

"Do you know where my lipstick is?" a woman's voice called from down the hall.

"Frost or matte?" the woman in the elevator with me called back.

"Matte," the far-off woman yelled back.

"Melbourne or Morocco or Haifa?"

"Haifa."

"That's what I'm wearing," my elevator companion shouted. "It's in the top left bathroom drawer, on the right-hand side."

I raised my eyebrows at her.

"And you better come quick, Heather," she yelled. "The guy in the elevator is pissed off."

As she gripped the elevator door, I noticed that her nails were the same shade of Haifa as her lips.

"Tell him I'm going as fast as I can," Heather shouted. "Doesn't he know the elevator takes forever?"

"It's taking forever because of you," I muttered.

Another ten seconds passed, but Heather did not present herself. Milton Rosenbaum began to look every which way and make little whimpering noises.

"That's not the right color, it's not red enough," Heather shouted, still inside her apartment with the door open.

"You want South Beach then, which is actually a frost," my helpful elevator companion replied. "Check my makeup bag, in the pocket. Maybe you can mix two colors?"

"That's it," I said. I lifted the woman up by her waist, deposited her just outside the elevator, and shooed Milton Rosenbaum out.

"Go, little boy. Follow your mommy," I said to the dog, using my shoe to block him from reentering.

Meanwhile, the woman tried to push back in, but I fought her out. We slapped at each other—me with only one hand, because the other was employed pressing the Close Door button; she with Haifa-coated ice-pick nails—until the door closed completely. I heard a final scream of rage, but by then the elevator had begun to descend.

When I got to the lobby, my mother was gone. It was drizzling outside, and two or three taxis were waiting in front of the building's entrance, as they did every night. They knew that a high-rise like The Harvey—many of whose tenants were students at nearby schools—never really went to bed. Someone was always needing to go to the emergency room, or wanting to go out drinking, or sending someone they had just slept with home in the middle of the night.

I knocked on the first driver's window and asked if he had seen a woman in a gray sweat suit come by. He said she had gotten into a cab, which had driven off.

"Which airport was she headed toward?" I asked.

"What am I, a detective?"

I stood in the rain, which was getting heavier, and looked down the road in both directions for the red taillights of my mother's taxi, but there was just the white reflection of streetlights in black puddles. It was too late. My mother was long gone and there was no way to bring her back. She had probably gotten the cab a second after she'd hit the lobby.

Now she was unreachable. A few years back, Nathan and I had bought her a cell phone for her birthday, but she never carried it; she kept it in her car for emergencies, and her car was back in Lakeside, with the life she'd left to come help me. When I remembered that, I almost started to cry.

"I said, do you want a cab, or what?" the cabdriver asked me. "It's raining in my window."

I said no and walked back inside.

PART FOUR

DOSSIER

HERE IS where I lose you.

This is all good and fine, you say, but before we go on, before there can be forgiveness, I need to tell you more. All of the key questions, I have carefully stepped around thus far, I know that. I know you know it too: What was I thinking when I wrote those lies? What did it feel like? Where did the ideas even come from? Wouldn't it have been easier just to tell the truth? How did I ever get away with it?

The questions are there, they hang in the air unspoken and they just won't go away, no matter how I try to ignore them, no matter what song and dance I might offer you. Until the questions are answered, you say, we cannot go on. After all, the criminal defendant who wants to plead guilty to his crimes, serve his sentence, and be allowed to return to society, is required not only to declare his crimes, but also to allocute—to confess to the details of them.

It's not enough for him to say he's sorry and accept his punishment. No, the murderer, the rapist, the check kiter, the embezzler must, in his own words, state for the record exactly what he did wrong, and how he did it. That is what everyone wants, the victims especially. They want to see whether the defendant bends a smile when he explains how he lifted the wallet out of the little old lady's purse. Is his regret genuine? Or does he enjoy, just a bit, the reliving of what, at the time at least, might have seemed like the perfect crime?

Give up the details; I know, it's necessary. And you ask me to believe that the more I tell you, the easier it will be for you to forget. But I fear that when I tell you what it actually did feel like, when I tell you what I was thinking when I fabricated, you will never be able to forgive. Indeed, it may be the very particularity, the selfsame specificity, that makes it unforgivable.

• • •

Still, here are the details.

The first time I invented a story was early in my tenure at the *Weekly*. It was a story about Felix Rizzoli—now a footnote to history, but then, and for several years to follow, a young D.C. player. Rizzoli had been an analyst on the State Department's Policy Planning staff whom President Clinton respected for his reserve and discretion. In July 1995, after the Senate held the Whitewater hearings, the President abruptly elevated him to a spokesman position. The bespectacled young man who always wore tweeds was suddenly on the nightly news, fielding questions from the White House press corps.

Unlike his predecessor, who had returned reporters' barbs, Rizzoli was calm, and tried to defuse them. When challenged, he said things like, "That's an excellent point. I'll have to raise it with the President." Attackers who had expected to follow up with another challenge were left empty-mouthed.

At first, the conventional wisdom was that Rizzoli was too much of an egghead for the job; the public wouldn't connect with someone who had written a thesis on Adlai Stevenson. Soon, it was widely believed, the mistake would be realized, and Rizzoli would be demoted. But then, only weeks after the conventional wisdom had been firmly established, a new, contrarian conventional wisdom set in—Rizzoli was a great success and, in fact, his nerdiness was his genius.

A *Weekly* attack piece was inevitable.

This was my break, I thought: Rizzoli happened to have been a junior at Lakeside High when I was a freshman. Even better, he had been my gym leader, supervising my daily P.E. period.

At the magazine's weekly story conference, I pitched the piece— explaining that Rizzoli was hardly the timid academic the *Herald, Post,* and *Times* had portrayed him to be. In actuality, he had been "Rowdy Rizzi," a notorious bully. Everyone liked the reversal. At just the time when the conventional wisdom had settled on the idea that this was a good job for a nerd, we would be saying Rizzoli wasn't a nerd in the first place; he was a thug in geek's clothing.

I remembered a crucial game of dodgeball. Rizzi, as P.E. leader, had been a veritable bombardment fanatic. The game terrified me, and so my response when I got a ball, which was rare, was simply to hold on to it as an S.D.I.-like defensive measure—I could throw it at incoming missiles intended for my head, and deflect them. Rizzi didn't like this and during one game, near the end of the semester, he grabbed the ball out of my hands, and then urged the other team to throw their balls at me. "Glass is unprotected," he yelled out. "Get Glass."

And they did. All of them. I felt like I was being stoned.

All the writers at the *Weekly* were excited by the idea. There was energy here: "What else?" they asked. "What else?" I knew that if the piece was good enough, it could be a cover story—my first. But I didn't have anything else. Not yet, anyway. So what I said was, "There's much more," and that I'd write up a draft and circulate it.

I hoped Nathan would have some good stories—he'd been a little kid when Rizzi reigned, but he'd had his run-ins with him too. Unfortunately, he didn't remember anything except a sort of general meanness, and "something to do with a seesaw."

I called Rizzi's former classmates and teachers too, but they didn't really have any good anecdotes either. Reporters think in anecdotes; most other people do not, except maybe at Thanksgiving dinner. A former math teacher said Rizzi was "callous." Excellent, but how? "He just was," the teacher said. A neighbor said he was "hot under the collar." Yes, yes, tell me about it. When did you notice that? What did you see or hear that made you think that? "I don't remember," the neighbor said. "We all just knew it."

Inside, I began to panic. I needed this piece to work, and for it to work, I needed a few little set pieces involving Rizzi, illustrating his character. I checked in with the usual gossips—the same Lakeside parents, ironically, who would later rumor-monger about me—but they had nothing. No anecdotes at least, just lots of nasty adjectives.

For my story to even *be* a story, I needed another item, a capper—

a final, smoking-gun detail that would finish Rizzoli off. The article could run with dodgeball and something else, but it could never run on dodgeball alone; it would look too petty. In journalism, one anecdote exposes a youthful indiscretion. It takes two anecdotes to reveal an inner truth.

So I made the capper up.

It was about Rizzi cheating on a test, by looking at my paper. I said *he* was never caught, but that *I* came very close to being caught, and even blamed as the cheater. I also said Rizzi had gotten angry at me—actually, threatened to hit me—for initially covering the paper with my hand, even though, trembling with fear, I had eventually removed it and let him look on.

I was so close—I'd gone to the same high school as Rizzi—but so far; I just didn't have enough for a piece on him. It might have occurred to some other reporters, I think, to fabricate in this situation—but it would have been just a crazy notion, a temptation to be immediately dismissed as immoral and impossible. The difference was that I actually *did* it—I did what others only imagined. And what people later wondered, when they finally learned what I had done—what Allison had wondered aloud, and what my parents must have wondered, and what I knew Brian and Lindsey could never comprehend—was, Why did I cross the line? Why did I actually *do* it, and not just think it? What made me both so weak, and so heedless?

Here is the answer: In part, it was because I wanted to be recognized as having written a great article—not just a good one, but an exceptional one. I wanted it more than other people, perhaps, because I wanted it not venally or narcissistically, but desperately, even pathetically. I didn't really want the money, or the public acclaim, or to be on television. (Though I didn't mind them either.) What I truly wanted was to be well regarded by the people around me—actually, to be loved by them.

In the moment I considered fabricating, then, I felt the strong pull of that need. And it seemed to fall into a groove inside me—a certain channel in my personality. I am compulsively imaginative, and by that, I mean I am always speculating, wondering, considering, and writing the world around me into a story. I remained a child this way long after I graduated from college, and at the time I fabricated, it had not yet been in me to grow up: to face the difference between my stories and realities, between the way I imagined things to be and the way they actually were. I was suggestible; I was escapist; I was immature; I was rebellious; at some level, I think, I was angry—furious at the drab, indifferent world, which never came close to living up to my Technicolor imaginings of it. The world, to me, was not a stage, it was a weary office where success cost a pound of flesh and promised little satisfaction.

And so, when I thought of fabricating, my thoughts slipped smoothly into that same groove of imagination, elaboration: I don't have a good anecdote for this, dammit, I'd think. This piece is not good. It sucks, it's awful. *I'm* not good, I'm not a good journalist. What if Rizzi had cheated on a test or something? That would be so great; it would complete the story. Actually, I think I heard he *did* cheat on a test once. I think if he had cheated, this is how it would have been: He'd have cheated off someone, and been not grateful, but angry. That was the type of guy he was—the kind who hated you for your own weakness, even your own generosity. I bet at some point, he probably did cheat, and that was probably just the way it went. In fact, I'm beginning to remember now, maybe I didn't just hear this story about Rizzi; maybe he cheated off of *me.*

And then I started to type. The gap was breached, and there was no going back, or at least it felt that way to me. I had left the truth on the other side of some divide, a gulf, and there was no returning.

I kept typing.

But what about the fact checkers? How did I outsmart my seasoned editors? Was I some kind of evil genius? Some journalists wrote articles suggesting as much, but it wasn't really that way. Just as I wasn't really a wunderkind, I wasn't a malevolent mastermind either.

A story I wrote about animal rights activists who break into people's homes and try to liberate their pets provides a good example of how I got away with it. I called it "The Catnappers." Here's a brief excerpt:

Derek Juliano grabs the Yorkie and runs for the front door, which Patricia Conway holds open.

"Little girl, you're going to be free," he says to the dog in his arms. A pink bow in her hair bounces as he runs.

Conway yells at Juliano to run faster. "They'll be home any minute," she says. "Come on. We've got to get out of here."

. Juliano and Conway have a plan ready in case they're caught. They'll say they're dog groomers and must have come to the wrong house accidentally. They don't know if it will work. They have never been caught.

Outside the house, Conway and Juliano, holding the dog, run to a small ravine fifty yards away. I chase after them. Juliano places the dog at the edge of the ravine, near a steep slope. "You're no longer a slave," Conway says to the Yorkie, as she ceremoniously removes the dog's tag. "You're free to live your life the way *you* want to."

"Be fruitful and multiply," says Juliano. "They shalt not neuter thee."

They chant together: "All things bright and beautiful, all creatures great and small, all things wise and wonderful, the Lord God made them all."

"Amen," I say.

The three of us pile into the getaway car, which is parked near the ravine entrance, and Conway and Juliano bow their heads for a moment of prayer. I watch the Yorkie.

She begins to run back toward her home.

"She's going back," I say to them.

Juliano and Conway jump out of the car, recapture the dog, and return her to the ravine. Again, the dog runs back toward her home. After repeating this another time, the pair, out of breath, bring the dog, who is very nervous, back into the car.

"This happens sometimes," Conway says. "Dogs have been

subjugated for so many generations, they sometimes think they want to return to their captors."

"Canine Stockholm Syndrome," Juliano explains.

We drive the dog six miles to the far end of the ravine, where Juliano and Conway insert her into the wild, too far away to find her way back to oppression.

After I finished writing "The Catnappers," it was edited by Ian. "There needs to be a time peg," he said. "The reader needs to know why this is important now." I added a paragraph noting that Juliano and Conway were part of a nascent movement to give mammals full constitutional rights. (While this was technically true, the movement, at the time, was so nascent as to be barely embryonic.)

But Ian said that wasn't enough. I added another line, explaining that the movement was "gaining steam," and he approved it. Then he passed the story to Victoria, a seventy-five-year-old Canadian woman who was the grandmother of six and fact-checked virtually the entire magazine. Every year, for the past ten years, Victoria had announced her retirement and every year, days before her retirement party, she had said she just couldn't bear to leave.

I know exactly how Victoria fact-checked the story, because I had played a large role in assessing the system. When Robert took over as editorial director, he asked me to review the magazine's procedures. The *Weekly*'s system was considered a very good one, modeled on the industry's standard, but he thought perhaps it could be even better. Unfortunately, in choosing me, Robert had unwittingly chosen the worst possible person—someone with an incentive to undermine the system, not to improve it. In the end, though, I mostly just left it alone; it was already susceptible enough to the unscrupulous.

Under the system as it had been, and as it remained despite my mandate to improve it, Victoria dealt with spelling first. She would read a story and circle all proper nouns with an orange pen. She then confirmed the spelling against *The New York Times, The Washington Post,* the *Los Angeles Times,* and *The Wall Street Journal.* If there was any discrepancy—and surprisingly often, there was—she would research the etymology of the word, make a determination, and issue a memo to the staff. Spelling was Victoria's passion. During staff meetings and in the lunchroom, she would quiz writers on her memos and become dismayed that few had read them. Famously, in 1988, Victoria became so upset that a writer, despite her many memos, had spelled Qaddafi with a K, that she resigned from the magazine for a week.

After spelling issues were resolved, Victoria, using a blue pen, underlined every factual statement in the story and then, using a green pen, she numbered them. She then looked to verify each fact, and on a lined sheet of paper, she would record the source for the fact in red pen. In doing so, she consulted a list entitled "Acceptable Forms of Verification" (which I have included for your perusal below).

If a particular statement could not be authenticated with standard reference materials, Victoria would circle the fact's number in black ink and ask the writer to prove the assertion. Once he or she did so, Victoria would record the proof beside the number, in purple ink. (Again, she consulted "Acceptable Forms of Verification," to make sure that what the writer had provided was sufficient.) Keeping the colors in order was deemed essential to the system. Writers at the magazine were often warned about the slippery slope of color-coding carelessness. A glossy color chart explaining the significance of each color was handed out to all staff members periodically.

Because I had been charged with reviewing the magazine's system, I knew its weaknesses, and I'm ashamed to admit that I took full advantage of them. I saw that the fact-checking system was, at base, designed to assist reporters in writing accurate stories. It operated under the very reasonable assumption that the writers wanted their stories to be true. And so I knew that all the color coding—and the degree to which it was insisted upon—provided a false sense of security. The system was still vulnerable to writers who wanted to subvert it. And unlike other writers, I needed to do just that; I felt I needed to find the holes.

Thus, while other writers found fact checking to be a nuisance and tried to avoid it, I—ironically, in retrospect—always concentrated on the process. I always made it easy for Victoria. Indeed, more than that, I actually did her work for her, as if it were a kind of courtesy. I underlined the supposed facts in a copy of my story in blue, and numbered each of them in green. Then I supplied verification (in purple of course) to support each of the underlined statements. Eventually I even got her to work off of my initial markup, instead of her own. (Manipulative, yes, but not exactly brilliant.) And at each step of the way, I frequently falsified.

Here's Victoria's rulebook—with some additional comments from me on how one goes about coming up with "acceptable forms of verification":

ACCEPTABLE FORMS OF VERIFICATION, IN ORDER OF PRIORITY

1. *The New York Times*—The gold standard. If it was printed in the *Times,* it was accepted as true by the *Weekly,* absent overwhelming evidence to the contrary. It did not matter that the *Times* does not itself regularly employ fact checkers.

    For my "Catnappers" story, I found a story in which the *Times* referred to a Yorkshire terrier as a "Yorkie." This proved to Victoria that the breed existed, and the nickname was acceptable. Never mind that it was common knowledge, Victoria still had to check it off. Seeing it in the *Times* was deemed better than having a live Yorkie yapping at your feet.

2. All other newspapers. For "Catnappers," I used the NEXIS database to print out a story from a Nebraska paper that defined Stockholm Syndrome as a "psychological condition in which one begins to sympathize with one's captor." This was accepted by Victoria as proof of the term.

3. All other printed material. I photocopied part of a map to prove to Victoria that there is a ravine in the city in which "Catnappers" supposedly took place. This was considered exemplary verification by me. Topography and weather were checked only if they were absolutely essential to a story.

4.   Reporter's notes. Facts that could not be verified by any outside publications—say, my supposed interviews with the catnappers—were checked against a reporter's notes. Victoria would check to make sure that every detail in the story corresponded with a note the reporter had made prior to publication.

Notes, of course, lay at the root of my fabrication. My notes themselves were often fabricated. To hide the fabrication, I made sure they were formally perfect. I made sure to include a first page for every person interviewed (whether real or fictional), with the name spelled out in large block letters, with dashes between them, so Victoria would be confident I had asked the subject to spell his or her name. And I always added the requisite accompanying phone number, though sources were never called without talking to the reporter first.

I should note that for the lottery story on which I was finally caught, I was in a rush, and so was Victoria, so I'd created only the sketchiest of notes for her. They were so bad I'd trashed them after the process was over, thinking I'd replace them with a better set; but then I'd moved on to another story and forgotten all about it. That was why I'd had to fabricate more for Robert. For most other stories, I was far more careful, and the notes looked perfect by the time Victoria received them.

AN UNACCEPTABLE FORM OF VERIFICATION

1.   The reporter himself. Nothing was assumed to be true just because a reporter said it happened. It must be written down somewhere. In this respect, the *Weekly*'s system was tighter than those of many other publications, which accepted "On Author" verifications—at least informally—and as a result, soon found themselves effectively not fact checking at all.

Every so often a freelancer, annoyed by this policy, would say, "So if I just write it down, will it be okay?" Victoria said no. But in reality, though, it worked this way—at least when I was the reporter:

For "Catnappers," after reviewing my fact-verification packet, Victoria told me I had missed a fact: "You need to verify that the dog was very nervous when she was brought into the car," she said.

I told her I believed it was a matter of opinion. (Opinions, unlike facts, need not be checked.)

"Whether or not the dog was very nervous is a fact," she replied. "Either she was or she wasn't."

"How can we ever know that for a fact?" I asked. "The dog can't speak and tell me about her anxiety."

"It can't go in the magazine unless you can prove it's true," she retorted.

"All right," I said. "I'll try to figure out something."

I called a veterinarian and read the article to her.

"Did that really happen?" the vet asked me.

I didn't answer her question. Instead, I said, "I'm calling because I need to know if you think it's true to say the dog would be nervous?"

"This whole thing is horrible," she said.

"Yes, it is," I said. "But I need to know for the fact checker—"

"How do you live with yourself?" the vet asked. "You watched them do it, and you could have stopped it, and yet you did nothing? What kind of person are you?"

"The dog was shaking a bit when she was in the car," I continued. "Her legs trembled. Does that indicate she was nervous, very nervous?"

"I hope you rot in hell," the vet said and hung up.

I wrote in a notepad: "Dog's hind legs trembling means 'I'm extremely worried,' according to vet." Then I wrote down the vet's name and number and brought the page to Victoria. She read what I handed her and said it was sufficient.

Don't blame Victoria. The truth was, she had no choice. No one was going to let a story be held up because of questions about whether a dog was nervous. But no one was going to let Victoria turn her work in until she had checked off every single item, either.

Don't blame Robert, either. He had reasonably trusted his staff to apply a fact-checking system that was common throughout journalism, and had even entrusted me with trying to improve it. And under that system, he was alerted only when there was a fact-checking problem, and I always made sure my stories didn't raise red flags. So unless Robert had decided to simply take over Victoria's job and turn it into a full trial-style interrogation and cross-examination, there was really nothing he could have done to catch me. Indeed, even if he'd told Victoria that every single source a reporter quoted had to be called, it still wouldn't have worked.

When Victoria asked to call a subject to check a quote or fact, I often said things like, "The source was nervous about the press, she didn't want to talk to anyone but me. . . . I'll call her up and double-check it right now, though."

I would then go to my office, wait ten or fifteen minutes, and then tell her that the source had approved the quote. Or, worse, to make it more plausible, I would say that the subject okayed the quote, but with a few tiny sentence-structure changes, or with an additional sentence or two.

If Victoria still persisted on calling a source in the story, I would drop the individual from the article and moot her demands. I'd say the source just wasn't right for the piece, or make up some other journalistic reason for eliminating him or her from the story.

I say all this not to excuse or exculpate myself in any way, but to explain. My only purpose here is to answer your question—the how question. And perhaps to ask your forgiveness for the answer I must give.

I can never exculpate what I did: It was simply and purely wrong— and what I did with Victoria only worsened it. The problem wasn't her, or Robert, or the system itself. The problem was me: I saw immediately that this was a system based on trust, I convinced Victoria to trust me, and then I abused her trust. My only point is this: I did not have to be an evil genius to do it. The fact-checking system just wasn't designed with someone like me in mind, and that said far more about me than about it.

• • •

That, then, was the how. And here is a little of the why—the beginning, perhaps, of the why. When the first few fabricated stories were
done, and fact-checked, and the articles were turned in, my editors
loved them; more than that, they loved *me*—I felt it. My colleagues
did, too. So did editors from other magazines, who called to tell me
they had enjoyed my piece, and to keep their magazines in mind if I
had an idea that might work for them.

And the more stories I fabricated, the more Robert and Ian considered me for cover stories; the more plum assignments they gave
me; and the more freelance offers I received. And so, in the years that
followed my first fabrication, I would pitch many more stories that I
knew I never could honestly write.

My pitches were famous in the office because they bubbled with
excitement. It wasn't always the content of the proposed articles—
I sometimes wrote about exceedingly dull Washington topics—it was
that my excitement to write the story was catching. But what I was
enthusiastic about, of course, was not the story, which was merely a
tale I'd told myself; it was the next chance to make them all fall in
love with me all over again.

That was how it was, and how it felt, and how I did it. But, you ask,
what about the deeper why—and the what happened next?

The what happened next I can certainly tell you, but the rest of
the why will have to wait. I'm not being cagey, I promise; it's only
that I had to wait for it, too. Throughout the time that followed my firing, I slowly and gradually came to see the real why, and the deeper
how, the how I needed to learn: how to stop lying.

PART FIVE

DESPERATION

AFTER MY mother had left for the airport, and I'd finally gotten down to The Harvey's lobby and realized I'd missed her, I got into bed and looked for sleep, but I couldn't find it. Finally, after hours of tossing and turning, I decided just to get my day going. I waited until 5 A.M., because that was the earliest hour I thought I could convince my body that it was enjoying an early start, rather than an endless night.

I got up, brushed my teeth, showered, shaved, dressed, made myself breakfast, and then realized I had nothing else to do. I knew I should start looking for a job—any job—but I didn't want to face the process, not for a few days at least. I knew I'd be rejected everywhere, and I didn't want to learn where I'd end up. I might even have to return to Lakeside, where a friend of my parents might take pity on me.

Desperate to avoid starting what I knew would be a painful process, I logged on to the Internet. There were four emails from Cliff. I read only the most recent:

Dear Steve,

I don't know if you're getting my emails, but I thought I'd try another time. Allison told me you moved out. Again, I am so sorry about everything that happened. Is there a new number where I can reach you?

Please call me. The interview will be at your convenience. You tell me when and where, and I will be there. You can even limit the topics we discuss. Call me, and we'll set the ground rules.

Again, please call. Time is of the essence.

Your Friend Always,
Cliff

I didn't write back. I didn't want to give anyone an interview, and especially not Cliff. I'd seen Cliff's face at the airport—the glint of glee—and I knew exactly what kind of an interview he had in mind. If he'd promised an interview to his editor, that was his problem, not mine; I decided.

I felt lonely and alone. Still online, I searched for a chat room in which I might distract myself. A dating room titled "Sexy Librarians" sounded the most promising. I clicked to enter. Several men and women—or at least, persons with male and female screen names— were inside. A woman named Beth had challenged everyone in the room to name a Janus word—a word that is its own antonym. Her example was "sanction," meaning both "to approve" and "to penalize."

"Jumbo shrimp," one person wrote. "Jumbo means big and shrimp means small."

"I don't think you understand," Beth wrote. "It has to be one word."

"Military intelligence," another offered. "Military = dumb. Intelligence = smart."

Several people wrote LOL after that one: "Laughing Out Loud." One even wrote ROTFL: "Rolling on the Floor Laughing." (Laugh inflation is one of the unexpected consequences of the Internet. Everything is funny. Then later, when you really do laugh, there is no acronym to express it.)

"Cleave," I typed. "As in: After accidentally cleaving the diamond in two, he cleaved it back together again."

"Boo!" Military Intelligence condemned my attempt.

"SURVEY SAYS: NO!" Jumbo Shrimp yelled.

"Yes, Steve! Anyone else?" Beth asked.

"Baby Grand," Jumbo Shrimp offered.

"I still don't think you get what I'm asking for," Beth wrote. "It needs to be a single word."

"Will you take Bad Sex?" Military Intelligence tried.

The room went crazy with that one.

"U R a comic genius!" wrote Sandman92543.

"Who cares if it's a single word?" added Harriet54638. "Why does Beth get to make up the rules?"

"Beth's a fascist," Sandman92543 declared.

"Dust," I wrote, ignoring them. "After my grandmother dusted the cake with sugar, I had to dust the excess off the countertop."

I realized I could probably waste my whole day coming up with Janus words, and it would be weirdly satisfying. At least it would distract me from thinking about what my life would probably be like now.

"Thank you, God," Beth wrote. "Who are you, Steve?"

"Down with Steve," Jumbo Shrimp typed.

"Steve is the opposite of himself," Military Intelligence added.

I offered one more: "Seed. The farmer seeded the watermelons in order to seed his fields."

"Steve is a seed," Jumbo Shrimp wrote.

"Kill him," Military Intelligence added.

"I think I love you, Steve," Beth typed. "Do you want to go into a private room?"

Beth and I wrote to each other for the next three hours. She was not, in fact, a librarian. Originally from San Francisco, she was a senior at Marymount University in nearby Arlington, Virginia, and loved to read science fiction. She said she had "the mind of Christopher Hitchens and the body of Christy Turlington."

Wow.

We talked about how we both loved sushi and speed Scrabble, and how we had never connected with someone else on the Internet. Every so often, I would throw another Janus word at her and she would emoticon uncontrollably.

"Dispense. You should dispense with your expired medications when the pharmacist dispenses you new ones."

":))))))))))))))))))

":))))))))))))))))))

"@>---------------"

That last one was a rose.

Sometime around 6 P.M., Beth said she had to go to class, and then to a Chili's near the college, where she worked part-time. We made plans to chat online later that night. I signed off—sad to lose Beth, but also anticipating the next time we'd meet online—and I went downstairs to get the mail, the only chore I had to break up my day now.

There was an envelope from my father, postmarked two days earlier—when my mother had still been here, I noted—but addressed to me. It contained a single newspaper clipping, with a note saying, "This might cheer you up a bit."

I suspected that, as during war, my mail had been aggressively censored: The only reason I did not see heavy black ink cross-outs was that everything containing anything even arguably bad or depressing had been withheld in its entirety by my family.

Here is the clipping, which came from the *Chicago Courier,* one of the city's tabloids. I had read this columnist for years, and had even written to him when I was in eighth grade to say I liked a column he had written attacking junior high sports. Though my father seemed to think the clipping was positive, I was less sure:

THROUGH A GLASS, DARKLY
by Joe McGuire

I've heard enough commentary, for the moment, about what's wrong with Stephen Glass, although I'm willing to admit, there's a lot to say on that score. What has been less frequently noted is how Glass actually shows us what's wrong with journalism.

Before you say Stephen Glass doesn't deserve my defense, let me make it very clear: I'm not defending him. But I'm not that interested in lynching him either. (Others will do it far better than I.) I'm more interested in indicting the Glass generation—or more specifically, the position in which they've been placed.

As longtime readers of this column know, I started out on the police beat in Amarillo, Texas. I worked long hours, I was introduced to cops, victims, culprits, hardened reporters, and cheap scotch, and I would never have had it any other way.

Now let's look at Glass and his contemporaries—the elite twenty-somethings, drafted straight out of college newspapers, where if they were even reporters at all, what they reported was academic scandal. I saw tempests—murders, rapes, and assaults and their aftermath. They saw only teacups: Should Latin be a separate department, or part of Classics?

We're way beyond the New Journalism now, and into the era of Newbie Journalism. In prior generations, these fragile flowers would at least have had some kind of hazing ritual—a beat like mine, although maybe in a larger city, with better scotch. But no longer. Magazines like *The Washington Weekly,* and others in D.C. that I could name, now throw these kids blindly into the world with pencils and notebooks. They don't bother to train them, figuring they're too smart to need it.

Training is something these kids desperately need, though— enough training to resist the sort of writing they're asked to do, which is the very easiest kind. It's snarky, it's glib, it's superior, it's often downright mean, and it purports to report objective facts while sneaking some very subjective conclusions under the radar.

Worse, if they don't write it the first time, their editors come down on them hard: After all, kids, if you're not willing to bat, you can't play ball. Put your earnest, nuanced, fair-to-the-subject draft in the drawer.

The kids know what's expected, and they do it—that was what got them good grades in college, wasn't it? And now they want to be on TV, maybe start making the real money too.

Journalists used to know they'd always be poor. It was a blue-collar job, better than laying bricks, mostly because it didn't take a toll on your knees. But ever since Robert Redford played Bob Woodward, a journalist can be a celebrity. These kids know that, and worse, it's just what they want. You see the bars they go to these days? People wear all black; drinks are $10. Almost makes you wish Nixon had never been caught.

What's wrong with the way the new kids are expected to report and write? Pretty much everything. For one thing, it fails to appreciate that while some facts are objective—say, did it rain in

Peoria last week?—many are deeply subjective, based on percep-
tion and nuance.

What I notice, won't necessarily be what you notice. What I
care about, isn't necessarily what you care about. The reporter will
always bring creativity to his task; the key is that readers can see
where it enters in.

And that brings us back to Glass. Glass should never have
done what he did. He broke the basic contract between writer and
reader, that elemental trust. But at the same time, he should never
have been asked to do what he was asked to do, either.

Glass, like the rest of his cohort, was asked for sarcasm and
irony, both tactics to place the writer far above his subject (and the
reader). He responded with full-out invention, a fantasia for public
consumption, into which he invited the hornswoggled reader,
who—brought there on false pretenses—must have thought this
was some kind of strange, messed-up world.

In the end, though, I don't care much about Glass. I'm worried, instead, about my daughter, who says she wants to be a journalist and seems well-suited to it—at least, to the kind of reporting
I grew up with. Will she get used to writing mean, even when she
doesn't feel it? Will she adopt positions because they're controver-
sial and contrarian, without caring if they're actually correct? Will
she report only via the telephone, without ever having a beat to
cover? Will she prefer commentary to reporting, journalism's real
blood-and-guts? Will she see journalism as a profession, and not a
vocation—something you do if you don't feel like going to law
school or taking the MCAT?

I want more for her, and so even if the *Weekly* offers her a job,
I'd tell her not to take it. She'd be better off in Amarillo.

I wasn't sure what to think of Joe McGuire's screed. I agreed with a
lot of it, but I resisted even thinking anything so critical of journalism:
It felt too much like kicking the victim. Whatever larger lessons might
be drawn from my predicament, I wanted to concentrate on the small
ones: the lessons I hoped could someday help me make a new life.

•   •   •

For now, though, I was too lonely to focus on much of anything. So I drove to Chili's, where Beth ought to have arrived for work. I didn't think I would introduce myself—I didn't want to look like a stalker—but I needed to know she was real.

When I arrived at the restaurant, I took a seat at the far end of the bar, close to where the servers picked up drinks. From there, I studied the wait staff as they walked past me. There were nine college-aged waitresses, all pretty; but none had a name tag, and none resembled Christy Turlington. Fortunately, none looked like Christopher Hitchens either.

I started becoming anxious: Where was Beth? At the hostess stand, I saw a chart of the restaurant's seating, which had the servers' names on it. I had the impulse just to grab it, but I restrained myself. Instead I studied the hostess. It took her about four minutes to seat a party. I figured that would be shaved to one minute when she saw me nosing around her stand. It was a tight window, but if everything went right, it should be enough. I could consult the chart, and figure out who Beth was, before the hostess returned.

I waited until the hostess had a large party to seat, and swooped down on her podium. I found Beth's name, but I couldn't figure out how the chart matched up to the room. So I started rotating it, trying to get everything lined up.

Then the hostess, while still seating a customer, spotted me. She dropped the menus on the table and made a beeline for me. It took less than one minute. A lot less.

"Can I help you?" she asked.

"Yes," I said. I was still holding the seating chart in the air. "This is a map of the restaurant, isn't it?"

"It is."

"That's very cool," I said.

She took the map from my hands, and held it close to her chest. "What can I do for you?" she asked.

"I just came over to find out where the bathroom was, but no one was around, so I thought I might look at your map, and then I got really taken with it. It's very interesting.

"I'm into maps," I added.

She just looked at me.

"I collect them."

Still she was silent.

"You seem to have all the chairs and tables organized so perfectly."

"We do," she said after a moment, judging my threat level as medium to low. "So, did you find the bathroom?"

"Do you know the Four Color Theorem?" I asked. She looked around for someone to seat, but there was no one waiting. She had to talk with me; there was no other choice.

"The Four Color Theorem holds that no more than four colors are ever needed to illustrate a conventional map so that no two adjoining countries are the same color," I explained in a single breath. "I thought you might find that interesting.

"Because you work with maps," I added after a moment.

"To be honest," she said, "I don't."

"Could you show me how this map works?" I asked. "Like, point me toward the bathroom—on the map?"

"I'm sorry, I can't."

"Why?"

"I'm not allowed."

"But it's just a map of the room. I could look at the room and see everything there is to be seen. What more could it tell me that I can't already see?"

"You're making me very uncomfortable."

"I'm into orienteering," I said. "Urban orienteering."

"I'll give you to the count of three to leave, or I'm going to call the manager—"

"We navigate our way through commercial buildings with compasses and things. We have scavenger hunts and races. I think you would actually enjoy it." I heard myself fabricating—lying, to put it more bluntly—and I cringed. Were these white lies? They wouldn't really do any damage, would they? They might even do some good— they might bring me closer to Beth. But I couldn't afford even white lies anymore. Should I tell the hostess I'd lied? I started to ponder the question, but she started counting.

"One—two—"

I was out the door before she said three.

I sat on a bench outside the restaurant, head between my knees, and cursed myself. I couldn't tell the truth even here. What was wrong with me? My mother was right: Other people didn't have these problems. I was like a car that always pulled to one side. I could correct for it constantly, but if I stopped paying attention for even a moment, I'd slip off the road, into some parallel world of my own imagining.

To me, lying always seemed like a good solution—no, it was more than that: the best solution, the only solution. And yet, there had been others. Couldn't I have simply asked for Beth? I felt like an idiot—because I was an idiot, I realized. And a liar too.

Around eleven o'clock, I checked my email and found Beth online; she'd kept our date. I didn't have the nerve to tell her I'd surreptitiously looked for her at Chili's. It seemed like stalker behavior—because it *was* stalker behavior, I saw now.

We typed some more and then, with my fingers beginning to go numb, I suggested we talk on the phone. Our phone call went on for more than an hour, and within the safety of anonymity, it drifted naturally to talk about sex. She told me she had fantasized about coming over tonight and sleeping with me.

I immediately agreed, and told her my address. Then I quickly began giving her directions.

"That wasn't an offer," she said.

"It wasn't?"

"You're right," she said. "It was."

Half an hour later, my doorbell rang, and with it I was overcome by a sense of wonder and revelation. That morning, with nothing to do, I had logged on to my computer, chatted with a stranger, traded Janus words, and now, a little more than twelve hours later, she was standing outside my apartment waiting to have sex with me. In that one moment, all of the promises of the Internet seemed to have been realized, and all of the sadnesses of my new life seemed briefly to fall away.

I adjusted my posture, casually held on to a beer bottle, half of which I had spilled out in the sink a minute before, and swung open the door.

It was the hostess.

"But, but . . . the map said . . ."

"There are two Beths."

"Two Beths?"

"Uh-huh," she said.

"Really? Two Beths?"

"Make love to me."

And I did.

The next morning, while Beth slept, I snuck out to get groceries. I was nervous: I had planned to go only to the twenty-four-hour supermarket, and only late at night, to ensure that no reporter, no neighbor, no person I knew would spot me. I would have worn camo if I'd thought it would help.

In retrospect, of course, I see the paranoia. I had been accustomed to D.C., where supermarkets are heavily frequented meeting places— the Safeways even have nicknames (the Social Safeway, the city's best dating service; the Soviet Safeway, where the shelves were bare yet the lines were long; and the Secret Safeway, which was tucked behind a movie theater and nearly impossible to find). But in Virginia, super- markets are anonymous and luxuriously huge. If anyone had seen me, I could have run through the football-field-length aisles to get away, and slipped behind a pile of produce. You could have lived undetected in that supermarket for months, like the *Mrs. Basil E. Frankweiler* children in the museum.

Now, venturing into the Giant in the light of a weekend day, I bought everything I thought a girl might want for brunch. Yogurt, in case she watched her weight. Bacon, so she would know I didn't think she was fat. Tofu, in case she was a vegan. If candied insects had been available, I would have purchased them just in case.

Breakfast was a creation of Roman proportions.

Beth awoke to the smell of omelets. "Mmm. . . . That smells good," she said, still hazy. "Eggs?"

"And fruit," I said. I pointed at a cantaloupe half on a breakfast-in-bed tray. I had spooned out the seeds and replaced them with raspberries and blueberries.

"What kind of cheese would you like in your omelet?" I asked.

"Whatever you have is fine. But I don't think I can eat all this. I usually just have coffee."

"Cheddar, mozzarella, Swiss, or sharp?" I insisted.

"Um. Cheddar," she said hesitantly.

"And how about yogurt? Nonfat, low-fat, or regular?"

"Nonfat, I guess," she said. "But—"

"Boysenberry, strawberry, cherry-vanilla, or pineapple-banana?"

"I'm going to the bathroom," she said. "You pick."

I picked by laying everything out on the table for her.

"All right, big guy, I've got some questions for you," she said, after we had finished a fraction of the feast. "I think I have the right to know a little about the person who just fucked me. Don't you?"

"I do," I said. But I didn't. My hands started shaking and I spilled a dollop of yogurt on my lap, but she didn't seem to notice.

I told her I was a former journalist contemplating a career change. She said she was impressed, so I didn't tell her about the firing. I hoped that revelation could wait a date or two—until she liked me more, until she trusted me a bit, until she wouldn't just walk out when she heard. So for half an hour or so, I answered her questions as vaguely as she would allow; I didn't lie, but I omitted.

When she was done, she told me to make love to her again, and I obeyed. Then she told me she had a class, kissed me, and left.

For the first time since I had last seen Allison, I had gone twenty-four hours without missing her. I decided my life was about to change for the better.

Now that I thought about it, Beth was nicer than Allison anyway—kinder, more understanding. Sexier. And maybe through her, I could start again. I fantasized a little future for Beth and me—including marriage, and kids who would laugh about how we met, their parents' nerdly computer match. They'd laugh about their father's early career troubles too—the brief, unhappy interlude before he'd married their mother and she'd turned his life around.

Later that morning, I went to a neighborhood video store—thinking that, with nothing much else to do, except dream about Beth, I might like to watch a movie. But once I arrived at the video store, nothing seemed more depressing than sitting in my all-white apartment trying to watch a movie while the daylight streamed in. I turned to leave.

"Can you hear me?" the man behind the counter shouted. A small tag identified him as Glenn, the manager.

"Are you talking to me?" I finally asked. Then I realized he had to have been: We were alone in the store.

"Why are you here in the middle of the day?" Glenn asked. "Why aren't you at work?"

"Do you want me to leave?"

"No, I want to know if you want a job," he said. "I had to fire two people today. It's minimum wage with free rentals."

I nodded, and he told me I was hired and to come in the next day. And that's how I ended up a shift supervisor at Action Video without ever speaking a single declarative sentence.

It was true: With Beth in my life, my luck seemed to have changed. Yesterday I had been jobless and without any prospects. Today I was on my way to becoming an international DVD magnate. Not far along that way, but on it, at least. I was determined to be a perfect employee—and never, ever to lie.

• • •

The next afternoon, I started work. Part of my job was to supervise two employees, Oskar and Philippe. What I didn't know when I accepted the position was that experienced members of the Action Video team avoided the daytime shift. In fact, the two prior supervisors, when refused transfers to the night shift, had simply quit.

During the night hours, most of the staff were experienced, having been with the company for years, or they were students looking to pick up some extra cash. But during the day, Action Video had fewer customers and paid a lower wage. As a result, many people who might have worked there chose instead to go to one of the Internet start-ups nearby, or one of the coffee shops that served the dot-com kids, or even the new mall down the road, where the Gap was offering a fifty-dollar signing bonus. After all, this was 1998, the height of the boom years, and labor was in short supply.

It was in this context that Glenn explained to me on my first day that my coworkers weren't "like you and me."

"What's wrong with them?" I asked.

"Don't worry. They're not psych patients or ex-felons or anything like that," he said. "They're perfectly good people. It's just that they're . . . different."

Glenn explained that the store had had trouble retaining daytime employees. Of the ten he had hired this year, only these two were left, and Glenn said they were barely hanging on. It was up to me to help them make it through. Then Glenn disappeared into his office.

"This is going to be fun," I said to my two new coworkers. "If you ever have any problems, please let me know. I'm going to work hard to make sure you're happy."

Oskar and Phillipe eyed me warily.

As my first duty, I emptied the comment box, only to find used gum, a retainer, and a crumpled note that said, "You guys are weird as shit."

I worried about what I had gotten myself into. Abandon hope, all ye who enter here. Was this some kind of bizarre joke on me? I'd thought that my personal hell would be populated with journalists, but perhaps I'd been wrong; perhaps it would simply be a world as strange as those I'd fabricated. But then, what other world would have welcomed me like this? I resolved to feel at home here.

Ten minutes later, our first customer, a mom toting a baby around her waist, arrived. "Welcome to Action Video," I yelled to her the second she walked in. "Come on, guys," I said to my coworkers. "Make the customer feel welcome."

"If there's anything we can help you with, just ask," I told the customer.

Without my help, she found a new release and brought it to the front desk. Philippe tried to check out her purchase, but because he held the video in the direct sunlight, the scanner's laser wouldn't pick up the bar code. He banged the video on the counter. "I wish for a wave," he said.

"What?" the customer asked.

"I wish for a wave to extinguish the sun. A great big wave," he explained. "Or a wind . . ."

"A wind?" the customer said.

"To blow away the sun," Philippe said. "A wave won't do it."

"Excuse me?" the customer said. She was nervous now. I saw her shift the baby closer to her, and look toward the door.

"I'm so sorry," I jumped in. "It's part of our new movie preview program. He's reciting lines from a Kevin Costner movie that's coming out soon. We haven't worked out the kinks in this new program, have we, Philippe?"

"A wind of biblical proportions," he said.

"Rated R," I added, and the customer laughed.

Then I had an idea: I stood behind Philippe, to cast my shadow over his register. The scanner instantly beeped, and an expression of total joy crossed his face. Quietly, he finished the transaction and shuffled away.

After the customer left, the store was empty for a while, and I took down several of the movie posters and repositioned them to block all possible sunlight from the window behind the cash register. Darkened, it was less depressing—as if it were the normal time to rent, nighttime.

"That was a nice way to treat Philippe," Oskar commented as I worked. "People aren't always so kind to him."

"They should be," I said. I tried to forget that the way I'd been kind had been by lying once again. My anti-lying resolution had lasted less than ten minutes. In my mind, I kept pleading emergency circumstances, but I knew I couldn't let myself off so easily: The Chili's trip hadn't been any emergency, and I'd lied there too. Suddenly, I wanted to ask my mom what she thought—did she remember my lying on other occasions when I was little? And did she have a theory why? But I was nervous to call—right now, I couldn't take another fight, nor could I bear to remind myself of how much I had disappointed her—and so I didn't.

Instead, on my lunch break, I called Nathan and asked him whether he thought I would ever stop lying. "They just pop out of me sometimes," I said. "I tell myself I'm not going to lie. I even promise myself. And then something happens and before I know it, I've lied. What should I do?"

"The only thing you *can* do: try not to lie again," he said. "Try as hard as you can. What do you want? To go back and change it somehow?"

"Yes," I admitted. "That's what I want."

"Well, you can't. All you can do is try not to lie next time."

When I got home from my first day of work, I checked my voicemail and email again. There was still nothing from Beth; worse, I learned that the email address she'd given me was now defunct. I called the Chili's, but there was a new hostess there. She told me Beth had quit because she had gotten her "break," somewhere in D.C.

I was crushed; everything with Beth had seemed to be going so well. Now she seemed not only to have no interest in me, but to have disappeared altogether. I began to rethink every detail of the hours she and I had spent together. Should I have cooled it with the Janus words? Breakfast was too elaborate: It had freaked her out, I decided. She had just wanted coffee—the one thing I had forgotten.

She probably had a caffeine-deprivation headache when she left. I had given her a headache. And, I admitted to myself, I had lied to her. What was wrong with me? Why couldn't I tell the truth? Maybe Beth, like Allison, had sensed—perhaps only subliminally—that I was withholding some secret from her, and had decided to keep her distance.

I would have kept obsessing about Beth, but I had to work, and I was newly grateful for my Action Video position.

The next day, I went in early. That day, and the next, I watched Oskar carefully and he seemed completely normal, despite what Glenn had said—just another guy in his twenties trying to make some money at the store. So, on the third day, I asked him to join me for lunch at the nearby food court.

The lunch progressed without incident. In fact, we had an interesting conversation about books and movies and politics, and I thought that through Oskar, I might just find another clique for myself; I might find a new home. I couldn't imagine why Glenn had made me, the new guy, Oskar's supervisor. Why hadn't he promoted Oskar and hired me to work under him instead?

Then, on the walk back to Action Video, during a lull in the conversation, Oskar put on his Walkman headphones and began chanting in a loud monotone, as if he were at some rally, "I hate the Christian God. The Christian God hates me."

He repeated it over and over, his red hair shone in the sun, and there was a manic gleam in his eye.

Although Oskar was wearing the Action Video uniform, a pants-shirt-and-apron combo that featured little pictures of movie stars—I had to wear it too—I didn't see much harm in his one-man protest, until he walked into the store and continued to march through the new-release aisle.

Gingerly, I removed his headphones. "That's for another time," I said, and told him to return to his work.

Ten minutes later, I heard screams coming from the romantic-comedy section. "Manager! Manager!" a customer yelled. "What's going on?"

It was another young mother—we had a large children's section that attracted the moms—and she shielded her child's eyes, although I don't know what she was afraid the boy would see.

Oskar had put his headphones back on and was marching and chanting again.

"I'm very sorry," I said. "It's part of a performance-art thing to promote the DVD release of *The Last Temptation of Christ*. I'm not sure the customers are really into it." Liar, liar, liar, I silently chanted to myself. But still I kept lying.

I checked the customer out myself, and asked Oskar to re-alphabetize the videos in the back.

It had been a long three days at Action Video, but none of the customers slipped anything into the comment box as they left, so I counted it a success. I was still lying, I knew that—but weren't they excusable lies now? No lies were excusable, I reminded myself—not for me, anyway. But wasn't there some kind of emergency exception? The two previous shift supervisors had quit, and I was determined not to. I would be different. I would keep my job, and I would make sure Oskar and Phillipe would keep theirs, and the world would be a better place. My lies were good, they were very good; they were making everyone around me happier. Glenn had already complimented my performance as a supervisor. I solidly had his approval now. It all felt familiar—too familiar.

I arrived back at The Harvey exhausted and dispirited—for I'd seen that my small success once again was the result of my lies, and I wondered how I could ever stop the pattern. Before I could go upstairs, the desk guy stopped me; a letter from FedEx was waiting for me.

I expected the letter to be from Cliff and was ready to throw it away unread, but then I saw that the return address was actually my father's. I opened it to find a note written on his professional stationery, in his loopy, slanted, virtually indecipherable hand:

Dear Stephen,

I hope I head off Mom's letter. Don't worry too much about it. She's upset, but these things come and these things go. Please understand that she's going through a bad time. After everything that happened out there in Washington with you, things got worse when she came back. Especially at Curls. She was sitting there, getting her nails done, when Linda Davidson showed up. She said to Mom, "How are you?" Mom said she was fine. "That's not what I hear," Linda said. "How can you be fine at a time like this?" She said it in front of all the ladies at the salon. You know what Linda is like. She has nothing to do but criticize, criticize.

Your mom and I love you very much. You have always been a good boy. Once in a while, people ask me if I'm upset and I say no, which is the truth. They don't know the whole story. No one knows the whole story.

There's an anecdote that Rabbi Umfer once told at a Yom Kippur sermon. He said this Jew who was a jeweler was contacted by a king. The king had a beautiful diamond that he looked at all the time. It was his favorite diamond in the world. Then one day it got a crack. He began calling all the goyish jewelers and ordered them to fix it, but none of them could.

Finally, someone recommended he get the Jewish jeweler, which he did. He told the Jewish jeweler to fix it or he would kill him. The Jewish jeweler studied the diamond for days. No matter how hard he tried, he could not fix it. And then he had an idea. He cut more scratches into the diamond, so that they made a picture of a rose. He gave the diamond to the king, who loved it and made him a hero. I think it's a good story for you to think about.

Don't worry too much about the Mom situation. You'll put things back together. You always have. We can't wait to see you in the fall for the Jewish holidays. Make sure to bring your sport jacket home with you.

> Love,
>
> Dad

As much as I appreciated my dad's letter, it created new anxieties for me about my mother's letter, which had not yet arrived. Soon, however, those anxieties were dwarfed by new ones.

The next morning, I happened on a copy of *The Washington Banner,* one of the city's free, alternative newspapers, at the coffee shop where I stopped on the way to work. The *Banner's* cover proclaimed: "STEPHEN GLASS—THE NAKED TRUTH, p. 12."

As I paged through the paper, I started to feel sick. There in the center of the page was a large photo of me, taken while I was in college. I remembered the photo being taken at 6:30 A.M. in my dorm room, after I'd pulled an all-nighter at the newspaper. My hair was standing on end and my smile was a large open-mouthed grin.

The college paper—the paper that for so long had been so proud of me, the place that had been my home for four years, the paper I had visited just a year before to advise current students— must have sold them the photo. Newspapers do that. It's standard procedure, but it hurt me anyway. For so long they had been my family. I wondered how much they'd been paid. But the picture was nothing compared to the article it accompanied, which I focused on next:

SLEEPING WITH THE ENEMY
by Beth Theophilus

Stephen Glass, the 25-year-old *Washington Weekly* reporter who was notoriously dismissed from his job—and, indeed, from his entire profession—at the start of this summer, has come to mean something different to everyone.

For his former colleagues, Glass is the greatest con artist of his generation: an individual so skilled in deception that he passed off dozens of fearlessly fabricated and patently implausible news stories as true.

For his friends, Glass was the confidant they only *thought* they knew, a man who has forced them to question the honesty of all of their friendships, one by one.

And for the pundits, Glass is evidence of the dangers of a world in which reality inexorably slips into entertainment. But for me, Stephen Glass is the man I met on the Internet one night last week and fucked.

I pause here because I'm honestly torn about whether to tell this story. When Stephen and I met, first in an online chat room and then in person, he did not know I was a journalism major, and he did not know I knew what he had done. Was I committing the very kind of ethical violation he had?

I decided quickly that the answer was no. The more I thought about what had happened between us, and weighed the information I had gleaned from our night and morning together, the more I knew I had to write it all down. I was a witness to history, and no one could tell this important story but myself.

It is Stephen himself who forces my hand. While the rest of us turn upside down the wreckage of his lies, and sort through how he got by so many fact checkers, editors, and readers, Stephen stays mum in his Jeffersonville apartment—refusing to talk, refusing to help us to understand why.

I spent less than twenty-four hours with Stephen, yet fortunately that brief time was enough for me to find out the crucial "why"—the ghost in this fabrication machine, as it were.

While Stephen himself was evasive in response to my questions, his apartment and lifestyle spoke volumes. Obviously untroubled by his betrayal of journalists everywhere, and unscarred by his firing, Stephen struck me as cheerful and, indeed, randy.

Not since Monica Lewinsky has someone exhibited such callous disregard of the consequences of his or her own actions. I could hardly stop myself from challenging him: "Don't you realize what you've done?" But I remained quiet, knowing there was a deeper purpose to be served.

Before I met Stephen Glass, he had destroyed my dreams. A naïve journalism major, I . . .

It went on like that. Beth had four conclusions:

Conclusion 1: Stephen slides seamlessly between reality and fiction.

Evidence: "When Stephen was about to have an orgasm, he screamed out: 'I'm going to go off!' I told him I had never heard the moment of climax called 'going off.' 'It's another Janus word,' he said. 'As in: every time the fire alarm goes off by accident, I hope it will just go off as soon as possible.' But, gentle reader, 'go off' is obviously not a true Janus word, because it is *two* words."

Conclusion 2: Stephen is not sorry.

Evidence: "I practically begged Stephen to show remorse. At one point I asked him, if he could do one thing differently in his life, what would it be? He said he would have met me sooner. But we could hardly have met any sooner. After all, we had first started chatting only that day!"

Conclusion 3: Stephen is truly dangerous. He does not understand the gravity of what he has done and therefore will strike again.

Evidence: "When asked about his occupation, Stephen did not say he had been fired. He merely said he was a 'former journalist,' looking to get into another profession. Imagine Jeffrey Dahmer describing himself as a former food taster, looking to get into a new line of work. Now imagine being that food. I couldn't bear to listen anymore, because I knew I would only hear lie after lie after lie."

Conclusion 4: Stephen continues to lie.

Evidence: "Stephen claimed to practice a sport called urban orienteering. I have searched far and wide, but have found no evidence that urban orienteering is a sport."

Yes, she was right about that last one: I was still lying. I'd wished that she had understood that when it came to her, the root of my lies was weakness, not malice. I'd wanted to be with her desperately. Why couldn't I get a break, a little sympathy? I wondered. Then I remembered I wasn't entitled to that anymore; I wasn't entitled to anything; or perhaps what I really was entitled to, was this.

For several hours, I felt as if I were in shock. I tried to call Nathan, but he was out. I wanted to call my parents, even though I realized that I couldn't tell them all this, and even if I could, since my mother and I were in a fight, she probably wouldn't want to listen.

Finally, at some point, I went down to the lobby and checked my mailbox. Other than coffee and work, it was still the only daily ritual I had, and so I always did it whenever I was at a loss for something to do.

But the box was empty; my mother's letter—the one my dad had mentioned in his letter—still hadn't arrived.

I had turned to leave, when a man standing near me in the mailroom asked if I was new to the building.

"Yes," I told him, and I started to walk away.

He reached out his hand. "My name is Dotan Braverman. And yours?"

"Steve," I said.

"Steve . . . ?" he asked. His voice trailed off so I could fill in the last name.

"Nice to have met you," I said, and headed toward the elevator.

He yelled for me to wait up. I waited at the elevator and Dotan, carrying an armful of mail, drew very close, threateningly close, to me.

"You're Jewish, right?" he asked.

"Yes," I said at full volume, which sounded too loud because we were standing so near each other. I backed up a step, but he matched me, drawing close again.

When the building's lone elevator finally arrived, Dotan followed me inside. "We're the only two Jews in the building," he said after the door shut.

"Okay," I said. "It's not some secret kind of club."

"All I'm saying is, we got to stick together."

"Whatever you say."

"We just got to watch each other's back. Can you do that for me?"

"I'll do my best."

"I'm serious," he said.

"I am too." Although I wasn't. My indifference had quickly given way to anxiety. What did Dotan really want with me? His paranoia fed my own and I began to wonder how much he knew about me and my past, and how much I had to fear him. Had he read Beth's article too? He probably went to the same coffee place—it was only a block away from The Harvey—and they'd had a huge stack of *Washington Banners*. Had he recognized me from the photo, and made up this crazy Jewish brotherhood thing? I worried that he might call the *Herald* now, and tell them something about me. I don't know what I imagined he would reveal, but it didn't matter; telling them anything would hurt. All that mattered was that he was yet another person whom I had to protect myself from. How far would I have to go to escape into anonymity?

The elevator stopped at the sixth floor.

"You ever need anything, you come to my room," Dotan told me. "I'm in 613. Get it?"

It must have been obvious that I didn't, because he quickly added, "It's the number of *mitzvot* in the Torah. Hilarious, huh? I didn't even request it. God works in mysterious ways."

He gave me the thumb-and-pinky shaka sign, told me to "hang loose," and walked off. I felt a little better; on the threat spectrum, he now seemed farther from "journalist" and closer to "crackpot."

Over the next week, I read Beth's article another thirty times—I unsuccessfully tried to limit myself to no more than two times a day—and each time, I was shocked and saddened all over again. I knew I couldn't date anyone again, not for quite a while, but I still longed desperately for human contact, a human connection, and a safe atmosphere in which I no longer felt I had to lie or keep silent.

I hoped to find it at a place called Squiddy's.

Eighty miles northwest of Washington, in a blue-collar Maryland town, there is a small, unassuming lap-dance club. The establishment is a boarded-up former mattress store, square and made of taupe-colored stucco, set back from the highway, between a Taco Bell and a Chevron. There is a sign, but it's small and dark and easily missed when driving by at night. Unlike other adult clubs, Squiddy's doesn't advertise or do anything to publicize itself. There are no free lunch buffets or happy hours, and porno stars don't come by on weekends to sign autographs and sell videos.

No one could possibly know me there, I hoped. (I had found the place on the Internet, and users boasted of its low profile.) Even journalists hoping to spot a congressman indulging a secret lascivi-ousness wouldn't go that far. It was the dregs—the underbelly's underbelly.

Inside the club, a live, undersized squid languished in an algae-encrusted aquarium, the patchy patina on its glass walls like the scum on the enamel of a mouth full of never-brushed teeth. The squid lived alone in the tank except for a mossy scuba diver figurine. In the diver's mask, bubbles caught for a moment and then emerged to stream upward and vanish. The squid's name, according to a Post-it note stuck to the glass, was Mr. Squid.

"I think he's lonely," I said to one of the dancers.

She said nothing.

"He just floats there, not even moving his tentacles," I added.

Her hand was touching my shoulder. I could smell her perfume, a potent cinnamony scent. The music was blaring, and several men at the bar were shouting at the dancers on stage to take it all off. They always took it all off during the third song; that was their routine, I had read online. But even here, where a lap dance was available to anyone with ten dollars, the men felt the need to pressure the women to move faster still.

"Do you think Mr. Squid is lonely?" I asked her. "I mean, I don't know if he can experience loneliness, but do you think he wishes he had a friend in there?"

"Do you wish *you* had a friend?" she asked me.

I turned and looked directly at her. She was very tall and very blond, but haggard in her tall blondness. She accentuated her height by wearing four-inch stiletto heels. Aside from the shoes, she was wearing only an aqua-blue bra, a bikini bottom, and a fading glow-stick bracelet.

"Would you like a dance?" she asked.

Before I could answer, she took my hand and led me to the rear of the club. There were six lawn chairs sitting in a row, and three beach umbrellas. Behind them, cutout construction-paper fish were pasted on the wall and cutout bubbles ascended from their mouths. I worried that the club doubled as a kindergarten during the daylight hours.

She pushed me lightly on the shoulders and I fell back into one of the chairs. She leaned over me. Her breasts hung over my head and a dash of silver body glitter floated down onto my face.

We had a minute before the song began. "I don't think we've formally met," I said. I wanted to begin my honesty policy immediately, and so I did. "My name is Stephen Glass and I'm from Jeffersonville," I told her. I reached a hand upward to shake, and she took my thumb in her mouth.

For the first time in weeks, I had offered my real name to a stranger unnecessarily, and it felt wonderful. I decided then that I had been more right than I knew; I could be totally honest here. Indeed, the strip club could become a kind of clinic for me: Here, in the privacy of people who knew nothing about me, and cared not a whit, I would learn to become myself again.

"My name is Stephen Glass." I said it—virtually sang it—again. "I'm from Jeffersonville."

"I heard you the first time," the dancer replied, when she'd finished fellating my finger, wonderfully unaware of the importance of this moment—of my proud announcement of my name. "I'm Kimmy, and I live around here," she grudgingly offered.

"This seems like a nice place to live," I said.

"Really? Have you ever seen any of it outside the club?"

"No, I guess not."

A Madonna song faded out and the Backstreet Boys' "As Long as You Love Me" began to play. On that cue, Kimmy reached one hand behind her back and pulled off her bra. She leaned farther toward me, our lips just millimeters apart, and gently employed her knee in my lap. She licked her upper lip, her tongue narrowing further the infinitesimal distance between our mouths.

"I was a journalist," I said to her. "Until I got fired."

"I'm sorry," she said.

There wasn't a hint of judgment in her eyes, and I felt bolder and braver, and I began to think it was possible I might someday come to love her. You laugh, don't you? But I longed for benevolence. I wanted someone to reach out to me, to connect with me, and to learn everything I had done wrong, and to forgive me for it. Is it so crazy that I fantasized that Kimmy might be that person? Her job, after all, was to seek out my desperate needs and to fulfill them, if only for a few minutes. And I was the type to try to help her do her job as well as I could.

Yes, Kimmy would haul me out of this mess. I was certain of it. As I would save Kimmy from her plight here, she would save me from the place in which I was stuck, too.

I needed to know more about this woman who was pulling at my penis through my sweatpants.

"So, Kimmy, what do you do?" I asked.

She drew back slightly. I hoped I hadn't spit on her when I spoke.

"Why? You got a special request?" Kimmy turned around and sat on my thighs, facing away and grinding her butt against me.

"I mean, outside of here. What do you do for a living?"

She bent backward and threw her head over my shoulder. She blew air into my ear. *"This* is my living," she said. She took my earlobe into her mouth.

"Of course. I'm sorry. I meant, what do you want to do when this is done? When you're no longer a dancer? What're your dreams?"

"You sure talk a lot, Stephen Glass from Jeffersonville."

Kimmy flipped over. In one motion, she flung her legs over my shoulders and pressed her hands against my knees, in a sort of assisted handstand. Contact was never broken. Now she was using the top of her head on my crotch. I never knew a person could have such finesse with the cranial crown.

"Do you have a boyfriend?" I asked. I spoke loudly now, because her ears were in my lap.

She didn't say anything, but releasing one hand and balancing on her other three limbs, Kimmy slapped her own ass. Worried that she might not have heard my question, I ducked my head down below her pelvis so we could talk better. Now we were face-to-face, except that her face was upside down.

"Can you hear me?" I yelled.

"I hear you," she yelled back, but somehow still in a sensual way.

"I asked if you have a boyfriend."

She slapped herself once more, and still did not answer.

I pushed the chair back a foot or two and she wobbled, still inverted. "This is really uncomfortable for me," I said to her ass. "Do you mind getting down? I'd like for us to get to know each other first."

In another fluid motion, Kimmy dismounted. I think she sighed, but I couldn't quite hear her with all the music. I motioned for her to sit in the lawn chair beside mine.

"I'm only allowed to use one chair at a time," she said.

I got out of my seat and gestured for her to take my place. She did, and I sat on the floor in front of her, legs crossed. "Is this better?" I asked.

"It's your money."

"Now we can get to know each other a little," I said. The Backstreet Boys began to fade out, and No Doubt's "Just a Girl" started up.

"Only if you got another ten dollars," she said.

I handed her the money. "Can we play Truth or Dare?" I asked.

"That won't work," she said. "I can't dare you, because I'm not allowed to tell the customers to do anything, and you can't dare me, because if it's legal, it's included in your dance."

"How about Truth or Truth, then?"

"I don't think so," she said, and began to use her foot in my lap.

"Please. I'd really like to play," I said. I was running out of money. I had just cashed my Action Video check and more than half of it was gone, but still I handed her another ten dollars.

"Thank you, but no," she said. "You are, however, the proud owner of another lap dance."

"Come on. Please? I'll start: I was fired when I was caught making up stories."

"Uh-huh."

"Look, I've told you something, now you tell me something."

She paused and looked at me intently. "You're very strange, Stephen."

"Great. Now we're having an honest conversation."

"So that's what you want. *You're very strange, Stephen. You're very, very strange.* Is that what turns you on?"

"No. I want you to tell me about yourself. Tell me something true."

"Fine," she said. "Truth: You're sitting on the ground."

"Um, all right. My turn again . . . Truth: I think you're very beautiful."

She looked at me guardedly.

"Your turn," I said.

"Truth: Unlike you, *I'm* sitting in a *chair.*"

"Truth: I love your eyes."

"My turn again?" she asked. I nodded. "Truth: This is the first time a guy has ever sat on the floor during a lap dance with me. If you weren't such a freak—"

"Can we stop with the seating arrangements?" I pleaded. "Say something you think, or feel. . . . Or, how about your real name?"

"I don't want to share that."

"Please?" I said. "I gave you mine."

"No," she said. "Just no."

The song started to fade out and Kimmy began to stand up. I offered her ten dollars more. I only had thirty remaining in my wallet. I needed to move faster.

"Do you ever date your customers?" I asked.

"Yes," she said, but I was suspicious.

"Really? Is that true?" I asked.

"That's the answer you want."

"How do you know?"

"It's the answer every man in a strip club wants."

"But is it true?" I asked. It takes a liar to catch a liar, or maybe not: Maybe a liar is the worst person to catch another liar, for his whole life turns not just on others' suspension of disbelief but on his own. You can't convince someone else of a lie if you don't believe it yourself—or at least, that had been my experience.

"Is it true?" I repeated again, suddenly wanting very much to know.

"For you it is," Kimmy responded.

"Do you think you could go on a date with me?"

She didn't answer. I have always been timid in starting up relationships. I had a crush on Allison for more than a year before we went on a date. And, in fact, in the end it was Allison who asked me out. She arranged for us to go to a movie together with other people, who then conveniently canceled. During the middle of the movie, Allison turned to me and said, "How do you think this will ever happen if I have to do all the work?"

This time, I was determined to take charge.

"Look, I'd be the best boyfriend you ever had," I said to Kimmy. "I'm caring and sensitive. And I would make you happy. I'd do whatever it would take." I meant it.

"I am happy," Kimmy replied.

"Not as happy as you'd be with me, I promise. No one would work harder than me to make you happy."

"If that's the case, why aren't you dating someone already?"

"Because I was fired," I said.

"Your girlfriend left you because you were fired?"

"Yes," I said. "And because I lied to her."

"What about your friends?"

"Most of them left me too. The ones that didn't leave me, I left."

"That's fucked up. All because you were fired, and you lied?"

"It was a very close-knit group," I said. "If it had been the other way around, I probably would not have remained friends with the person either. I mean, *now* I would, but not then. I'm different now. There's almost nothing someone could do that I wouldn't forgive."

"Well, of course, because now you have to. You feel you have no choice," she said. There was a moment of silence. "You know, I got fired at the BigMart last year, when they found out I was working here at night," she continued. "Word floated around that I was a dancer, and some of the old lady cashiers ratted on me. I lost some friends, but I didn't lose everyone. I'm glad I had friends outside the BigMart. You should have, too."

"I think I could love you," I said.

She stopped and made a sound. It was a sound of pity, and of contempt. "I don't even know you. You're just Stephen Glass from Jeffersonville. You know even less about me."

"I'm telling you I'm very attracted to you. And I'm telling you I would try very, very hard to make you happy."

The song ended, but Kimmy didn't make any movement toward getting up this time. "No," she said.

"No?"

"That's right, no."

"Just give me a chance."

"What makes you think I want you to rescue me?" she shot back. "Just because I work here? Did you think that you'd come here and meet someone even more desperate than you, and she'd go out with you because you could *save* her? Did you think this would be *Pretty Woman*?"

"Honestly?"

"Truth or Truth, right? It's your game."

"Yes, I think I had begun to hope for that. Not when I came here, but when we began talking."

"Fuck you, Stephen."

I said nothing.

"Forget it, forget all this shit. Here, sit down where you're supposed to be. Now, what do you want me to do? Do you want me to touch my tits? Do you want me to talk dirty?"

I still said nothing.

"Dammit, Stephen Glass from Jeffersonville, tell me what you want me to do."

She put one leg over my shoulder and began gyrating in the chair, her expression completely absent, her mind in some other place. I waited, motionless, until the song ended. "I'm sorry," I said. "I don't know what's happened to me." I gently removed her leg, stood up, and shuffled away.

"You have one more dance," she called after me. "Come on back. The guy at the bar bought you another dance."

I stopped and looked at the figure she was pointing to. His head was down and he was writing on a napkin. It wasn't Cliff, or anyone I recognized, but a cold shiver of absolute fear ran through me: I was sure he was a journalist. I wondered what my parents' friends would think when they read that I was not only a liar but a pervert too.

I ran up to the man, who was in his sixties and unshaven. He was wearing a camel-colored sport jacket with a gray oxford underneath. Both were tattered and coffee stained.

"What the fuck do you want with me?" I accosted him. "Can't I have any private life?"

The man looked at me blankly and said nothing.

I grabbed his cocktail napkin. "Who do you work for?" I yelled at him. "Does the world really want to hear another installment of my life?"

I yelled for Kimmy, who slowly made her way to the bar, while the man just stared at me. "I told you I had been a journalist, didn't I?" I asked her.

"Yes," she said. "But—"

"And I told you I had been fired for making up stories, right?"

"Yes, but—"

"I was honest with you, and told you stuff that made you think less of me, right?"

"Much less," she cracked wise, and smiled, for the first time that evening, at her own joke.

Triumphantly, I turned back to the old man, who was looking on in bewilderment.

"So if your headline says 'Fabulist Stephen Glass Frequents Strippers,'" I said, "it better also say 'And Turns Over New Leaf.'"

"He's not a reporter. He's a voyeur," Kimmy finally said. "He comes here every night and pays for people to get lap dances so he can watch."

I looked down at the napkin I had been waving about. It was a small sketch of a frog, holding a sign that said GLORY BE.

I pressed the creases out of the napkin as best I could, and handed it back to the old man. "I'm sorry," I said. "I'm so sorry. I thought you were someone else—something else."

Filled with shame and horror, I bolted through a fire exit near the stage, holding my breath for the sound of a door alarm, which miraculously never came. I hurried through an alleyway littered with broken bottles and condom wrappers and fast-food bags, and then I ran across the parking lot to my car.

Was I really as paranoid as my encounter with the frog man suggested? Or did I just have an intuition of catastrophe that hadn't yet been fulfilled? Like the journalists I feared, I had become an expert reporter on the beat of myself and my self-destruction. Like them, I was just waiting for everything to go terribly, terribly wrong for me once again. And if it wasn't inclined to, it seemed I'd make sure it would anyway.

A few weeks later, over the July Fourth weekend, Nathan arrived to visit me. I apologized again for drafting him to play a role in my cover-up. *The Dartmouth Review* had briefly made an issue of it—he had been made into a sort of fabricating Mini-Me.

"Please stop apologizing," Nathan said, after he had been in my apartment a few hours. "Otherwise I'm going home. The most tiring thing about all of this is to have to constantly reassure you."

"But I feel like I can't make it up to you."

"Steve, I hate to break this to you, but what *The Dartmouth*

Review writes is not a big deal to me. You know what the result of this was? This really cool sophomore Wiccan finally slept with me. You know how Dartmouth is—it's like, the frat guys, the Wiccan/feminists, and everyone in between. The Wiccans thought it was sexy. They even invited me to go to their forest rites."

"Did you join their coven?" I asked, fascinated.

"I wasn't ready to take that step. Look, Steve, if that doesn't make you feel better—and it would, if you saw this girl—then you should read some of the bad stories that were written about you, the ones Dad never sends. According to them, I was a 'popular dreamboat' and you lived in my shadow, consumed by jealousy. The only more successful Lakeside High student than you, was me."

And then, at my brother's request, I never apologized again, although I still wanted to.

Instead, I told Nathan about Kimmy—I'd been embarrassed to mention her on the phone—and I could see, as he listened, that he was thinking about what had happened with Beth too, and was starting to worry. I think he could see how bad things had gotten for me. So he made a bargain with me: one more experiment into the underworld of sex, and then it would be over.

I wished I could have shown him I could quit cold turkey, but the longings for contact—any contact—were too strong. So I opted for the one last time that Nathan had offered me. For our venue, I chose the massage parlor Delightful Spa, from a suggestive, but not too blatant, advertisement in a flyer we had in Action Video's backroom adult section.

"Maybe this isn't such a good idea," I said to Nathan, as we got close to Delightful and I began to have second thoughts. "What if there's a bust?" I was still nervous from my close call at Squiddy's, not to mention the disaster with Beth.

I pulled into a parking spot. Then I put the car in reverse and backed out again. "We need a plan," I said. "We need to make sure it's not a sting operation."

"You realize that by pulling in and out of the parking spot across from the spa, you're calling attention to yourself? If the L.E. is here, they're sure to be watching us now."

L.E.—law enforcement—is what johns call the police. As far as I knew, Nathan hadn't been a john before, but he had watched a lot of *COPS.*

"I can't stay here," I told him. I drove a lap around the mini-mall and was soon right back in front of Delightful. Nathan had started looking at the wheel. I wondered if again, yet again, control of my car was to be taken from me. But then a horrifying sight distracted me.

A suburban woman and her teenage daughter, who was dressed in a bright red soccer uniform, were walking on the sidewalk. The girl was talking and windmilling her arms. In between the offices of a chiropractor and a travel agent, the girl stopped her mother. The girl then dribbled an invisible soccer ball ahead a few paces. The mom crouched slightly, pretending to be a goalie. The girl ran toward her, tacking left and right, shaking off defenders, and at the very last second, just before she collided with her mother, kicked the invisible ball toward the invisible goal. The mother made as if she missed, and the girl, standing directly in front of Delightful's door, raised her arms in triumph.

I thought to myself, They don't know, they cannot know, the iniquities my brother and I want to perpetrate in that building. I froze at the wheel, ready to leave, but Nathan forced me to re-park.

"All right, Plan A," he said once we were in the space again. "If the L.E. busts in, tell them you meant to go to the chiropractor next door."

"No one's going to believe that. I'm going to be naked in the massage parlor with some nude woman, and oil everywhere, and I'm supposed to say, 'You mean, this isn't the chiropractor?'"

"You just have to say it confidently."

"What's Plan B?"

"Say you're just getting a massage. There can't be anything wrong with that, right? It's obviously legal."

"Maybe she's not a licensed masseuse. Did you think of that?"

"And maybe the person who cuts your hair doesn't have a license either. We can't worry about little shit like that."

"She does have a license. I see it every time I go to her. It's taped to the mirror."

"Steve"—even my patient brother was exasperated by now—"just go in there and get a massage. Take it slow. Sometime during the massage, she'll drop a hint that extras are available, and then you decide at that point if you're comfortable with them. If you're not, just politely decline."

I was beginning to suspect that Nathan had actually done this before. Five years younger, he still always did everything first.

"What else?" I asked.

"There's nothing else," Nathan said. "We either do this or we don't. We cannot plan for every contingency. It's a whorehouse."

I rang the doorbell and the chime played the first seven notes of "Take Me Out to the Ball Game." But no one came to the door.

"Ring it again," my brother said.

I did. Still no one came. Maybe there was some kind of secret ringing code and we didn't know it. Maybe they knew the feds were casing the joint. I headed back to the car.

"Where are you going?" Nathan asked.

"It's a sign from God. We're going to get busted," I said. "He's giving us another chance to walk away."

Nathan rang the bell a third time. "You think God gets involved in such little things?" he asked.

"Yes," I said.

"Then where was He during your time at the *Weekly*? Where was the second chance, when Robert was marching you from building to building?"

"I think He gave me more than enough chances," I said.

I was halfway to the car when a wizened woman wearing a black kimono opened the door. My brother greeted her. "Is he coming too?" she asked Nathan, pointing to me.

He said I was, and I scuttled back, and into the building, as quickly as I could.

• • •

The madam led us into a spacious waiting room where all the furniture was pink or green, and the carpeting was a bit of both. Near the door was a large cement vase filled with Starlite Mints. I took one.

"For after," the old woman said.

I put the mint back.

"We would like a one-hour massage," Nathan said.

"Separate," I added. The woman looked at me blankly.

"I'm sorry," I said. "That was obvious, wasn't it."

"How old are you?" she asked me.

I told her my age and she told us to wait. The woman disappeared behind a green curtain.

"She didn't ask *your* age," I commented to Nathan.

"No," he said. "She didn't."

Ahead and to the left was a long corridor. Along the hallway were a dozen or so curtained doors to what looked like massage rooms. All of the rooms' walls stopped a foot shy of the ceiling. The sound of women giggling trickled out from above them.

"Do you think that's for some building code reason? Maybe to avoid having to get permits when they built it?" I asked Nathan.

"Do you really want to spend your time here speculating on construction law?"

"No," I said, but I still thought about it.

Tiny speakers, hung from the ceiling, played a "love songs" radio station. After a minute or so of our standing there, listening to Michael Bolton, a man from behind one of the curtained doors shouted, "That's the ticket!"

"What do you think is taking her so long?" I asked Nathan after a minute more.

"Just chill."

A little while later, the old woman returned. "Can I see your ID?" she asked me. I handed her my driver's license and she walked back behind the curtain again.

"What do you think she wants with my license?" I asked Nathan. What I wanted, of course, was not legal at any age.

"She's Xeroxing it. I know it," I said before he could answer.

"Why would she want to copy your license?"

"Maybe she's one of those identity thieves."

"Stephen . . ."

"Look, I don't want anyone to know I was here. If she just told people I had come here, no one would believe her, but if she has a copy of my license . . ."

"You've got to stop talking."

The old woman soon returned, and handed me back my license. She asked for sixty dollars from each of us, which we gave her. Then she led us to separate rooms, down the corridor of the giggling women.

My room was the size of a large closet, and smelled of rosewater. In the center was a massage table with a towel spread out on it, and to one side there was a chair and a small counter with three boxes of tissues, a bottle of baby oil, and a tub of Vaseline. There was also a sign on the wall: BEWARE! THIS IS A MASSAGE PARLOR!!! NO ACTIVITY OF ANY KIND MAY BE DONE HERE.

Not knowing what to do, I sat on the table. The disc jockey announced that they were having a Michael Bolton marathon and played another one of his songs. It was interrupted by more giggling, waterfalling again through the gap between the wall and the ceiling. The unseen man cried "That's the ticket!" several more times, with increasing passion.

I remembered that I had a pen in my pocket, and on the sign above me I drew a little caret between NO and ACTIVITY, and I inserted the word SEXUAL.

Then I realized that the newly revised sign might scare off some customers, so I added: SENSUAL ACTIVITY, HOWEVER, IS PERMISSIBLE.

I then looked at the sign and decided the whole message was too formal, even cold. I added, AND ENCOURAGED!

Another minute or two passed, and I began to believe they had forgotten about me. Bored, I was about to open the door and go back into the reception area, when the old woman returned.

"You still have your clothes on!"

I looked down at myself, observed that I did, and nodded.

"But you've had so much time."

"I didn't know I was supposed to take them off."

"Why are you here?" she asked.

"For a massage," I said.

"With your clothes on?"

"No," I said.

She pulled the curtain that served as the room's door closed, and I removed all my clothes. I took the towel that was spread out over the massage table and wrapped it around my lower torso.

Soon she came back in. "Leave that here," she said, pointing to the towel.

I put the towel back on the massage table, and stood before her naked.

"What have you done?" she screamed.

"I don't know," I said.

She left the room, but returned thirty seconds later with two other women. They were talking animatedly in a foreign language and pointing at the altered sign. One of the women looked at me and rolled her eyes in disgust. I began to put my clothes back on.

"Keep them off," the old woman yelled at me.

I did as I was told, standing naked among the women, not understanding what they were saying. Eventually, they came to some agreement, and the old woman told me to follow her.

She led me through the empty corridor and into the sauna, and then she left me alone.

In the sauna, I thought about how people's bacteria get stuck in the wood benches, just waiting to infect the next human to come by. In an orthodox Jewish home, once a wooden spoon has touched something that is not kosher, it can never be made kosher again. Silver and stainless steel can be redeemed by boiling. But wood, because it keeps all those unkosher molecules tucked away between its little splinters, is tainted forever.

I refused to sit down. I didn't have a towel, and I didn't want my butt on the same spot where someone else's had once rested. The sauna floor, which was very hot, stung my feet, so I stood on one leg, switching every so often. Bored, tired, scared, I read the only thing in the sauna—a two-year-old copy of a country-music magazine, *Dixie Rhythms*.

After maybe two minutes, the door opened up and the old woman pushed my naked brother into the sauna.

Nathan's body is much like mine. He has brown curly hair and olive-shaped eyes. His pectorals and biceps are broader, from working out in high school while I spent my free time in the ham-radio shack, but his posture has all of my flaws, the shoulders that roll too far forward, and in. The hair pattern down his chest is similar too.

I couldn't, of course, help but see myself.

"Hey," he said.

"Hey," I replied.

I offered him the magazine. He said, "No, thanks," sat on one of the benches, and watched my alternating-leg routine.

"Germs," I explained.

"Relax. This is our roots," he said. "Somewhere in Russia our great-grandfather and his brothers went to the *shvitz* together."

"It wasn't like this," I said. "Waiting for whores."

"You don't think so?"

I put *Dixie Rhythms* down on the wooden bench and sat on top of the magazine. Beside me, Nathan lounged comfortably on the bare bench. A few minutes of silence passed.

"How do I tell them I'm sorry?" I blurted.

"Mom and Dad, or everyone?"

"All of them."

"Mom and Dad will get over it someday. Sooner than you think, probably."

"And everyone else—how do I tell them?"

"You can't," my brother said. "I've thought about this a lot—I read everything they write about you, Steve. You'll never be sorry enough for the journalists. You'll never win them back and get into their good graces again, not in this life. You could work harder at good deeds than Mother Teresa, and you'd still be the fabricator."

I remembered that the *Weekly* actually had run a story once called "Mother Teresa, Malefactor."

"The only way you'll ever give them a modicum of satisfaction," Nathan continued, "is to let them run your obituary. Here lies Stephen Aaron Glass, who was wrong and broke the rules. Very important rules. And he was bad too. Very bad. He suffered all his life, and then he died painfully.

"I don't mean they think about it that way," Nathan continued. "They don't. Robert doesn't go home to his wife and say, 'I really wish Stephen Glass had a stroke.' He doesn't actually fantasize about seeing you dead. It's more like he condemns you forever. He believes you've committed an unforgivable sin. Worse, he believes this sin fundamentally represents who you are. He believes he rooted it out of you. He discovered that deep down, you are a bad person, and now he has to let everyone know, because he is a good person and good people have to protect themselves and others from bad people."

I realized Nathan's speech, his opinion, must have been a long time in the making. Nathan was like that: He'd be quiet for a long time, thinking, and then let you know how he felt. I agreed with everything he'd said, but it scared me to hear that he'd come to the same conclusions I had, on his own. He wasn't even a journalist; he just read what they wrote. He could see it anyway. He knew.

"I know you're right," I said.

"I don't mean to be hard on you," Nathan continued. "But these people aren't going to forgive you. That's the way they see the world: no mercy. When you were a journalist, you thought that way too. Remember the Harry Madison story?"

Madison had been a rising Republican governor who some in

the GOP believed might be a future presidential candidate. By calling for state-funded daycare, he'd attracted broad support from
Democratic women. For my piece, I'd spent several days following
him. In my article, I'd painted him as a sexist, all on the strength of
a single joke about blondes I'd overheard him tell his campaign
manager; in every other respect, he was exemplary. For once, what
I'd written was true, but in retrospect I saw that it was also trivial,
and unfair. The story was picked up by newspapers across the country. Local reporters piled on; they reported that old high-school
friends had heard the governor make off-color jokes, too. A dozen
blond college women protested outside Madison's office, and all
three networks and the cable news stations carried footage of their
march. By then, Madison wasn't a presidential hopeful anymore: It
was already over for him.

"It didn't matter that Madison hired more women than his predecessor, or that he supported women's rights or anything," my brother
reminded me. "That joke sealed it. There's no second chances with
journalists. They don't see that people can be two ways—Clinton can
be a great president and a low-down dirty dog. Or, people can be
mostly one way but they can work at it, and over time they can
change.

"So someday, when Robert hears you're doing well in your life
again, when you're a veterinarian or a political candidate or a consul-
tant or something, he's going to get angry. He's going to say you're
pulling the wool over everyone's eyes again. He'll probably talk to the
papers, and try to make it uncomfortable for you, and hope you fail
again. It's not just that he's never going to be on your side, Steve. It's
worse—Robert's always going to be against you. And that's just the
way it is."

Finally I had to break in: "Thanks, Nat, I feel so much better." I
was on the verge of tears—I couldn't listen to it anymore.

"No, no," Nathan said. "I don't want to make you feel bad. My
point is, you have to go on. You asked me, how do you get them to
know you're sorry? You can't. Your personality is that you need everyone to like you, you've always been that way. If it doesn't happen, you

get anxious, really anxious, and you try to find a way to make it happen. This time, it just won't: If you try to get their approval again, you'll be trying forever. I don't want to watch you do it.

"And another thing"—Nathan was on a roll now—"you've got to start by making today the last time you go to a place like this, like you promised. I know you think you can't date anyone anymore, that no one will have you, they'll all treat you like Beth or Kimmy did. But it's not true—or even if it's true for a while, it won't be true forever. This is not what you deserve. It's only what Robert thinks you deserve."

There was silence for a minute or two more. Beads of sweat rolled off my chest and down my stomach, into rivulets that flowed down my belly. The smell of two brothers baking filled the room.

"Stories end two ways, Steve," Nathan resumed. "Everyone dies and it's a tragedy, or everyone gets married and it's a comedy. You still get to write your life any way you want—even if you can't get it published in a magazine, write it for yourself at least. Just don't let them write it for you."

We didn't say anything more. The air was hotter now, and singed when it was inhaled.

Nathan seemed exhausted from his long speech. I knew he must have kept it bottled up for months. I also knew that the reason he'd watched every TV show and read every article about me was so I didn't have to—he'd quietly kept track for me, metering just how bad it was and figuring out how I should try to deal with it all. I knew there must have been some bad things about him in there too, and not just in the *Dartmouth Review* pieces, but he'd never said anything to me about them.

I saw all the ways he was trying to protect me, and I thought about how I hadn't been much of an older brother lately, and how he had.

And I saw that Nat was right: Apologies were not going to save me now. Neither would being a charming person, and neither would seeing, and serving, people's needs and wants. What they wanted and needed, I just couldn't give them anymore. What they wanted was for it never to have happened—for me never to have done it. Or, perhaps, for me never to have even existed. I couldn't give them that, even if I had wanted to. And another truth was this: I didn't.

I wanted to be alive, to continue with my life and figure out what I actually wanted to do with it. I hadn't been cut out to be a doctor or a journalist, that was for certain, but maybe there was something else I could be.

Having come to the end of other people's desires, or at least of my ability to meet them, I began to wonder, for the first time in a long time, what my own desires might be—might have been—underneath. They might not always have been pretty, but at least they were my own.

The old woman returned and pointed at me to follow her. She led me back to the massage room, where a woman in her early forties wearing a miniskirt waited to rub me down.

I lay on the table facedown, and she squirted baby oil on my back and began to press on the muscles below my shoulders.

"Would you like any extras?" she whispered in my ear.

"Yes," I said. "I'd like a happy ending."

PART SIX
DÉNOUEMENT

TWO MONTHS after I was fired, and a week after that day in the sauna with Nathan, I had finally convinced myself that the worst might be over. For the first time, I'd been able to sleep through the night, and recently my anxiety had seemed, on most days at least, to have died down to a tolerable level. My job at Action Video was going well, and although I didn't have a girlfriend, I wasn't desperate for one either; Nathan had persuaded me to be patient. Best of all, except for Cliff's daily emails, which I deleted, I hadn't heard from any journalists in a few days. I felt almost happy.

But it didn't last long. I called to order a pizza and when the deliveryman arrived at my apartment door, he asked if I was *the* Stephen Glass.

"You know, are you the guy in the *Post* today?" he asked when I didn't respond. "It's you, right? You sure look like him."

I handed him a twenty. "Can I get seven back?" I asked.

"Yeah, It has to be you. You're wearing different glasses, but you definitely have the same nose. Same ears too. And brown curly hair. Except it's longer in real life. And bushier. You need a haircut."

"My change, please."

"Man, I hope you don't mind me saying this, but you totally fucked up."

There was silence.

"I apologize," he said, and counted out seven singles. "I'm sorry. I really am."

I didn't believe his contrition. No one, no matter how apologetic they are, appears sorry in a maraschino-red Domino's uniform.

I closed the front door on him, walked to my kitchenette, got a plate and a glass of water, and opened the pizza box. Three slices, almost half the pie, were missing. In their place was a sealed Number 10 white business envelope. My name was printed on the outside, in a bold hand, along with the instructions, "Read Me Before You Eat Me."

Inside was a note, written like a ransom demand out of the movies, with tiny letters individually clipped out and pasted awkwardly together.

HOLDING UR SLISES HOSTAGE. DO NOT KALL POLIS.
WILL FON W INSTRUKTIONS.

PIZZA BANDIT

Thirty seconds later, my phone rang. I let it go to the machine: "Hey man, it's the Pizza Bandit, pick up the phone. I just delivered your pizza, so I know you're in there. Don't be scared, dude, the note was a joke."

He said his name was Greg Picken and he was a freelance journalist, talking to me on his cell phone from just outside my door. He delivered pizzas for extra money.

"I sent you an email a few weeks ago, asking for an interview. Do you remember? Probably not. You didn't write back. So when your order came through, I thought I might get your attention this way. You know, the participatory journalism thing? Anyway . . ."

The machine beeped and cut him off, but a few seconds later, the phone rang again. "Hey, it's still me. Look, I prepared something that explains why you should talk to me. Let me get it." I heard him rustle papers, both through the phone and through the door. "Okay, here it is. My Top Three list for why you should give me an interview. Top Three, because I didn't have time to come up with seven more reasons. I had to write it on the drive over and I had another delivery to make. Plus, Top Ten lists are so cliché. So here goes.

"One. A lot of people are saying a lot of really bad shit about you, and you need to set the record straight.

"Two. It'll make you feel better. I wrote that one in case the shit they're saying about you is true, in which case the record's already straight.

"Three. I haven't made up my mind yet about what you did. Which, if you've seen the coverage out there, is saying a lot.

"So you've gotta speak to me. How do you plan on convincing people you're right if you don't talk to someone?"

I hadn't planned on trying to convince anyone I was right. I was wrong, dead wrong.

The machine cut him off again. A few minutes passed, and I assumed he had given up. But then I heard him push an envelope under my door. I opened it cautiously. Inside, dripping with tomato sauce, was a solitary blistered pepperoni. The amputated pork appendage was wrapped in a note, which stated, "Agree to the interview, or another slice gets hurt."

And then the phone rang again. Again I let the machine pick up. "Shit, man, it's getting annoying to have to call you back every time the machine disconnects me. Come on, didn't you think the pepperoni thing was funny? I'm a natural at this shit. Please pick up the phone, or at least open the door again so I can return your slices. I have them out here on napkins. . . . They're still warm.

"Whoa! I know what's wrong. You think I'm a bad writer because the spelling in the ransom note was all messed up. It's not my fault, I swear. After you ordered, I only had a few minutes to put it together, while your pizza was cooking. Most of the letters came from one of the menus. Do you realize there are no *c*s on our menu—"

I couldn't take him anymore. I picked up the phone. "There's a *c* in *cheese*," I shouted, as if deranged.

Then I replaced the receiver and unplugged the cord from the wall. And as I did so, I thought suddenly of Allison. I thought of what it must have been like for her, and I felt sad and ashamed that I had hidden in Lakeside while she had suffered this, or something like it— maybe something worse—in D.C.

Two days later, *The Washington Herald*'s gossip column published a photo of me angrily paying the Pizza Bandit. The Bandit's name, Greg

Picken, was listed as the photo credit. He must have set up a camera with a timer to take a picture when I opened the door.

Beneath the picture was the following extended caption:

> Stephen Glass, the former *Washington Weekly* journalist who was fired for fabricating dozens of stories, gets pizza delivered yesterday. Deliveryman Greg Picken said Glass seemed unfazed by the scandal.
>
> "I asked him why he made up the stories," Picken told us. "Stephen just brushed me aside as if it wasn't important."
>
> Glass's tip was decidedly average. He gave Picken $1.75 on an $11.25 pizza, or just over 15 percent. If only that much of his journalism had been true.

The caption hurt, but by now it felt like par for the course. At least they hadn't found a way to say I'd lied again.

A few days after the Pizza Bandit's visit, I got a cold email from Samuel at the *Weekly*. It said he'd be sending my packed-up possessions to me in care of a D.C. post office: the one near Dupont Circle, where I had last lived. (Apparently no one at the magazine cared to learn where I lived now.)

I tried to remember what I had left in the office, beside my files, which I knew they would keep. Mostly family photos, I decided—including one that I loved of Nathan. He is age eight, in Israel for my Bar Mitzvah, drunk on the free samples at the Carmel winery. (Nathan had a childhood drinking problem that mysteriously went away by the time he was about eleven.) There was no copy of it, and Nathan might never be that drunk again.

After my experience with the Pizza Bandit, I realized my apartment was really no safer now than the outside world—maybe less safe—and missing my family, I started to want my photos back. I decided I had to pick up the box.

· · ·

I drove to Dupont Circle later that day, and pulled into a parking spot on Florida Avenue, near the Washington Hilton. From there, I looked carefully at the post office. I tried to peer in, to see the other postal patrons. Postal patrons—that's what they call us, although I don't know of anyone who feels like they patronize the post office, it's more like we suffer it.

That's when I spotted Cliff. He was sitting on a ledge near the entrance. Next to him were two large coffee cups and a half-dozen ruffled newspapers. Someone at the *Weekly* must have tipped him off that I'd have to come here someday soon, and they'd been right: Here I was.

I ducked low in the driver's seat and watched him. Cliff was studying all the young, dark-haired men who came into the post office. It was bright outside and many customers were wearing sunglasses or talking on their cell phones, making it hard to see their faces. Cliff would dart in front of each of these men and take a look at him. When he saw it wasn't me, he would raise his hands, apologize, and go back to the ledge.

I remained in my car and waited for Cliff to leave. He was one man, I thought: he couldn't stay here forever. But two hours passed, during which I stayed put and so did he. By now, my whole body hurt from crouching behind the steering wheel. Every half hour, I tried to stretch, by extending my torso horizontally across the front section of the car, but it didn't help much. The car was hot, and I was getting sleepy. I took off one of my shoes. I had once heard that it's impossible to fall asleep if your feet are different temperatures. Untrue. Meanwhile, Cliff remained perched on his ledge. Every few minutes he stood up and rubbed his butt and knees. He seemed to be getting sleepy as well. Two out-of-shape, pasty men in an endurance competition—who would prevail? It was Hands on a Soft Body.

Didn't he ever have to go to the bathroom?

An hour later, that question was answered. After about twenty minutes of pacing, Cliff disappeared around the side of the post office to take a whiz. I was about to get out of the car and make a bolt for it, when I saw his head poke around the corner of the building. He was keeping an eye on the entrance while he was peeing.

Cliff finished his business and returned to his ledge. I took my hand off the car door handle and continued to wait.

Around 3 P.M., a Domino's pizza truck parallel parked in front of me. A man got out, carrying a pizza box, and walked up to Cliff, who handed him some money and took the box. When the deliveryman turned to the side, I saw it was the Pizza Bandit. Coincidence? I thought not.

Cliff and the Bandit laughed together. Cliff offered the Bandit a slice. He smiled, took one, and sat down on the ledge beside Cliff. Cliff asked the Bandit some questions I couldn't hear, to which he nodded. Cliff then walked into the neighboring bagel store.

I decided this was my break, and I speed-walked toward the front entrance.

"Hey wait," the Bandit called to me as I reached the door. "You're Stephen Glass."

I got on line without answering him. He followed me inside. Then Cliff ran into the post office at breakneck speed, erupting through the twin doors.

"That's him," the Pizza Bandit shouted, pointing at me.

"I know," Cliff yelled back. "He's a friend of mine."

I stood perfectly still and kept my eyes fixed forward. There were at least seven people in front of me, yet only one window was staffed. Some of the customers turned and looked at the Pizza Bandit, Cliff, and me. Wholly unimpressed, they returned to waiting.

"Thank you," Cliff said to the Bandit. He handed the Bandit a twenty-dollar bill.

But the deliveryman didn't move. "I'm going to stay and watch," he said. "I'm going to write about it myself too, you know."

"It's my story," Cliff protested, outraged.

People's heads turned in line. One person muttered, "Be quiet."

"This is not a library," the Bandit responded, addressing the line generally, unsure of who had spoken. "Plus, it's a public place," he told Cliff. "That's not a threat—that's a promise."

Cliff waited for him to finish, but it soon became clear that the Bandit was done. "I'm sorry, but what's not a threat?" Cliff asked.

"*That's* not a threat, *that's* a promise," the Bandit repeated.

"I still don't get it," Cliff said. "What is *that*? What is not a threat, but is a promise?"

"*That* is *that.* Besides, our stories aren't the same. I'm going to do a story on *you* doing a story on Glass."

"No you're not," Cliff snapped. "I am the journalist here."

"I've got some great stuff. Want to hear my description of you?"

"Come on," Cliff said. "You can't do that."

"It's a free country."

"I am trying to do an interview here," Cliff proclaimed.

"And I *am* doing an interview too—with you," the Bandit insisted. He was writing down everything Cliff was saying.

The line moved a step forward, and as soon as the elderly white-haired man in front of me took a step, Cliff attempted to step between us, so he could face me. But he inadvertently bumped the man, who stumbled forward and shot him a dirty look. Immediately, I took another step toward the man, so Cliff couldn't try to insert himself again.

Cliff sighed, exasperated. I realized he must be desperate: Based on what he'd perceived to be the strength of our friendship, he had promised an interview to *District* magazine. Then he'd told everyone he had it, when in fact I hadn't spoken a word to him yet and didn't seem inclined to, ever. Even the Pizza Bandit had been more success-ful (if only by aggravating me)—indeed, he'd been in the *Herald*—and that had to rankle.

Service at the window moved quickly until the elderly man in front of me was up. He was trying to send a parcel to one of the for-mer Soviet Republics, but had addressed it only in Cyrillic letters.

"Soviet Union," the man said to the postal clerk.

"It no longer exists," the clerk said. "Where in the *former* Soviet Union do you want it sent?"

"Azerbaijan," he said.

"This is going to Azerbaijan?"

"I'm from Azerbaijan."

"That's nice and all, but where is this package *going to*?"

The clerk pulled out a map of the Eastern Hemisphere. The man pointed to Azerbaijan and then to himself.

"No," the clerk screamed, "Where is it going?" She mimed throwing the package like a football at the map.

Behind me, Cliff said my name a few times, but I didn't acknowledge him at all. Cliff needed me to say something, anything. In the end, *what* a subject says to a journalist is secondarily important to the requirement that the subject actually speak. I focused only on the white-haired man, silently begging him to finish up quickly. Next to us, the Bandit—who'd stepped out of line—did some kind of karate move. "I'm pumped," he said to Cliff. "Tell me why you're taking this tack in the interview. Tell me what you're thinking. Give me the play-by-play."

"I don't have time for this," the postal clerk said to the white-haired man. "It's going to Uzbekistan. If it's the wrong destination, the Uzbeks will send it on to the right -stan. It'll get there somehow."

The white-haired man nodded in appreciation, though not in understanding. And finally, I stepped up to the counter, and told the postal clerk I had a package waiting for me. The worst was over, I hoped; I'd be out of here in a few minutes.

Cliff and the Bandit flanked me at the window. They were crowding very close, to hear what I was saying to the clerk.

"Are these men with you?" the clerk asked. I shook my head.

"Then get back," she said to them.

"We're here to observe," Cliff said.

"The public has a right to know," the Pizza Bandit added.

"I don't care what the public has a right to," the clerk said. "Get away from my window." Cliff and the Bandit stepped back.

"Can I have your ID, please?" the clerk asked me. I passed my driver's license under the window.

"Stephen Glass?" she asked.

"That's right," I said.

"Are you *the* Stephen Glass?"

Cliff, who was scribbling furiously in his notebook, leaned in, and so did the Bandit. I hesitated.

"Yes. He is," the Bandit yelled out. "I asked him the same question myself. He's the one!"

"Can I have your autograph?" the postal clerk asked me. She slipped a piece of paper through the window. "My husband's a big fan of yours."

I looked down. This was something new. A fan?

"He watches you all the time," she added. "The Magpies are his favorite. He says you're the best young midfielder in Europe."

"You mean someone else," I said. "That's not me."

"You're not the soccer player?" she asked.

"No," I said.

"He's the one," the Pizza Bandit yelled again. "He's the one."

"You're sure you're not?" the postal clerk asked.

"I'm sure," I said. "I wasn't even good at gym."

"I should have known. You have an American driver's license. How could you be a British soccer player?"

"Don't listen to him," the Pizza Bandit said. "I tell you, he's the one. Why do you think we're here?"

The Pizza Bandit then turned to face the line of customers. "Hello, everyone," he shouted. "This man, standing at the counter, is Stephen Glass, infamous journalist and Britain's greatest soccer player."

"Could you just sign your autograph anyway?" the clerk asked me. "My husband will kill me if he thinks I let you slip away."

"I can't," I said. "I'm sorry. Can I just get my package?"

The postal clerk went into a back room and returned with the box, which I signed for. She handed it to me. "Please, can't you just sign another?" she asked, before I left the window. "Who's going to know? It would mean the world to him."

"I'm really sorry," I whispered. "I really am. But I just can't."

With the bulky package in my arms, I began running for the door. Cliff jogged alongside me. The Bandit moved slightly more slowly, because he walked out of the post office backward, like cowboys do in Western movies so no one in the saloon will shoot them from behind.

"Please," Cliff said. "Just a few questions."

I reached the post office door, opened it, and ran for my car.

"I was your friend, and now you won't even answer my questions?" Cliff shouted at me as I ran. "How is that fair?"

I loaded the package into the backseat and screeched out of my parking space. As scared as I was, I was glad I'd gotten out of there after telling only the truth, as well as saying as little as possible. A quick fib might have gotten Cliff and the Bandit removed from the post office, but I hadn't resorted to it—and not only because if I had, it would inevitably have made the paper. For once, I hadn't even thought to lie.

When I got back to my building, I immediately ran into Dotan, the resident whom I had previously met at the mailboxes. He insisted that I come up to his apartment "to discuss Judaism," and, still shaken by the post office experience, I agreed. I didn't want to be alone, and though I feared spending time with him, for now it seemed like the lesser of two evils.

Dotan welcomed me into apartment 613 munificently, and offered to take the box out of my hands.

"It's sensitive," I said, and laid it on the kitchen counter with the *Weekly*'s return address facedown.

Dotan's studio was an exact copy of mine. Even the TV and the couch were positioned similarly. "We set our rooms up the same way," I commented.

"Jewish feng shui," Dotan replied.

He offered me some hummus and pita bread, which I accepted, and told me about his girlfriend, Debbie, who was on her way over. Debbie was a doctoral student at Georgetown, he said, writing her dissertation on the linguistics of screams. She had recorded hundreds of people's screams. "That's how we met actually," he said. "Debbie put an ad in the paper asking for people to scream for her, I responded, and it was love at first sight. It didn't hurt, I'm sure, that I also have a world-class scream.

"Would you scream for her?" he asked. "You look like you might be a good screamer. She's always looking for more people. She hopes to build the largest scream library in the world. She has some movie stars' screams too. Not the screams they do in the movies, those are all acted. Real screams. The way they scream in real life."

"I don't know if I could just scream on demand."

Weirdos, I thought: I attract them because I am one of them. They sense it somehow.

"Debbie'll coach you through the scream," Dotan assured me. "She does it all the time. All you have to do is think about your life going really awry."

"I'm not sure," I said. I didn't want Dotan getting me in front of any microphones. First thing I knew I'd be screaming, then suddenly he'd be interviewing me.

"I know you can do it. I know you can make yourself angry," he said. "I saw the photo of you in the *Herald,* with the pizza."

I looked down at the floor and adjusted myself on the couch. My fears about Dotan had been realized. He knew about my past, and was using our tenuous connection to expose me further. Even if he didn't want to expose me in the papers, I was sure he wanted to know me because of my notoriety. He wanted to be able to tell people: "I know Stephen Glass, the guy who made up all those articles. Yes, we're friends. In fact, I just saw him the other day." But I would never really be a friend, or even a person, to him. No, I would be a story for him to absorb into his personal narrative, the one that runs in each of our minds every day, and that we share with others so they can somehow understand us. And I didn't want to be that: an anecdote for him. I'd rather be alone. I started to stand up to leave, when Dotan spoke again.

"I saw the *Banner* story too. I couldn't believe that woman," he said. "Trapping you that way. Sleeping with you and pretending to like you so she could get a story. That's horrible. For me, that would be like if Debbie were just dating me to get my scream."

"I guess I should thank you. I appreciate that," I said. It had been so long since someone, other than my parents or Nathan, had said something supportive to me about any of this. I was wary, but I wanted to hear him out. In my mind he'd been put on probation; I was still suspicious, but a little hopeful too.

"No need to thank me," Dotan said. "I'm not doing anything for you, just telling you what I think. And I'm not the only one. My rabbi thinks so too. He's spent a lot of time thinking about what you did. He was a big admirer of your writing. I think you should meet him. I think you'd like him."

"That would be nice," I said. My voice was neutral; I didn't want to commit to meeting any rabbis.

"Why don't you come with Debbie and me to Shabbat services tonight?"

"I don't know," I said. "I'm kind of busy."

"Honestly, what are you doing?"

"Um . . ." I had been planning to stay in my apartment and maybe watch a video.

"Come just for a bit," Dotan said. "If you don't like it, you can leave at any time. No one's going to hold you there. Debbie might ask you to scream for her sometime, but you don't have to if you don't want to."

"Let me think about it."

"There's some total hotties there too, and you know what they say."

"No," I said. "What do they say?"

"Conservative in the head, reform in the bed."

"All right, all right, I'll go." I still wanted a girlfriend badly; suppressing the longing had amplified it, too. More than this, I wanted contact. Some days I spoke to no one but Oskar and Phillipe. Them, and the customers to whom I was apologizing for whatever they'd done that day.

Dotan, Debbie, and I arrived at the synagogue at about 7:15, a half hour before sundown. The sanctuary's long walls were painted a creamy yellow, and along one end, a bronze statue of two skinny arms holding out the Ten Commandments stretched the length of the room. Someone had just vacuumed the flaxen floor, leaving behind the back-and-forth trail of bent, clean carpet fibers.

Sticking up in this cavernous golden mouth were hundreds of bone-white seatbacks, like rows of teeth, attached to the pews for the comfort of the congregation. Rabbi Gordon, however, looked entirely uncomfortable. He was kneeling in his dark suit in the second row, one hand on the floor and one hand behind his lower back.

"I'm sorry I'm late," Dotan said to him as we walked in the room. "Rabbi, please stop. I'll take care of the books."

Rabbi Gordon rose slowly. As he stood up, each of his joints cracked like twigs underfoot. He was only in his midforties, I later learned, but had a drawn face and seemed far older, and tired. A prematurely white, closely trimmed beard extended from his ears to the space under his chin and covered part of his neck. The area under his nose, where a mustache should have been, was shaved clean. His eyes were a soft brown, matching his hair, which was neatly parted on the left.

When he was fully standing, which took almost a minute, Rabbi Gordon recentered his yarmulke on the back of his head and smoothed the wrinkles out of his shirt and pants. "Thank you, Dotan," he said. "Please double-check the third row carefully. Mrs. Shymel didn't have her book last week, and she gets very upset."

The rabbi turned to me. "It's a special large-print one," he said. "Looking at this place, you would think it was a ballpark for the retired, with the cushioned, raised backs. But the ladies won't come without them."

Dotan was bent over in the row where the rabbi had been, but he jumped up and ran back to us. "I'm sorry I didn't introduce you," he said. "This is a friend of mine, Stephen."

"I know who he is," the rabbi said. He extended his right hand, which I took and which held mine for a long time. "Why don't you follow me for a minute?" he suggested. I warily agreed.

"I'll keep doing the prayer books," Dotan yelled out, his head popping up and down between the pews.

"I've known Dotan since he was reading *K'tonton*," the rabbi said as we walked to his office.

"I remember *K'tonton*," I said.

K'tonton, which comes from the Hebrew word *k'ton,* meaning "small," was the name of a Tom Thumb–like boy in a series of children's books about Jewish identity. Born into a normal-sized family, K'tonton was always getting lost in the house, or on a trip to the ocean, or spirited off on a runaway dreidel.

Where is K'tonton? Where is K'tonton? The family would spend most of the story searching for him, only to find their smallest son in the cake batter, moments before the mother was about to put the pan into the oven.

Reading *K'tonton* was the highlight of the seven years of Hebrew school my parents required Nathan and me to attend. We were sent there to learn the Jewish rituals, stories, and language that had been passed down for more than five thousand years. But in actuality, what I learned was different: Hebrew school was where I first came into conflict with authority, over a language I initially resisted learning to speak and ultimately rebelled against dramatically and self-destructively. When I thought about Hebrew school that day at the synagogue, I realized suddenly that at the *Weekly,* I'd still been that annoying, disruptive, plaintive boy: I hadn't grown up as I had thought, but rather had been frozen somehow—with all my resentment, my discontent, and my secret, subversive questions and plans intact.

During most of my years there, I was taught by Mrs. Shulevitz, a used-up Israeli woman who smoked cigarettes in the classroom. She had once seen *The Paper Chase* and taught Hebrew by the Socratic method.

"Zvi," she would instruct—that was my Hebrew name, it means "deer," and when the word was uttered, I looked like I was trapped in the headlights—"Zvi, translate from the reader, page twenty-eight."

I would begin slowly, jerking from word to word, sounding the letters out right to left, promising myself I would translate them at the end of the reading, and hoping if I just went slowly enough, the period would end.

"Stand up taller, Zvi," she'd yell at me. "Like you are speaking before the Knesset."

I would fix my posture by raising my back, but my head remained stooped over my book. I couldn't make eye contact with her.

"This is no good," Mrs. Shulevitz would shout from her desk. "You are too slow. What kind of reader are you? Start from the beginning again. Stand taller. You are going to get scoliosis."

I would try the passage again, but with no more success. I never did any Hebrew homework so I didn't know the words. It took all the time I had during the week to do my *real* school homework, and when she pressed me on why I knew virtually no Hebrew, I told her the truth. Real school came first.

"Is that what you think, Zvi?" Mrs. Shulevitz yelled. "You think junior high is real school and this is fake school? Is that what you think?"

I started to sit down.

"Stand up. I'm not done with you, Zvi. This school is more real than you can believe. Come to the front of the room."

She pulled down a map over the chalkboard. "You see Israel? Can you even find Israel on a map? Zvi, point to the State of Israel."

I did.

"How big is it?" she asked me.

"I don't know," I said.

"You don't know?"

"Small," I said.

"Wrong," she said. "Tiny. Almost not there. And who is this, I'm pointing to?"

"Egypt," I said.

"And this?"

"Lebanon."

Syria. Iran. Iraq. Jordan. Qatar. U.A.E. Libya.

"You know who they are, Zvi?"

"Arab neighbors?"

"Neighbors. Pshaw. They are enemies. Neighbors don't invade you, and make it part of their constitution to drive you into the sea. Do they?"

"No, I guess not," I said.

"They are why you must study, Zvi. Someday you might be called to protect Israel, and how are you going to do it without knowing Hebrew?"

I said nothing.

"I'm talking to you, Zvi. How are you going to do it?"

"Not well," I said.

"If you do not improve, I will send you back to *K'tonton,*" she said.

Oh, please, send me back to *K'tonton,* Mrs. Shulevitz. Little stories about little boys lost, being rescued in the nick of time. Please send me away from these long lessons on the Hebrew past tense.

And she sent me back to my seat.

Rabbi Gordon showed me to the couch in his office, and I sat down. The room was wallpapered in books. On the upper half of the shelves, from head height to the ceiling, the titles were inscribed in Hebrew lettering, little ribbon bookmarks rising above the books' spines. The lower half of the stacks was loaded three or four volumes deep with English titles: histories, biographies, and, I noticed, even a few spy novels.

Magazines were scattered on the coffee table in front of me: *Time, Newsweek, The New Yorker, The New Republic, U.S. News and World Report, Commentary, Harper's, Hadassah, Scientific American,* and, of course, *The Washington Weekly.* There it was, the newest issue. This was the first time I had seen the magazine in months, and it hurt and was strangely familiar at the same time—like coming home to a house that wasn't yours anymore.

On the cover was a blowup of one of those old Charles Atlas ads found in the back of comic books. A scrawny man says: "Darn it, I'm tired of being a skinny scarecrow. Charles Atlas says he can make me a new man!" Above the cartoon was the headline: THE CASE FOR BEING OUT OF SHAPE.

Rabbi Gordon saw me looking at the magazine. "I've gotten it for years," he said. "Robert and I went to City College together." He paused. "Back then, I was always a bit scared of him. Robert was the best student I knew, and we were both planning to go to rabbinical school when we graduated. I remember thinking we would both probably end up at JTS and then when we'd be applying to shuls, he would get the better one. He was so much smarter. My wife, Gwen, she knew him there too, would always tell me before finals that I had to study harder to catch Robert. She drew a little sketch of Robert once and tacked it up above my desk. This is what you need to beat, Gwen would say. I'm not so aggressive anymore. And Robert became more interested in the secular world."

"Are you still friends?" I asked. The words came out of me slowly and muffled, as if from under water.

He chuckled, showing he knew what I was thinking. "No, and your secrets are good here. Once in a while, we bump into each other at a conference or something, and then we pretend to be nice to each other. Sometimes he even says we should have dinner together, but I know we never will. I've stopped saying we should. It only makes it worse three years later when you haven't actually followed up."

The rabbi and I sat there quietly for a minute and I enjoyed the warmth of his bottomless sofa. I appreciated that he had shown vulnerability he hadn't had to reveal—all to prove that if I suspected he might be against me, I was wrong: He was for me, instead. He didn't mind if I thought he was petty or competitive, or that his wife was pushy; he was willing to let me think all those things, as long as I also knew he was on my side. He could be seriously flawed, and that meant so could I.

Besides my parents and Nathan, Rabbi Gordon was, I think, the first person who was unequivocally in my corner—not that he thought what I had done was acceptable or minor, but that he wanted above all for me to survive it. All this he had communicated without saying any of it.

"Shabbat is going to begin in a minute or two," the rabbi said. "I need to be going in."

"Thank you," I said, and we walked back into the synagogue.

The sanctuary was half full now. Men and women in their late thirties and early forties hovered around the entrance, hairpinning yarmulkes on the heads of their young sons, who were running every which way. Under the pay phones—which were still rotary so that the rabbi could put a little circular lock in the dial on Shabbat, when you weren't supposed to make calls—three seventh-grade girls sat cross-legged on the floor in their smart dresses. Ten steps away, a pack of junior-high boys—standing in a half-circle looking all formal and proper in their little-man suits and short-man ties—pretended to do anything but crave them.

Old ladies, sitting by themselves or with gaggles of friends, filled in the first three rows. When the rabbi walked in, their faces became illuminated with the love for a husband that should have been, the high school boyfriend they should never have dumped, the father who should never have died. The rabbi nodded solemnly to them. They were his faithful, the ones who came even when there was a snowstorm or a toothache or theater tickets. Without them, there would be no shul.

Dotan was sitting with some friends in one of the back rows, and he waved me over. As I sat down, the service began, but I found it hard to concentrate on it. I started daydreaming about Hebrew school again.

After Mrs. Shulevitz sent me back to my desk, she announced a pop quiz. There were groans in the classroom.

"Do not be angry with me," she said. "Be angry with Zvi. He is the one who has let you down. He is the one who has revealed your secret."

Avi, the smartest boy in the class, raised his hand. "What secret is that, Mrs. Shulevitz?" he asked.

"That many of you are just skating by! You think junior high is the *real* school? Ha! You must work harder. I only ask you to give it your best. Is this your best, Zvi? Because if it is your best, you're in trouble. Well, is it, Zvi?"

"No," I said.

"Stand up when you speak to me," she said.

I stood up.

"Is it, Zvi?"

"No," I said again.

"We'll see. You all better do well on this quiz, because I am sending your grades home to your parents."

Mrs. Shulevitz then blew angry cigarette smoke on the class. (Out of a sense of fairness to the dead, I note, as Mrs. Shulevitz always did when she was criticized for smoking in class, that she used only a kosher brand of tobacco. As proof, she kept in her desk a full-page ad from *The Jerusalem Post* inserted by the Dubek corporation, Israel's largest tobacco company, stating that their cigarettes had full kashrut certification. "*Glatt* kosher! I can send you a copy of the ad!" Mrs. Shulevitz would say to the concerned parent who called because her fifth-grader had come home smelling of smoke. "Is your home kosher? No? Well then!")

For the quiz, Mrs. Shulevitz told us to read a few passages in our textbooks and answer the questions at the end of the chapter. Everything—the passage, the questions, and our answers—was to be in Hebrew.

I can honestly say that I tried. The story seemed to have something to do with a boy who saw a lion escape from the zoo, or perhaps the circus. Or maybe it was all on TV. Possibly it was from the point of view of the lion. I had no idea. I understood only every third word or so. And the stories had only the most limited connection to real life, so I was working in a contextual vacuum. It was like trying to drag a dream about a foreign world out of the murkiness of sleep, weeks after it had been dreamt.

I flipped to the questions, hoping they would give me clues to the text. Here is what I read:

1.   What did Benjamin XXX the lion XXX at lunch XXX he was XXX?
2.   In that case, then what XXX XXX XXX the lion?

"Are you translating, Zvi?"

I was concentrating so hard, I hadn't noticed Mrs. Shulevitz step up behind me. She did not permit students to translate Hebrew into English on quizzes. "You must think in Hebrew," she said, at least once every class. "There is no time in conversation to translate every word."

I told Mrs. Shulevitz I had been thinking in Hebrew.

"You better be, or you will be a failure," she said.

Considering each Hebrew word and trying to remember what it meant, I began to sketch in my notebook. It started innocently enough, as just a way to vent anger. Choppy, two- or three-inch straight lines, like I was slashing the page with my pencil—a way to express the hopelessness and misery of everything around me without breaking the rules, without causing myself any more shame, without getting into any more trouble.

Enough, Mrs. Shulevitz. Slash, slash, slash. Neat vertical lines in a row. I attacked another page. Slash, slash, slash. More playful this time. One vertical line and a horizontal line crossing it. Artful serifs, now. Like a serial killer leaving his signature cut.

More slashing and crossing of little lead lines on the page.

Yes, I saw it too.

Swastikas.

Dozens of them.

Big swastikas and small swastikas and in-between-sized swastikas.

Over and over again, I covered Mrs. Shulevitz's precious little assignment with Hitler's sign.

These small ones here are for humiliating me, Mrs. Shulevitz. These here, the medium-sized ones, are for not understanding what I am going through, or even trying to understand. I am in seventh grade, for fuck's sake. And this big one in the center, Mrs. Shulevitz, you see this one, this one is for shaming me.

Mrs. Shulevitz took my arm and dragged me into an empty office. She used the phone to call someone, and spoke incomprehensible Hebrew at an impossibly rapid-fire pace. Even if I had known the words, she still would have been too quick.

Mrs. Shulevitz looked through the rest of my notebook but found nothing else. She left the room and locked me inside.

A minute or so later, she returned, with all of the contents of my locker in a trash can. She dumped out the can and began to rummage through its contents, tearing through my junior high homework, ripping pages, crumpling assignments for math and social studies and history and typing—what did she possibly think she would find in my folder for typing class?—and putting it all out of order.

"Wait," I said. "Please wait. I need that stuff."

"*Shecket,*" she snapped. Be quiet.

Ten minutes later, all my junior high papers were in a tattered heap. She had found nothing else. Mrs. Shulevitz sat down across from me and smoked. Her hair was twisted every which way and there was sweat beading on her face, and she told me she knew there was more.

"There is nothing else," I said.

"Maybe not this," she said. "Maybe there aren't more swastikas, but there are other things you're hiding." More than ten years would have to pass before she finally would be right.

She left the room again, locking me in once more. Five minutes later, she returned with the rabbi. He looked at the pile of demolished paper and asked me what had happened. Mrs. Shulevitz answered for me, telling the rabbi what she had found. She held up the defamatory notebook: "Need I say more, Rabbi?"

"Let him talk, Lois," the rabbi said.

Mrs. Shulevitz was angered at being silenced. I explained how she had humiliated me, and Mrs. Shulevitz jumped in and said that what she had done wasn't the point. "Get to the point," she said.

"It's all the point," I told the rabbi. "I have to show the context."

"He has committed a crime," she said, and held up the notebook again.

The rabbi told Mrs. Shulevitz to leave the room. Once she'd left, I told him everything that had happened and said I was sorry for the drawings. "I am not an anti-Semite," I said. "I received the highest score in the class on my Jewish Identity exam."

He left me alone again, although he did not lock me in, and he spoke with Mrs. Shulevitz outside the door in Hebrew.

"Lo. Lo. Lo," she yelled. No. No. No.

A minute or two later, the rabbi returned with her. He said nothing of what had happened, but pronounced us teammates for the upcoming Jewpardy! trivia contest. We would have to study together every day for the next month to get ready for the statewide competition.

What happened next was probably exactly what the rabbi had anticipated. At first, Mrs. Shulevitz refused to work with me and I had no interest in working with her. We sat at separate tables in the synagogue library, preparing with the thousands of flashcards the rabbi had left for us. But as the days went on, we began to talk more and more, and eventually we came to rely on each other.

No, Mrs. Shulevitz and I never became friends; we never even became friendly. But from being forced to spend so much time together, each of us learned that the other had a complicated life that we did not know enough about to understand, let alone judge.

Mrs. Shulevitz and I lost in the first round of Jewpardy! and I didn't think about her much again. The rabbi assigned me to another teacher, and when I became a Bar Mitzvah, I elected, without hesitation, to leave Hebrew school forever. (Nathan would stay on, however, and eventually become fluent.)

Then, during my senior year of college, I heard that Mrs. Shulevitz had died of lung cancer. Her kosher cigarettes apparently were no healthier than the *trayf* ones made in America. My parents told me they had heard that no one showed up at her funeral. No former colleagues or students. The rabbi had moved away, and she had no family.

The synagogue paid for the funeral, and the ceremony was performed by one of the old religious men who wander Jewish graveyards saying prayers for a fee over the dead relatives of busy people.

I'm sorry, Mrs. Shulevitz. I truly am.

The cantor concluded the Aleinu and led the sanctuary in the Mourner's Kaddish, the final prayer of the Shabbat service. *Yis'ga'dal v'yis'kadah sh'mey ra'bbo. . . .*

And we all said, "Amen."

"We have some new people here tonight," Rabbi Gordon announced. "I hope you will welcome them. Please convene in the Siegel Multipurpose Room for the kiddush."

I began to follow Dotan out of the pew, when an elderly woman blocked my exit. She was no more than five foot two, although the force of her personality gave the illusion that she could play professional football.

"Shabbat Shalom," she said. "You're new here. I'm Rose Shymel. What's your name?"

"Stephen," I said.

Dotan said something about having to go set up the kiddush room and stepped around Mrs. Shymel, leaving me alone with her.

"Stephen who?" she said.

"Um. I'd rather not . . . I'm kind of private. . . ."

"Who's this cute boy you're talking to, Rose? Keeping him all for yourself?"

A woman who was an inch or two shorter than Mrs. Shymel, and whose hair was hairsprayed more than four inches vertically, descended upon us. She said her name was Ethel Blumenthal, and asked me for mine.

"He doesn't like to say," Mrs. Shymel said.

"What do you mean, he doesn't like to say?" Mrs. Blumenthal asked.

"He says he's very private."

"Private?"

"That's what he says."

"With us?"

"With us."

"Can you believe that?"

"Come over here and get a load of this, Shelly," Mrs. Blumenthal yelled to another elderly woman, who was talking to the Sabbath Goy about some problem with the pew's back support. (Because religious Jews can't work, spend money, or even turn on the lights on the Sabbath, each synagogue hires a Sabbath Goy who, being a Gentile, has no objection to doing such things.)

"What do you want?" the woman yelled back. Then, seeing me, she came over. "New face, Shabbat Shalom. I'm Shelly Himmel, what's your name?" she asked.

"He won't say," Mrs. Shymel said.

"What is he, in the CIA?" Mrs. Himmel asked.

"Are you in the CIA?" Mrs. Blumenthal asked me.

"No," I said.

"Are you a Republican?" Mrs. Shymel asked. "It's okay if you are. My father was a block captain for the Crown Heights Republican Party."

"I'm not very political," I said.

"Ashamed of your parents?" Mrs. Blumenthal asked suspiciously.

"No, no," I said. "I love them."

"Then what is it?" Mrs. Himmel asked.

"I'm just very private," I said. I was very uncomfortable. I wanted to leave, but Mrs. Shymel was standing in my way.

"Wait, before we go any further, we've got a problem and it's not about his mishegaas," Mrs. Shymel said. "Sophie can't make it tomorrow for mahj, so we're going to have to cancel."

"That's the highlight of my week and she rips it out from under me. I wondered why she wasn't in shul tonight. She doesn't want to have to face us," Mrs. Blumenthal said. "Who else do we know who can play? It's not an option to cancel. I'm not going to live that many more years, and we only play once a week. Canceling one session reduces the quality of my life."

They listed a dozen names, but all the mahj players they knew were either dead or in Florida. Exasperated, Mrs. Blumenthal asked if I knew how to play. I said I did, and they were shocked.

"Who your age knows how to play mahj?" Mrs. Shymel asked.

"I do," I said.

"Mr. No Name knows how to play mahj. Imagine that."

"You didn't learn how to play from a Chinese person, did you?" Mrs. Himmel accused. "Chinese mahj is not Jewish mahj."

"I know how to play Jewish mahj," I said. "Brighton Beach Jewish mahj. I even have my own card. My mother orders it for me every year." (Mahj cards, for the uninitiated, set out the winning tile combinations, which change yearly.)

"Are you single?" Mrs. Blumenthal asked.

I said I was.

"Because I have a beautiful granddaughter," she said.

"Granddaughter? What about me?" Mrs. Himmel said.

"We all have beautiful granddaughters," Mrs. Shymel said. "Do you live around here?"

"I live in the same building as Dotan Braverman. He's the reason I came tonight."

"My granddaughter lives in that same building," Mrs. Shymel said. "Would you like to go on a date with her?"

And so I learned that contrary to Dotan's claims, there was indeed another Jew in The Harvey: Mrs. Shymel's granddaughter. Finding out that Dotan had been lying from the moment we met made me sick inside. I felt I had been wrong to let down my guard. What were his true motives in befriending me? I realized I still had no idea. I began to wonder what I might have told him that I would later regret. I needed to leave.

"I have to be going," I said. "I'm meeting some people."

Mrs. Shymel gave me her address and asked me to promise I would meet them for mahj the next day. I said I would try. But I wondered if I should just flee the triumvirate as fast as possible.

"I don't have that long to live," Mrs. Blumenthal said, perhaps sensing my ambivalence. "Do this mitzvah."

"And I'll bring deli," Mrs. Himmel said.

Again I promised to try to make it. Then I finally managed to extricate myself from the gaggle and head toward the front entrance. But Rabbi Gordon caught me just before I was out the door. "Not staying for kiddush?" he asked.

I explained what had happened with Mrs. Shymel et al. "They think it's just making small talk, getting to know me, being friendly and warm," I said. "But for me, it's hard."

He nodded. Then he asked me to come into his office, which I did.

There I sat on his sofa again. "I know it's not their fault," I explained. "They just wanted to know my last name. I've thought about legally changing it. But then I remembered what happened with Jeff Gillooly."

"Who?" the rabbi asked.

"Tonya Harding's ex-husband—you know, the one who was involved in the attack on Nancy Kerrigan?"

"Who?" the rabbi asked again. Clearly he didn't get out much.

"A figure skater. Anyway, Gillooly went to jail, did his time, and eventually most people forgot about him. Then the news got out that he was changing his name to Jeff Stone, and he made the papers all over again. Suddenly everyone's writing stories about how he's changing his name. When I thought about that, I realized you can't get away from your name. My name is like the Mark of Cain. It haunts me."

Rabbi Gordon slowly rose from his chair. He climbed the little ladder propped against his bookshelves and took down a thick blue volume. He looked through it quickly, opened it to a page he had chosen, and handed it to me.

"This Mark of Cain stuff is forever misunderstood," the rabbi said. "Cain, who is a farmer, kills Abel, right?"

I nodded.

"When challenged by God, Cain asks: 'Am I my brother's

keeper?' and God effectively says yes, and punishes him. You know all this, right?"

"Yes," I said.

"Okay. God's punishment is to banish Cain from his profession. He says the soil will no longer yield to him, which will force Cain to wander the earth. Apparently not a good prospect in the post-Eden world. And now here's the interesting part. Cain then cries out to God, saying his punishment is too great. He says that forcing him to become a nomad is effectively condemning him to death. Anyone who meets him might kill him. Hearing him, God promises Cain that anyone who kills him will have sevenfold vengeance brought down upon himself. And to warn people against hurting Cain, God marks him. The Mark of Cain is not just a sign of shame. It's also a marker that you are under God's special protection."

I sat back down in the sofa, and couldn't help but smile a bit. Special protection? I thought He would have written me off by now.

"Don't get too excited," the rabbi said. "Robert isn't going to be humiliated in the press seven times over."

I nodded.

"Why do you think God did that?" the rabbi asked me.

"I don't know," I said.

"Try," he coached me.

"Because he wanted Cain to bear only the punishment God thought he should have to bear?"

"And no more," the rabbi said. "That is exactly right."

I think he saw that my eyes were beginning to tear, because he cleared his throat. "We'd really enjoy having you come by sometimes," the rabbi said. "I could put the word out that you're to be given some space. I believe the Sabbath Three would respect that if it came from me."

"Thank you," I said. "But I need to be honest with you. I'm not a very religious person. I'm really just grasping at straws here, and I wouldn't want you to think that I'm using your temple to get out of my problems, or that I really understand the Torah or anything. I dropped out of Hebrew school. I'm not even sure I believe in God.

I don't want to mislead you here, because—well, for obvious reasons.

"But," I added, "I might still come, if it's okay with you, even knowing all that—what I said, I mean." Despite my suspicions about Dotan, I found myself wanting to talk to the rabbi more, even though I knew that I probably couldn't today. And that startled me: He was the first person I actually wanted to talk to more about what had happened. I wanted to consider his questions and answer them not just for him, but for myself—instead of avoiding them. In Dotan, I had hoped to find a friend with whom I could pretend that everything at the *Weekly* had never really happened, or that it was an event in my past so insignificant that it never really needed to be discussed. In the rabbi, I hoped to find a counselor who knew everything I had done wrong, and still could help me build from there.

The rabbi stood up and shook my hand. "People come here for many reasons," he said. "I hope I see you again."

The next morning, I decided to go to Mrs. Shymel's for mahj after all. I felt that after the rabbi had been so kind, this was the least I could do in return. And I didn't resent going as much as I'd thought I would. For one thing, I'd volunteered myself. For another, mahj gave me an excuse to finally call my mother, and a safe, neutral subject about which we could talk. It was a way for me to reach out to her and offer her a connection back to me, to do something I knew she would be happy I had done, spending time with three old Jewish grandmothers, women much like her own mother. Even so, I was terrified to call— my mom had been hopping mad when she left; I remembered it clearly. But I knew it had to be done.

The phone rang, and she picked up.

I said nothing.

"Is this Cliff Coolidge?" my mom demanded. "Because, Cliff, if it's you, I've had just about enough. Can't you leave my family alone? You have no business with my son anymore."

It was a tiny ray of hope. She was still defending me.

"Reveal yourself," my mom thundered. I'd previously thought that only my dad could thunder, but my tiny mom actually thundered into the phone. Then she threatened, "If this is a reporter . . ."

"Mom?" I squeaked.

"Stephen?" She sounded both angry and hopeful that it was me.

"Mom, before you say anything, can you please know that I am so sorry, and I know what you were trying to do, and I just didn't appreciate it at the time. And now I do. I'm so sorry. I know that you were there because you love me, and you just wanted to help me through it. . . ."

"It's past, Stevie. It's really all right. Your father calmed me down, and I'm starting to appreciate what you were saying too. That's why I didn't call. That's why I never sent the letter I wrote you. I think it's important that you do this on your own, and I know you can, I really do."

"I'm so sorry I disappointed you," I said.

"You're going to impress me, Stevie. You're going to pull yourself out of this and that's going to impress me."

"I love you, Mom," I said. I wanted to also say that I couldn't worry about impressing her anymore, only myself, but it sounded mean and I kept the thought to myself.

"I love you too," she said, and I knew everything between us would be all right again soon, even if not immediately. I knew, too, that we probably wouldn't have to dissect the fight ever again, and I was relieved. In our past arguments, my mom and I had spent hours on the postmortem, analyzing every word from every angle, and so the aftermath would always be far longer than the time we ever spent fighting. But this time our period of silence, our time apart, had allowed us each to think it all over, and appreciate the other's position. Now it seemed there was little more to be said about a fight we both knew we'd needed to have.

"You've got to hear what the Wordens concluded after their inquiry," she said after a moment.

"I can't wait."

"They called another press conference, and no one came but *The*

Lakeside Letter—dirt-digging again. So—get this—their conclusion is that while there is 'probable cause' against you, more information is needed. Probable cause! What are they, the U.S. Attorney's office?" She paused. "So the saga continues. You have to laugh, Stevie, or else you would cry."

I knew she meant herself—that she was probably often on the verge of tears, still—but it was kind of her not to come out and say it. It hurt me to think of the looks the Wordens must give my mom when she jogged around the neighborhood in the morning, and Mrs. Worden would be outside, retrieving the newspaper, with Dr. Worden standing at the door behind her and glaring. "Dagger eyes" wouldn't come close to describing it.

So I changed the subject. "Mom, I want you to know that I went to temple this week." Yes, it was a shameless play for approval, and I was backsliding a bit. But at least it was true.

"Stevie," my mother said. "You don't have to tell me that. We only expect you to go on the holidays."

"But it is true! I met these grandmas who asked me to play mahj with them. They desperately need a fourth, and I'm planning to go later today. I think I might even begin going to temple regularly."

"Yeah, sure, and there's a rabbit who lives in the moon. I really don't think you should exaggerate like this anymore, Stevie. If you even went to temple once in a great while, Dad and I would be happy."

"You can call the rabbi," I said, and I tried not to be too disappointed. I knew that for a long time I would face this kind of skepticism—even from my parents. But I was determined to prove myself anew each time.

"I'm sorry. I don't need to call him," my mom said. "I should just trust you, Stevie, and I'm glad you're doing this. But I've thought about it and I think you need to do something else, too."

"I'm not moving back to Lakeside," I protested.

"It's not that. I want you to start therapy. Dad and I agree on this."

"Mom, I told you what happened with Dr. Kantor—"

"I know," my mom said. "But Dad got some names from a friend at the hospital, people I think you'll like better."

"I don't mean to be resistant, but these psychiatrists, they're all meddlers, busybodies, and judgers."

"I think you're overreacting."

"I'm overreacting? *You* have one of these people tell you, with all the authority of all those degrees on the wall, in front of the person you think you love, that you're basically a murderer. Then you see how much you like it."

"Just try, Stevie," she said. "Remember Mr. Harding?"

"The only thing I remember about him is that one time when he was teaching physics he dropped Davie Fenton's T-shirt in the liquid nitrogen and then broke it against a wall. Harding forgot to bring a replacement shirt, so Davie had to walk around topless for the rest of the day. The guy was insane, the worst teacher I ever had."

"But you don't think *all* teachers are bad, right? So why not give another psychiatrist a try?"

I hemmed and hawed for a moment. I had no good answer. "All right, I give up. I'll take the names."

"Good. I'll email them to you."

"Now can I talk to you about mahj for a second?"

I asked her about a strategic point, and she told me I melded my jokers too early in the hand; I should hang on to them. Then I quizzed her some more, and at the end of the exchange I thanked her and told her I'd let her know how much I won. We'd probably be playing for a penny a point.

"Make sure you bring a coffeecake or something," my mom added. "It's more important than the game to them, the food."

I told her I would.

"And call the psychiatrists, okay?"

I told her that I'd do that, too.

By the end of the call, it had all been forgiven, I hoped—my evicting her from the apartment when she was trying to help me get settled, the airport run in the early morning, the snide comments of the country club ladies, and even the mean *Dartmouth Review* articles about Nathan.

That was the great thing about my mom, I decided: Angry as she might have been, she also passionately wanted me to survive this. That was why, I thought, she'd flown to Jeffersonville with me in the first place, and why she'd finally flown back to Lakeside, too.

On the drive over to Mrs. Shymel's, I promised myself repeatedly that under no circumstances would I stay any longer than two hours. That was the absolute minimum amount of time, my mother had said, that one could stay at a mahj date without offending anyone.

I arrived ten minutes earlier than expected, coffeecake in hand. Mrs. Shymel lived in a large, boxy house in Kalorama, just a few blocks from the string of embassies along Massachusetts Avenue. A housekeeper answered the door, greeted me by my first name, and led me through a maze of rooms to the backyard.

There I found Mrs. Shymel, Mrs. Himmel, and Mrs. Blumenthal, standing neck deep in the shallow end of a swimming pool. Mrs. Himmel, the shortest, barely cleared the water's surface with her chin. "Look who's here," she announced. I worried that if she opened her mouth for too long, she might drown.

"Mr. No Name came!" shouted Mrs. Blumenthal. "He came! He came!"

"I told you he would come," Mrs. Himmel said.

"No need to *kvell* about it," Mrs. Blumenthal replied. "He's not your child."

"Where's your bathing suit?" Mrs. Shymel asked me

"You didn't bring a bathing suit?" Mrs. Blumenthal added.

"Have a roast beef sandwich," Mrs. Himmel said. "Or turkey. Do you like turkey? It's from Felsenthal's in Bethesda."

"I didn't know we were going swimming," I said.

"We always swim before mahj," she said. "We have to do our exercises. What, you think mahj is a good enough workout?"

"I'll wait here until you're done," I told them.

"Absolutely not," Mrs. Shymel said, and then called for the house-keeper. "Martha, get this boy one of Charlie's swimsuits."

Two hours, I said to myself. Whatever they want, I'll do, but just for two hours. No mitzvah should require more than two hours.

The housekeeper showed me to a bedroom and opened a dresser drawer containing a half-dozen Speedo-style swimsuits, all of which were wildly patterned with paisleys, checks, and plaids. One had BAR MITZVAH BOY printed in rhinestones across the crotch. She told me to take any suit.

"Are you sure Charlie isn't going to mind?" I asked the house-keeper. Wearing someone's bathing suit seemed to me much like wearing someone's underwear. I wanted to have a little more informa-tion about the man with whom I was going to be so intimate.

"Mr. Shymel passed away last year," the housekeeper said.

Ten minutes later, wearing only Mrs. Shymel's dead husband's orange-and-black tiger-striped Speedo and my glasses, I returned to the pool.

"He looks just like Charlie," she said to her friends. "A young Charlie!"

"He does, doesn't he?" Mrs. Blumenthal said.

"Turn around. Let's have a look at you," Mrs. Shymel ordered. "Your last name isn't Shymel, is it? You're not some long-lost relative, are you?"

I pretended not to hear her and stepped into the pool.

"You're too skinny," Mrs. Himmel said to me, as the water lapped gently at her chin. "Why didn't you take a sandwich? Something's wrong with the sandwiches?"

"I didn't want to eat before I went swimming," I explained.

"We don't do that kind of swimming," Mrs. Blumenthal added. "This is water aerobics." She then told me to stand beside her, against the wall of the pool. The two other women also lined up.

"Tevye!" she shouted out. *"Fiddler On the Roof!"*

The three women raised their hands above their heads, pretended to fiddle, and walked to the other side of the pool. I followed behind them. I wondered if my humiliation could be any more complete, and if God was giving me credit in the Book of Life. For this, I was sure to live forever.

"Raise your hands higher," Mrs. Blumenthal yelled at me.

"Higher," Mrs. Shymel yelled. "You can't cheat your body."

My arms were about a mile above the women's heads, holding the neck of an imaginary fiddle and also a very active imaginary bow.

"If he had eaten a sandwich . . ." Mrs. Himmel said.

"No rest for the weary," Mrs. Blumenthal shouted when, ten feet later, we reached the other side of the pool. *"Music Man!"*

The three women marched back to the other side, playing air trombones. I followed behind them.

"Thirty-second rest," Mrs. Blumenthal said when we got to the other side.

"Your form needs work," Mrs. Shymel said to me.

"It's my first time," I protested.

"Enough talking. Goose-step!" Mrs. Blumenthal shouted. The women and I high-stepped back to the other side.

"Don't you think that's a little insensitive?" I asked Mrs. Blumenthal as we were kicking. "I mean, with the Holocaust . . ."

"Don't start with us about insensitive," Mrs. Himmel said. "I was in Auschwitz," she informed me. She stopped in the middle of the pool, halting the entire kick line with a wave of her hand. "You, on the other hand, won't tell us your last name. You won't even take a sandwich. It's not insensitive. It's therapeutic."

"She knows," Mrs. Shymel said. "She was in a health field."

"What did you do?" I asked.

"I was an optician," Mrs. Himmel said.

"Stop talking," Mrs. Blumenthal said. "While we're waiting, everyone is getting fat. We might as well be eating."

"Let's eat, then," said Mrs. Himmel. "At least we'll see what's wrong with these sandwiches that I Won't Tell You My Last Name won't even touch."

"Rockettes!" Mrs. Blumenthal yelled, and the four of us draped our arms around one another in a line and kicked our way to the other side.

Fifteen minutes later, in the middle of our fourth round of Tevyes, a woman in her early thirties appeared at the side of the pool and I realized that my humiliation could indeed deepen. Deepen, and grow.

She was tall and had shoulder-length brown hair and her eyes were exactly the same color as mine, green with a hint of yellow. Her nose was perfect, but somehow not pert. And the sides of her bee-stung lips curled into a devilish little smile. She wore a chocolate-colored velour hoodie that fell below her waist, and as she walked toward us, I could see the bottom of a green bikini peaking out underneath.

"Hi, Grandma," she yelled out.

Having immediately fantasized about dating and marrying this woman, I very much wanted to know which of the women in the pool was her progenitor, if only to preview what she would look like forty years from now. But I had no idea which of the three elderly women she was speaking to, because immediately upon her entrance, all of my exercise partners broke away and rushed the side of the pool with an enthusiasm matched only during Mrs. Himmel's spurts of food-pushing.

"Sylvia, look at your *shayna punim*," Mrs. Blumenthal said.

"I'm so glad you came," Mrs. Shymel jumped in. "Was there terrible traffic? You must be tired. Sit down."

I swam over to the side of the pool, to be near Sylvia too.

"You can't look at her yet, Stephen," Mrs. Himmel yelled at me. "She's like a rugelach. You have to finish your dinner first. Do another round of Rockettes."

With no one to hold on to, I walked to the other side of the pool kicking my legs, arms extended, alone.

After I did a few more solo laps, the grandmothers rejoined me and we finished the day's workout, which culminated in a few laps of "Michael Jackson"—backward moonwalking.

"Works out the back of the legs," Mrs. Blumenthal explained. "People walk forwards all day, and they forget to exercise the other side."

Mrs. Shymel's housekeeper placed a stack of towels on the chaise next to Sylvia, and it was then that I remembered I was only wearing Charlie's tiger suit, which, now wet, tightly hugged my cold-water-shrunken testicles.

I didn't want Sylvia's first sight of me to be like this. But there was no way I could get to the towels without being seen. So I lifted myself out of the pool, crossed in front of her, and, without rushing, so as to seem completely confident, I simply announced, "This isn't my bathing suit."

"I know," she replied. "It was my zadie's."

"And he looks so much like Charlie," Mrs. Shymel said to Sylvia. "Stephen, walk over here so she can see."

"I don't know," I said.

"Come on," she said. "It's like having a 3-D picture of Charlie. Please."

"Okay," I said, and I stood up and walked toward Sylvia. I cringed in shame. She gave me a very strange look, strange even for these odd circumstances, and I prayed it was just the Speedo that had inspired it.

"No, do it again, Stephen," Mrs. Shymel said. "Like you're at a fashion show. Swing your arms a bit and turn at the end. Look forward, not at us."

I did as I was told.

"You see, Sylvia," Mrs. Shymel said. "That was the man I fell in love with."

"My friends call me Syl," she said, and held out her hand, which I took warmly.

"You kids and your names," Mrs. Shymel said. "You, Sylvia, amputate the beautiful name you were given. Your great-grandmother's name—"

"—and Sylvia Plath's," Syl added.

"And you, Stephen, won't tell us your last name."

"I'm sorry," I said. "It's just that I'm very private."

"And he doesn't eat," Mrs. Himmel added. "Can you really trust him?"

"I'll figure it out eventually," Syl said.

A half hour later, the three grandmothers and I were seated at a table in the living room. Mrs. Shymel mixed the mah-jongg tiles, and we each built a small wall in front of our racks. Mrs. Himmel was East, so she broke her wall first and the pieces were distributed and then traded. I sat in the West position so I could watch Syl, who lay on the sofa reading a magazine.

I paid little attention to the game and often had to be reminded by Mrs. Himmel that it was my turn. Instead I watched Syl, the slow motion of her breath raising and lowering the magazine propped on her stomach.

"Bogdanovich?" she said when she caught me staring at her. "Your name is Bogdanovich, isn't it?"

I smiled. "You're reading a movie magazine," I said.

"You won't even confirm or deny it?"

"No, because soon that will lead to a game of hot or cold, and in no time you'll have it revealed."

Caught, she pushed her lips to one side. "I can tell it's not Bogdanovich," she said. "There's no fear in your eyes."

We played for hours, far longer than I had ever anticipated staying, but I didn't mind. Indeed, with Syl there I didn't even notice that so much time had passed. After the game was over (I lost spectacularly, to the tune of $3.43) and the tiles were put away, Syl announced she was going for a swim, and I wandered outside a few steps behind her.

"We-didn't-really-get-to-meet," I said, but it all ran together.

"That's okay, we've met before," she said. It wasn't an accusation or even a correction, but a mere statement of fact. We had met previously and she wanted it noted. But where? How could I possibly have missed her?

Syl unbuttoned her jeans, which fell into a little pile at her feet, and unzipped her hoodie, revealing the green bikini underneath. She slipped into the water almost soundlessly.

I walked around the pool and stepped out onto the diving board, placing my feet half over the edge, teetering back and forth by just thinking about adjusting my weight.

"When did we meet?" I asked.

"In the elevator," she said.

She dunked her head, came back up, and squeezed the water out of her hair, pulling it into a long ponytail.

And now that her hair was pulled back, I remembered her. Syl was the woman with the small white dog—the woman I had lifted out of the elevator, the night I was chasing my mother to the taxi. The one I'd slapped at. The one who'd slapped at me.

"I'm sorry about that," I said.

"Don't worry about it," she said.

"I was having a hard time."

"Your mother . . ."

"Yes, my mother."

Syl began to swim toward the deep end, but it was clear from her first stroke that she wasn't swimming toward me. She was swimming laps and I, by standing on the diving board, just happened to be positioned at one end of her course.

The night was quiet except for the splish-splash of her cupped hands pulling at the water. She swam back and forth and I admired her form, coming and going, without embarrassment; as long as her head was submerged, she couldn't see me gazing at her, dreaming of her.

After about twenty minutes, Syl stopped swimming and lay down on a raft. I remained nervously stationed on the diving board.

"What do you do?" I asked, but immediately I detested myself for saying it. Not only did it seem like the standard, stuffy Washington question, implying that one's identity is entirely dependent on his or her occupation, but I no longer had an answer I was proud to share in return.

"I work for OmniOnline, the internet service provider. I write welcome-screen splashes," she said. "You know, the upbeat messages you see when you sign on. Like, 'Shania Make You Shimmy?' That's me. They're supposed to get you excited about being online."

"That's interesting."

"No, it's mindless."

"At least a lot of people read what you write."

"If you call it writing. It's one step above refrigerator poetry."

"It's definitely writing. Tell me what you wrote for them today." I hoped if she kept talking, she would forget to ask me what I did.

"Well, first I hunted the web for ultra-optimistic news stories. For instance, I found a story about a birthday party for the oldest man in the world. That's what OmniOnline wants, because no one opposes longevity. Then I wrote the headline—that's the so-called writing part.

"It's actually kind of tricky," she continued. "I can't suggest in any way what he did to live long, or what he even thinks about living long. If I did, someone could be offended, and we're not supposed to offend anyone. If you say it's his diet, every nutritionist in the world will write in. Say it's exercise, and the couch potatoes protest or, worse, they sign off and go to the gym. God forbid you say it's his positive attitude, the pessimists will start a petition."

"So what did you write?"

" 'Very Big Day.' "

We both laughed. Syl was funny and smart, I realized; so much for my first impression of her in the elevator.

"Anyway, I'm really a poet," she explained. "I just keep telling myself that. The OmniOnline job lets me work from home and gives me enough time and money to write poetry, which is what I love. I've only published a few poems so far. But one was in *The Pacific.*"

"That's great," I said. "I read *The Pacific.*"

I used to write for them too. Several months earlier, I had published a long story in *The Pacific* called 'Children of the Corn.' It was about people who worried that eating genetically altered foods would change their own genome. Surprisingly, given that mine was the byline, it was actually entirely true, but I knew no one would believe that now. What I had done had destroyed even the truths I had written, as if it had made them lies too.

"So what do you do?" Syl asked. "Or is that a secret too?"

"I work in a video store," I said.

"Really? I did that during high school."

Her answer upset me, and it showed.

"I'm sorry," she said. "I meant, it's something we have in common. Which one?"

"Action Video."

"I've been there," she said and then paused before adding, "It's a strange place."

"It can be," I said. "But the guys who work there are great. You just have to get to know them. I'm a supervisor." I felt defensive, and protective of Philippe and Oskar, but at the same time I wanted to make sure she knew I wasn't simply more of the same.

"That's cool," she said.

We looked up at the sky and Syl played with the little bikini knot that hung between her breasts. It was a sign that she was either edgy or bored, I wasn't sure which. I was surprised she hadn't left yet. I gazed up at the stars, to make it less obvious that there had been a lull between us.

"You're going to fall in," she said. She was right. Looking up, I had stopped paying attention to my balance, and I was about to tumble over the edge of the board. I took a few steps back and carefully sat down on it, leaning my arms low like an ape before my butt ever touched down. I made it.

"Why is it that you came over to see your grandma today?" I asked.

"Honestly?"

"You don't have to say if you don't want to."

"My grandma made me promise to come. She's tried to set me up a million times, and I never really let her. It's always these clunky things where she tells me I should call some guy I've never met—

who, mind you, *she* has never even met either—and ask him out. What am I supposed to do? Call him up and say, 'I hear we have a lot in common: We both have cute, old Jewish grandmas'? That wouldn't even be enough of a foundation for a one-night stand. So I always refuse.

"This time, though, I couldn't get out of it. She had in fact met you, and she said she had already told you I was coming, and since we live in the same building I figured I had to show—otherwise she'd appear at my door someday, with you in tow. How about you? You really came *to play mahj*?"

"I promised my mother," I said.

"Chasing your mother again." She laughed, but nicely.

We talked about the stars, and how many more you could see from this Kalorama backyard than from our own apartments, even though they were so many floors higher up. I would have talked with her about anything she wanted, just to keep her there with me. For a while Syl and I were silent, and she looked down at the water, and I wanted very much to kiss her, but I didn't know how to approach it.

After a half hour or so, the lights in Mrs. Shymel's house were extinguished, and we were all alone. In the starlight, Syl told me gossip about people in our building. The Betty White look-alike on the floor below me sold pot to half the apartments. The "blind" couple on the eighth floor subscribed to newspapers and satellite TV; it was apparently a disability scam. (I held my breath until she finished discussing that one, remembering my own faux deafness.) And a group of six businessmen shared an apartment on the second floor so they could bring their lovers during lunch breaks. The doorman kept a schedule so that the men would never overlap.

And Dotan, he tried to get everyone to go to synagogue.

"Dastardly," I said.

"Evil," she replied.

I thought of how Dotan had said he and I were the only Jews in the building, and how, because he knew Syl, he must have known it wasn't true. I asked her about it.

"He always says that," she replied. "He tells it to everyone and then he drags them to synagogue and they learn the truth. He likes to say it because it makes it sound more urgent: Only you can save Judaism."

"It's not urgent?"

"No," she said.

"Few things are urgent," I said. I was reaching for topics.

"Except, maybe, are you going to kiss me anytime soon?" she asked.

"Yes," I said. "I would really like that."

Inspired by her directness, I decided to match it. I jumped off the diving board and into the water, clothes on and all, and planned to swim debonairly over to her. But it didn't work out right. The impact of the water knocked my glasses off, so I had to dive to retrieve them, and swimming fully clothed made any graceful stroke impossible. It looked more like I was thrashing my body through the water at her, like an otter on the Discovery Channel.

But when I arrived at her raft, some minutes later, Syl was still there, willing to kiss me, and we did.

The next day, after work, Syl and I met at Jeffersonville Java, a coffeehouse near The Harvey. She wore a light blue tank, gray capri pants, and black shoes with chunky heels. Her hair was blown out and curled ever so slightly at the bottom, revealing precious little ears, unscathed by the puncture of earring holes.

"You never had your ears pierced," I said.

She grabbed both of her lobes between her fingers, as if protecting them. "I wouldn't want to maim them," she said. "They're my one perfect feature. Everyone has one perfect feature."

"I'm not sure I have one. I have a *worst* feature."

"Okay, what's that?"

"My feet. They're hideous."

"They're feet. How terrible can they be? No one's feet look *that* good, I hate to break it to you."

"They're so bad my mom told me never to show them to a potential bride until after we're married."

"And then surprise her with them?"

"Only if I have a prenup," I said.

"They can't be that bad."

"They're gruesome."

"Take off your shoes," she demanded.

"Here?"

"Doff 'em," she said.

"It's a coffee shop," I said. "People eat here."

"Then where would you suggest?"

"Your apartment, maybe?"

"You'll take them off in my apartment? Where I live, eat, and work? But you won't remove them here, in a public spot?"

So right there in the coffee shop, I took off my shoes and socks, and propped my size-fourteen soles up on the small silver-colored table, between our two cappuccinos, which they dwarfed.

"What's the problem?" she asked. "They're a little pale; you don't seem to give them any sun. And the toes could be a bit shorter, but I really don't see any major problems."

"They're completely flat," I said.

"So, they can't draft you."

I couldn't believe she was putting a positive spin on my feet. I hoped it was a general characteristic—this looking to the small, irrelevant positive in the face of huge negatives.

While Syl was wiggling my toes, the manager came to the table and told us we were going to have to leave.

"I'm sorry," I said. "I'll put my shoes back on. I wasn't thinking."

"Too late," he said. "No shirt, no shoes, no service."

"We didn't require any more service," Syl said.

But the manager had already begun to clear our table, taking Syl's half-finished cappuccino out of her hand. As he did, she accidentally-on-purpose spilled a little of the liquid on him, and he yowled.

Then Syl removed her own shoes, told me to follow her, and led us in a musicless, two-person barefooted conga line around every table, until we finally reached the exit.

"People need to be free," she shouted at the manager as we got to the door. "Liberate your feet!"

One solitary coffee drinker raised his head from the newspaper and applauded: three small, crisp claps.

Outside, we sat on the curb, put our shoes back on, and laughed. "What do you want to do now?" I asked.

"Let's figure out what your best feature is," she said, and we went back to her apartment and spent the rest of the night doing just that.

The next day, I left work at the video store early. I wanted to ask Syl back to my apartment that night, but I needed some time to hide away anything that bore my last name. Even as I knew I'd go through with my plan, I also knew I'd eventually regret it. But, for now, I was ashamed to admit, the lying would once again win out.

When I returned to The Harvey, Dotan was waiting for me in the lobby. He said that a reporter had been walking around the building, asking everyone about me and trying to interview them.

"I called security and they told him to leave, but as he was walking out the door, he gave me this note to give to you," Dotan said.

I felt relieved. Dotan wasn't going to help the journalists; he'd helped protect me from them instead. And I felt bad for doubting him. Dotan had the clarity and integrity of the single-minded, and I should have seen that immediately. The only ruses he'd employ would be harmless ones, designed to get me into one of those toothy-white-cushioned pews—it was where he thought I belonged, and where, for the first time, I thought I might belong too.

• • •

Here is the note Dotan gave me. It was written in tiny print on yellow legal paper:

Stephen,

I do not appreciate that you are making this so difficult for both of us. As your friend, I have worked so hard to make sure *your* side of the story is reported, the one thing that has been missing in all of the media attention.

You, however, have simply blown me off. You rudely skipped our dinner plans back in May. You refused to even speak to me on the plane. You don't return my phone calls. And I don't even want to go over what happened at the post office. What more do you want from me? I have tried to be your friend, to help you and to help the truth get out there.

I'm sure we'll catch up soon and put this all behind us. Please call me.

Still Your Friend,
Cliff

I felt relieved that Cliff had left the building, and that the letter just seemed like more of the same—more of what I'd come to expect from him—and so I began again to focus on preparing for the evening.

There was plenty of evidence of the Glass surname in my apartment to hide from Syl: the bills, the mail, books with my name scribbled on the edge. I password protected my computer, so she couldn't open any files while I was in the bathroom (not that I really thought she would). I even turned the answering machine to silent, so she wouldn't happen to hear a phone solicitor offer "Mr. Glass" a better long-distance plan.

Then there was the box, the large carton shipped to me by Samuel. On each of its six sides, in large block letters, it said my name. Even though I had wanted it so much that I'd run the Cliff gauntlet to get it, I hadn't had the heart to open it yet—would it have my nameplate, or had they thrown it away? What about the presents from Brian and Lindsey? Had they taken them back?

I tried sticking the box under my bed, but it wouldn't fit. And it was too big for the kitchen cabinets, or any of the closet shelves. It just sat out in the open like an uninvited, unwanted guest. In a rush, I decided my only option was to disguise it. I dressed the box in my largest shirt and a baseball cap, and set it at one side of the tub. Extending from the box to the other end of the tub, I laid out a pair of blue jeans. In the lap, I put an open book.

Finally, I closed the shower curtain and hoped BoxMan would go undetected. And if she found him, if Syl came upon BoxMan and wondered what he was, I hoped she would conclude that it was just very bad scarecrow art.

Later that night, after a movie, Syl came up to my apartment for the first time. I poured us two glasses of wine and she sat on the couch, her legs folded beneath her, and I sat down next to her, and we listened to music. She'd brought a CD with her: Bob Dylan's *Blonde on Blonde.*

Syl closed her eyes and pressed her back against the couch, arching her spine. Watching her, I seamlessly slipped away into the music myself. When she got up to use the bathroom, I held my breath, but apparently she either didn't look in the tub, or if she'd seen the strange shadow behind the curtain and pulled it aside, she'd let BoxMan pass without comment. Syl silently returned to the couch.

Songs passed and perhaps an hour later, the Dylan CD came to an end. But still we said nothing, and there was no discomfort in the silence. And then, when it somehow seemed for the first time to be the absolute right moment, I reached over to her and unbuttoned her blouse. Syl rotated her body slightly to allow me to, and then undid my shirt. For a while we just held each other quietly, and then we made love.

The next morning, I woke before Syl. In case she wanted a shower, I disassembled BoxMan, who was still sealed with tape, and hid him in parts, as if he were a dead body. The box itself was still too big to hide away, but I threw a sheet over it and put a lamp on it, as if it were a side table; I wondered why I hadn't thought of this solution before.

I was tempted, as before with Beth, to fetch a full buffet of breakfast foods for Syl, but I checked myself. I had realized that my need to please sometimes backfired and ended up alienating and overwhelming the person instead. And on a deeper level, I was also wondering if my need for Beth's (and everyone else's) approval had been desperate and out of bounds—did I really think I'd needed to, or even that I could, win her with a scooped-out, berry-laden cantaloupe?

So with Syl, I decided, I would limit my indulgence to coffee with a comprehensive selection of sweeteners and milk—brown and white sugar, Equal and Sweet'N Low; skim, whole, and half-and-half. I knew Syl loved coffee, and I cursed myself that I didn't have a cappuccino machine. I could be Starbucks for her, I fantasized. I could be her supplier, her dealer.

But wasn't that just the same desperate search, writ smaller (and in sugar)? I decided to just get her a cup of coffee. There was milk in the fridge if she wanted it.

When I returned to the apartment with the coffee, Syl was already awake. Propped up against the headboard with a few pillows, she was reading the newspaper that had been delivered to my door.

"I know your secret, *Mr. Aaron,*" she said, when I climbed back into bed. She showed me the little white subscriber tag that read "Stephen Aaron, Apartment 811."

I froze. I hadn't meant to deceive her. After the Pizza Bandit incident, I had switched my last name to my middle name on all my subscriptions. I'd refused to buzz anyone in after that, and in case someone got in anyway, I didn't want him to be able to find me just based on the paper lying outside my door. Now another "white lie" was getting me into more trouble.

I wasn't even sure why I got the paper at all anymore. Recently I had lost my taste for reading about Beltway scandals and the downfalls of others. These had always been, to me, the best stories—the take-downs, the assassinations. But now I thought mostly about the "subject" reading the story, and how it felt to him or her. My point of view changed my reactions completely. I even began to identify, in the obituaries, with the deceased.

Syl kept holding the label aloft, waiting for me to comment. I thought for a moment about telling her the truth about my name, but "I'd rather not talk about it" was all I said. I liked her so much, and even if she was going to leave me in the end, I was selfish: I wanted this little time with her anyway.

I couldn't bear to tell her, and fortunately, she saved me. "You don't have to talk about it," she replied sweetly, and, for a while at least, we didn't speak of it again.

Over the next month, Syl and I were virtually inseparable. Every morning I awakened her with an iced coffee with skim milk and two packets of Equal, stirred vigorously, and when she came to, we talked nonstop. There seemed to be an endless number of stories and thoughts and things of every kind that we wanted—no, needed, *urgently* needed—to share. She called me into the bathroom to keep talking and listening while she showered and brushed her teeth and washed her face and even blow-dried her hair—I learned to shout over the noise—because otherwise, it seemed, there just was not enough time.

Each of us made minor adjustments to fit the other, of course. While I didn't want to slip back into my old patterns of trying to please people too much, trying so hard to win their affections that I'd be willing compromise everything, I knew there was something beautiful about pleasing people you love. And while the line between pleasing and overpleasing is difficult to pin down, I could not—nor did I really want to—defeat entirely my need to please others, especially Syl.

I remember my first alteration for Syl. It was on the second night we slept together, when I removed my shirt at the foot of the bed. It was a regular dress shirt and I disrobed as I had every day since I was a child, unbuttoning the top few buttons and then, with both hands, lifting the bottom of the shirt over my head.

"Put it back on," Syl said, and I did. She got up from the bed. "Do it this way," she instructed. She unbuttoned the top two buttons and then took my right hand and used it to pull the back of the collar up and over my head. "That's how lacrosse players do it—much sexier."

That night, I put on my contact lenses and practiced in the mirror dozens of times, until I could do it in one fluid motion. I could do it with T-shirts, dress shirts, even my one cheesy tank top. And each time I did it, it never failed to delight her. The hell with the lacrosse players.

During the afternoons, Syl would do OmniOnline's bidding, sneaking in time for her poetry every free minute she could find, and I would go to Action Video and try to break Oskar and Philippe of their strange patterns, or at least try to keep them from doing something that would get them fired.

Philippe had taken to donning sunglasses, which violated company policy, and wearing zinc oxide on his nose and cheekbones, which was not provided for in the dress code, but which I allowed, on the ground that makeup was permitted. Oskar, meanwhile, remained unrelenting in his campaign against the Christian God and was caught inserting antipapal tracts into video boxes.

While I had to remove the pamphlets, of course, I gave Oskar his own shelf—labeled "Oskar's Offerings"—where he could recommend to patrons any movies he liked, albeit without commentary. Then, so as not to insult Philippe, I added "Philippe's Picks."

Oskar chose *Priest, The Mosquito Coast,* and *Stigmata.* Philippe chose to leave his shelf blank, explaining that he just liked to have some space of his own, and he liked the idea that people would think all his picks had been rented already.

• • •

When evening came, Syl and I went on long walks with Milton Rosenbaum—who, I learned, was named after her deceased grandfather and preferred being called by his full name.

Each night the three of us went up Secession Street to a small ice cream shop and got cones—Milton Rosenbaum preferred peanut butter flavor—and all the while, Syl and I waited to see who would say I love you first.

She did, but only by seconds. When she said she loved me, I said I loved her, and I don't know if either of us quite felt it until it was said, but once it was spoken, it was fundamentally true.

I was so happy I couldn't speak again for a while. I bought Milton Rosenbaum an extra-large cone, which he scarfed down, and then he licked the pavement until we had to drag him away, paws splayed.

Meanwhile, Cliff stopped by The Harvey several more times, trying to catch me at home, but he was always turned away, either by the gruff doorman or a vigilant Dotan. And the media stories about me continued—incredibly; didn't they have anything else to write about?

Mentions in the papers and on TV were less frequent than they once had been, but not uncommon. Once I happened to be watching when Robert appeared on *Press Box,* a late night TV program about the media, hosted by Gil Garvey. Robert wanted to publicize the completion of "Project Shards of Glass." He announced that in reviewing all of my articles, the *Weekly* had found that seventy of the eighty pieces I had written contained at least one unverifiable fact.

"Wow. You rechecked everything he wrote? That's an immense task," Garvey commented. "It must have taken hundreds of hours."

"It did," Robert said. "But with this report, I think we can tell our readers confidently that we have vanquished the enemy."

"We should also tell our viewers that you've recently signed a book deal to write about all of this. Tell us about it."

"It's called *Defender of the Truth: Regaining the Moral High Ground in American Journalism*. It's a full recounting of what happened when I unmasked Stephen's lies. Plus a broader examination of journalism as it's practiced today. I think it'll be quite compelling."

"I'm sure it will be," Garvey agreed. "One thing some of your critics might say is that you've gotten famous through all of this. I mean, now you have a book deal, in which you'll be the hero of your own story. Not that you wouldn't be otherwise—this whole incident is very black hat versus white hat. But what would you say to them? Are you enjoying the spotlight at all?"

Robert paused for a second, turned away from Garvey and looked directly into the camera, and then said, "Absolutely not. That's like saying the burglary victim enjoyed getting robbed. Or that John Walsh, the guy on *America's Most Wanted,* is happy that his child was taken from him because it got him a TV career. Stephen Glass did something wrong to me, and to a lot of other people, and I'm just not willing to take it lying down. For instance, we've worked very hard to improve the fact-checking system at the magazine."

"Yes, I've heard that," Garvey said. "One trade publication I read said that your new system is the most stringent in the country—a model for other magazines. Is that right? Before you answer, I should let our viewers know that they also said your past system was solid—it seems Glass would have evaded anyone's fact checkers—and now it's even stronger."

"Absolutely. We're committed to not letting anything like this ever happen again."

"Do you know anything about what Stephen's doing?" Garvey asked. "We've invited him to appear on this show many times, but he's never responded."

"No, Stephen and I haven't spoken since he was fired," Robert said. "But I can tell you this, in all of my years of journalism I've never known someone as greedy as Stephen Glass. You watch, somehow he'll turn his disgrace into a windfall. Maybe he'll wait it out for a while, but eventually there will be the appearances on talk shows and he'll write a book too, talking about the stress he was under, and how sorry he is. Trying to blame it all on anyone but himself."

"So you think he might actually write again?"

"I hate to say it, but I do. It's like asking on V-E day, will there ever be war again? Just because we have seen the devastation and defeated him, doesn't mean that we can let down our guard against him now."

"And on those sobering words, we'll take a break," Garvey said.

When *Press Box* returned, Garvey asked Robert to talk about the *Weekly*'s current cover story: "Clinton: Our Most Moral President." Robert made the argument without a wink to the viewer, without a moment of hesitation.

What Robert had said didn't hurt me as much as it once would have. The media now seemed to exist in a parallel universe, far away from the one in which Syl and I lived. Except for intermittent guest appearances by Cliff, my life had a whole new, though smaller, cast of characters—as if it were itself a TV show, one in which the first crew had gone on strike, and all the scabs were suddenly working. Robert had been replaced by Glenn; Allison, by Syl; Brian and Lindsey, by Oskar and Philippe. (Believe it or not, I thought every understudy was better than the corresponding player.)

And what about my role in the drama? It was a quiet one: When I wasn't at Action Video, I mostly spent my time alone with Syl, except when we were at Shabbat services, where we always saw Dotan, Debbie, and the grandmas. Feeling that God had to get credit for at least some of my new good fortune, I had begun to go every week. When the rabbi saw me there with Syl for the first time, I could have sworn he smiled, but I didn't understand until quite a bit later why.

Hearing of my attendance somehow, Cliff called Rabbi Gordon for an interview. But the rabbi refused to speak to Cliff, and even pre-empted his next move: He told Cliff that while he was very welcome at the synagogue as a worshiper, he definitely was *not* welcome as a journalist. And Cliff never showed—which was a good thing, since the Sabbath Goy had told me he was fully prepared to evict Cliff "Mossad-style."

After several weeks of attending Friday night services, I asked Rabbi Gordon if I could again meet with him privately. The rabbi welcomed me into his study, and when I sat on his couch, and smelled the familiar scent of the old books and his aftershave, once again I felt remarkably free to be frank.

He offered me a bagel and lox, which I accepted. And after a brief disagreement about whether there were any good bagels in Washington (I thought not; he, as usual, was more optimistic), I said what I had been wanting to say all this time. "I haven't told Syl my last name," I blurted. "Or anything about what I did."

I explained to the rabbi that I had often considered confessing my true name—and thus my true history—to Syl, but I had always pulled back from the edge.

I explained how I had tried to become obsessive in the rest of my life about telling the truth, actively thinking about my truthfulness as much as possible, to keep myself on course. Syl thought it was hilarious that I carefully counted my change, to make sure I had never been given too much. (If I got too little, I never brought it up. The last thing I wanted to do was get someone fired.) I had stopped lying to cover up Oskar and Phillipe's eccentricities; I just apologized to the customer directly instead. Meanwhile whenever I spoke to someone, I corrected myself, sometimes several times in a conversation, to make sure I was precise. And caveats, oh did I make caveats. Whenever I discussed something I hadn't actually seen for myself, it always came with a source—the paper I had read it in, or the TV show I had seen it on. I was never without an Acceptable Form of Verification. And I always made clear that I could be remembering wrong. I never wanted to even be *thought* to be lying ever again. No mistake of mine would ever look innocent, and so from now on I would be extra careful to always be scrupulous about the truth.

But with Syl, it was different. The further I fell into love, when it was supposed to be easier and easier to be honest, the more difficult it became to break the news of my history to her. And so I remained silent.

"She thinks my middle name is my last," I explained to the rabbi. "She got it from a newspaper subscription label, and I didn't correct her. And I know that every day I don't tell her, it's going to be harder to tell her the next day. I don't want to become one of these men on *Unsolved Mysteries* who gets married, and never tells his wife about his other life, and then he turns sixty-five and the Social Security checks start coming, and someone winds up dead."

"I don't think I've ever seen that show. But I did look up the Jeff Gillooly stuff. I don't know how I missed that," the rabbi said. "What do you imagine will happen when you tell Syl?"

"Individual Armageddon. A personal doomsday. I'm serious. I imagine that everything in my life will fall apart all over again. I imagine it will be the new worst day of my existence."

"Let me tell you a story about my last trip to Israel," the rabbi said. He explained that according to Jewish legend, the Messianic Age will begin when the Messiah passes through the Golden Gate of the Old City in Jerusalem. Some rabbis believe the Messiah will live on Earth for some time, unaware that he or she is the Messiah until he or she passes through the gate.

"Secretly, deep down," the rabbi admitted, "that's what I was counting on. I had no evidence I was the Messiah. I couldn't levitate, or move things with my mind. I didn't even really make more than my share of peace among the people around me. But somewhere inside me, I had this hope. Now this isn't a very attractive thing to admit, but seeing as I'm not him—I'm only a Messiah wannabe—I think it's okay to confess it."

"Of course it's okay," I said. "I had a Hebrew-school teacher who told me that every day I didn't keep kosher, was another day the Messiah didn't come."

"They're hard on you kids," the rabbi said. "In any event, the Golden Gate was sealed up by the Turks in the sixteenth century to prevent the Messiah's entrance. Most rabbis say we shouldn't worry too much about this. If the Messiah can arrive, after all these years, he can certainly get through a sealed gate, too.

"Every time I visited Israel, I avoided getting anywhere close to the Golden Gate, because I was truly scared. I was scared that when I got near, and the trumpets didn't blare, and the rocks sealing it didn't come tumbling down, and I turned out not to be the Messiah, everything would somehow change for me. Messianic dreams weren't a big part of my life, but they had represented a tiny hope that had been with me for a long time, and I worried what I would feel when I lost it.

"And that's what happened this last winter. I held my breath. I walked near the Golden Gate—or as near as I could get, it's a difficult world nowadays—and sure enough, there were no trumpets. I took a few steps back and approached it again, just to be sure God saw me, but still nothing happened. And it wasn't so bad. I even felt a bit relieved. My wife, who had been to the Golden Gate several times and has known for years she isn't the Messiah, found out for certain that she's not Mrs. Messiah either.

"Here's the moral of the story, Stephen: In the end, you need to face what you know is coming. I know there's a chance Syl will leave you because of your past, but I think it's also possible she has struggled too, at some time in her own life, and she'll find it within herself to forgive you. You may even feel great relief when you tell her. Wouldn't you prefer to have what you have now, and have her know about your past too?"

"Of course," I said. "But how can I know she won't break up with me right then?"

"You can't. But you can know this: You can know that God won't give you more than you can bear."

"How do you explain that to the Jews in Auschwitz?"

"I'm not going to address that, Stephen," he said, with a hint of annoyance. "That's the old you poking its head out."

"The very old me. Since I was three, probably," I replied. "I used to bring this up all the time in Hebrew school, and no one's given me a straight answer yet."

He laughed, but still didn't fill me in.

"So do I have to tell her today?" I asked.

"No, you don't have to do it today, but if you're back here in a month and you still haven't said anything, I'll be disappointed."

The next day, I reached into my closet and—alone, trembling—opened the box from the *Weekly,* the last bodily remains of BoxMan. The Nathan photo was there, all right, and I had forgotten the huge burgundy stain on his white shirt. But my few awards and the gifts were gone—Brian and Lindsey apparently had taken them back after all, just as Lindsey had revoked her friendship. All that was left were the family photos and a few items of clothing—an extra sweater, a *Washington Weekly* cap. I wondered if the hat's inclusion was a gesture, a taunt, or simply thoughtless.

Beneath all this, there was a small, partially unwrapped, unfamiliar white box. I opened the box nervously, to find what looked like fragments of Styrofoam; among them was a ribbon, still tied but now holding nothing within its loop. What the hell? I thought. Then I picked out of the rubble a neatly folded handwritten note, with a Spanish sentence and below it the English translation: "The party is still to come, Stephen." It was signed "Jorge 'Throw' Gomez."

I tasted the Styrofoam, suspecting what it must be, and there it was: the unmistakable flavor of the desiccated American treat that had traveled on the lunar lander, and then to Throw's children in Paraguay, and now to me, in my own remote location.

There was another letter in the box too—this one was stamped and postmarked and "Personal and Confidential" was scrawled below the address—and it took me a while to work up the courage to open it, because of its return address. But after a few hours, I got into my bed and unsealed it carefully.

Felix Rizzoli
The White House
1600 Pennsylvania Avenue, NW
Washington, DC 20500

Stephen—

How does one recover from a story that's untrue? How does one do it—especially when he's ashamed of the wrong he actually *has* done in his life? How does one do it, when no one will believe him when he says, *This* one, *this* story, is not true? You've got to believe me. I promise. It didn't happen. The reporter's lying.

The answer is: He doesn't. A man cannot recover from it. Or at least, I never have.

After your story came out, I told people it wasn't true. I was insistent. I even wrote a Letter to the Editor, which the *Weekly* printed. But no one really changed their minds.

My enemies, I'm sure, believed every word you wrote and doubtless faxed the story all over D.C. My friends at least said they believed me, but I knew they couldn't help but think a little less of me. They couldn't help but ask themselves, and in a few instances, even ask me, "If it wasn't true, why did he write it?" Stephen, I had no answer for them, and I still don't. What supposed wrong were you trying to vindicate? I remember how I used to be in high school, and I'm not proud of the boy I was, but you made me out to be even worse. Why? And who among us is proud of how they were in high school?

I wish you had let those days rest, but if you had to revive them, you did so in the cruelest possible way. I don't know if you know it, but I fought dyslexia for years. I couldn't cheat for the same reason I couldn't pass the tests: I couldn't read properly. I was too ashamed to say it in the Letter to the Editor, but I want you to know.

I want you to know, too, what happened to me afterward.

Several weeks after your article came out, the Chief of Staff called me to his office. He asked me if your piece was true. I said it wasn't. He nodded—he obviously didn't believe me, but he wasn't going to say so—and said it didn't matter. What mattered, he said, was that it was *believed* to be true, and as long as that was the case, I was on probation. If there was another, similar violation (similar, of course, to one that never happened, but then you knew that), he would cut me loose. I started holding my breath and never stopped. I still haven't, Stephen. Think about that.

Now you're fired and disgraced, and that suits me just fine. But don't think anything you say or suffer could ever make up for what you did.

Rizzi's letter was a blow and after reading it, I wept. This was the part of what I'd done that I hadn't yet dealt with, and I hadn't done so because I just couldn't face it. Often I had invented stories about imaginary people who were part of fictional institutions, which had put forth invented arguments about purported events that had never happened. That was hurtful to my editors, colleagues, and readers, I know, but it wasn't as hurtful as what I'd done to Felix Rizzoli. And here's something worse: Rizzi wasn't the only one. I had mostly been a fabulist, but every so often I'd been a faker too.

I went to my computer, printed out the stories that attacked real people, and reread them. I marked up everything I had invented, and I made a list of the names of the people I'd hurt. And then I looked at the list and asked myself, What was—and what is—wrong with me? I also asked myself what Rizzi had asked me: What supposed wrong had I been trying to vindicate? These people had lives, and I'd tried to rip them down. What *was* wrong with me? What had I wanted to prove? And why them?

I saw it, suddenly: They were all successes, all people who were loved and respected, who had done well for themselves, who had lived up to everyone's expectations—more than that, they'd exceeded them. They were all children of whom their parents were rightly proud, so proud. They had actually done what I'd only aspired to, and at some subconscious level, I must have wanted to bring them down, to prove they and I weren't so different after all. But of course we were. They were the real thing; I was an imitation.

I was, and I am, so sorry for how I hurt them. It pains me to even think about it. I apologize now: an insufficient apology, I know, to substitute for the one that should have come so long ago, and never did. I want to offer it even though I understand it will afford little comfort to the people I wrote about (especially since few will believe it). But I do mean my apology; I did read Rizzi's letter, and I did feel the gravity of it and the sadness, and the way he knew it would never quite go away.

The horrible power of a lie is that its taint often outlives its rebuttal; its stain fades but never truly disappears. Somewhere out there, someone still thinks Rizzi was a cheater; and worse, someone else remembers he did something bad, but can't quite remember what. Some things are never quite outlived, but only borne. He knew it, and I now know it, too.

I had inflicted so much harm, and what I'd done had finally come home to me, yet I still kept lying, albeit mostly by omission. Syl had stopped asking about my true identity, believing she had uncovered it already, and it looked as if she'd never learn it, except from me. Yet I didn't tell her. The reason I was able to get away with this for so long was that Syl lived in her own world. We rarely talked about current events, and the press notices passed her by. She read only fiction and poetry, though she read them obsessively—she kept a book in her purse, one on her nightstand, and even one in the trunk of her car where the tire jack should have been. "It'll help me out more, in an emergency, than anything else," she explained. (I nodded in agreement, but made sure there was a fully charged cell phone in the glove compartment.)

Syl wasn't a fan of magazines, and especially not of Washington magazines. On the car radio one afternoon, a journalist referred to Washington as "the most powerful city in the world," sending Syl into a frenzy. "The most powerful city in the world?" she yelled at the radio. "By what fucking standard? Can you name a single truly great piece of art that has come out of this town? Any genre—literature, movies, painting, visual arts, even the *culinary* arts. Can you? Can you?"

"He can't," I said and flipped the car radio to Tape. She always had the same Dylan cassette in, *Blood on the Tracks,* and by now I had learned to like it.

I sang along with "Idiot Wind": "They're planting stories in the press/Whoever it is, I wish they'd cut it out, but when they will, I can only guess. . . ." It was a private joke between me and myself, and I thought it was funny. I wished I could tell Syl but I feared it, too. As I sang, I unsuccessfully tried to adopt Dylan's nasal, devil-may-care attitude. I probably verged into Kermit the Frog, but even so, Syl never told me not to sing.

Keeping my identity secret was made even easier by the fact that Syl had no interest in going out to the restaurants, bars, and functions my former colleagues favored. "You have to ask yourself what these people do all day, how bad their lives must be, that they would find these things diverting," she explained.

Instead, she refused all invitations to what she called The Member Parties. Syl had coined the term because at one such party she'd attended years ago—before she'd stopped going to them—a legislative assistant had hit on her by bragging about his job with a powerful Member of the House of Representatives. He told her he was celebrating that night because his boss had greatly appreciated his research on a highway bill.

"Working for The Member has really been a terrific opportunity," he said. "What people don't realize is that highway policy is incredibly important and interesting. My research—and this is what The Member actually said—will break down the 'entrenched barriers' preventing trucks from bringing more products to market. Do you watch C-SPAN? No? That's too bad. What The Member means is that things like the clothes you're wearing and the drink you're holding, will be cheaper if they can be moved more efficiently. Of course, it's not all in the clear yet. Naturally, the train guys are against us, but The Member said to me personally that we have a shot at this one. Have you ever worked on the Hill for a Member?"

"No, I'm a woman," Syl said. "I take my commands from a vagina."

And so we avoided the press, and everyone else, and in our solitary bubble the weeks passed us by. Finally, during the middle of that sticky August, we reluctantly agreed to go on a double date with Dotan and Debbie. They had been asking us for weeks—with Dotan reminding me time and time again that he was the force behind our newfound happiness, although he was obviously unaware that his constant invitations were detracting from it.

Syl and I had tried to avoid going out with them in every polite way possible, pleading business or exhaustion. Eventually, though, it became too awkward—we kept bumping into them in the building on nights when we were obviously doing nothing but watching videos ("Oskar's Offerings" were surprisingly excellent)—and so we finally agreed. To be precise, I agreed for both of us. Syl was perfectly comfortable with the discomfort.

The way it came together wasn't elegant. Dotan caught me in the mailroom once again, and once again reminded me what a shame it was that we were never able to put together a double date.

"It really is too bad. Totally our fault, of course," I said. "Syl and I are just swamped these days. We'd invite you to join us tonight, but we're going to the Crab Cave. You know, all *trayf.*"

"That's perfect. We've got nothing going on and we've been dying to go there," Dotan said, explaining that they didn't keep kosher outside the home. Left without any other choice, I stammered out a reluctant invitation and then I went up to Syl's apartment and told her what had happened. I told her I felt bad that they had asked us so many times, and we'd always said no.

"We don't owe them anything," she said. "We can lead our own lives. If anyone should feel bad, it's *them.* They need to learn to take a hint."

"Please? It will make them so much happier than it will make us unhappy. The world's overall happiness will be increased," I said, and although Syl is not a utilitarian, she consented.

What Syl did not know, what she could not know, was that I was more upset about going to dinner with Dotan and Debbie than she was. I trusted Dotan now, at least to a point, but I nevertheless feared that the more time Syl and I spent with Dotan and Debbie, the more likely they were to divulge my disgrace to her.

I didn't think they would be cruel about it. Rather, I figured they must assume my girlfriend would know all about my past—it was a reasonable assumption, after all. I expected Dotan would broach it in a kind way, maybe to show support, as he had done after Beth's "Sleeping with the Enemy" article came out. But I would be killed by the friendly fire just the same.

My best bet was to keep the conversation on any subject other than work or the news. Difficult, I thought, but not impossible. I would get Debbie talking about screams. She could go on for hours about them: "Did you know that people's screams have regional accents?"

Fortunately, a crab joint is probably the best possible kind of restaurant to avoid sensitive topics. The alternative—a long, slow, leisurely dinner at a quiet and expensive restaurant, with service too good to complain about—would have left us with nothing to do but learn more about one another. But at a crab house, the activity of dinner—breaking crustaceans with little hammers and knives and extracting tiny bits of flesh—always gives everyone plenty to muse about.

"Oooh, look at this one," someone might say. "So much meat."

Still, even assuming I could keep the subject off my past, I didn't know how I could possibly avoid any mention of my last name. I had taken careful precautions to never be placed in a position in which I had to overtly lie to Syl. I paid for groceries with cash, so the checker would never say, "Thank you, Mr. Glass," and Syl would never see my credit cards. I made reservations in her name, which she liked, since it doubled as a feminist act. And, I continued to hide my mail.

I knew these were lies, even if they were omissions, and I knew I soon would regret them, but I did it anyway. Lying to Syl didn't feel like it had at the *Weekly*. In a way, it felt so much worse, because I was always conscious of it; I couldn't get it out of my mind. I knew—I was always aware—that I was lying to the woman I loved. Once, after I spent a weekend nursing her back to health from a flu, she told me I was "perfect," and I nearly cried.

I knew I was repeating myself, behaving the way I had with Allison. When Syl found out about my past—and at some point she would, it was inevitable—she would surely be dismayed to learn that she had been in love with someone who wasn't quite me. But even though I knew I had to come clean, I still couldn't bear to actually do it.

My crab house ploy worked. Dotan and Debbie never spoke about work or my past, and my last name never came up. Mainly they talked about wanting to go out with us again.

"This is great," Debbie said when we sat down. "We don't have many friends who will go to places with this much *trayf*."

"So where do you go, when it's just the two of you?" Syl asked, trying to make conversation.

"We don't really like to go out just the two of us," Debbie said. "We got our whole lives to do that."

"We did on our anniversary," Dotan noted, while using his front teeth to pull some flesh out of the joint of a crab's knee.

"He's misremembering. We didn't," Debbie said. "Not this year anyway. We have friends who started dating the same weekend we did, so we thought it would be fun to have a double anniversary date."

"The more, the merrier, is what I always say," Dotan added.

"Do you know anyone who started dating the same weekend as you guys?" Debbie asked me.

"No," I said. "We don't."

"That's too bad," she said, and we all fell silent for a while.

Toward the end of the meal, when Syl and Debbie were talking about a wedding Debbie had just been to, Dotan asked me in a hushed voice if I had seen anything he should be "made aware of."

"I'm glad you brought this up," I said. "Because you mentioned something like this when we first met and I really don't know what it is that you think we should be watching out for."

"That's the right answer," he said. "You tell that to them when they press you."

"I'm serious," I said.

"As am I," he replied. "They're always out there. Even when you don't see them, they're there, and you have to be aware. They will change everything."

And it was then that I finally knew for sure that Dotan never wanted to hurt me, or use me, or expose me, because it was then that I began to truly understand him. I believe Dotan feared that the world was dangerous and threatening. In every contact with another person, he felt he ceded a tiny bit of control over the story of his own life. And so his hold on his own construction of his existence seemed tenuous—and what more do we have, but that?

This was the reason he was so worried that there were things he needed to be "made aware of," or that there were people saying things about him. By going out with other couples all the time, and becoming active in the synagogue—even by identifying so strongly as a Jew—he got a bit of his own story back; he was reassured to see how other people saw him, and to see that they saw him as, in many ways, much like themselves. His story was like their stories. He'd only wanted to make sure that I—the odd young man in terrible trouble, so frequently in the paper—was not really as alien as I seemed. He had been happy to find out that, indeed, I wasn't. And in a way, so had I.

I relaxed for the rest of dinner, feeling less on my guard, and I even suggested we go out for ice cream for dessert. Afterward, when we were home again, Syl made me promise that we wouldn't have to go to dinner with them again anytime soon, but she admitted it hadn't been as bad as it might have been.

Syl liked to get out of Washington and go to random places—places, as it happened, where it was unlikely that anyone had heard of me—

and I was deeply grateful. It was as if she were being considerate of my feelings somehow, without even being aware of them.

One Tuesday night, we drove to Pat's and Gino's in Philadelphia and held our own cheese-steak taste test. On a long weekend, we drove all the way to Tennessee, because neither of us had ever been there, and ended up captaining teams in the state's annual Tomato War, a dodgeball-like activity employing overripe vegetables. (Syl came out not only winning but virtually spotless. I looked like a man-size ketchup packet had exploded on me.)

And we always had factory tours. While other couples met for drinks, we begged managers for after-hours visits of The Capitol Cake Company plant and the Washington Mustard bottling facility. Instead of breakfast in bed, we watched the Sunday predawn marshmallow-puffing process at the Maryland Marshmallow plant. And pretzels—oh those twisted pieces of dough, we met their makers by the handful: Herr's, Anderson's, Hammond's, Martin's, Snyder's, Pennsylvania Dutch, Utz, and the Sturgis Pretzel House in Lilitz, Pennsylvania, where we both earned a certificate designating us each an "Official Pretzel Twister."

I knew this might not be the kind of compatibility that couples therapists looked for (it seemed a bit too offbeat and overspecific for that), but it worked for us, and I was happy with it. And my parents agreed. My father even said my relationship with Syl was a sure sign I was finally "back on track."

"Soon you'll be a hero again," he said to me one night on the phone, after my mother had gone to bed. He often used the word *hero* as a strange synonym for "good guy."

"Dad, I'll never be a hero again." I'd learned long ago not to fight his odd usages, but just to follow them. "There are some people who will never forgive me and once we all accept that, I think we'll be happier."

"Why should I accept that? You're a hero to me," he said.

My mother greeted the news that Syl and I were seeing each other with equal enthusiasm. She proposed coming to Washington to meet Syl, but I refused, saying it would scare her off. She said she liked Syl already, and there'd be nothing scary about it, but in an act that I knew took a great deal of inner strength, she nevertheless agreed not to come.

To celebrate Syl's and my one-month anniversary, I planned a Saturday-night trip to sleepy Running River, Virginia. I suggested we play bingo at the volunteer firehouse there; the games were famous throughout the area. Syl agreed, though she seemed strangely hesi-tant. I asked if there was something else she'd prefer, but she said no, this would be nice.

We arrived in the town hours before the firehouse opened for bingo and so we drove through the hamlet's tiny commercial district. A sign proclaimed Running River "The Home of Howdy Doody."

"Why do you think they named him Howdy Doody?" Syl asked me. "I mean, can you imagine the Hollywood meeting? Some ventril-oquist says he's got an act that's a surefire hit with children. It's called 'Hello, Shit.' And the producers love it, but tell him he has to rename it 'Howdy Doody,' to make it more family-friendly? And he says, 'But you're compromising my art'?"

Syl seemed on edge that day, in a way I had never seen her before. "And what is it with the bingo song?" she asked a minute later. " 'There was a farmer, had a dog, and Bingo was his name-o. B-I-N-G-O. B-I-N-G-O. B-I-N-G-O. And Bingo was his name-o,' " she sang. And then she explained: "Name-o? That's a rhyme? It may be the worst rhyme in all of English song. You can't just stick an *o* at the end of a word. It's what third-graders do when they're pretend-ing to speak Spanish. Please-o go-o to-o the-o store-o."

To placate Syl, I tried to come up with a real word to replace "name-o," but was unsuccessful and eventually gave up. The best I could do was "and Bingo was very lame-o," which Syl noted was at least slang, though nothing you could use in Scrabble.

For a second I was creepily reminded of Beth and wondered, What is it with me and the word women? But I soon calmed down. Syl was a poet, I reminded myself, not a journalist. She wasn't even especially observant. Sometimes she would space out and put her FedExes in the regular mailbox, or feed the dog Count Chocula.

And almost every day she would disappear for several midafternoon hours. When I'd once asked about it, she was evasive. At first I thought she might be seeing someone else, but I later figured she was just going on walks, and lost track of time thinking about her poetry; she'd said she liked to walk when she composed because it meant she was better able to "keep the meter straight." The truth was that Syl didn't live in the real world, and that was just fine with me.

We found that there was there was no real commercial district, and nothing much to do, in Running River. In one place there was a collection of brick buildings that we thought might contain the firehouse, but it turned out to be a religious wellness institute, where it appeared that people went to lose weight by learning to fear God.

Eventually the hour for bingo arrived, and we found the A-frame firehouse, which looked like a ski lodge with Dalmatian-patterned window dressings. Once inside, we took seats next to each other at one of the long lunch tables, the kind with attached benches.

Aside from us and the firefighters, there were probably one hundred elderly women, along with a few of their husbands, in the room. "We should have brought the grandmas," Syl whispered to me guiltily. The women positioned good-luck totems on the tables, all around them—rabbits' feet and horseshoes and Beanie Babies and plump Buddha figurines, and even Japanese porcelain "good luck" beckoning cats with one paw raised. Waiting for the game to start, they played with the totems and talked to one another excitedly about the twelve hundred dollars some woman from out of town had won the week before. The men, wearing baseball caps advertising farm machinery and tire companies, didn't speak or acknowledge one another. They drank their beers quietly, with a defeated look. This was probably what they gave up each week in order to watch Sunday football in peace.

"I like your dog," I said to the woman sitting next to us, when Syl went to get the bingo cards. The woman wore a sweatshirt that had a picture of a Lhasa apso ironed on it. Above the dog it said: THIS IS MY DOG.

"I liked her too," the woman said. "But she's dead."

"I'm sorry," I said. "I thought because the caption said 'is' and not 'was,' it meant she was alive."

"She *was* alive when I made the sweatshirt," the woman said. "But now she *is* dead."

I nodded in agreement. I had no idea how to continue the conversation.

"My girlfriend has a Lhasa apso too," I finally said and pointed to Syl, who was on the other side of the room. "They're great dogs. His name is Milton Rosenbaum."

"*Whose* name is Milton Rosenbaum?" the woman asked.

"The dog," I said.

"The *dog's* name is Milton Rosenbaum?"

"Yes," I said.

"That's a Jewish name," the old man across from us said, breaking his silence for the first time.

"Yes," I said. "Our dog is Jewish."

"How'd that happen?" the woman asked. "Did you get him in Israel?"

"No," I said. "He's an American Jew."

There was silence.

Fortunately, Syl soon returned and handed me my cards. "I like your dog," she said to the woman, noticing the sweatshirt, as she sat down. "I've got a Lhasa—"

"We heard you got a Jew dog," the old man interrupted.

"I'm glad I didn't happen to get a Jewish dog," the woman said. "I'm not against Jews or anything. I just think it would have been hard. We're both Christians, and have been our whole lives. I wouldn't have known what kind of food to give it."

"Milton Rosenbaum doesn't have any dietary restrictions," I said to the woman.

"Does he work on Saturdays?" the old man said. "Jews, you know, celebrate the day of rest on Saturdays. Frankly, it never made any sense to me. God rested on the seventh day, and the seventh day is Sunday. Just look at any calendar."

"Milton Rosenbaum doesn't work any day," I said.

"Anyway, he's more of a secular Jew, like us," Syl added pointedly.

"Do you think it's possible our dog was Jewish too?" the woman said to her husband. "He loved bagels."

"And he watched *Seinfeld* with us," the man added.

"I think you may have had a Jewish dog and not known it," I said.

"Wow," the woman marveled.

"Man, you live with a dog for ten years and you don't even know the most intimate things about them," the man said.

"They're a secretive bunch, the Jewish dogs," Syl added.

"Faced with generations of persecution, they've grown accustomed to blending in," I added.

"I know," the man said. "We saw *Schindler's List.*"

"All those years unrecognized, Percy must have felt so alone," the woman said. She looked like she was genuinely disturbed and surreptitiously she started rubbing the embossed decal of her dead dog, as if to comfort it somehow.

And then the announcer called out, "Let's get ready to bingo!"

Syl had bought me twenty-seven cards—a good, although not an expert, player's hand—but bought only one for herself. "You sure it's going to be fun for you, with only one card?" I asked.

"This is all I want," she said.

The caller began drawing numbers, and each time he did, Syl checked her single card in no time at all. Afterward, I noticed, she was very still and cold and seemed to be focusing very determinedly on the card in front of her, even though she had already checked it. She wouldn't look at me.

I wondered if this was just how she played games, or if I had done something to upset her. I was going to ask, but then I remembered how annoying I could get when I constantly asked people if they were okay. Nathan had told me not to do it so much, so I kept quiet.

Despite what you might think, competitive bingo is an exciting game. Everyone is zipping up and down their columns. Arms fly. People moan. There's even body English. The tension in the room is worse than when I took the SAT in Lakeside, and that was so bad it made one student scream. (He was dismissed from the exam.)

Syl, however, was far from excited. She sat there in a different world, checking her single card and drifting away. As the numbers were called, she seemed to get paler and paler. I wondered if this was going to be a space-out moment, at the end of which she'd try to eat the card like a cracker, or rip it in half like a movie ticket.

"Everything okay?" I asked her, while searching for O-67.

"I'm fine," she said.

"Do you want to go home?"

"I said I'm fine, Stephen."

"And Bingo was very lame-o," I sang to her in a whisper, but she still said nothing and someone, somewhere, yelled bingo. I tried Dylan: *"She was born in Spring, but I was born too late / Blame it on a simple twist of fate . . ."* I knew she liked that line because in fact, her birthday was in May, and I was several years younger than she. But I got no reaction.

" 'Hello, Shit'?" Still nothing.

It was during the third game when things began to heat up for me. I had almost filled the entire top row of one of my cards. I was only missing I-21.

I began chanting the number quietly: "I-21, I-21, I-21, I-21."

But the drawer could not pull it out of the bin. He pulled I-19 and I-20, but no I-21.

"Come on," I said softly. "Give me an I-21."

"I-"

"Yes, yes, yes," I said.

"-22."

"Fuck," I said.

"No cuss words at the table," the old woman with the dog shirt said.

"I'm sorry," I said. I could feel the tension in the room escalating.

Other people were close, too. Please give me I-21. Please, please, please.

And then it happened.

"I-21," the fire chief yelled out.

"Bingo," I yelled. "Oh baby." I pumped my first in the air. I did a small touchdown dance involving a couple of poorly executed break-dance moves. Syl looked at her feet and seemed uncharacteristically mortified.

"We got a bingo there in the east corner of the room and look at him go," the fire chief proclaimed. "He must be a newcomer. Danny, go check out the man's card while we get to know him. What's your name, fella?"

"Stephen," I said.

People started throwing out their cards, preparing for the next round. Danny, a fireman, walked toward me.

"Where're you from, Stephen?" the chief shouted.

"Jeffersonville," I said.

"You're far from home. Thanks for coming down. Is this your first bingo?"

"First of many, I hope," I said.

"What're you going to do with the money?"

"I don't know."

Danny stood next to me and shook my hand. He had the $500 prize in his breast pocket.

"All right, Danny," the chief instructed. "Read them off to me so we can double-check Steve's card."

"Um, chief, we got a problem," Danny said.

"What's that?" the chief asked. "This guy a Democrat?"

The audience laughed. Syl remained very still, fighting something.

"Sure seems like it—he's only got the top line."

"Oh, city boy, looks like you *bongoed*. This was a picture-frame game. You had to have all four sides."

My fellow players began to hoot and boo; even my tablemates grumbled. "Get the hat," someone yelled out.

A large dunce cap was put on my head. "You have to wear that for the rest of the night," the chief said. "We can't do anything but shame you."

"Shame, shame, shame," the bingo players chanted in unison.

"I understand," I said. "I accept my punishment."

"Jewish dog owner," the old man mumbled.

"I'll help you this round," Syl volunteered, but she still looked grim about it—or perhaps embarrassed on my behalf, I couldn't quite tell.

"I'm sorry," I whispered, but she said nothing.

During the next round, it immediately became clear that Syl was an all-star bingo player. Within seconds, she could check all twenty-seven of my cards. She didn't used the black dauber to mark them off, either: she did it instantaneously, from memory.

"I could do more," she said, and I ordered another twenty-seven.

"You're amazing," I commented. "You have an incredible memory." But still grim, still not daubing, she said nothing. She must really hate the game, I thought. I screwed up—she's supposed to be enjoying our anniversary, and she hates it. She's so good at it, it's clearly boring for her. She's tolerating it only for my sake.

With the combination of the sheer number of cards we'd bought, and Syl's skills, we were soon getting close to bingo every game, and for me, at least, the excitement crackled. It was almost sexy. We would say the numbers we needed under our breath and then somewhere on the tablecloth of digits, they would magically come up.

"Get me another set," Syl said, dolefully, and again I ordered another twenty-seven. Still she used no dauber; still she was infallible.

At eighty-two cards, Syl and I had more than anyone else in the hall, and as might be predicted, on the next game we got bingo. This time, we both stood up. Syl got up slowly, as if in a daze.

"The Democrat dunce and his dame," the chief called out. "Don't throw out your cards, anyone. This one needs to be checked."

Danny came over and looked at our winning card. The game was blackout, and we had indeed filled every square. He handed the $750 prize to Syl.

"You can remove the dunce cap," the chief announced, nodding at me. "You have redeemed yourself."

I jumped up in excitement. Syl ran from the hall.

I ran after her. She was getting into the car. "We have to leave," she said. She handed me the money. "I don't want it."

"I thought we'd spend it on something for the two of us," I said.

"No," she said. "We should never have come."

"What about our cards? We still have cards to play."

"Leave 'em for the Nazis. I need to go home."

So I got in the driver's side, started the car, and we began to make the long trip back to Jeffersonville. For more than an hour, I said nothing; the money remained on the dashboard between us; and Syl sobbed. I wondered if it was the Bingo Brownshirts who were to blame.

"I can't believe I did it," she said, over and over again. "I can't believe I did it."

Once, I asked her what she had done, but she only began to bawl harder and so I remained silent. By the time we were halfway home, Syl and I had both been quiet for some time, just staring out the windshield into the blackness. Then suddenly she spoke. "There's something I need to confess," she said. She wouldn't look at me.

"Okay," I said.

"You won't hate me?" she asked. "You promise?"

"I promise I won't hate you," I said. "I love you."

"I'm a gambling addict," she said, and then she inhaled deeply and looked at me.

I put my hand on hers, and told her I loved her, and waited for her to go on. Secretly, and I am ashamed to admit it, I was a little happy. She was flawed like me—not as badly, but she was flawed.

"I go to Gamblers Anonymous regularly," she confided. "That's where I go in the afternoons. I don't tell anyone. It started in college. My parents wouldn't pay my tuition unless I majored in computer science. My dad thought that unlike poetry, it was the job of the future.

After my freshman year, after studying fucking flat recursion and machine language, I decided to pay for college on my own. So I went to the financial aid office and met with a counselor, but the amounts seemed huge—I thought I'd never be able to repay the loans. Around the same time, I was approached by the Cal Tech company. You know about those?"

I shook my head.

"Computer science majors around the country organize themselves into card-counting teams," she explained. "They call them companies. In Las Vegas it's legal to count cards, but the casinos can bar you from playing and they're quick to catch on. With companies, though, the counter and the bettor aren't the same person, so the casinos have trouble tracking them.

"Anyway, the casinos know about the companies, and they're always on the lookout for pale-faced, pimply boys who score big. But female computer science majors are rarer, so the Cal Tech company offered me a premium to work with them. My job was to lose big money at the table, but count the cards. When the deck was favorable, I signaled to someone else, who placed an even bigger bet, and we cleaned up. I was also supposed to draw attention away from the winner by being a bimbo. I dyed my hair blond and got a bunch of push-up bras and ho outfits.

"It turned out I was good at it—the card counting, and the bimbo act too. By the end of the summer, the casinos were flying me to Vegas every week, comping me the best rooms. I was their dream: a stupid, blond rich chick who lost by the boatload. The company said my share could be as much as $100,000 for the summer. But I ended up making $200,000—my four years' tuition and then some. I was ecstatic.

"Then, I became greedy. When school started again, I broke away from the company. I thought I could count and play at the same time. But it was too much, I wasn't ready. During one weekend of blackjack, I lost my $200,000, and then $150,000 more—I'd built up that much credit with the casino. I had to call my parents for help, and they had to mortgage their totally paid-off home. My dad was going to retire a few years early. That's not possible anymore. He has to pay

Caesar's. I try to contribute, but I don't make much of a dent. My mom got an ulcer from it all."

A car passed us on the left, making a screeching noise as it accelerated.

"Do you hate me?" she asked.

"I love you," I said, and I rolled down the window, held my hand out, and let the wind blow our winnings away. The bills fluttered, dipped, and disappeared. Neither of us said anything more for a while. I held Syl's hand tightly and kept driving home.

I couldn't believe I had been put in the position of being able to forgive someone else. If my fabrications had been about wish fulfillment and fear fulfillment, as the *Now* article had suggested, this was both a wish fulfillment and a fear fulfillment for me. I hoped Syl didn't sense how much more I would have forgiven her for—how much she could have cheated and stolen and lied, and how I still would have loved her just as much, just in the hope that if I someday told her the truth about what I'd done, she somehow could still love me too.

I wasn't in any position to judge her or anyone else now, and anyway, I didn't think I could ever have judged her harshly—not Syl, not even on my most arrogant of journalist days.

"Okay," she said. "It's the free confession hour. Confess something now and be forgiven. Tell me something damning. I need to feel like I'm not the only fuck-up in the car."

Had she read my mind? I said nothing. I just looked at the yellow line on my left and kept driving straight. This was the fear fulfillment part: I'd known it had to come. And yet maybe in a perverse way, it was a wish fulfillment too. This couldn't go on much longer. I had to go with this opportunity to set things straight; it might be my last chance. I thought of Rabbi Gordon: I didn't want to see him the next time we were in services, and not to have done this.

"Come on. You must have done something wrong, Stephen," Syl persisted.

"I have," I said.

"Well, out with it. How bad can it be?"

"Worse than yours. Way worse."

"What'd you do, kill someone?"

"No," I said.

"Then tell me. It can't be worse than losing your parents' home at the blackjack table."

"It is."

Syl turned in her seat and looked at me. I was eerily reminded of Robert. Next she takes off the seat belt. Then she rises in her seat. The car begins to slide into the shoulder, the gravel snapping against the undercarriage of the car. . . .

"What is it?" she demanded

"I'm not Stephen *Aaron,*" I said.

"Okay, well, that's bad. I've been sleeping with someone whose last name I don't know. I thought we were beyond all this 'my last name is private' stuff, but I guess not. But it's not *that* bad."

"It's worse," I said. "My real name is Stephen Glass."

"Why is that worse? I like that name."

"It's not the name, it's what I did. Before I worked at the video store, I was a journalist at *The Washington Weekly.*"

"Go on," she said. "I think I might have read about this some-where, but I want to hear it from you."

"I was a reporter there, and I wrote stories. Lots of them. And a lot of them weren't true. I made them up. Sometimes just details, sometimes out of whole cloth. I mixed true things with false things, so readers would think the false things were true. I even said untrue things about real people, hurtful things that caused them serious trou-ble." I thought of Rizzi.

"Then when I was caught"—I rushed on, to make sure I told her everything—"I made more things up. I refused to own up to what I did. I invented evidence to back up the lies, and eventually it all came crashing down."

"And everyone knows about this? Everyone but me, *your girl-friend*?"

"Yes," I said.

"Dotan and Debbie? When we were at that dinner?"

I nodded.

We were quiet for a few minutes.

"It was the free confession hour," I pointed out lamely.

"But I didn't expect something like *this*," she protested. "I thought you might say you'd been arrested for pot or DUI or something like that."

We pulled into The Harvey's parking lot, and I parked in my spot.

"Did Allison know while this was all going on?"

"No," I said. "She found out when I got fired."

"Then how do I know you're telling me everything now?" Syl demanded. "How do I know anything you say is true? How do I even know you love me, and you're not just saying that?"

I was quiet and looked at my lap. "You can't know," I said. "I can't ever prove it to you. I'm asking for you to trust me. I love you very much. I have never loved anyone in my life as much as I love you. I need for you to trust me. Remember how I said, when we first met, that very few things are truly urgent?"

She nodded.

"Well, this is *urgent*. I've changed, I'm not the same person. I've seen the pain my lies caused. My mother can't go out with some of her friends anymore, because she sees how harshly they judge her— they think she's a bad mom, and it hurts. Reporters hound my dad at work, and my brother became notorious at Dartmouth because I made him help me in the cover-up. I put my own brother in jeopardy. Allison left me and it hurt me a lot, but I know it hurt her too, and I was the cause of it. My best friend, Brian, got so angry at me he stopped speaking to me. He hates me now.

"And it's not just my family and friends. I hurt strangers, people I didn't know, people who owed me nothing and did nothing to deserve it—I mean, not that anyone did, but some especially didn't. One of them wrote a letter that will stay with me all my life. I'll be an old man and still be able to quote it. It's burned into me. That letter finally made me feel it, all the hurt. I got the job at the video store so I could prove to someone, anyone, maybe just myself, that I could do honest work."

I paused, almost out of breath, then continued: "Syl, I know I need to work on this. I tried to go to therapy with Allison and that didn't work out, but that's why I went to synagogue that day when I met your grandma—to talk with the rabbi. It's why I'm still going. I thought he could help me, and I think he *is* helping me. I'll find a good therapist and go there too. My parents sent me names and I've been meaning to call, and I will. I'll do whatever it takes to allow you to trust me. You need to tell me what's going to happen to us."

It took her a few moments to respond. "You're lucky I'm not like I used to be," she said tartly. "A few years ago, before going to G.A. and everything, I would have just turned my back—couldn't relate to you. Now I'm more sympathetic, maybe *too* sympathetic."

She was quiet for a few moments more, and then went on: "I took this philosophy class in college. It was one of the few computer science requirements I actually enjoyed. I remember I learned one really important thing from it. Do you ever wonder if you're the only one in the whole world who's alive, and maybe everyone else in the world is really a robot, but is lying about it?"

I didn't respond. I was scared that it was a trick question. Sometimes I did wonder.

"At some point, everyone thinks that," she reassured me. "The course spent weeks wrestling with the question of, How do you test this? How can you prove it's not true? Well, the final exam answer is, You can't. At some point, you have to just go it on faith alone."

"So, you're thinking . . ." I knew she was working up to a point, but I couldn't wait for it. The suspense was too much. Did she have faith in me, or not?

"I'm thinking I have a really bad headache and need to get an Advil—"

"And . . ." I encouraged her nervously.

"And then we're going to go to your room, and you're going to tell me about your lying, and I'll tell you about my gambling, and we're going to be totally honest and hopefully, at the end of it, we'll both have enough faith in each other to go on."

We talked late into the night and though it was touch and go, we somehow made it through. In the morning I woke up, saw Syl lying beside me, and felt ridiculously fortunate. I knew I didn't deserve it, this stroke of luck, but I embraced it all the same, as if I had finally, through no virtue of my own, gotten the universe's approval. Was God protecting me after all? Maybe He was, maybe the rabbi had been right. Maybe the Mark of Cain was a shield too and not just a stigma. I could go on wondering if He existed, but like Syl said, I couldn't prove *she* existed, and I had to believe in that.

Syl was the second chance, I realized—one of the ones I'd been given. It wasn't the video store job, or even my mom forgiving me. It was Syl.

I went to work that morning fresh and new and happy. It was to be this way then: Syl and I, confessed squanderer and admitted liar, together evermore.

I arrived at Action Video twenty minutes early, wearing a tie with my uniform. Today was my two-month anniversary at the store, and Glenn had said he wanted to meet with me for a routine performance evaluation.

"Hello, Mr. Happy Pants," Oskar said. He was waiting by the front door for me.

"Good morning, Oskar," I said. There was a lilt to my voice. I was thinking about Syl.

"You're not going to be so sunny in a few minutes," Oskar warned.

"The sun is bad," Philippe said.

"Why's that?" I asked. My question was directed to Oskar. I knew Philippe's reasons for hating the center of our solar system.

"The Christian God is looking for you," Oskar said.

"Is that so?" I was looking through the new videos, paying little attention to either of them. Oskar was getting on my nerves a bit.

"He might hate you too," Oskar suggested.

"How about you, Philippe? Are you scared of the Christian God?" I asked, to try to get Oskar's focus off me for a moment.

"The sun is wicked," Phillipe said in a low voice that barely reached my ears.

"Worse than yesterday?"

"Worse than ever."

I sighed, wondering if I'd made that much progress here after all, and leaving Philippe and Oskar alone at the counter, I walked to the employees' back room, where I clocked in. I checked my tie in the bathroom, to make sure it was knotted correctly, and then I knocked on the door to Glenn's office.

He shouted for me to come in. He had glued an Enter button from a computer keyboard to the wall outside of his office. On the inside, beside the door, he had glued a Return key.

Glenn's office was a narrow sliver along the edge of the video store, more like a corridor without doors than a room, and when I reached the end of it, I sat down. Glenn walked around his desk and joined me in another chair on my side of the table.

"I like to do it this way," he said. "It makes me less intimidating."

I wasn't sure Glenn could ever look intimidating. He was a reedy man, probably weighing less than 150 pounds, with a constricted face and a bush of twisted blond hair. He was always cold and wore a scruffy corduroy jacket over his uniform, even in the summer.

"Feeling comfortable?" he asked. "Do you want some water or something?"

"I'm fine." But I wasn't.

"Good, well, let's start with the basics."

Glenn told me he was impressed with my work. He said he liked the way I managed Oskar and Philippe, and was going to give both me and them a raise—something he'd never done with daytime employees. He said he had observed me with customers and believed I treated them fairly and helpfully, and that he had actually received several compliments about my work, which was "very rare in this customer-driven industry." And he said he had informed "HQ" that my rearrangement of the horror and romantic-comedy sections had resulted in one-third more customers renting a second movie from those categories.

"I feel like you're a part of our family here," he said. "We think you have a lot to offer the Action Video organization, and who knows where this arrangement could someday lead. You're a bright star, Stephen Glass."

I said thank you.

"There's only one thing left. The district manager reminded me that I never asked you to fill out an employment application. It's really silly, but HQ requires it, so we got to do it. Do you mind if we do it now?"

I said that was fine, but I was worried.

Glenn returned to his side of the desk and took out a form and a pen. "All right, what's your full name?" he asked me.

"Stephen Aaron Glass," I said.

He asked me my date of birth and my address, and asked to see my Social Security card and driver's license, which I showed him.

"Do you use illegal drugs?" he asked.

"No."

"How about any convictions or arrests or summonses, except for traffic violations?"

"None of those either," I said.

"Didn't think so. You don't seem like the type," he said. He was writing down my answers before I even verbalized them. "Wouldn't really matter if you did, though, assuming it wasn't a huge deal," he continued. "We try to help people who've served their time, paid their debt to society and all. Them, and all those like Oskar and Philippe, who society maybe owes a debt to.

"All right then, the last question," he said. "You haven't ever been fired, have you?"

He checked the No box on the application before I had spoken, and he reached out his hand to congratulate me on my formal hiring just before I said, "In fact, I have."

I told him everything. Once, near the end, when I told him how sorry I was, my voice quivered and jumped a bit, but I stayed calm. I needed to finish, and I needed him to hear it all, even details that were probably unnecessary. And then I needed him, like Syl, to tell me it was all okay; he knew me now, and my past didn't matter. I was a good employee, a good shift supervisor. I had increased rentals. I was a bright star, Stephen Glass.

Glenn just sat there the whole time, pressed deep into his executive chair as if the force of what I had done had blown back his slight form.

When I was finished, I folded my hands in my lap and waited, and hoped. Glenn waited too. He looked down his desk and looked up at me and rubbed his face. "I'm sorry," he said finally, "but I'm going to have to dismiss you."

I nodded.

"I just can't hire someone who has done that. Ultimately, this business is about honesty. From small chains, like this, to the biggest companies—all businesses, I guess—are about honesty."

"You should know that I really liked working here, and I believe I did a good job." I said it more for myself than for him. It was pointless to protest.

"I know," he said. "But I can't keep you. I would give you a good recommendation, though. A very good one. But I have to ask you to leave."

"I understand."

There was silence. Glenn watched me and I watched my hands. I knew I needed to stand up soon.

"Well, that's that," he said.

"Yes, that's that," I said.

"You'll need to turn in the uniform. We can't have people out there impersonating Action Video employees, can we?" He laughed a little, to show it was a joke.

"Can I wear it home?" I asked. "I don't have a change of clothes with me."

"Yes, of course," he said. "Just mail it back to me tomorrow. But I'll need the name tag, please. If you don't mind."

"Of course," I said. I slid the pin off my shirt and passed it across the desk. "I'll be going now." I stood up and began the long walk to the door.

"When you tell an employer you were fired for conduct like that, the employer has to act on it. HQ wouldn't have it any other way," Glenn said defensively, responding to a protest I'd never made.

He seemed half upset with me, and half upset with what he felt he had to do.

"I understand," I said, and I turned and walked out the office door, and into the store.

Although I had been fired once again—twice in a single summer—this time I found I didn't feel ashamed, only terribly sad. I even felt strangely proud of myself. This had been a kind of test for me, I knew, and I'd passed it. What I'd had to do was refrain from lying, even if it greatly advantaged me to do so, and for once I'd resisted the temptation. It should have felt better than it did, but at least it was a beginning.

I walked to the front counter, where Oskar and Philippe were still stationed. Amazingly, they had managed to rent two videos in my absence: I noticed the empty boxes for *Die Hard 2: Die Harder* and *Little Women,* clearly a couple's choices, and I thought of Syl.

Right away, Oskar and Philippe spotted the vacant space above my left breast pocket, where my name tag once had been. When I approached, Philippe covered his ears with his hands, like the Hear No Evil monkey. Oskar's face was flushed with anger.

"Did the Christian God get you?" Oskar asked.

"I think I narrowly escaped him," I said.

I told Oskar I would miss him and I told him to remind Philippe, when he unplugged his ears, that dark always follows day, and with it he would be relieved of the brilliant sun.

Out in the parking lot, I climbed into my car, the same car Robert and I had taken to the Democratic Hotel, and drove on the same road, although going in the other direction. Again I drove at a funereal pace, but this time it was luminous outside. And all I could think was, Why can't it rain? It's supposed to rain at times like this.

In the movies, in books, on TV, in Shakespeare's plays the weather replicates the content of the story—but not now. The sun, the god-damn luminous sun, beamed down on me in all my misery.

And then I realized that it was sunny for everyone else's story. It was sunny for Robert, who'd valiantly trounced journalism's enemy. And it was sunny for Brian, who was working on his next piece no doubt. And for Lindsey, who, I'd read that morning in Gil Garvey's media column, had just gotten engaged to that *New York Times* reporter. It was probably sunny for Allison too somewhere, now that she was no longer dating me. And their sun, their rightfully earned sun, was no longer for me, not anymore. And there was no one to blame for all this goddamn sun, and the way it never fell on me, except myself.

Somewhere between the video store and who knows where—I was driving without a destination, too upset to head back to The Harvey just now—my cell phone rang. It was Syl. She could barely speak. And I thought, Here is where she fires me too. But what she actually said, through her tears, was, "His penis is blown up like a softball."

"Whose penis?"

"Milton Rosenbaum's!" She was sobbing.

"Of course," I said. Who else's penis could she have meant?

"I think he's dying. He's screaming in pain. Blood is exploding out of him. We're driving to the animal hospital right now. Can you meet us there?"

"I'm actually only a block or two away," I said. "I'll be right there." I could hear Milton Rosenbaum yelping in the background.

"You're not at work?"

"No," I said. "I'll explain when I see you."

"Okay. And, Steve, some guy called for you on my cell. He asked where you were, but he wouldn't say who he was, and I told him to fuck off, I had a sick dog on my hands. Was that the right thing to do?"

"Was it a reporter?"

"Yes, I think so. It was a 202 number and he sounded officious."

"It's fine. Syl, just worry about Milton Rosenbaum."

Animal hospitals, the world over, smell unlike any other institution. The odor has the tang of formaldehyde, the sourness of spilled beer, and the violence of an antiseptic cleanser. The smell is how a dog knows he's at the veterinarian the moment he crosses the threshold, even before he's been forced to stand on a cold, high, steel examining table so someone can shove a thermometer in his ass, which is when things usually begin to go downhill for Milton Rosenbaum.

I arrived at the animal hospital a minute or two before Syl got there, and waited outside for her. When she popped out of the taxi, I took Milton Rosenbaum into my arms and Syl and I ran into the hospital at full speed, as if we were paramedics on *ER* delivering a gunshot victim to surgeons.

Catching the hospital's stench, Milton Rosenbaum, who himself smelled even worse, began to squirm and twist. But I held him tight, and then tighter still, and he gave himself over to me.

"Out of the way. Out of the way," I yelled at no one in particular. "Sick dog coming through."

Running through the emergency room's door, I carried Milton Rosenbaum to the admitting station. Behind the window was a gray-haired nurse in her late sixties. She wore horn-rimmed glasses and had her hair up in a bun. Beside her, sitting upright in a chair, was a three-legged dog. Around the dog's neck was a hospital ID with his picture and name, Triage.

"I've got a very sick dog who needs immediate attention." I squeezed out the words as I tried to catch my breath.

"What's the matter with him?" the nurse asked evenly, as she passed me a clipboard with a form for us to fill out.

"His penis is exploding," Syl said. "He screams in pain. Blood is pouring out of every orifice."

I lifted him up so the nurse could see his bloody genitalia. His manhood was inflated in the middle like a snake that had eaten a mid-sized mammal.

"We'll call Milton when it's his turn," she said, unimpressed.

"It's Milton Rosenbaum," I said. "He likes to go by his full name."

"Okay, Mr. Rosenbaum," she said. "Please take a seat."

Syl and I sat down in two of the attached orange plastic scoop chairs. On Syl's lap, Milton Rosenbaum lay with his feet quivering in the air, spread out to make room for his newly massive penis. I stroked his belly and looked at the outsized photographs on the walls of dogs and cats undergoing surgery and dental cleanings. There is no patient privacy at the animal hospital.

Syl and I sat in silence for a few minutes, watching Milton Rosenbaum apprehensively. Every so often, he would raise his little head and cough, and flecks of blood would land on Syl's sweatpants, and I would stroke his little head and tell him everything was going to be all right, even though I was pretty worried it might not be.

There were other animals in the waiting room too. Across from us, a woman and man sat on either side of a calico cat. One of the cat's hind legs was bent over the top of its head—not an unusual position for a cat, but the leg seemed to be stuck there.

"What happened to the cat?" I asked.

"My boyfriend rolled on top of Woochie while we were sleeping," the woman said.

"I told you I was sorry," the boyfriend yelled. Then he stood up and went to the vending machine, which he banged with one of his fists.

"They don't have Doritos," he said when all of us, people and animals alike, looked at him.

"I think he has a problem with anger," his girlfriend said to no one in particular.

"I heard that," he yelled back. "Don't be saying that kind of stuff about me behind my back."

I smiled weakly and returned to petting Milton Rosenbaum.

"Do you work at Action Video?" the woman with Woochie asked me.

"No," I said.

"Oh, I thought because of the uniform," she said. I looked down at the tiny Marilyn Monroes on my thigh.

I turned to Syl, who was looking at me anxiously—worried, I could see, not about me but for me—and I told her I had been fired. I told her everything that had happened, blow by blow, and she listened and when I was done, she touched me gently on the shoulder. "That's terrible, Stephen," she said softly.

"Sounds like an asshole," the woman across from us with the

distended-leg cat said. I had forgotten she was so close by. One thing about Syl: When you talk to her, she sucks you in so deeply, you can easily forget there are other people near enough to overhear.

"No," I said. "He was just doing his job."

Finally, the admitting nurse rang a bell. I started to get to my feet, but was disappointed. "Hizzoner," she called out. "Your turn."

A twenty-something man sitting behind us stood up, carrying daintily in his hands a limp green lizard with a crested head. They were shown to an examining room. Meanwhile, Milton Rosenbaum coughed up more blood and it seemed certain he must be hemorrhaging inside. Syl turned to me and said, "Stephen, please do something."

I went back up to the admitting nurse. "We need to see a doctor immediately," I said. "Our dog is dying."

"We take the animals in the order they arrive," she said.

"A limp lizard gets preference over a dying dog because he was carried in first?"

"That lizard is a bearded dragon and he's calcium deficient," she said.

"Give him Tums," I said. "My dog is shitting blood."

"Hizzoner needs his shots or he will die."

"Can a lizard even know he is going to die? Because if Hizzoner doesn't know he's going to die, if he's not even aware that he's alive, then let's ease his pain and move on. Milton Rosenbaum has known he's dying since the day he was born, and right now he thinks it's the last stop before it's all over. Pay no mind to his 'don't worry about me' routine, he wants your attention. He thinks he has a bad case of Ebola."

I knew I was losing it, but I couldn't help myself: I needed to make her understand why Milton Rosenbaum was more important than this goddamn reptile.

"I think you should sit down," the woman said.

She was getting testy. Sensing his owner's frustration, Triage leaned forward and snarled at me. But his three-legged bend was more of an inadvertent bow.

"My ferret thinks he's got M.S.," an old man in the corner of the room shouted in our direction. I turned toward him.

"I don't know," he said. "I just thought we should jump in before any more of the cold-blooded budge in line."

"Is the ferret before me?" I asked the woman behind the counter, but she shook her head.

"Ferrets are illegal in Jeffersonville," the ferret owner explained. "So they get put at the end of the line. Only after the cops come and give me a ticket, will they see him. As if it's Frisky's fault. This is probably the kind of hospital that wouldn't have treated John Wilkes Booth's broken leg either." He said the last bit louder, so the nurse would be sure to hear.

"We don't treat people," she said defensively.

"Stop it, Steve," Syl commanded me from her seat. "You're not getting us anywhere. Leave the ferret alone."

"I'm sorry. I just got frustrated."

I returned to the chair next to Syl. Milton Rosenbaum coughed up some more blood and it soaked into Syl's sweatpants, and I felt sorry that I had accomplished nothing remotely effective to help the miserable little dog and, indeed, probably only agitated the nurse more.

We sat there for a few more minutes, comforting Milton Rosenbaum, who was shaking and sneezing and completely disoriented, when the electronic doors swung open.

Standing there, sweating and out of breath, were Cliff and a photographer.

"I knew it. I knew it. I'm good. You said your dog was sick," Cliff said when he spotted us. "I've been to every animal hospital in the area."

The photographer immediately began taking pictures of Syl and me holding Milton Rosenbaum, with his bloody coat and his swollen penis. We looked like sadistic animal testers from a PETA poster. The white light of the flash pulsed through the room.

"Stop taking pictures," the ferret owner yelled. "Frisky's sensitive to light."

Cliff waved at his photographer to stop. He slowly and cautiously made his way to Syl and me, as if we might otherwise escape, and calmly sat down across from us, next to the woman with the broken cat.

"Steve, it's good to see you again," Cliff said. He was ebullient. "Look, I simply need to talk to you for my article. I want it to be fair and balanced, and it's going to press in a matter of days, so I need to interview you now. Now. This minute. I don't care what's going on here."

I said nothing. Milton Rosenbaum moaned in pain. Syl held my hand.

"Why don't we start with my first question," Cliff said. "Will you tell me what happened, in your own words?"

There was only quiet. Everyone in the animal hospital was watching me. I studied the floor.

"I've been doing a lot of research on you, and I just want to make sure I get everything right," Cliff persisted. "Let me tell you a little about what I've learned, okay? Then maybe you'll understand why it's important that you talk. Sylvia, this may be of interest to you, too. I interviewed Robert—that was Stephen's boss, Sylvia. We went over every story you made up. He says your motivations were very clear— all you wanted to do was become famous and rich and glamorous. You wanted more than anything else to be the hot Washington journalist, and you were willing to do whatever it took. Was that what made you lie, Stephen? That's what he says."

"I've got to leave," I said to Syl.

"Please don't," she said. "I need you here. Milton Rosenbaum needs you here. If it gets any worse, I'm going to need you to find someone to help us."

The dog looked at me, but there was only pain behind his eyes. The whites were huge and growing, and the pupils were endlessly sad.

"I've talked to Brian and Lindsey, and they say you deceived them too," Cliff continued. "They say they don't know if they should believe anything you ever told them now. Lindsey says you told her you fought with your mom a lot, but now she thinks you only said that because you knew *she* fought with *her* mom a lot. Is that right? Did you do it just to connect with her? Did you tell her whatever she wanted to hear? That's what she thinks, Stephen.

"You have an opportunity to set the record straight right now, on that and everything else, all the bad things that have been said—that are even now being said. Just tell me whatever it is you want people to know about you, and I'll print it word for word, just as you say it. Otherwise, I'm going to print that you listened quietly and said nothing and perhaps *that's because you have nothing to say.* You're in check, Steve. You have to make a move or forfeit. You have to talk or be punished for your silence. So which is it?"

Milton Rosenbaum moaned. I sat there, still and silent, and stroked the dog, and listened to Cliff, and said nothing.

Cliff tapped his pen on my shoulder. I flinched slightly. "That got your attention," he said. "Why not just tell me what you were thinking when Robert was hunting down the lottery story? When you were at the hotel, and walking him through it. How was it you thought you could lie even then?"

With every word or so, Cliff poked his pen into my shoulder another time. "Or, what about just a few words on why you did it?" he tried. Harder pokes now. "That's what everyone wants to know. Why throw a brilliant career away? And that last article—you made up several individuals, you made up a law firm. Didn't you know you'd get caught? Were you trying to get caught? I think you were. In retrospect, Steve, your stories were ridiculous—literally *in*credible."

I stayed silent. With each baiting phrase, I became more adjusted to the poking and recoiled less. I simply withstood it.

Cliff continued: "Clovis thought you were a con man. And he's the literary editor, so of course he told me to read a book to understand you. He gave me *Confessions of Felix Krull.* Krull's a bad guy. Have you read it? Come on, you can tell me that. That's nothing.

"I was also looking into your high school days. You were on student debate—you remember that, don't you? Okay, do you remember Mr. Kerchner? Ron Kerchner? The coach for JFK High? He judged the debates sometimes. Do you remember him?

"I'm asking because Mr. Kerchner remembers *you.* He remembers one time when he was judging a competition you were in. You were debating a bill about paying reparations to Japanese-Americans who had been interned during World War II. You argued that the bill should be rejected for being underinclusive. You wanted it to cover everyone who was interned, not just the Japanese-Americans. Someone during the Q and A session asked you, Who else was interned? And you said some German-Americans were held too. Do you remember that?

"You said it without hesitation, Steve. Mr. Kerchner said that after the round was over, he took you out to the water fountain and told you that, in fact, no German-Americans were interned during World War II. He said he knew because his family was from Germany. You said you'd *assumed* people other than Japanese-Americans were interned. And he told you that old saying: Do you know what someone who assumes is? It's one who makes an ass out of you and me.

"Were you trying to make an ass out of you and me, Stephen? Stephen, please look at me. Don't you understand? If you don't talk, they'll think you're a monster. People's worst views of you will rush in. They already have begun to rush in. That's what happens in a vacuum. If you say nothing, there's nothing to counter everything that's been said about you, and everything that's been said about you becomes the truth. It's a natural process. At some point, you can no longer fight it."

Cliff drummed the left arm of my eyeglasses with his pen. The vibration from the impact carried through the metal frame into my ear, where it sounded like a jalopy's engine ceaselessly knocking. Still I did not move.

"Why don't you leave him alone?" the woman with the cat asked Cliff. I wished it had been Syl; I wondered what she was thinking now. Would she change her mind about me?

"It's my job," Cliff told the woman in an even, calm voice. Any reporter who's any good has been asked this before, and knows the answer cold. I had said it myself, I remembered, when Harry Madison's campaign director called to ask why I had printed the blonde joke, out of everything else I'd heard Madison say that day.

"My job is to help the public understand what has happened," Cliff said to the woman, and then he turned back to me. "I don't mean you any harm, Stephen, but if I don't hear your side, harm will come. You were a journalist, you know it too. It just works out that way."

"Sylvia, talk to Stephen," Cliff pleaded. "Tell him to talk with me. I don't think he knows that because he's never spoken about this, no one thinks he's sorry. I think deep down he probably *is* sorry, but I can't prove it or even put it in the article without some evidence, and that evidence has to come from him. Or you—it could come from you."

But Syl said nothing. And somehow, unlike me, she was able to do it in a way that didn't look like she was blowing him off or ignoring him. With the shrug of a shoulder and the tilt of an eyebrow, she made clear it was *he* who was invading *her* space, and this angered Cliff.

She stared out at him; she was formidable. He started to sweat and become red, and he started making fists with his hands. He stormed up and down the row of chairs in front of us.

"Do not make me into the villain," he yelled at Syl. "I have done nothing wrong here. It is Stephen who has done wrong, can't you see that? It's *he* who fabricated the stories. *He* is the one who got people to trust him and then deceived them. That's his pathology, Sylvia. He thinks he's just making people feel better. He thinks he just wants to make the people around him happy but, in fact, what he wants is their trust, so he can destroy them. You know, I once heard that the reason it's called a confidence game is not because *he* gives you *his* confidence, but because *you* give him *yours*.

"Don't look at me that way." Cliff spun around. He was talking to everyone in the room now, the woman with the broken cat, the man with the criminal ferret, and the nurse with the three-legged dog. Being pet owners, they had all seen wild things that non-pet-owners could not even imagine, and yet still none of them had ever seen anything quite like this.

"I am not the one at fault here," Cliff protested. "What have I done? I have tracked *him* down for weeks. I have searched high and low so *he* could tell *his* side of the story. A side that will probably just be another lie. And yet I have spent time and money and sleepless nights, and worked my ass off, for *him* to be fairly represented in my article. I have done all of this for *him,* don't you understand that? And for *you* too, the people who might read the story, so that you can know the truth, something *he* didn't ever deign to share with you. I'm not at fault, there's nothing wrong with *me*—I've done this for you and for him. And still he won't talk to me. Who's not being fair now? Huh? I'm asking you. I'm asking all of you. Someone talk to me, please."

But everyone, and every animal, was silent. The only noise was the high-pitched whistle that Milton Rosenbaum's trachea now made when he breathed.

And perhaps because the quiet was too loud for him, Cliff all at once reached over, grabbed Milton Rosenbaum out of Syl's lap, and held him up over his head, like a boxer displaying his championship belt.

"You will talk to me," he said to me. "Now you absolutely must say something."

"Put down the dog," the man with the ferret said in a calm voice, as if Cliff were holding a gun. "Just put down the dog and take a step back."

"I won't hurt him. I promise you, I won't hurt him," Cliff said. "I just need Stephen to talk with me. I need to interview you, Stephen. I have been reasonable. I am a reasonable man."

The old man took a step toward Cliff.

"Don't come near me," Cliff screamed and pumped the dog above his head. Drops of blood fell to the floor.

The old man took another cautious step.

"Don't go near him," Syl yelled. "You heard what he said!"

The old man stopped.

"What do you want from us?" Syl asked Cliff. "Do you want to kill my dog? Is that it?"

Milton Rosenbaum, who was so disoriented he probably had no idea he was now more than seven feet off the ground, coughed again. His bloody drool fell onto Cliff's shoulder. I thought of calling hospital security, but the situation seemed too volatile; I felt I couldn't leave.

"I want thirty minutes," Cliff said. "Just thirty minutes when Stephen answers my questions. That's all. I'll give you your dog back, I promise. I just need thirty minutes."

"Do it, Stephen," she said.

"But, Syl . . ."

She was crying. "Stephen, I'm not a journalist. I don't care about journalism. I don't care what they write in the paper about you. I love you. But I also love my dog. I am not going to let Milton Rosenbaum get hurt, and maybe even die, because you won't give this man half an hour of your time. So talk to him, please."

"Okay," I said. "Cliff, give us the dog and I'll do it."

"And pictures too," he said.

I looked at Syl.

"And pictures too," I assured him. "Now give me the dog."

"I can't give you the dog first," he said. "You're a pathological liar—how do I know you'll actually do it?"

"Fine. Give the dog to the man with the ferret. He'll hold it in escrow while I answer your questions."

"No, no, no, you could be in cahoots together," he said. "He's obviously on your side."

"Then—"

"Stephen," Syl yelled at me. "Stop this, and just do what he wants."

"Okay, thirty minutes, starting now, go ahead," I said.

Cliff lowered the dog from above his head, and sat in one of the orange seats. With one hand still gripping Milton Rosenbaum's collar, and another holding a tape recorder, he began: "My first question is: Why did you do it? Why did you lie?"

For a few seconds, I said nothing.

"I thought you were going to answer my questions," Cliff said, grabbing Milton Rosenbaum's collar tighter.

"I'm thinking about my answer," I said, and after a moment I added, "I lied because I wanted people to love me."

"No, no, no, that doesn't count. I don't believe you, and neither will anyone else. You can't give fake answers. That wasn't the deal.

Lots of people want someone to love them, but *they don't lie*. If you don't say something better than that, something we can believe, I'll—"

Suddenly Milton Rosenbaum, in a moment of clarity, saw Syl and me sitting across the aisle from him, and looked up at the man who was holding him, and began to scream. And with that, a rage that had been simmering for all this time within Syl, suddenly burst through. Cliff did not see it coming. In an instant, she strode up to Cliff's chair and kicked him once between his legs, with the full sole of her foot, as if she were tramping down garbage; and he screamed too.

Cliff slid to the floor, bent in half, and Syl, as composed as one can be in a bloody sweatsuit, took Milton Rosenbaum's collar from Cliff's debilitated grip. Everyone in the room applauded, as if someone had dropped a cafeteria tray.

"You're up, Milton Rosenbaum," the nurse called out just then, and Syl and I walked into the examining room with our shivering dog in my arms, and none of us looked back.

Behind me, the ferret man said something I couldn't make out, but I heard Cliff reply in a weakened voice, "Well, I got my interview. I got my interview. And what is so wrong with that?"

But I knew he hadn't gotten quite what he wanted: He hadn't gotten the half hour he'd promised his editors. But maybe what he had gotten would be enough for him.

In the examining room, the veterinarian told us that as sick as Milton Rosenbaum looked, he would nevertheless eventually get better. She diagnosed him as having gastroenteritis, coupled with a food allergy that caused him to itch all over. Milton Rosenbaum scratched the itch by biting himself until he bled, she explained. Then, after swallowing his bloody skin, he regurgitated it. I was feeling extremely faint at this point in her explanation, and I still didn't quite see why his penis was twice as big as his paw, but the vet said that was "normal" under these circumstances and I trusted her.

She was explaining to us how to administer the antibiotic—it involved a syringe, and again I was getting woozy—when there was a rough knock at the door. Syl looked at it, and knew. "Don't answer it," she pleaded with the vet.

"I have to," the vet said. "I'm still in my residency, you know."

Cliff entered in a fury, his tape recorder outstretched. The doctor shrank back, flattened to the wall. He went for Syl first, but I stepped in front of her, worried she'd attack him again and get the worst of it this time.

"It's like a horror movie," Syl screamed at him. *"You just won't die."*

Meanwhile, Milton Rosenbaum, perking up, started in on a low growl, a sound I'd never heard emanate from the little dog before.

I struggled with Cliff, and pushed him out the door, for his own protection and everyone else's. Then I closed the door behind us, so that we were back in the waiting room, and Syl, the vet, and Milton Rosenbaum were safely enclosed.

"Please leave," I said to Cliff. "You lost your hostage. I am not going to give you anything else."

"Just answer one question for me, and I promise I'll go," he said. "Why won't you talk to me? You used to be a friend of mine."

I looked at the floor, and then at him, and despite my intention to just turn my back and walk away, I spoke. "I can't give you an interview, because you'll never really understand. I don't know that any journalist could. I don't think I could have understood it while I was still a journalist. You think that if I talk to you and you report it word for word, you'll have the story right, because it'll be accurate. But accuracy's not all that you're looking for. Journalists always say it is, but it's almost never true. You're looking for a good story; accuracy's only half of it. You'll get the facts right and then you'll beat me over the head with them."

I paused for a moment and swallowed; my eyes were starting to tear.

"Talking won't be better for me, Cliff. When you're ashamed of your own story, silence is better. When you're silent, people will at least think, or at least *you* will still *think* they think, that they haven't yet heard from you, so there must be more to it. But once you've told your story and it doesn't come out any better, then they've heard it from you, and they know they've heard it all. And you wish you had stayed silent. It's so much better not to talk."

Despite myself, I cried—it was the effect of everything together, it was hearing myself say this, and having thought our dog was about to die, and being relieved to learn he wasn't, and having gotten rid of Cliff, I'd thought once and for all, and now seeing him back here once again. Most of all, it was seeing myself through his eyes now, and seeing myself so ugly.

Through my tears, I couldn't help myself, but I saw it: He had gotten his exclusive after all. I had even wept. What more could he ask for?

I felt Syl tugging at my arm. "We can go now," she said. "The vet's releasing Milton Rosenbaum, and I got his antibiotic. I have to inject it and you're going to have to help me."

Her voice was so calm, and I realized she didn't care that I was crying, that I'd broken down; she wasn't ashamed of that, or of me. I realized, too, that she was assuming our life would go on long after this, and I started crying even harder.

I was a mess, and she led me away. Cliff fairly skipped out of the emergency room, and every cat and ferret and rabbit and guinea pig turned to look as he left, so loud and jubilant was his exit.

The next morning, I woke Syl up with coffee, as I did every morning, and asked her if she would like to move to New York. There was nothing holding us in Washington anymore. She could live and work anywhere, OmniOnline had made this clear, and I could live anywhere but here.

"When?" she asked.

"I don't know," I said. "Soon, though."

"How about today?"

At this point I normally would have asked Syl if she was mad at me for suggesting she uproot her life so suddenly. "Are you sure?" I would have asked her, over and over again. "Do you really want to do this?" To appease me, she would have had to say "It's all right" so many times that in the end, the move would have become her choice, and not my asking something of her.

But on this day, I simply said "Thank you." I was exhausted from years of looking outward, retrofitting myself to meet everyone else's needs or wants or expectations—or whatever I'd perceived them to be, anyway. For the first time in my life, I decided I would set out both on my own terms and without a plan, and for the first time in my life, it felt completely right.

For once, I counted on Syl to care about me, and about what I needed, just as much as I cared about her, which was a great, great deal. She was an intuitive, impulsive person and I trusted her impulses. I even hoped they could rein in my own anxiety—the cease-less worrying that churned inside me all the time. Syl knew when she was right, even without knowing why; I never knew for sure, but for now, I'd have to count on my instincts, as she did.

"Are you going to call your parents and tell them?" Syl asked, while we were packing.

"I'll call them after we get there." That was unlike me too, and I knew that, and I thought it was good. I wouldn't ask their advice, worry about their reaction, get their permission. I would just let them know. And it would all be okay.

Syl smiled, and made arrangements for us to stay with a friend in the East Village until we found a place of our own. I called U-Haul and rented a truck, and we turned in our apartments' keys. (The Har-vey's studios were in such demand—don't ask me why—that we knew they would quickly be re-rented.) I carried her over the thresh-old of one of the building's elevators, to celebrate for one last time how we'd first met. And then we left The Harvey, pulled onto I-95, and headed north.

Somewhere around the Delaware Memorial Bridge, I heard Gil Garvey interview Cliff on the radio about his upcoming *District* mag-azine cover story, "Heart of Glass." It purported to be the authoritative article on one noted fabulist. Cliff told listeners that while I had claimed in the interview that I'd lied for love, he had not believed me then—and did not now. I was lying even then, he explained; I was up to my same old tricks. I had learned nothing. Syl turned off the radio before I could reach for the dial.

Three hours later, in the Holland Tunnel, as we passed the blue line that signals that you are entering New York, I said good-bye to Washington forever. I had moved to that city the day after graduation, expecting I would come upon my life there. I had hoped to find a job and a girlfriend, and then a career and a marriage and a family—the secure, comforting place in the world I had longed for. What I had told Brian had been true: I really *had* wanted to be there forever.

But instead and unexpectedly, in the summer of 1998, when I was twenty-five years old, and no longer at all sure of where I was going in the world, I for the first time realized that that was not—and it never had been—the place for me, not remotely so. And I was not the person I'd thought, or hoped, I was.

The tunnel released us into the clear blue light of a Manhattan summer afternoon, and I thought about what I might do with the second part of my life, this fragile thing.

Here is a life broken in two. I have tried to put the halves back together again.

I am still trying.

Acknowledgments

I will never be able to repay my parents, who have continued to love me and trust me and have faith in me. I have put them through more pain than any child should inflict, but somehow, after each blow, they continued to stand beside me. I owe them more than I'll ever have.

I am incredibly fortunate to have Michael Glass for my brother. He is the surest friend one could ask for, and he provided much-needed encouragement at every turn. His thoughts are incorporated throughout. Michael's short films—*Balls, The Prime Rib,* and *The Pride of Ownership*—speak to the essence of loyalty and fairness and the importance of family; I know of no better spokesman for the cause.

Julie Hilden read and commented on the manuscript literally dozens of times, saved me from myself hundreds of times, and calmed my nerves thousands of times. Most of all, Julie showed me that it was still possible to live a life I could love. Read her forthcoming novel, *3,* and you'll see how amazing she is.

Geoff Kloske is an unparalleled editor. He is a remarkable talent and I am indebted to him. Many thanks also to David Rosenthal and Carolyn Reidy, who made sure this book always had the support it needed. Thank you, too, to Aileen Boyle, Caroline Bruce, Fran Fisher, Nicole Graev, Irene Kheradi, Elizabeth McNamara, Victoria Meyer, Melissa Possick, Emily Remes, Walter Weintz, and Gabriel Weiss at Simon & Schuster.

Lynn Nesbit, my agent, managed this project perfectly. She is a strong advocate and an insightful reader. Every author should be in as safe hands. Many others at Janklow & Nesbit—especially Ben-

342 ACKNOWLEDGMENTS

nett Ashley, who stepped in when I needed him—were also exceedingly helpful.

Thank you as well to the following: A.B.; J.B.; J.B.; P.B.; P.B.; S.B.; T.B.; C.C.; L.C.; S.C.; T.C.; P.D.; J.F.; J.F.; A.G.; E.G.; E.G.; T.G.; M.G.; E.H.; K.H.; L.G.; F.J.; C.L.; J.L.; R.L.; S.L.; W.L.; B.M.; J.M.; O.M.; R.M.; S.M.; M.N.; B.P.; G.P.; J.P.; K.P.; C.R.; D.R.; P.S.; E.S.; S.S.; M.T.; R.U.; C.V.; and G.Z.